A MAN FOR

T 99080

Mereck's voice filled Netta with sensuous yearnings. The ties of his white shirt slid open, baring the hard planes of his chest. She stared as his powerful muscles flexed with his movements. Her pulse quickened. Would his bare skin feel hot to her hands? Would the hair on his chest tickle her palms? The room seemed hot. She sipped her watered wine. It helped not a whit.

MIDNIGHT'S BRIDE

SOPHIA JOHNSON

ZEBRA BOOKS
Kensington Publishing Corp.
www.kensingtonbooks.com

ZEBRA BOOKS are published by

Kensington Publishing Corp.
850 Third Avenue
New York, NY 10022

All Kensington titles, imprints, and distributed lines are available at special quantity discounts for bulk purchases for sales promotion, premiums, fund-raising, educational, or institutional use.

Special book excerpts or customized printings can also be created to fit specific needs. For details, write or phone the office of the Kensington Special Sales Manager: Attn. Special Sales Department. Kensington Publishing Corp., 850 Third Avenue, New York, NY 10022. Phone: 1-800-221-2647.

ISBN-13: 978-0-8217-8049-7
ISBN-10: 0-8217-8049-2

First Printing: October 2007
10 9 8 7 6 5 4 3 2

Printed in the United States of America

For my daughters, Valeri and Lorrie,
who listened to my ideas for Mereck's story
and laughed when I told them of
Netta's cooking skills, him, or rather,
the lack of them.

From the first page, they declared
Midnight's Bride *their favorite tale of*
the trilogy. They thought Mereck a sexy, Alpha
hero, a man both savage and tender.

What other medieval man
would have had a wedding night like his?

With many thanks to Della Jacobs,
my ever-so-patient critique partner.

Prologue

Blackthorn Castle, Scotland, 1050

Young Mereck of Blackthorn spied the old crone bent nearly double by an unsightly hump on her back. She shuffled on gnarled feet and crooked limbs up to the gates of Blackthorn Castle and demanded entrance. 'Twas a surprising voice for one so misshapen, for it soared above the clatter of the crowd and the din of carts and horses' hooves on stone.

"Aiyee. Me name is Beyahita. I come to tell the tale of the *Baresarkers.*"

Hearing the misshapen one's words spread fearful shivers down Mereck's neck and back. Though he longed to run, he edged close. She haggled with Lady Neilson, who oft sought ways to lighten dreary winter nights with tellers of tales. The wizened old Beyahita was keener than the most aggressive story teller as she bargained for food and shelter. Each night she proposed to tell a tale about the Baresarkers of Welsh legends, men who became part beast, neither truly human nor fully animal, when enraged.

That moonless night, after everyone had supped in the

great hall and the children were snug abed, Mereck stole from the room he shared with his half brother, Damron, and his three cousins. His teeth clattered together, and he hugged his small cloak about him. As he edged along the shadows of the great hall, Beyahita began her first tale. Given her wizened appearance and quavering voice, her eloquence was surprising.

"A robust male child, aptly named Gruffyd, was born at midnight the last day of June, in the year 943. The bairn took his first, hesitant breath when his mother sighed her last.

"'Twas soon found Gruffyd was as no other man. He could hear others' thoughts."

She paused, her piercing gaze seeking Mereck in the darkest corner of the smokey room. She gestured with claw-like hands. Her voice strengthened.

"Possessed of Lucifer's temper, he would become so enraged he knew not what he did. He foamed at the mouth and howled like an animal. Those who witnessed his rages named him Gruffyd the Baresarker, after the cults of Odin's horrific warriors.

"Gruffyd grew to be a man larger than most. He took as his bride a fragile maiden named Elgin. She, too, gave birth on a moonless midnight. Soon after, she became brainsick, for she babbled that Gruffyd had stolen her mind. She refused to eat. She shuddered when he drew near. Her loving husband despaired. One day, when Gruffyd placed the babe named Aeneas to Elgin's breast and turned aside, she shrieked and sprang from the bed. She raced to the top of the keep with the child. Her husband followed. When he reached her, she sought to hurl herself and their newborn son to the rocks below. Loving her mightily, Gruffyd strove to pull her back from the edge. With the strength of madness, she tore from his arms. He wrenched the babe from her grasp as she leapt to her death."

Mereck shuddered and pressed against the wall. All the hall's inhabitants leaned forward as her voice dropped low.

"'Twas soon whispered that by stealing her thoughts, Gruffyd thieved Elgin's mind and left her crazed. Men who dared repeat the story vanished soon after they spoke of it." She stared around her. Her voice rose with each word. "When they found the missing men, they saw they had been foully murdered, their tongue and body parts severed as if by a ravening beast."

No one noticed Mereck, bastard son of Donald Morgan and a captured Welsh woman, Aeneid ap Tewdwr, hidden in the dark shadows. Nor did they note the crone's eyes gleam as her gaze fixed on him there. Mereck did.

Each night, she spoke of another cursed generation. After Guffyd, she told of Aeneas and Fallon, Gilbride and Lienid. Each of the wives birthed their children on moonless midnights. All became brainsick and died after childbirth. Her gaze ferreted out Mereck, his body quivering with sick horror as he absorbed the legend.

One night as rushlights spluttered and died, Beyahita began her last tale.

"'Tis whispered on the wind that yet another son of Gruffyd's direct line was born at midnight the last day of June, in the year 1043, a century from Gruffyd's birth. This bairn was doomed to kill his mother in childbirth and is destined to destroy any woman he is so foolish to love." She cackled like one demented and pointed a skeletal finger at Mereck.

It was Mereck's birth date. His mother that Beyahita spoke of. He buried his face in the heavy cloth of the tapestry. He did not want to be a Baresarker. He just wanted to be a boy. Like Damron, his half brother, loved by a mother and a father.

He would never give his heart to a woman. Never love.

For now Mereck knew why his mother had died.

He had killed her.

Chapter 1

Wycliffe Castle, England, 1073

Lynette glared at the man who stood before the fireplace. Shorter than she, his dirty breeches bagged over scrawny bones. His tunic, stained with the food he had eaten in the past several days, drooped off one narrow shoulder. Baron Thomas of Durham had mayhap a dozen gray hairs on his head, even fewer teeth, and could not hear past the width of the table.

"Blessed Mary! He is older than you, Father," Lynette cried. "I thought I would lose my morning meal when he touched my hand. I cannot bear to think of him as husband to me. Nay! I'll *not* do it."

"Aye. You will." Baron Wycliffe's jaw set, his eyes glared his hatred. "Pretending to be great with child will not change it," he said as he stabbed a finger into the bulging pillow hidden beneath her clothing. "This is your tenth suitor in as many months. Your sisters tire of waiting for you to find the perfect spouse. The man does not exist." He slammed a fist on the table. Spittle flew from his lips with his bellowed words. "Hateful girl. You are all of eighteen summers. You will soon be too old to tempt even such a man as Baron Durham!"

"He is as skinny as James of Hexham was fat." Lynette rolled her eyes in disgust. "Every time he looks at me he drools through the few black teeth he has in his head. Hmpf! He tries to squeeze my breasts and asks if they are soft as a plump kitten."

The doddering old man leered at her through watery eyes. She glared back at him.

"I'll stay in my room until he is gone. I'll not marry him. Not now. Not ever."

"Aye. You *will*. Refuse and you will feel my stick across your back," her father shouted. "You will have naught but water and stale bread until you come to your senses."

He yanked her out of her seat, near toppling her to the ground. As if they performed a play for his amusement, her intended groom beamed with delight.

"I relish spirit with me bedsport," Durham said. "Show the girl we mean business, milord. We'll have our weddin' soon as she drops the babe." He cackled with glee, but his toothless grin faded when the baron grasped her hair and dragged her from the great hall.

At her bedchamber, he shoved Lynette through the doorway then slammed the door behind her. The heavy key grated in the door's lock. It was not the first time he had done such. He ordered it placed there after her first suitors bolted from the castle. Each time she sent a man sprinting across the drawbridge, her father beat her and tried to force her hand. He did not reckon with her strong will.

The sun had started to wane when Lynette's stepsisters unlocked the door. Watching her handmaid and servants carry a tub and buckets of hot water into the room, Lynette was instantly on guard. Her father had never before allowed her to bathe after he confined her. 'Twas part of her punishment.

"We hope to bring you comfort while you think on marrying the baron tomorrow." Priscilla spoke in such a prim and proper manner as to make the shortening of her name apt. "Here is your favorite soap to soothe your spirits," she said as she placed a small vessel of heather-scented soap on the stool.

"And I brought a tray of cheeses, bread and wine. Father seeks to force your hand, and we wished to help you through this trying time." Elizabeth patted Lynette's shoulder, but she failed to hide the glitter of malicious excitement in her eyes.

"Two goblets? Who will share with me?" Lynette studied their faces. Why would either girl do anything pleasant? They forever wailed and complained, urging their father to marry her off without any thought of her feelings. Though she distrusted them, she welcomed the hot bath and was grateful for it. She was even more thankful when they left the room.

She undressed and stepped into the tub, willing the hot water to relax her. If she could stifle her anger, surely she would think of a way to escape the morrow's horrible event.

"Mayhap I can pretend to have a wasting sickness? No sane man would wed a woman who cannot keep food in her stomach." She raised her brows at her handmaid and waited for her reply.

Mary shook her head. "Nay, lady. How could ye lose a meal if ye have naught but bread and water?"

"Oh, aye. That will not work." Lynette soaped her hands until small bubbles formed, then admired the colors reflecting there. "If we put droplets of mud on my face, and when it dried, colored it with berry juice, would it not look like I had a pox? Surely Father would fear catching it. For certs, after a day or two his anger will cool and he will change his mind."

"Huh. 'Tis more likely the baron will swathe yer face in veils, hurry the weddin', then toss ye both through the gates." Mary took Lynette's arm and urged her to rise.

While the handmaid poured fresh water over her, the door again creaked open.

Lynette turned and gasped, for unseen hands pushed a wobbling Baron Durham into the room. His eyes glittered with anticipation. Now she knew why her stepsisters had brought the food, wine and two goblets.

"Oh, me pretty," Durham crooned. "Water drips from yer pretty, pink tits. I will lick them dry for ye." He smacked his sunken lips together as he shuffled across the room.

"Get out, or I'll have Father throw you from the castle," Lynette shouted and pointed toward the door. Folding her arms over her breasts, she plopped down in the water to hide the rest of her body from his greedy stare.

Drool trickled off his chin leaving wet trails down his tunic. He lurched to a stop a pace from the tub. He looked like she had turned him to stone. She wished she had. He clutched his chest. His eyes bulged, and he coughed violently.

"Begone!" She stabbed the air and glared all the harder.

Finding a spurt of strength, the baron shouted, "Uncover that which is now mine," followed by an obscenity she had never afore heard. A leer spread over his wizened face. The final shout that burst from his lips must have drained him of his last energy. He listed sideways. His arms flew out, grappling for balance. He tottered a moment. He gasped loudly for air, then slithered to the floor like a cracked egg.

Her screams, and those of Mary, no sooner sounded than her father and stepsister charged into the room.

Lynette scrambled from the far side of the tub and grabbed her chamber robe. Her family had arrived too quickly for them to have been anywhere but lurking outside her door.

Her stepsisters spied the old lecher's body on the floor. Their shrieks bounced off the stone walls, the shrill sounds mingling and tangling like knots, till Lynette's ears rang. The baron slapped first one face then the other.

"Oh, my beautiful skin," Prissy wailed and grabbed her smarting cheek. "'Tis your fault, Lynette. You made Father angry apurpose." Tears gushed from her eyes as she bolted for the door.

Elizabeth screamed, "You killed that old man to spite us."

Seeing her father's arm rise again, Elizabeth wrapped her arms around her head and sprang forward. Too fast. She slammed into Prissy's back and propelled her through the doorway. They fought like two chickens, squawking and scratching until their father's roar sent them running.

A burly servant arrived to drag the dead man like a discarded sack of grain from the room. He was not out the door before the baron and Lynette started to argue. As in all their disputes, she ended with the same plea.

"Why can I not go to Wales?" She thrust out her chin and clinched her hands on her hips. "Caer Cadwell is mine. If you release my dowry to me, I will hire knights for my protection."

"Ha! And will they protect you from the werewolf Baresarker specters of Caer Cadwell? From the howling spirits of their crazed wives?" He rubbed his hands with glee.

Tremors of fear shuddered through Netta. On dark, stormy nights, she could hear her stepmother's voice whispering in her ears. *Ye think 'tis the wind that wails on dark nights? Nay, ye foolish girl. The new Baresarker howls his need for another mate. Brutal he is in his bed-sport. A wife lasts but one night. Mayhap two. He leaves them aside the gate, broken and bloody. Not a spark of life in them. Do ye hear him? He waits, hidden, for you. One night he will crush you in his arms and spirit you away.* At this point, she would shove Netta into a storage room as dark as a pit in hell, then lock her in.

"'Tis naught but a legend! There is no Baresark." Netta swallowed and lifted her chin, determined to believe this chant she had oft repeated to ward off their spirits.

"You will wed," her father bellowed. He raised his walking stick and rained blows over her back. She ducked under his arm and leaped to scramble across her bed. The oak stick slammed against the wooden tub and broke in half. Pulsing veins bulged on his forehead and neck as he hopped with rage.

"See what you have done? See?" He spluttered as he stared at the splintered wood floating in the water. "Stupid woman. You think to hire knights to protect you? Hah! You have no skill to command a force of savage Welshmen. I've had my fill of you. You seduced the baron to excitement apurpose. You killed him, displaying yourself in such a manner."

"Displaying myself? I was in my bath," she shouted, pointing to the soapy water. "You shoved him into my chamber then lurked outside. I'll not marry a doddering old fool, a filthy young one or any horrid man you pick."

"Oh, yes you will. The next man to come through the castle barbican will be your husband. Be he knight or swineherd with warts on his lips and hair growing from his ears like a forest, I care not. And that, accursed girl, is an end to it."

He stomped so hard leaving the chamber the floor timbers shook. In his rage, he neglected to lock her door.

Afore full light the next morn, Netta listened, her ear against the door's crack. Hearing her maid's footsteps draw near, she whipped the door open, grabbed her arm and yanked her inside so fast the girl flew like a stone shot from a catapult.

"Ackk!" Eyes rounded with surprise, Mary wobbled and grabbed a bedpost to steady herself. "I came fast as I could, milady."

"Blessed saints, be quick!" Netta flicked the backs of her fingers at Mary and then removed her own tunic. As her head cleared the material, her black curls fell over her eyes. She shoved them away to see the maid still hesitated, biting her lips.

"Well?"

"What?" Mary leaned closer and whispered, puzzled. "Be quick about what?"

"I need your clothes."

"Me clothes?"

Netta grasped the hem of Mary's tunic and whisked the garment over her head. Mary yelped in surprise, her arms flapping like a fowl's wings. Before her arms settled, Netta disappeared beneath the folds of the garment.

"'Tis him. I heard the gatekeeper raise the portcullis." Netta's voice was muffled as she fought the coarse cloth. "Surely 'tis a knight who brings many warriors? Their horses clattering over the drawbridge echoed like thunder." Popping her head through the opening, she wriggled the garment down over her slender body.

"What do ye plan, milady?" Mary's teeth chattered, and she rubbed the chill bumps on her bare arms. She groaned when Netta started untying the laces of Mary's leather shoes.

"To dress as you, of course. I must needs use your clothes," Netta mumbled.

Mary seemed in a stupor and did not move. Netta tapped her on the ankle. "Your shoes, too."

"Oh, nay, milady." Mary shook her head and backed away from Netta. "Ye're fixin' to waller in more trouble."

"This time I will not get caught." Netta crawled after her.

"Ha! Ye said that yester morn. Afore ye put the pillow under yer clothes and went to greet old Baron Durham."

"It worked, didn't it?"

Mary pursed her lips. "Aye, too well. He raised sech a clamor the master came a runnin' and found ye."

"I'll be more careful." Netta grinned wryly. "You cannot say I lack practice. I must see what this new suitor is like."

"What can it change?" Mary shrugged and lifted her hands, a sympathetic look on her face. "Even the goose girl heard yer father's yell that since ye killed the baron ye will marry the first man to come through the gates this day."

A huff burst from Netta's lips. "I did *not* kill Baron Durham." She squared her jaw. "Father killed him when he tried to prove I was not about to drop a bairn. I was in my bath. You should know; you were there. He was old enough to be my father's sire. Anyone of that age could pass on." She grabbed the shoes Mary reluctantly shed.

"The master will beat ye again, like he vowed."

"Let him. I must needs take the chance. I will not go blindly into this." She squeezed Mary's hand. "Do not worry for me. I mean only to peek down into the great hall and see who Father will force me to wed."

Blessed Saint Agnes, I beseech you. Do not let him be as horrid as that brainsick old man.

Mereck of Blackthorn would soon return to the Highlands, for he had finished all but this one remaining commission in England. Over the past sennight, he had heard rumors aplenty of how Wycliffe's daughter had thwarted all suitors. Last eve, a tinker joined their campfire and regaled them with yesterday's happenings.

"Why she done killed old Baron Durham," he had said. "He thought she was near to drappin' a bairn."

"That killed him?" Mereck's left brow had risen in disbelief.

"Nay," the tinker chortled. "'Twas by coaxin' him aside her bath. He got a look at her neked body."

"You believe the sight of her killed him?" Mereck probed.

"Never heard of old ones dyin' from seein' a neked slip of a girl." He scratched his groin and thought a moment. "Nay, musta poisoned him. What 'bout all the others? Some could not run fast enuff to be rid of her. Stumbled o'er their own feet, they did. She's to be giv'n to the first 'un thru the gate soon's the sun rises, but not e'en swineherds wud chance weddin' sech a one now."

Mereck chuckled as he led his men through the portal of the barbican and into the bailey of Wycliffe Castle. The first rays of dawn barely peeked over the horizon. After pointing at his standard bearer, men atop the walkways gawked at him. Mereck glanced over his shoulder. Caught by a breeze, two banners cracked in the wind. One the Morgan standard, the other, black letters on a field of scarlet. He scowled at the lad, who quickly lowered the second.

An unusual number of people milled about in the bailey, and his gaze caught the stable master and his helpers. A falconer stood nearby with a young merlin perched on his wrist. The chandler, carrying a rod of new-made candles dangling by their wicks, walked so slowly the candles did not sway. The cook, hugging an empty iron pot, eyed him from his head to his toes, while laundresses, clutching dirty linens to their breasts, shuffled through the dust and headed to the stables.

To the stables?

Why were they all not at their duties? 'Twas interesting.

Annoyed by his beard, Mereck scratched his chin and used his gift, his special gift, inherited from his Welsh mother. He freed his mind to search their thoughts for his answers. Words screamed from all directions, making him grimace with pain: *savage*, *poor mite*, *kill her*, *shameful*, *old bastid*.

Baron George of Wycliffe lumbered down the wooden stairs as Mereck vaulted from his saddle. He handed his destrier's reins to his squire and turned to his first-in-command. "See to the men. Dinna turn your back," he murmured as he glanced at the lingering crowd.

"Greetings, greetings, my good man." Wycliffe's smile was fawning as he approached. "I see your man bears Lord Morgan's banner. I have heard much of him."

"Thank you, Baron." Mereck's nod acknowledged Wycliffe courteously. "I am Mereck of Blackthorn, friend to Bleddyn ap Tewdwr, Caer Cadwell's overlord. I come at his bidding."

Mereck found it strange he was welcomed so heartily. 'Twas no more than two leagues from Wycliffe that a band of masterless warriors had set upon them, no doubt planning to rob them of their fine mounts. He had not the opportunity to change from his bloodied Welsh war garb.

Could the tinker from last eve be right that a father would marry his daughter to a stranger without thought of her welfare? Even so, would he not have denied someone like him? Blue dye stained one side of his face. He wore a blood-splattered ox-hide tunic, which came to just below his knees, wolf skins draped across his shoulders and leather arm bands from his wrists to his elbows. The size of his sword alone added an extra threat to his appearance.

At Blackthorn, if warriors such as his were to appear unexpectedly, he would have stood atop the gatehouse with a closed portcullis, his archers armed and ready until he learned the reason for the visit.

"Will Lord Bleddyn not come for his yearly call?" the baron asked as he led Mereck up the stairs and into the great hall.

"He is at Blackthorn Castle in Scotland, Baron. I came to England on another matter. Lord Bleddyn asked that I visit you and inquire how the heiress to Caer Cadwell fares."

The baron rubbed his hands together and grinned before he waved Mereck toward the high table. As Mereck crossed to it, he scrutinized the room before sitting across from Wycliffe. Long trestle tables and benches lined the walls, and servants scurried about wiping already cleaned tables and moving stools from one spot to another while avidly watching him.

"Such a lengthy journey must cause your wife to bemoan your absence," the baron said.

"Wife? I have no wife, sir."

"Do you spend much time in Wales?" George asked.

In reply, Mereck's brow quirked.

"You are Welsh, are you not?" the baron supplied. "No other would be at ease in such savage garb."

Mereck narrowed his eyes, and the baron stammered to a halt.

"I command the Morgan's warriors at Blackthorn Castle and spend most of my time in the Highlands. My mother was Welsh. I uphold much of her family's customs."

"Ahh. And what think you of Caer Cadwell? Would you wed to claim such as your own?"

"I am Damron of Blackthorn's bastard half brother and not suitable to be lord over such a demesne." Mereck let no flicker of expression betray his thoughts. No matter how angry, no father would give his wealthy daughter to a bastard, unless the suitor was a royal one acknowledged by his sire.

"Your bastardy means naught to me, sir." The baron's lips curled in a sly smile. "Your deeds as a warrior and leader of Lord Damron's army have made you famous throughout England." He near wriggled with excitement. "I spied your standard. Only the fiercest warrior in the land can have earned the name Baresark from his enemies."

Mereck's hands clenched under the table remembering the first time someone had pinned the title on him. He held his tongue, for he craved nothing more than his own lands, especially these particular lands. Why was the baron so eager to rid himself of his daughter? There had to be more to the story than the tales he had heard.

He felt someone studying him, as if soft fingers ran over his hair, down his back and arm. He shifted on the bench, feeling their heat before they jerked away. A woman. Her gaze physical. Determined. Studying the balcony above, he sought her form. He did not see her. She hid in the shadows.

Mereck felt the instant she left.

Netta's hand covered her mouth to still its trembling. The stranger sat, his back to her, talking to her father in a rich baritone. The melodious sound, in stark contrast to his powerful body, drifted up to her. She couldn't see his face. From what she did see, she knew what he was.

A savage. A giant of a savage.

Long wavy hair, neither brown nor golden, a mixture of both, fell about his shoulders. She saw flashes of blue dye at his temple. He wore wolf skins as casually as her father wore a cloak. Slender, sensuous fingers rubbed over his chin and hesitated as if annoyed to find the tangled beard there. Shifting on the bench, his blood-stained hide tunic rode up his leg, revealing a muscular thigh as substantial as a tree trunk.

The barbarian must have felt her scrutiny. His head turned. Afraid that he would spy her in the shadows, she wasted no time pulling back out of sight.

She had to see his face.

If she was very careful, she could make her way to the outer door of the castle. From there, she would have a clear view of the lord's table where the men sat. Spying a large bowl of flowers on a nearby table, she hugged them to her. She could look between the blossoms and still hide her face.

By the time she went down the stairs and to the entrance of the great hall, her nose began to twitch. Saints preserve her! Someone had stuck feathers deep in the arrangement. Her stepsisters, Priscilla or Elizabeth. Likely mean-spirited Prissy. She'd vow her life on it. Not only did Prissy know Netta loved flowers, she knew feathers made her sneeze.

Oh, saints! She held her breath. Too late. An explosive sneeze that would do justice to as large a man as the barbarian erupted from her lips. The flowers parted. Sea-green eyes stared into hers. She gasped in three hasty breaths. Another powerful sneeze burst forth.

The flower arrangement catapulted to the floor.

Chapter 2

Baron Wycliffe sprang from his bench, crashing it backward. "Netta! Hold." His bellow sent servants racing for cover.

Netta darted for the outer door, running as fast as her legs could carry her. She jerked it open and heard his furious shout.

"'Tis a thief! Seize her."

Netta flew out into the open and down into the dusty bailey, naked fear adding a burst of speed to her feet. Heavy footsteps thundered close at her heels. She squeaked like a mouse chased by the barn cat. Desperate to find a hiding place, she dashed forward. Where were all the castle folk she had seen gawking about earlier? Her pursuer gained by every step. Whimpering, she fancied she felt his hot, feted breath on her neck. The stables! She leapt through the doorway into the dark interior.

A large callused hand clamped on her shoulder and jerked her to a halt.

"Why do you flee, girl? What have you taken?" The words held a harsh thread of warning.

She recognized that voice. It belonged to the man in the great hall. Ugh. She smelled him too. Blood. Sweat.

Chain mail and horse. In great quantities. He held her like a grouse meant for the cook's pot, by the neck with feet dangling in the air.

"I have taken nothing. Unhand me," Netta gasped out.

"Nay. Not until I know you have not stashed the baron's coins on your person." He allowed her feet to rest on the floor, her back to him, but he did not release her.

Feeling his hands rove over her body looking for the stolen goods, she fought to defended herself. She scratched, hit, pinched and did everything possible to make the odious man release her. She gasped. He had thrust his hand down the front of her loose tunic and inspected her breasts! His roughened palm grazed over her nipple, sending shock waves through her.

"Cease, oaf." Outraged, she struck his hand so hard she flattened it further against her tender skin.

He did not stop. What he did do was close his fingers around her quivering flesh and squeeze gently. Deep sounds came from his chest. Much like a giant cat's purr. Horrified, Netta's arms came back, and she rammed her sharp elbows into his body as hard as she could. She yelped, not he. His stomach was like stone.

"You hurt only yourself when you grapple with me, girl. Come. Baron Wycliffe will determine what you have taken."

His deep voice and his warm breath on the back of her neck made her knees weak. Was she turning into a coward? Her father was still furious with her; she could not let the man give her over to him. She had told Mary she did not care if Father beat her again. Heaven help her. She lied.

The man grasped her shoulders and spun her around. She flinched, and a whimper of pain escaped her lips.

"What is this, girl?" His voice held displeasure.

Sensing what she had to do, she allowed fear to show

in her eyes. She had no need to pretend; her voice quavered on its own.

"Please, sir. Do not give me over to the baron. He is cruel beyond measure. He likes beating the servant girls, he does. The more we cry out, the more the master enjoys it." She guiltily sent a quick prayer to her favorite saint, Saint Agnes, to forgive her the lie. Father only enjoyed beating *her*.

She looked up at him and shuddered. Not only was he a giant of a man, he was a hairy one, too. He had painted half his face blue! She could not see the rest of it for all the hair that dwelled there. Many Saxon men wore beards, but this man had enough hair on his face to make two men proud. She tilted her head back to see more of him and met his eyes. Beautiful green eyes that searched her own. Their beauty was not only in their color, but in their expression.

Sympathy? How could that be? Confused, she kept silent.

"What would you have me do, girl?" He frowned down at her. "You heard your master demand I seize you. I cannot hide you behind me and pretend you are not there." His brows arched.

Not hide her? Aye, he could. As mighty as he was, another man could disappear behind him. Was that a smile behind his whiskers?

"Sir, can you not tell him you lost me amongst the people in the bailey?" She hoped the lout would take her suggestion.

"He called you by name. He will easily find you."

Rats and fleas! She had best be away afore her father became impatient and followed the giant. "Release me and I will join my mother. She works in the kitchens of Ridley Castle, just over the next rise." Saint Agnes received another prayer begging forgiveness for such a lie. "She will aid me."

"What if they deny you entrance?"

He sounded worried. Was he a barbarian with a conscience?

"The daughter of the house has need of a lady's maid, sir. She'll not turn me away."

No cause for another prayer there. She sighed with relief. Elise would be happy to shelter her, but how would she get there? She could not take her favorite mount. Before she could voice her thoughts, he solved the problem for her.

"My squire will take you up behind him. He will stay with you until he is assured they allow you entrance."

He made good on his word. Dwarfing her wrist in his big hand, he pulled her behind him to the last stall. A young man, a stranger to Netta, tended a huge destrier. He stopped and looked at them. The horse trumpeted and threw his head about in such a vigorous fashion he nearly knocked the lad to the ground.

"You there. Go to Marcus and tell him Baresark has need of a gentle mount."

Baresark? Netta jerked and near shrieked in fear. The man in Welsh legend her stepmother had told her tales of since she was but five summers old had come to life. Their threats rang through her mind and fright near buckled her knees. Her father had sworn that if she did not obey him, this fearsome warrior from the past would come at his bidding and drag her away to his dungeon.

How had he summoned him? Was her father a warlock? Trying to break the man's steely grasp, she jerked back so hard she feared she would wrench her arm from its socket.

The boy nodded and raced from the room. Why had he

grinned when called "you there," and why was he not afeared of this savage? Instead, his lips had spread even wider on hearing his master call himself Baresark. Was the boy brainsick?

Netta grimaced. Her skin felt over-sensitive. She began to fidget, drawing her shoulders forward to try to put space between her flesh and her borrowed clothing. 'Twas as if she had nettles in her tunic. She wondered why. Then she knew. His penetrating gaze, roving over her face and form in the dim light, felt like calloused hands exploring her curves. Bile surged to her throat. She gulped. Afore he learned she was his intended bride, she had to get away from him. Above her heart's pounding, she heard the sharp clop of a horse's hooves coming toward them. A large man led the horse, the squire followed.

"You wished a gentle mount, *Baresark?"* he asked, giving the name emphasis. "I can call none of the mounts gentle, but this be the calmest of the lot." Laughter sounded in his voice.

The large hand grasping her wrist tightened, then relaxed.

Netta could not see clearly, as the steed blocked out what little light there was. The squire knew his job well, for he immediately started to saddle the horse. The men began to speak, and she listened. Not because she was being nosey. It would not have done her any good, for the words were strange to her. What language did they speak? Possibly Welsh? The giant looked at her expectantly. When had they ceased talking?

"What? Is something wrong, sir?" She tried to stop her voice from quavering. Saints! What had she missed?

"Twice have I asked if you were ready to mount?"

She blinked. The squire grinned at her from atop the horse.

"Oh, aye. Methinks I was woolgathering." No chance

of any more of that. Before she realized her feet had left the ground, the barbarian had seated her behind the lad.

"Netta. Is that not the name the baron used? I will see how you fare at Ridley Castle." His gaze studied her.

Nay. He would never see her again if she could help it. From atop the mount, she saw his face. As if she had spoken her thoughts, the expression in his eyes changed. Were the tales of his being able to hear other's thoughts truth?

"Your interest will be welcome, sir." Ha, when loathsome toads walk upright on warty back legs. Her hand flew to her mouth to hush her thoughts. Saints! Did his lips twitch?

Wordlessly, he motioned toward the bailey. Clutching the squire's slender waist, she tried to disappear behind him. Did he feel her heart pound against his back? As they made their way across the grounds and out over the drawbridge, she listened for sounds of pursuit.

She did not relax her tense grip on his tunic until they were well out of sight of her father's castle.

No one would pursue them, for Mereck sent word to Baron Wycliffe that he had everything in hand. Netta had unusual courage. Especially for a woman. She had not fooled him for a moment. He had known it was she, Lynette of Wycliffe, on the balcony.

When he had chased the supposed thief, he knew who fled from him. He had purposely let her gain the lead until she entered the stable. He decided to send her out of harm's way when he learned her father had beaten her. No woman should suffer at the hands of any man—surely not by those of her father.

Had Wycliffe told Netta of the Baresark legend, and of the early rulers of Caer Cadwell, to frighten her of Wales?

He would have to take care she did not learn the man she feared as Baresark was also Mereck of Blackthorn, else he would have to force her to marry him. It did not set easy on his soul.

Ridley. The two estates bordered each other, and Bleddyn had told him Netta and Elise were friends. Ridley's daughter was the second reason for his journey to England.

Standing with legs braced wide and hands fisted on his waist, he chuckled.

Netta would soon be under his scrutiny.

Later that day, as the sky deepened to a stormy gray at dusk, Mereck tapped the betrothal contracts on the table and listened to Baron Wycliffe reciting Lynette's dowry. How many months before, nay, years even, had they been prepared?

"I note Caer Cadwell and its manors are passed through the matriarchal line, Baron." Mereck's gaze bored into the weak blue eyes of the man facing him. "How are the holdings protected to prevent losing them by the wrong choice of husband?"

The baron dusted his hands together as if ridding himself of something distasteful. "The man who weds my daughter must be able to protect her holdings by personal prowess, or by great wealth. Your warrior's reputation proves you capable."

Mereck watched the baron pick at his clothing. Why was Wycliffe determined to lure him into taking his daughter? The man was already speaking to him familiarly as if the contracts were all but signed. The girl deserved better than a bastard. Mereck grimaced at the hated word.

"Lynette's foolish mother insisted her daughter and her son-by-law must happily share a year's wedded bliss afore they are permitted to reside at Caer Cadwell."

Mereck nodded his head on hearing this. It seemed her

mother had been far more concerned for her welfare than was this strange man.

"Baron, knowing I can bring naught to increase your wealth, why are you willing for me to wed your daughter?"

"Lynette needs a strong fist to rein her in." Wycliffe eyed Mereck, appraising him like he would a wild boar in a hunt. "Suitors aplenty have vied for her hand." Anger caused his voice to rise. "She found ways to send them running without an offer. After the fifth man feigned an urgent summons from his father, I watched her more closely." He banged his pewter goblet on the table, sloshing wine onto the pristine white cloth. He muttered, "A clever girl. Too clever.

"Afore I called her to the great hall, she found a way to meet her new suitor alone. I caught her. In this very room." He twitched in the chair, his fat hands fisted until his knuckles turned white. "Dressed like a slattern, she was." The baron's words hissed through clinched teeth. He turned red with anger. "Spittle ran from the corner of her lips, and her hair was knotted and streaked with mud."

Mereck's tense body relaxed, and he fought a smile. The girl had imagination. His hand tingled with the memory of her soft breasts, and his blood surged on thinking of the beauty of her face and form.

"By God's sweet nails. She crossed her eyes 'til they stared at her nose." The baron sputtered and scowled so hard his own eyes were in danger of crossing. "She pointed at them to be sure he noted it. She talked like a fool and chanted what sounded like a curse. The man was well on his way by the time I reached the bailey."

Mereck had long since learned to restrain his ability to hear people's thoughts, for if they came from a mind filled with venom, blinding pain slashed through his head. Whatever the costs, he had to know what lurked behind Wycliffe's loathing. While he waited for the baron to recover his composure, Mereck cleared his mind and steeled himself to listen to the man's thoughts of his hated eldest daughter.

Wycliffe's hands tightened to fists. How he'd love to hammer them into that cursed Bleddyn, who had banned his crossing the Welsh border. How had that Welshman known Kyrie despised him as much as he loathed her? His wife had thought to secure her daughter's happiness? This savage will deal with the little witch as harshly as she deserves. Bleddyn will not dare cross Baresark.

He cleared his throat and spat into the stale rushes.

Lynette was not of his seed. She was the Welshman's get, Kyrie's first husband Rys. Mayhap a changeling. She should have died with her mother. He had forbad anyone to help with the birthing. Surely a sorceress entered and placed her babe amidst the blood on the bed. He had planned to kill the bairn; his hand had covered her nose and mouth. Her eyes had stopped him.

Remembering, fear flashed through him. He shuddered.

The minute he had touched the babe, her eyes had stared at him. Defying him! Shock like lightning had struck his palm. Anyone would have jerked back. Those eyes. The deep purplish-blue of a bittersweet nightshade. 'Twas a devil's eye, the right one with its honey-colored freckle, that frightened her suitors.

While Lynette remains at Wycliffe, he could not be free of her mother's memory. If he never saw the accursed girl again, he would be content.

Waves of physical hate filled Wycliffe. The restless hounds under the table whined. He kicked out at them.

* * *

Pain tore through Mereck's head. He fought the urgent need to bend forward and grasp it between his hands. A warm, wet nose nudged him under his outstretched leg. He ran his fingers through the dog's shaggy hair to soothe it. And to soothe himself.

He inhaled a shuddering breath and forced his body to relax. Across from him sat the only man in England, Wales or Scotland who would offer a bastard such vast holdings, the wealth to maintain them, and a beautiful bride. Even stranger than that, Wycliffe unknowingly was returning Mereck's mother's lands, Mereck's own heritage, to him.

His pain eased. He forced a smile and stood.

"Baron, be assured I'll return on the morrow to complete the contracts and bring my own. My man delivered Lynette to Ridley. Have no fear. She will trouble you no more. From this moment on she is *mine*. My charge. My responsibility. Lynette will accompany me when I return to Scotland."

He bowed and excused himself. After posting several warriors where they could intercept anyone trying to enter Wycliffe before his return, he rode through the misty rain toward Ridley Castle. He breathed deeply, cleansing his body and mind of the miasma surrounding the baron. As the air exploded from his lips, Marcus glanced at him with raised brows.

"What say you, Marcus? Will you take command o'er my men in Wales a year hence? Would you be happy there?" Mereck nodded at his first-in-command's astonished expression.

"The little servant? She was not a servant, was she?" Mereck smiled his answer. Marcus rubbed his jaw and eyed him. "The daughter of the house? Ah, then the tales were true?" He thumped himself on the forehead. "Had I known of it, I would have raced through the barbican afore you!"

Mereck's hearty laughter echoed through the trees. Stunned to silence on hearing that rare sound, his men stared.

The moment the helpful squire turned his back, Netta slipped into the shadows and entered the castle. She tucked her head down and prayed no one would recognize her as she used the servants' stairs. For certs, Elise would help her plan how to avoid an odious marriage. Glancing over her shoulder, she slipped into her friend's room.

"Netta! When did you arrive? I was about to go down to the hall. Come, we'll go together." Elise smiled happily.

"Shh, Elise, no one must know I am here." Netta led Elise to sit on the bed. She jerked the heavy rose-colored bed drapes closed, in case someone came into the room while they perched atop the warm furs covering the featherbed.

"Father has lost his mind," Lynette whispered in Elise's ear. "You must help me. That doddering Baron Durham died in my room. Father decided I would wed the first loathsome man who entered Wycliffe this morn, whether he be knight or swineherd."

Elise shrieked, "He died in your room? You are to marry a keeper of pigs?"

Lynette's hand flashed out to cover her friend's mouth.

"Even worse! The dreaded Baresark my father has always threatened me with arrived at first light. He is a bearded, barbaric Welshman. Father greeted him like a long lost relative. He wears animal hides and furs and leather bands around his arms in the old way. He probably has an enemy's skull in his travel pouch." Lynette shuddered with horror.

Elise grabbed the back end of her tunic and draped it around her head like a cloak. Only her shocked eyes were visible. "'Tis Baresark? A skull hung from his horse?" If

Elise's whisper had been any louder, they would have heard her on the other side of the thick chamber door.

"Shh. Nay, I saw no skull. It would not surprise me, though, for he is even more frightening than Father described. He oft said the savage keeps the skulls of respected enemies. They are supposed to bring him the man's wisdom." She stopped and listened. "Do you think anyone saw me come up here?"

Before Elise could answer, someone scratched on the door. Netta grabbed Elise's arm and whispered in her ear. "Hurry. See who it is." Elise scrambled off the bed, and Netta yanked the bed curtains shut.

Elise opened the door a crack.

"Milady, visitors have arrived. Yer father wishes ye to attend him."

Elise nodded. "I will be down directly. As soon as I find my shoes." She wriggled, trying to hide her well-shod feet behind the door. "Do not tarry for me." She slammed the door in the girl's face, then raced back to the bed to Lynette.

"Do you think the barbarian hunted you down like he did those poor creatures he wears on his body?" Elise gulped. "For sure that is why they have sent for me. I cannot go below."

"Act as if nothing is wrong," Netta whispered.

"Nay, I could not." Elise's voice wobbled, her hands shook.

"Someone will come to see why you have not obeyed his summons," Netta reminded her as she clambered off the bed.

"Let them. I'll not go below." Elise folded her arms and stood her ground.

Netta took Elise's shoulders and urged her across the room and out into the hallway.

"Do not be affrighted. No one knows I'm here."

Chapter 3

Shortly after Mereck arrived at Ridley Castle, he scrubbed himself clean, scraped the hair from his face and changed into a fine, white linen shirt, dark brown tunic and beige breeches. He stripped away all traces of the warrior Baresark. The next time Netta saw him, she would not recognize him as the man her father determined she would marry.

After the sunset bells of Vespers, Mereck told Baron Ridley and his wife of Wycliffe's harsh decree and of the betrothal contract he had signed that morn.

"Lynette is a keen-witted girl. Disguised as a maid, she came below to see what manner of man her father would force her to wed. He caught sight of her, called her a thief and bid me capture her when she fled." Remembering how she had winced at his touch, Mereck's brows drew together.

"The poor child." The baron's wife had tears in her eyes. "I am afeared he beat her soundly after you left."

"Nay. I would not allow such. I pretended to believe she was of no account and bid my squire to bring her here. No doubt, she is above. Hiding in your daughter's chambers. If she appears dressed as a servant, I would that you pretend not to recognize her in her disguise."

"Ah, now I see your plan. How fortunate you have arrived to escort Elise to her cousin at Blackthorn. When Lynette learns of it, she will surely think to escape by going with Elise."

In a soothing gesture, Baron Ridley patted Mereck's shoulder. "Aye. 'Tis unfortunate her father filled her thoughts with terror of the Baresark legend. As she comes to know and trust you, she will learn that though the legend and Mereck of Blackthorn are one and the same, she has no need to be afeared of you."

Netta huddled in the dark bed, awaiting Elise's return. The door burst open, and Elise entered, along with a servant and the appetizing aroma of roasted chicken. Netta's stomach grumbled, reminding her of her neglect.

"Put the tray on the table, please. What I have heard this night surprised me, and I forgot to eat. That's why I had you bring so much food," she explained loudly.

Noting a hand grasp the bed curtains to draw them back, Netta scrambled to the darkest corner of the bed.

"Nay," Elise fairly shrieked. "Do not worry with turning down my bed. I will undress later and do it myself."

Netta heard a disbelieving snort on the other side of the heavy fabric and almost laughed aloud. Elise was childishly dependent on others to do these chores.

"I will be fine. You may go," Elise added.

Netta parted the bed curtain just enough to glimpse Elise shoving the startled maid through the doorway. Once the maid disappeared, Netta leapt from the bed.

"Food." She raced to the tray and stood, sniffing the mouth-watering smell wafting through the white linen napkins. "I'm drooling like a bairn. I've had naught but bread and water since Baron Durham came to Wycliffe."

"Come. It will be warmer over here." Elise placed the tray on a fur rug close to a brazier of hot coals. After selecting a roasted chicken leg for herself, and handing Netta a thigh from the trencher, she sighed. "All has worked out for the best."

"What has worked out?" Netta asked.

"Our traveling to Scotland, of course." Elise waved the juicy leg at Netta.

"What?" Netta dropped her food in her lap. Startled, she looked down at the mess on her clothing. "Who is traveling to Scotland?"

Elise looked at her as if she thought her best friend dim-witted. "We"—she pointed the leg at Netta and then toward herself—"are going to Scotland." She beamed, but seeing Netta's mouth remained open, she hurried to explain.

"Mereck of Blackthorn is below. My cousin has had a terrible tragedy and has sent for me." Of a sudden, her eyes widened until the whites showed all around her blue irises. She gasped. "Oh, blessed saints in heaven. The wolves."

"What? What wolves?" Netta was beginning to think the only word she had spoken in this discourse was "what."

"You know. The wolves." Elise explained. Netta stared at her without speaking. "The wolves Galan and his friends told Brianna and me about. Do you not remember? I told you of it," Elise reminded her. "They said the ferocious Scots have pet wolves. On winter nights, they raid across the borders and take pesky English girls to feed the wolves." She twisted her fingers together and huddled closer to the brazier. "'Tis soon winter."

"Saints, Elise." Netta laughed. "What right-thinking

person befriends a wolf? Do not tell me you believed those silly tales."

"Galan is an honorable knight. He would not lie," Elise huffed.

"Aye, but he had made no knightly vows then. He was a boy. A tease. When you jumped with fear and cried, did he not comfort you and say he was sorry?" Netta grinned as Elise bobbed her head in agreement. "When your cousin scolded him, did he not look shamed?"

"Aye." Elise's face brightened. "So. You will go with me?"

"Go where?" Netta asked. All this talks of pet wolves made her forget what they were talking about.

"Where? Really, Netta. You should pay attention. To my cousin Brianna at Blackthorn Castle, of course." Elise tore off a chunk of dark bread and nibbled on it. Her eyes lit. "Mereck of Blackthorn will escort us. He did not laugh at me about the wolves." She looked accusingly at Netta. "He told Mother I may take one servant and only what we can put on a single packhorse. Mother will send my things later. Mereck is in a hurry to return to Scotland where our Bleddyn awaits him."

"Why did you not tell me Lord Bleddyn was in Scotland?" Netta's hopes surged. The Welshman would stop her father from forcing her into an abominable marriage and sure madness. "One servant? Of course I'll go, but I need clothing." She reached for another piece of chicken. "And a disguise," she added.

"My tunics will fall off you. Where did you get that ugly garment you wear? It keeps sliding from your shoulders. Why did you stop growing?" Elise frowned at her as if accusing her of being small apurpose. "I know," she said, one hand in the air extending her forefinger. "Cook has a daughter not full grown. I'll trade what you are wearing for something of hers. She won't mind."

They ate as they talked and made their plans. Seeing the trencher was empty, Netta eyed it with regret and licked the juice from her fingers. She had a hearty appetite—one suiting a woman as tall as Elise.

Switching from one foot to the other, Netta peered out the window opening as dawn lightened the sky. Hearing Elise returning from Matins, she dove behind the bed hangings.

"'Tis me," Elise whispered.

Netta jumped from the bed and grinned at the sight that greeted her eyes. A very frumpy looking Elise carried a heavy tray across the room.

"I hid the garments from the cook's daughter under my shift. Knowing you would be hungry, I told Maud I needed extra food." Elise frowned and shrugged. "Though several squires snickered and pointed when I walked past, no one suspected anything was afoot."

Her normally slender posterior was lumpy and shifted with each step. Trailing behind her like a tail was the sleeve of a brown tunic. Lynette muffled her laughter with a pillow and pointed. Elise craned her neck around, then grinned and wriggled her bottom until the clothing dropped to the floor.

Netta giggled and picked up the tunic to hold it in front of her. "No doubt they thought you could not clothe yourself any better than a babe. I had best put this on afore your mother comes to see how you fare."

"You cannot wear such coarse cloth next to your body. It will make you itch." Elise lifted her trunk lid and delved through her garments until she found a linen smock to protect Lynette's delicate skin from chafing.

"Why did you want berries? Cook had some to make a

special fruit pastie for Lord Mereck. He favors them. He praises her and kisses her cheek each time he visits. I whined and told her how sad I was to leave and be prey to savages and wolves, and she let me have a few berries." Elise looked guilty for having deceived the cook.

"They are for my disguise," Netta told her. Elise's eyes widened, so she explained. "I will blacken some of my teeth, and make a berry paste to make my right cheek appear as if it was marked from birth."

After donning the smock and brown tunic, she put the berries in an earthenware pot, then mashed them into a paste. She tried the dye on her cheek, but it was too thick and not dark enough. Adding wine, she again tested it.

"Is this unsightly enough?" She turned and faced Elise.

Elise shuddered and made a face. "Bleh!"

Netta plugged the pot with a stopper and set it aside. She blackened two front teeth with walnut stain she had prepared earlier, and turned to see Elise's eyes rounded wide.

"Yech, Netta. 'Tis disgusting."

"Good. Comely servants attract attention. Perchance your Mereck would want to sport with me. This will discourage him."

After hiding Netta's curly black hair beneath a scarf, Elise again surveyed her friend. "Keep your gaze lowered. No one has eyes like yours. They are bound to draw notice."

"Do you think your father will allow someone unfamiliar to attend you?" Worry churned Netta's stomach.

"Mother surprised me after Matins. She said I could choose any servant I wanted." Elise grinned. "Mereck himself suggested I take someone new. Someone who would not grow homesick for Ridley. Father agreed. Was that not fortunate?"

"Aye, indeed. What would I do without you? Wedding that frightful barbarian would ruin my life."

"And what would I do if you were not here to go with me to barbaric Scotland?" Elise blushed. "We are helping each other."

Netta hugged her. "Let us go to the hall for the noon meal. I'll follow and look the dutiful servant. We will learn if my disguise works."

The torches lit around the great room aided Mereck in spying Netta right off. She trailed Elise across the room, her back straight, shoulders squared with unconscious dignity. She smoothed her hands over her sleeves and stealthily scratched her arms. Thick, sweeping lashes framed her almond-shaped eyes. He willed her to look at him.

She did. Hmm. Beautiful eyes colored a purplish-blue. His stare discomfited her, for she quickly looked away, exposing her right cheek. He saw the red mark on her delicate skin. He had not seen it in the dim stable. Pity filled him. Was this one reason her father had been unable to secure a suitable husband for the lady? Why she shunned them? Most likely only unattractive young men and the aged came to seek her hand.

As Mereck watched, Elise elbowed Netta in the ribs. Netta's shoulders slumped, her head tipped humbly down as she shuffled off to sit at one of the lower tables. The last open seat was beside a sweaty shepherd sporting a very large wart between his eyes. Mereck could imagine his fetid odor.

Netta gathered her skirt close to sit on the bench. A visible shudder ran through her. Soon after she settled there, the man did not seem averse to using her sleeve to wipe his nose. Holding her hand over her mouth, she fled the bench. Her skirts flipped up to reveal shapely legs clothed in coarse white stockings.

Nearby diners laughed at Netta's abrupt departure. She grabbed a pitcher of wine from a passing servant and hurried over to the high table.

"Was your business this morn with Baron Wycliffe fruitful, Lord Mereck?" Simon Ridley asked, then took a sip of wine while awaiting Mereck's answer.

"Aye. Most gratifying, Baron." Mereck kept his face steady as Elise gaped at him. Netta approached the man beside him, the ewer of wine poised to refill his empty chalice.

Elise cleared her throat. "While you were at Wycliffe Castle, my lord, was all well with the baron and his family? Was there a great uproar and searching about the grounds, or warriors riding out with weapons?"

"Search parties? Why would there be search parties, Lady Elise? Has the baron perchance misplaced a daughter?" Mereck hiked his brows.

"Nay, sir," Elise said. "Many men come to Wycliffe to seek my friend Lynette's hand. They sometimes misplace servants."

"Hmm. Now you mention it, lady, there was something strange. Many peasants and sheep herders clamored to come through the gates." Mereck rubbed his jaw and looked pensive. "Each said they were the first to arrive. Many fights broke out amongst them over it. It seemed every man in the village sought an audience with the baron. They all offered to sacrifice themselves at the altar." He smoothed his hand over the cloth on the table, straightening a wrinkle there.

"The altar? What is this, my lord?" Lady Maud pretended she knew naught of the happenings at Wycliffe.

Mereck told her of the baron's harsh decree, while Netta moved closer, dutifully filling each chalice along the way.

"He cannot mean to do such," Lady Maud protested.

Remembering Wycliffe's unnatural hatred for his daughter, Mereck's lips thinned in distaste. His hand moved to grip his sword hilt. He regretted he could not have put it to use earlier.

"He did. I *saw* the betrothal contracts signed whilst I was there. They dinna require her signature. The marriage is all but fact, Baron. She is now under another man's control."

At the thought of who Netta now belonged to, warm waves of satisfaction flowed over him. His loins heated and began to stir. Netta was *his*.

"He did what?" Elise yelled and shot to her feet.

Netta leaned to refill his chalice. He caught her scent—roses and heather—and felt alarm crackle like sparks from her. A young man seated next to Mereck reached out and pinched her delightful bottom. Netta gasped and jerked upward. Wine flew from the ewer and landed in Mereck's lap. Eyelids narrowed, he turned an icy glare on the man.

Netta stared at the purple stain on his tunic. Her eyes widened and her chin began to quiver.

Elise hurried to stand between her and Mereck, the gesture protective, as she babbled, "He promised Lynette to the beast, my lord? Did you see the barbarian? I regret my new servant soiled your clothing. Take them off, and she will cleanse them."

"Lady, I do not think dining naked would be proper." His lips twitched at the abashed look on Netta's face. "The barbarian? I did not look upon the man to whom her father betrothed her, but I heard his vow to take the utmost care of her." For truth, he could not see himself at Wycliffe, but he had heard his own voice vow to care for her. His gaze swept over Netta.

He had thought much of the legend of late. Bleddyn was a mystic and healer, and Mereck had spoken to him of it afore leaving Blackthorn. Bleddyn believed it was a foolish legend that blamed a husband's love for their deaths. He deemed the Baresark wives died from difficult labors and unsanitary conditions. 'Twas common. Many women died of childbirth.

Lynette was the means to gain all he wished for in life. His mother's lands and holdings would be his own. As his wife, she would bear his bairns who would never have to hear the hateful taunt of "bastard." A family to call his own. His sons and daughters would have a father they could claim. One who would leave them security and a legacy.

He would protect his bride. But he would never love her.

The sound of Netta's racing footsteps on the stone floor faded as she fled the room.

Netta huddled in the window embrasure of Elise's room. Scratching her arms. Not only did the cook's daughter give her clothing to wear, she also sent along the fleas that lived there. Her shoulders drooped. She fought moisture filling her eyes. Heaven knew she had much to be miserable about—a father who sought to banish her from his life, escaping a betrothed who was a fearsome savage, a trip to the barbarous Highlands and now disgusting fleas.

If she was not so furious, she would wail.

Elise burst into the room, her mother close behind her.

Netta stood, jerked her head down and curtsied to the baroness. A particularly ferocious varmint made her twitch and shudder. Lady Maud's brows rose.

"What ails you, girl? Are you so infested with vermin you cannot keep still?"

Netta peeked up at her through lowered lashes. Elise's mother studied Netta with compassionate eyes. Would she recognize her? Netta's hands trembled.

"Aye, milady. I fear ye be right. I slept too close to a hound in the kitchens and he sent his friends to me clothin'," she mumbled.

"Elise, is this the young woman whom you begged me to let accompany you?"

"Aye, if you please, Mother. She will be my protector. She is not afeared of wild men or beasts!"

"What is your name?" Lady Maud asked Netta.

"It is Netta, Mother," Elise said. "I cannot go to that awful place without her." She began to wail piteously.

"No need to be upset, love. Come, Netta. I have a lotion that will aid you, and a strong soap that will kill the pesky devils." Lady Maud beckoned Netta to follow her, then stopped abruptly.

"Elise, have a servant go through the chest in my solar. Surely she can find something serviceable for Netta amid your old clothing stored there."

Netta's mouth dropped open. She drew near to the baroness, who surprised her by winking and giving her shoulder a quick pat. As they left the room, one woman stood tall and proud, the other slumped and shuffled, watching for any mishap that would deny her her freedom.

After attending mass at dawn and breaking their fast, Mereck's party prepared to leave. The bailey swarmed with horses and men, and the servants there to ease their leave-taking. A slight breeze stirred the dust, lifting it to swirl about them. Horses stamped and snorted, and sidled restlessly as their grooms fought to control the great destriers.

Mereck stood close-by as Netta spied the mount she was to ride. She scowled and studied the ugly beast. Had he purchased the sway-backed animal from a village serf?

Her back stiffened and her hands fisted on her waist. She turned to glare at him. Saints help her. Had he grown? He appeared larger today than he did yester eve.

Black breeches covered his massive legs, the pants cross-gartered with leather strips that disappeared beneath leather boots. Over a black shirt he wore his hauberk, a chain mail tunic that covered from his neck to below his knees. A thick red cloak, gathered at his left shoulder, hid all but the hilt of his great sword. His long tawny hair blew back from his face. His squire stood nearby holding a silver conical helm with nose guard in the Norman style.

Netta shouted above the clamor of shields, swords and the din of the many warriors. "This beast is the best you could provide, sirrah?"

Mereck raised a brow at the contemptuous form of address. Folding his arms across his chest, he stared down at her. She soon lowered her gaze, remembering her disguise.

"You expected to ride a fine-blooded mare? I doubt the baron mounts his servants as he does his family. Lightning is no beauty, but he is strong enough to carry you and some of your mistress' belongings."

"Lightning? Hmpf." Netta shook her head. "Only a deranged soul would name this broken-down horse Lightning."

The stable boys snickered. Mereck frowned.

At Blackthorn, Bleddyn had designed two special saddles. They had a high back and right side for a woman's hips to rest against, and a hump in front for her to drape her right leg around. A stirrup supported the left leg.

Before Netta could protest, Mereck gripped her waist and lifted her to the saddle. Taking her left foot, he placed it in the stirrup. With his head still bent, he caught her right ankle and guided her leg to the correct position on the saddle. A prankish gust of wind flirted across the bailey, and snuck beneath the edge of her green tunic. The garment flew up to reveal shapely calves. His manhood stirred, picturing one day having her legs locked around his waist as she urged him deeper.

Netta batted at the billowing fabric, forcing it down.

Pretending to be unmoved by the sight of her bared flesh, Mereck studied the mark on her cheek.

Hmm. The lady tried to hide her beauty behind fake flaws. What he saw was an unblemished face with a smooth forehead and black brows arched above beautiful, deep blue eyes. The spot on her right eye reminded him of a golden freckle. Her nose was perfectly formed, her lips full and begging to be kissed.

Ah, those lips. How would they taste when he nibbled on them? Like honey? The thought caused a rumble to well up from his chest. Netta looked down at him, startled.

He turned his attention to Elise.

If he had known what a demanding task it would be to get the lady started on their journey, he would have sent Marcus to fetch her. Elise ran back and forth between her mount and the members of her family so often he lost count. Each time he attempted to place her on the saddle of her beloved Buttercup, she held up her hand and bade him wait. She would then break into a run up the stone steps to again embrace either her mother or father.

He went, for at least the fifth time, to take Elise by the hand and lead her to Buttercup. He murmured encouragements as he courteously helped her mount and adjust to the new saddle.

Lynette glared shards of ice his way and muttered about arrogant men. Mereck placed his helm on his head and pretended he did not hear. He signaled for his squire to take his place behind Netta, and Marcus' squire to ride close to Elise. Earlier, he had ordered the boys to keep close watch over the ladies in case they should need assistance.

They waved good-bye and rode out from the castle walls. Netta prayed she would not see the dreaded Baresark in hot pursuit. By the time the sun rose high in the east, she began to relax. She mastered the saddle and the swaying beast she rode, but she could no longer hold her tongue.

"Oh, rats and fleas, Elise. This Mereck is a rude, obnoxious churl. How can you think so highly of him? He would better serve us to use this big heap of bones to feed the wolves than as a mount."

"Wolves? But Father said this morn that we need not fear wolves if we were careful and did not leave a trail of food in our wake. Or bang pots to attract them." Elise, eyes widened, darted glances at the trees crowding the sides of the road.

"Nay. There are no wolves here. Still, if we chance to meet any, we could offer this broken down steed to keep them busy while we made good our escape," Netta grumbled, but winced and patted the horse's shaggy neck as if to deny what she had said. "Lightning? No one of right mind would name this steed such. Snail would be more apt."

"Look. Another man heads into the woods. What do you think they do? Do they not pay heed to where they are going? They must quickly remember, for they are not gone for long." Elise squirmed in her saddle. "Do you think Mereck will soon stop at a keep?"

"I have not seen even a hint of a keep. He forgets he is not riding to battle. I doubt he recalls we are with him, much less that he would think of our needs."

Netta watched a man leaving the road. Shortly after, he rejoined the line of warriors to the rear. In but a moment, she realized his purpose.

"No wonder the dratted man does not call a halt. Men go off into the woods any time they want, whilst we must remain on our horses. Inconsiderate churl," Netta muttered, though she was glad this Mereck also wanted to go swiftly into Scotland. She had oft looked over her shoulder to search the area behind them, fearing the horrible savage pursued her.

Behind her, Mereck's squire Dafydd snickered. He pulled out of line, flashed her a cheeky grin, and made his way to his commander's side. Mereck swivelled in his saddle to study them. Though the nose guard covered much of his face, his eyes frowned. Soon after, they left the trail to enter a shaded area large enough to offer them comfort.

Elise, scurrying to dismount, did not see young Fergus, Marcus' squire, had come to aid her. She lost her balance and began to fall. Her arms flew out and walloped the squire across his face as he reached for her. She toppled into his arms, knocking them both to the ground. Elise landed softly—on the poor lad's stomach.

"Dinna think to attempt the same stunt, Netta." Mereck's voice was arrogant, but the corners of his lips twitched.

"Nay. I need no assistance, sir." Glaring haughtily at him, she drew back from his reaching hands. His green eyes flashed wintery sparks now. No longer soft, his lips thinned to a menacing line.

"Suit yourself, girl. But dinna expect me to cushion your fall."

"Humph! I expect no such chivalry from you."

Ignoring the narrowing of his eyes, she wriggled her right leg free. Her left foot refused to support her efforts to slide to the ground. After several useless attempts, she hissed in disgust.

She pretended she had no intention of moving.

Were Mereck's feet encased in stone?

Why did he not leave so she could ask Dafydd for help? This dratted horse was much too tall. She missed the willing hands that would have helped her at Wycliffe. Willing hands were here also, but she did not want his huge paws on her body again. Every time he touched her, strange flutters started in the pit of her stomach, and that place between her legs. Never had it happened afore. Netta frowned. She caught her breath, thinking he was really quite comely. What thoughts caused his eyes to sparkle like emeralds in the sun?

Leaning his broad shoulders against a tree, he tossed Dafydd his helm, then folded his arms across his chest. The wind ruffled his tawny hair while he waited, watching her as if he had all day. Standing close-by, Elise shifted from one foot to another, needing company in the woods. Netta was much in need of a visit there herself. Her face heated, realizing she could no longer delay dismounting.

"You may assist me." She waited. Was he bonded to the tree? Was it possible he had suffered a hearing loss in battle? Speaking louder, she informed him, "I have changed my mind. You may assist me," she repeated.

He did not move. Except his eyelids. They narrowed

even more over a frosty stare. She began to rethink her request.

"Please. I require your aid to dismount, sir."

He pushed away from the tree and moved close. She caught his scent. Not a stale odor like her father. Nor the sweaty smell she had begun to expect from her suitors. For certs, it was far more troubling. It made her heart beat faster, and a heated sensation flowed from her breasts to her stomach.

Mereck lifted her to the ground, his large hands causing her skin to quiver where he grasped her. Must he hold her so close to his body? She inhaled, deeply. Hmm. His scent. Juniper and musk. And man. She blinked in surprise as heat rushed through her. Smiling, Mereck released her and motioned for Dafydd to lead them to a private area.

If her legs were not so numb, she would show that sluggard Lightning a thing or two about fast moving as they headed for the woods. She and Elise were soon alone.

"Netta. What if wild beasts are awaiting us?"

"After the noise of our horses and the men stomping around, I doubt even a grasshopper is about."

Elise needed no more encouragement.

Not long after, Netta saw an arm-length piece of wood come crashing down through a nearby tree.

"Saints! You were wrong. A boar is after us." Elise hurtled toward her through the bushes.

Hearing muffled laughter from the clearing, Netta scowled.

"Huh! No beast, but a foolish warrior trying to affright us. Come. We should pretend we did not note it." Netta took Elise's arm and marched back to the clearing with her.

Mereck frowned at the men who watched them still

chuckling. The warriors hastily went about the business of eating dried strips of beef and bannocks made of barley flour.

Angus, Mereck's appointed cook, unpacked large sacks tied to a pack horse. Beneath a birch tree, the squires spread a wool blanket atop a cushion of leaves.

"Once you have served us, Netta, you may take your meal with us," Mereck ordered.

His words startled her, until she remembered she was to assume duties she had never performed. Elise started to follow, but Mereck steered her to the blanket and helped her to sit. Netta thought she saw a slight smile on his face.

She was unsure of how to continue. Shrugging her shoulders, she unfolded a cloth and began to pile bannocks, a large chunk of cheese, and several roasted chicken legs on it. She selected a hard piece of barley bread, and piled it with honey. Enough food for several men covered the cloth. But was it enough for her also?

Picking up the corners of the cloth, she started to lift it. She looked toward Mereck, where he lounged beside Elise and Marcus. Her stomach rumbled. Would it never quiet? She sat the cloth down, grabbed extra chicken and bannocks, and hurried to them.

"The woods are damp this time of year. I note Lady Elise has stepped in a puddle," Mereck commented as Netta joined them. His lips twitched, for Elise quickly folded her legs beneath her skirts. As Netta dumped the food on the blanket, he ordered, "When we make camp this night, you will tend to her clothing. You dinna want your mistress uncomfortable."

Netta bobbed her head. She watched Mereck serve Elise and himself, and then offer the food to Marcus, before placing it on the blanket near her. He did not serve her as he had Elise.

Netta kept her gaze lowered while she ate, for whenever she looked up, she found Mereck's green eyes studying her. She choked down a dry bannock. He had served himself and Elise all the honey she had scooped onto the largest piece of flat barley bread. She loved honey. Without it, her bannock was tasteless.

Did he not see he left her such a small portion of food, she would likely faint from hunger afore they camped this night?

Mereck's lips were twitching again. Did he have an itch?

Engrossed with her thoughts, she did not notice he had finished his meal until he stood. By his pointed look, he waited for her to note Elise had already risen. Netta shot to her feet, tossing crumbs from her tunic.

She picked up the blanket, shook it out and started to fold it. Mereck nodded his satisfaction before he went over to Marcus. The two were soon deep in conversation.

He was taller than Marcus, about nineteen hands tall. She eyed Mereck, assessing his weight. About fifteen stone, she decided. Broader about the shoulders than Marcus, also. The length of his legs caught her interest. As if feeling her perusal, they shifted restlessly, the muscles flexing with his movements.

Shards of apprehension sliced through her as she studied Mereck's muscular body.

His massive frame reminded her of someone. She frowned, searching her memory.

Who?

Icy fingers of fear whispered down her back.

Chapter 4

"This Mereck is the most unchivalrous warrior it has been my mishap to know." Netta, her forehead crinkled with annoyance, grasped Lightning's mane and leaned closer to Elise. "He is such an enormous man. He has his way about everything. Why, rats and fleas. I vow he would not shrink from murder."

Elise turned, her mouth agape. Mayhap Netta should soothe her afore she fell from her mount.

"If warranted when pillaging and raiding, of course," she added and shook her head. "'Tis all warriors do."

Elise straightened in her saddle and hiccuped. "My parents told me these men are not like the savage Scots we have heard about but are much like our own Saxon warriors."

Netta looked around at the men escorting them. "Highlanders do dress differently." She studied the men nearest them. "Some wear plaids belted around their waist or loose shirts over breeches. Marcus and some warriors still wear heavy hauberks and helms."

During their stop earlier, Mereck had removed his heavy battle apparel and donned a shirt. She glimpsed the bronze skin of his chest and a mat of tawny hair peeking through the shirt's opening. A thick leather belt held his plaid at his waist, and his broadsword hung from a holder strapped to his back.

"Have you not noticed?" Elise's brows rose. "Their parents failed to civilize them. Mother would be shocked and Father would scold and deem we cover our eyes."

"Shocked? Cover our eyes?" Netta peered around but didn't see anything startling.

"They do not wear anything under their skirts," Elise said in a loud whisper.

"Surely they are not naked." Netta lowered her head and peered through her lashes.

"While we supped, a man raised his skirt to scratch. Blessed Saint Mary. Do they all have hairy arses?" Elise's red face rivaled the roses in the Wycliffe gardens.

"Nay. For certs he must be the only one. Do not think on it." Netta's wide-eyed gaze searched for something to distract her friend—and herself. "Quick. See that goat jumping over a bush taller than himself. He ran like hounds are chasing him." She wondered if she herself would be much interested in watching for animals from now on. Men were far more intriguing. "And heather. Is it not lovely?"

Hmm. Was it possible the man Elise saw was unusual? She looked at Mereck just as an enlightening gust, and the horse's movements, hoisted the side of his plaid. Curly brown hair on his thigh rustled with the breeze. Her gaze glued to the sight of hard muscles flexing to control his spirited mount. Aye. This mode of dress was most interesting.

Netta ducked her head on seeing Mereck glance back at her. Had he noted her shameful study of his exposed flesh? She had no brothers, no cousins, uncles or male relatives living at Wycliffe. Only Father. He never allowed her to assist visitors who came to the castle. He assigned one of her stepsisters the duty of bathing them, hoping they would entice a wealthy man's interest.

Mereck turned often to study her and Elise. He frowned and waited beside the path for them to come abreast.

"Netta, do you not deem it needful to watch the path?"

"Nay, sir. I trust Lightning to follow in line," she stammered. Her gaze strayed to his bare knees peeking below his plaid. Her face heated like she suffered from an ague.

His probing, green gaze studied her. She glanced away, but wind again flirted with the material. She swallowed and stared. Oh my, how can legs be so intriguing? How would the hair on a man's body feel? Is it silky or coarse? Does it cover his arse like Elise had seen? Of a sudden, the savage she fled popped into her mind. He must be covered with coarse hair from his head to his toes. She shuddered, picturing it.

Mereck felt no pain on hearing Netta's inquisitive thoughts. Far from it. He swallowed a chuckle that near burst forth. Her curious gaze felt like soft fingertips whispering over his heated flesh. He adjusted the plaid to hide the telltale tent betwixt his legs and shifted uncomfortably in the saddle. Knowing she belonged to him made his heated blood pound through his body. His manhood hardened and jerked with impatience. Perchance, he would enjoy a wife who made him laugh. God knew he'd had little mirth in his life.

He looked forward to the day she would have the opportunity to explore him. She was comely, lovely even. Was her hair beneath that scarf as raven black as her brows? And the thatch betwixt her legs? Darker yet, shielding her secret delights?

He pictured her without her disguise. Without clothing.

Magnificently naked. His manhood acted like an untried youth's. Disgusted, he shifted again.

They rode till the sun began to dip and Mereck called a halt. He strode over the damp ground to lift Netta off Lightning. He stood too close when he swung her down, brushing her against his body. His heat seared her. Her face flushed. She avoided his eyes and hurried ahead, not reckoning with the wet earth. Misty rain had fallen much of the day, and her too-large shoes hit a patch of muddy leaves. Her feet skidded from beneath her.

"Uhfff." Her fall knocked the breath out of her. Ick! She crinkled her nose in distaste for the sour smell of rank vegetation hidden under the leaves. The unpleasant feel of her hips resting on squishy mud made her wish to grab Mereck's knees to scramble off the ground. When she looked up ready to grasp him, the sight that greeted her eyes near made her gasp.

Netta lay on her back, her head nearly between Mereck's feet. She blinked, fast as a hawk's wings, like a startled child. As he squatted beside her, her face flamed so bright he fancied he felt the heat on his ankles. Why was she so distressed over a simple spill in the mud?

"Dinna move. I would see if you have an injury." Mereck felt her head for any swelling, knowing how dangerous a blow there could be. Her head scarf hampered feeling her scalp. He tugged off the binding, releasing long, silky black curls to spill over his hands and onto the wet ground. He growled with satisfaction. One question was answered.

Netta tried to struggle away. He gripped her chin to hold her still.

Jesu. Such beautiful eyes.

Never had he seen as deep a blue. They were not small and set wide apart like the Saxon's idea of beauty, but large and placed just right. The portion of her right eye that caused such displeasure was as clear and bright as a golden wildflower in spring. Pleased, he studied the rest of her face while he held her prisoner with his hands.

Netta's brows curved full and elegant, her left cheek unblemished. Her forehead rose high and showed intelligence. Full lips trembled and tempted him to plunder them with his own.

His betrothed hid much that appealed to him.

Netta grinned up at him.

A wide grin that showed all her teeth.

She thought to discourage him? "Ahumpf." He strangled a chuckle, for the stain on her teeth was clearly faked.

"I dinna believe you are injured, girl, though you have wallowed in mud. See you wash properly." He eyed her hair and rubbed his chin thoughtfully. "Mud-caked tresses provide a favorite nesting place for forest insects."

She gasped and scrambled to her feet. He nodded to Dafydd and pointed to a pond just beyond the trees. The young man would see to it the area was safe.

Netta scrubbed her sudsy hair, fearing the creatures Mereck spoke of would fall from the trees and make a horrid writhing nest in her black curls. Finally satisfied no mud remained, she rinsed and scooped her tunic off the bank with the tips of her fingers. Mereck had spoken true. The back was covered with mud. She spread soap over it, then held it up and stared at it. Clumsy and unsure of how one went about washing clothes, she brought her hands close and bounced her knuckles together as she had seen the servants do. She looked to see the results. It was as dirty as before.

"Our laundress slaps the dirty spot," Elise advised over Netta's shoulder. "Like this." She swatted at the soapy fabric and succeeded in splattering soap in their eyes.

"Nay, they beat their fists together." Netta was sure of it. She pounded furiously, but the mud stubbornly clung to its new home. She gritted her teeth and muttered, "They were peasants. If they mastered the skill, it cannot be difficult to learn." She fisted her hands and ground them together, ready to tear the tunic to shreds.

"Oh, Netta. See how the mud rolls off?" Elise grabbed her stockings and imitated Netta's angry moves.

They grinned at each other and splashed from the water. Soon Netta was dressed in a light yellow tunic that Elise had worn when she was but ten and four. The garment was a perfect fit for Netta's small frame.

Elise dabbed the crushed berry juice on Netta's cheek and neck until she was satisfied with the effect. "Ech, how can you bear this horrid stuff on your face?"

Netta shrugged and uncorked the small vial of nut stain. "Which teeth did I blacken this morn? The two in the middle?"

"Uh, the middle? Was it not near the side?" Elise tilted her head and studied Netta. "Aye, I am near certain of it." She nodded and added the nut stain to Netta's teeth.

"We are ready to return, Dafydd," Netta called out as she tucked her concoctions away in her pocket.

Within a pair of heartbeats, the young man appeared and took the freshly washed garments from them.

Angus was already serving their evening meal when they came into camp. Mereck stood waiting. After they settled on the blanket and started to eat, he and Marcus discussed their plans for the following day.

Their preoccupation suited Netta, but she soon felt Mereck's gaze on her face. Could he see beyond her disguises? Lowering her head, she leaned closer to Elise and whispered, "Mereck watches me like a bug pinned by a cat's paw. What could be the matter?"

"Could it be the odious stuff on your cheek? Or teeth that beg pulling by a farrier's tongs? You disguised yourself well. We cannot let him know you are Lynette until we are so far from Wycliffe he will be unable to return you to your horrible savage."

Netta shuddered, imagining the giant wild man stalking her. She could not chance being hauled back and forced to marry a creature who filled her with terror.

"Netta, it has been many moons since we visited. You told me of Baron Durham, but how did you thwart Roger of Mortain's suit? By the time Father heard of him, Mortain was long gone."

Netta shuddered, remembering her fear of the cruel man. Between him and Baresark, she was not sure which man frightened her more. "I sought to discourage him when I told him I was no longer a virgin and was unable to have babes."

Elise gasped and put her hand to her throat.

"Netta, you spoke of such with him?"

"I wished only to be rid of him." She reached up and touched her cheek. "I can yet feel the sting of his hand. He demanded I allow him to sample my body. I refused, and he tried to beat me into obedience. Father's men-at-arms came upon us and escorted him from the castle. But not because Roger mistreated me. Father learned his sire tired of his cruelty to his tenants. To curb him, the baron tightened his purse strings, allowing him but a mere pittance in coins."

Netta shuddered and forced the unpleasant thoughts of the Mortain family from her mind.

Mereck's sympathy stirred at the thought of the Baron's cruelty in trying to rid himself of his daughter. Lady Maud had told him Wycliffe's hatred for Lynette was well known.

Bleddyn knew, for he saw to it Mereck was there at that crucial time. Had he not, another man would have laid claim to what rightfully belonged to Mereck—Caer Cadwell. His mother had escaped the slaughter of her family at Cadwell. Donald Morgan found her close inside the Scottish border and took her home to Blackthorn. Mereck was birthed the following year.

Netta belonged to Mereck now. His wife by contract, and soon-to-be-wife by vows.

His.

Caer Cadwell would again belong to a descendant of Gruffyd ap Tewdwr, his great-great-grandfather.

He bounded to his feet, startling the women. Elise scrambled up, but Netta did not move, not even when he crooked a finger at her.

He reached down and grasped her hand. She soon stood.

"Come, I will show you where you sleep this night."

Mereck enjoyed the feel of her soft hand enveloped in his, like a small, restless kitten as she tried to pull away. He did not release her until they reached the small tent Dafydd had prepared. It would be cozy on chilly nights, nights that would become colder yet as they made their way to the Highlands.

"Prepare your mistress for sleep, Netta, then seek your own pallet." He nodded toward the narrow bedding placed outside the tent. Beckoning to Elise, he held the tent flap open for her.

Netta spied the bedding prepared for Elise, dug in her feet and frowned. Why, it was twice the size of her pallet outside, with large, plush fur coverings inviting a warm sleep.

"Dafydd may remove my pallet. I will sleep with Elise."

"I think not. This is for your mistress, not her maid." Crossing his arms, Mereck looked down at her, his gaze stern. "You will sleep next to me, close-by your mistress should she need your services during the night."

"Why must I sleep in the open, sir, with insects and animals? This shelter is large enough for both of us." She tilted her nose up and stared at him.

His cold gaze moved over her, stopping for a moment at her hands on hips as she defied him.

"You will sleep on the pallet next to mine, girl. Dinna push me further."

She raised a finger in front of his nose to silence him. He glared down at her.

"Why must you be stubborn, sir? Elise will not mind."

Before she could speak again, he lifted her chin, forcing her to look at him. "Because I am *an unchivalrous warrior and an enormous man. I also have my way about everything, and would not shrink from murder, if it so warrants*," he added ominously.

Netta gulped, her eyes rounded wide on meeting his gaze. She remembered her own words at the noon break. She prayed the ground would open and swallow her into its depths.

Anger turned Mereck's light green eyes to cold emerald. Unable to look away, she studied his face. Tawny brown eyebrows and thick lashes added emphasis to commanding eyes. Hair not brown, not golden but a mixture of both flowed around his face and fell past his shoulders.

Its untamed look teased her memory. The fine hairs on her nape stirred. Eyes squinted, she tried to summon that missing face to mind. It would not come.

Her searching gaze studied him. Could one call Mereck's nose strong? Arrogant, even? Her gaze lowered to stop on his lips.

Oh, my! Full and sensuous. Soft. Enticing.

They twitched at the corners. Did her perusal amuse him? Blinking, she pulled back. Nay, she could not have seen this man afore. She would have remembered a face that sent such strange flutters through her stomach. Would she not?

"After you prepare your lady for bed, I will come for you."

Mereck's voice halted her wayward thoughts. His glint-eyed stare warned he would allow no further carping. Nodding, he left.

Peeking out the tent opening, Netta watched him assign the night guards. "He makes me so angry I want to stomp his toes." She stamped the ground instead. "I'm no peasant who must sleep in the open. I'll not do as he says."

"Oh, Netta, do not rile him," Elise pleaded.

"Why not? He relishes angering me," Netta fumed.

"Because of his temper." Elise's voice did not raise above a whisper. Her face blanched with fright.

"Everyone has a temper." Netta shrugged.

"Aye. But not like Mereck's. When King William and King Malcolm forced Lord Damron to marry Brianna, Lord Damron came to collect Brianna carrying the kings' decree. Why, she kicked his shins and boxed his ears. Lord Damron's cousin Connor said she had 'the fearsome temper of a Mereck.' Though I have never seen him so angered, I am afeared of causing it."

"Did Damron beat Brianna?" Netta's lips puckered in annoyance as she reached for the hem of Elise's tunic.

"Oh nay, I don't believe so," Elise said. "Still, it is much more than that. Damron and Mereck, born on the same day of the same father, had different mothers. Mereck's Welsh mother died after the birthing. Lady Phillipa, Damron's mother, took Mereck to nurse alongside her son." Elise's voice was muffled by her clothing.

Netta's eyes widened in surprise. How could Lady Phillipa be so forgiving?

"After their fathers' deaths and the time came to foster the boys, the lady took Damron and Connor to Normandy. Their grandfather kept Mereck in Scotland," Elise continued.

"How cruel! Why was he not allowed to foster with them?"

"Because of his terrible temper. They say he blames himself for his mother's death. He becomes fearsome if anyone dares call him bastard. It is an awful slight on his mother. At but ten and three, he skewered a man with his sword afore the man finished the word." She gasped for breath before she continued. "Oh, I beseech you, don't make him angry."

"Brianna married into a strange family. She must dislike them all."

"Oh, nay. Her sister Abbess Alana told my parents their love for each other is fierce." Elise nodded for emphasis.

Netta ran her fingers through her hair, troubled. "Why did Damron's mother not scorn a husband who sired a bastard?"

Elise shrugged. Netta felt pangs of sympathy for the young boy Mereck had been. How terrible for him, forced to stand by while his brother owned it all.

Netta helped Elise don a warm smock. She realized she

would have to sleep in her clothing, for with a hundred men watching, she could not remove her tunic. Maybe not a hundred, she corrected herself. They did not look to be on the courtly side, either. Scruffy best described them. The sounds of someone approaching the tent drew her attention.

"Netta, I wish to retire." Mereck's impatient voice boomed, "Come at once."

Netta jumped. Elise threw her a pleading look to remind her not to anger him. Netta rushed through the tent opening, knowing he would likely barge into their privacy and pull her out if she did not quickly appear.

"Oomph." Her eyes crossed. She shook her head. She had slammed into the solid length of Mereck. He felt like a massive tree. A very staunch tree. He wore a shirt, not armor. Was his body built of iron muscles? She detected no softness like her father's.

Dafydd and the other young squires, already rolled in their tartans, snickered at the mishap. She ignored them. Close behind Mereck a man laughed, the sound was more like the braying of an ass than a man. Hearing the hated sound, she grabbed Mereck's shirt, seeking his protection.

Roger? Bile flooded her throat. Had Roger of Mortain hunted her down for her father?

Chapter 5

Fear near buckled Netta's knees. Mereck's warm, muscled arms closed around her, drawing her close. The sound of his steady heartbeat against her ear soothed her. She clung to him.

For the first time in her life, she felt safe, protected. Holding tight to him, she steeled herself to peek to see who loomed behind him. Had Roger come to drag her back to Wycliffe? Laughter sounded again. On spying a grinning man talking to Marcus, relief washed through her.

Why did Mereck not let her go?

Feeling him stroke her back, she shivered. Her heart drummed to a faster beat. Pressed against his shirt, she drew in a deep breath. Juniper and musk. It came from his skin, this heady scent, making her legs quiver in a new way.

"I can stand on my own, sir. You may take your hands from me."

His deep voice rumbled from his chest. "Sleep now. You must rise early to help prepare porridge."

"Prepare porridge? Why would I do such?" Surprised, her head jerked back from his tantalizing scent. She missed his warmth when he drew away. The night was again cold, lonely.

"Are you not the cook's niece? Didna you work in the kitchens with her? You should be well trained to help him. Be grateful I dinna have you serve my warriors."

Netta's temper flared. She forgot her fear of moments ago.

"Are there any other duties you require me to perform, sir? Wash your shirts? Curry your horse? Or should I sharpen your blades and polish your armor? Oh, I misspeak. You do not wear armor over your little skirt." She ground her teeth and clenched her hands. She took several deep breaths.

Mereck stood as still as that tree trunk he resembled. She looked at his face. And wished she had not. He was angry. More than angry. Too late, she recalled Elise's warning.

"I will seek my rest now so I may rise early." Edging around him, she made a dive for the pallet.

She did not reach it.

Steely hands gripped her shoulders. He lifted her off her feet and spun her around so fast her thoughts flew from her mind.

"Ne'er use such a tone to me, girl. Were you a titled lady, I wouldna permit you to speak to me thus. Dinna attempt it again." Icy anger coated his words.

She nodded, far too frightened for speech. He released her. She dropped to her knees and scrambled under the wool plaid. Was this how a mouse felt burrowing into its nest?

She shivered. Well, rats and fleas. She knew what she was doing. Hiding. Never had she met a man as arrogant as he.

Hearing the rustle of clothing, she slitted her eyes open

and gasped. Mereck stood but two handsbreadth away. He unfastened the clasp pinning the plaid to his shirt. Turning his back to her, he removed the thick leather belt holding the yards of material around his waist and started unwrapping it.

"Get you to sleep, Netta. Dawn will rise long afore you are ready for it."

Saints! How could he know she watched him? Squeezing her eyes shut, she pretended sleep. But she could not resist another glimpse. She was too late. Wrapped snugly in the tartan, he stretched out on his pallet and placed the sword beside him all in one smooth movement. Heat radiated from his powerful body, warming her.

Mereck knew Netta would be a handful. She chaffed under the restrictions of her role, but she would fast learn to control her temper. He would see to it.

He slept lightly and awoke as the night turned colder. Slipping his arm around her, he drew her close and added his own covering atop hers. With ease learned from long years of practice, he removed the pins and freed her hair. Combing his long fingers through her tresses, their rose-scented fragrance pleased him. Holding her nestled against his warmth, he smiled when she sighed and burrowed closer.

Though he did not love her, he would make a passable husband. Never again would Netta feel unworthy, unwanted. Their children would have ample love from both parents. Moreover, they would bear a name proud to call their own.

As deep dark turned to gray, he rose and soon was fully clothed. After lighting a torch, he secured it in front of the tent then nudged Netta's hip with his boot.

"Rise, girl. It is time to awake Lady Elise and fetch porridge to break our fast."

"Nay. Why, it is the middle of the night," Netta grumbled. Pulling her cover over her head, she snuggled into the warmth hoping to slip back into the dream she was loath to relinquish. Who had held her so tenderly and whispered he wanted her? The face was a blur. But the memory of warm arms enfolding her while someone placed soft kisses on her forehead remained sharp.

"Ah." She took a deep breath. Mereck's scent permeated her covers, sending little shivers through her—until his voice intruded.

"Noon will be upon us afore you know it, girl."

He snagged her cover with his sword, pulling it away.

A blast of cold air hit her, startling her to a sitting position, hands grasping for the plaid.

"By the saints! Do you try to freeze me, sir?" She blinked as bare knees came into sight. She did not dare look higher up his hard thigh. The thought jolted her to her feet. She grabbed her plaid and scrambled into the tent.

"Wake up, Elise. We must prepare to leave. I cannot believe these people sleep so little," she groused.

"Wake up? Is it morning?" Elise sat bolt upright on her pallet and blinked. "Yipes, I'm blind," she wailed. "I can see naught but shadows."

"You are not blind," Netta soothed. "It is dark still. The torch outside the tent makes shadows within." She pulled the furs off Elise and started helping her to don her clothing.

"Mereck ordered me to serve as I did afore. Hurry, lest I swoon from hunger." Her stomach made its own demand known, adding emphasis to her words. She glanced over her shoulder at the tent flap hoping Mereck had not heard.

She started to tidy her hair and realized she must have

taken it down while she slept. To her surprise, when she rushed outside to retrieve her pins, she found them laid in a row on her pallet.

Once she secured her hair in a tight coil atop her head, she applied more of the berry mixture to her face. Her skin tingled. Her nose twitched. If the mixture became rancid, would it harm her flawless skin? She shuddered and hurried from the tent.

Angus briskly stirred an iron pot over the fire.

"Good morn, lassie. I ken ye wud be hurryin', so I have bowls ready fer ye. All ye needs do is add either honey or salt. Sir Mereck prefers a pinch of salt. Marcus likes honey. Mind now, just a pinch of the salt." He looked up and smiled.

Netta blinked.

Two of Angus' front teeth were as black as hers. The same two. She smiled back, then snapped her lips together. Had the stain worn off during the night? Angus chuckled and bent over the pot. Seeing her chance, she picked up a tiny piece of burnt wood fallen from the fire and glanced about to see if anyone watched. She rubbed it vigorously over her teeth. What a dratted coil. Had she covered the correct teeth? She wished Elise were there to tell her.

A deep voice spoke close to her shoulder. She whirled, letting the wood drop behind her.

"We would break our fast, Netta. You may bring our porridge and ale now."

Mereck ceased speaking and studied her face, his eyes questioning.

"What, sir? What is it?"

"Did you stoke the fire, Netta?"

"Nay. Should I have?"

He shook his head. "Squires assist in such matters." He

turned to stride over to Marcus. His shoulder brushed a limb with dew-misted leaves, raining glistening droplets on the golden hair covering his arm.

"Let me help, Netta." Elise hurried over after Mereck moved away.

Netta sprinkled a pinch of salt on the first bowl of porridge then turned to nod at her.

"What happened to your face?" Elise took a square of linen from her pocket and scrubbed Netta's mouth and chin. "You have black smudges all over it."

Netta groaned, rolled her eyes and smiled so Elise could see her teeth. "Did I do it right? I could not tell if I blackened the same teeth," she whispered.

"Oh dear, were they not the second and third teeth? I am not sure. Perchance you should do them all to avoid a mistake?"

"Oh, nay. I forgot the walnut stain this morn. Burnt wood tastes horrid, you know. Mayhap no one will remember which teeth, as long as two are black."

Feeling Mereck's impatient stare, Netta looked down at the bowls of porridge. Had she started to prepare them? She nibbled her lower lip and put a healthy pinch of salt on Mereck's cooked oats then added honey to the other three. There. She had done all that Angus had said. She grabbed Mereck's bowl and a cup of ale and hurried over to him. It took her two more trips for Marcus and herself. Elise brought her own.

The men waited politely until Netta served everyone. She seated herself and watched Mereck scoop up a spoonful of porridge and put it in his mouth. Eyes opening wide, he gulped it down then grabbed his cup of ale and downed every drop. Was the man over fond of ale? She hoped not. Men who became bleary-eyed and slurred their words were oafs of the worst sort.

Of a sudden, he stopped eating and looked at her. She was puzzled and a little uneasy. Did he not like the porridge? If not, it was his own fault. If he would put honey on it, the oats would be much tastier. Should she suggest it on the morrow?

Though the taste of ash ruined the first mouthful of her own food, she soon finished eating, grateful when Angus came to collect the bowls. She and Elise hurried to the stream to refresh themselves before they mounted.

Netta felt freer than ever before in her life riding through the forest that morn. Her father had never allowed her to visit any farther away than Ridley Castle. She took a deep breath of fresh air perfumed with pine and smiled up at the heavens. No misty rain fell today. The air was cold and refreshing. Not long after the sun reached its peak, the wind picked up.

Her gaze strayed from the path to follow a man into the woods. She gasped and covered her mouth, stifling an embarrassed giggle.

"No wonder Father forbade me to help with bathing guests," she whispered.

Curious, Elise's gaze followed Netta's stare. The man came out of the woods and took his place back in line. She looked back at Netta. "Huh? Why?"

"My old nurse told me men have all manners of strange body parts," Netta whispered. "She warned I would lose my wits if I looked at them." Her head bobbed, agreeing with the memory. Curiosity soon got the better of her, and she blurted out what she wanted to know.

"Did you e'er chance upon Sir Galan, or one of his friends unclothed?"

Elise's eyes widened. Netta could tell by the abashed

expressions flitting across her friend's face that the young men had indeed exposed her to more of an education than Netta's own. Netta pressed for an answer to her curiosity.

"Do men have a tail-like member in front?"

"A tail? Why would you think it a tail?" Elise asked.

"The last man who went into the woods did not go deep enough. When we came around the bend, I saw him studying a tree. He had his tartan up around his waist." She broke off, embarrassed.

"Oh. They have what you saw and two hanging things like small turnips covered in thin wool. They go together." Elise's eyes lit. She pointed at the stallion ahead of them. "See? Like that horse."

"But, uh, the man's dangled." Netta's voice faded. Her face felt aflame.

Strangled snorts from the squires alerted her they had overheard her query. Unwilling to let them know her appalling ignorance, she improvised on a conversation she had overheard one day at Wycliffe.

"That part of him was small and pitiful. I chanced upon my stepsisters discussing this woeful lack. They declared the most powerful knights have the longest members."

"Why would a great warrior have a bigger member? Or are they great warriors because they are so big?" Elise scrunched up her face, puzzling over her own question.

"Nay. A well-kept secret is passed from father to son. On their twelfth name day, their sire shows them how to make this happen. After finding a round stone of a certain weight from the river, the boy wraps it in cloth. He then uses linen strips to make a sling, and he ties the rock to himself."

"Saints! Would that not hurt?" Elise grimaced and shuddered.

"I would think so. They have to be very careful. The stone cannot be too heavy, and the boy cannot run. This must needs be done only on the last cycle of the moon—the men's cycle." Netta bobbed her head knowingly.

Talking excitedly, the squires steered their horses around the women and urged their mounts up behind Mereck.

Soon after, Mereck pulled his giant brown destrier, *M'Famhair,* to the side and stroked the beast's neck while he waited. His horse looked to be at least eighteen hands tall.

Drawing abreast of the huge beast, she peered out of the corner of her eye at Mereck. He motioned them to follow as he entered the woods.

Netta gulped, sure now that the squires had told Mereck of her foolish tale. Shivers rippled down her spine. Was he angry? The further they went from the group, Elise's face became as frightened as Netta felt.

For certs. They were in trouble.

Silent still, he helped them dismount and tethered the horses. Something about the way he walked made her heart skip a beat. Why did it do that? It should not, for he exuded such pure dominance she gritted her teeth. He halted in front of them and Elise gasped.

Netta stepped in front of her friend to shield her. Heat radiated from Mereck. Their bodies nearly touched as they stood toe to toe, so close her eyes almost crossed. She stretched them wide and stared at the opening of his shirt. Golden hair covered tanned skin. The strong pulse beat at the base of his neck intrigued her.

The scent of juniper rose from his heated skin, and she sniffed. Her father had always smelled of sweat and horse, but Mereck's scent made her nose twitch and her pulse quicken. She shifted, restless, and wondered if all of his skin smelled the same. Feeling crowded, she cleared her throat. He did not budge. Reaching behind her for Elise's waist, she eased her back.

Mereck at last broke his silence.

"I realize you are untried women who know little of men. What made you think boys do such things?" He stared down at them.

"What things, sir?" Netta forced her mind away from its intriguing study of his skin. "Oh. The stones. They do not truly help? Then if not for this exercise, why do men linger by the trees?"

"Who has talked to you of such?" He near shouted his question. The muscles in his jaw twitched.

"Such what?" She tilted her head back and blinked.

Mereck glared back, waiting. She decided she had best answer.

"Uh, do you mean about 'that' thing?" Netta squirmed. "No one has. I overheard Elizabeth whisper of it with Prissy."

Somewhere near her shoulder blades, Elise groaned. Her shoulder blades? Was Elise standing in a hole?

"There is no truth to the tale, Netta. If you seek knowledge of a man's body, come to me for the learning." He rubbed his jaw, eyeing her speculatively. "A servant girl of your advanced years ignorant in such matters? Hmm. The nights grow colder. Mayhap I will school you on the subject."

Elise grabbed Netta's waist, near toppling her over, and whispered, "What does he mean?"

Netta spread her arms for balance and scowled at him for frightening her timid friend.

Drats! It seemed Elise knew no more about the mystery between a man and woman than Netta did. She knew not how he meant to *school* her, but she knew the suggestion was improper. Intending to belt him in the mouth, she tried to pull from Elise's grip. Elise tugged at Netta's ear to whisper again.

"His temper! I beseech you. Remember his devil's temper."

"If you are finished insulting me, sir, may I remind you your men must be a league ahead by now?"

Netta ground her teeth to keep from shouting, for she had promised Elise she would take good care of her. She could not do that if she pricked Mereck's temper so badly he stomped her into pulp on the forest floor.

He studied her. Was he pleased she did not attempt to argue with him? His gaze fell to her lips. The color of his eyes changed to murky green. For truth, he seemed no angrier than before, but they assuredly darkened. How strange that a man's eyes would shift colors in such a way. What caused it?

Mereck's full lips drew her attention. The tip of her tongue darted out to dampen her own. Were his lips soft? If so, they were the only softness on his body. Glancing up, she saw he studied her lips just as thoroughly.

"Can we not go now?" Elise whispered behind her.

Days later when they made camp at dusk, Mereck came over to her.

"Netta, help Angus prepare the evening meal. My warriors hunted plump hares to make a hearty stew. He will tell you what needs be done."

She was concerned for Angus. Each daybreak, when she went to serve the porridge, he beamed at her. And each morn, different teeth were black. Was it some sickness of the mouth? It seemed contagious, for each day more of the men smiled, revealing their own black teeth.

She sighed and nodded, hoping Angus would not learn she had never cooked before. She watched him draw turnips, carrots and onions from sacks that had been tied to a pack horse. A large cauldron of water boiled over the fire. He peeled and threw in several onions, before he chopped off the head and feet of the first rabbit and gutted it. She ducked behind him and covered her eyes to rid her of the sight.

"Here ye go, lass. Prepare this'n and put it in the pot," he ordered and turned to slap the hapless creature into her hand.

Netta stared at it. She had no idea how to go about it. Seeing Angus glance back at her and frown, she held the unsightly thing by one leg. What went into "preparing it"?

She looked around and saw nothing to give her a hint. For certs, he meant for her to start cooking it. Maybe as it boiled the fur came off and they transferred the naked meat to the pot of fresh vegetables.

Netta held her hand over her mouth to keep from retching. She stood far back from the pot and slid the meat into the boiling water. Soon the horrid thing emitted a noisome odor. It made her eyes run.

It also gained Angus' attention.

He stared into the pot, then turned to look at her. His brows raised so high they near met his hair. Soon others in the camp smelled the awful stench and came over as well.

"Angus, mon, are ye thinkin' to poison us now?" Ewen asked.

"'Tis dinner wrapped for the winter he is makin'. Canna you see the coat is still on the wee creature?" Marcus grinned at Netta.

"What did you think, Netta? Have you e'er eaten food

where you had to fight the fur for the meat?" Mereck quirked a brow at her.

Holding her soiled hands away from her, she stared in horror at the bubbling water and the creature bobbing about in it. Her shoulders slumped, and she could not stop her chin from an embarrassing quiver.

"Begone if ye wud have a meal." Angus scowled at the grinning men and shooed them off. He frowned at Mereck, then nodded his head toward Netta.

"Come, Netta. Ewen will help Angus with the cookin'." Mereck turned a steely gaze on the freckled warrior, who did not dare quibble about the duty. Calling for Dafydd to bring soap, he grasped Netta's wrist and led her back to the stream where she had bathed earlier.

Netta's chin near touched her chest. She did not look at him or speak. He must think her a mindless nit. A cook's niece who knew naught of cooking. Even as a lady, they should have taught her more about how to run the kitchens, but her stepmother had ignored this part of her training so Lynette would be free to fetch and carry for her stepsisters.

Before she could brood further, Dafydd delivered a small bowl of soap and a soft cloth. Mereck led her to a flat rock and motioned for her to kneel. Wordless, she raised her hand for him to give her the soap. He shook his head and tugged her to kneel beside him.

He drew her arms forward, pushed up her sleeves, and then scooped great handfuls of water over them. He lathered his hands and washed over her arms until the unsightly mess was cleaned away.

She could not take her eyes from his beautiful hands. Never before had she thought a man's hands to be comely. Mereck's fascinated her. They were large, of course. As was the rest of him. They looked strong, their palms calloused.

Thin white scars crisscrossed their backs. Battle wounds? Watching the long, graceful fingers moving over her skin, she blinked.

Her heartbeat quickened. Her breath caught. If they caressed her in the same way, could they be any more gentle? She felt a sense of loss when he rinsed off the soap. He reached for a drying cloth. She tried to take it from him.

He shook his head and dried her arms.

Still, they did not speak. She stared up at him, mesmerized, for his green gaze never moved from hers.

She did not stop him when he laved her face and jaw.

Tenderly, he moved the cloth toward her eyes. She closed them.

His calloused fingertips explored her lips.

She trembled and opened her eyes. His own had darkened to deep, sleepy emerald. Tilting his head to the side, he lowered his lids and slightly parted his lips. She stared, fascinated. Warm, calloused fingers moved to grasp her chin. His lips approached hers, a hairbreadth away.

Chapter 6

The tip of Netta's tongue dampened her lips. She swayed toward Mereck, eyes locked on his tempting mouth. Would his kiss be soft and pleasurable, or would it be like Roger's—cold and hurtful? At the thought, she jolted back and sprang to her feet.

"We must return. Mistress Elise will be upset. She is not at ease around men." Blood raced through her veins, heating her face and neck. Was it this that made her voice so hoarse?

"As you wish." Mereck stood, a soft smile on his lips.

When they returned to camp, she hastened to Angus and Ewen. "I'm sorry I ruined your stew by my lack of cooking skills. Is there some chore I can do to help?"

"Dinna think about the wee mistake, lass." Angus patted her shoulder. "When all is ready, ye may serve as ye did at dawn. Sit and soothe yer mistress. She is no braw henny like yerself and is hidin' in the shelter."

"Aye, rest, lassie. Helping Angus is a right pleasant chore." Ewen winked at her. He turned his back to Angus and filched a small turnip from the stew. Popping it in his mouth, he rolled his eyes and rubbed his stomach. She started to chuckle, but he put his finger to his lips, a comical expression spreading on his face. "Dinna give me away, wee lass," he whispered.

Why had they grinned when they saw her? Instead of being angry that she had caused them extra work, they seemed amused. Netta's shoulders relaxed. She smiled and nodded her thanks.

She found Elise sitting on her pallet, her knees drawn up and her arms wrapped tight around them. Her eyes were wide as a frightened kitten's.

"Elise, come. Help me spread the plaid beneath the trees." She took her friend's hand and urged her from the tent. "We will sit until Angus tells me 'tis time to serve the meal."

Elise jumped up and hugged Netta. "I was so afeared for you. Was Mereck very angry?"

They found an area cushioned with pine straw and spread the plaid atop it. A canopy of rustling branches above made soft music in the breeze.

"Nay. He was most strange. He spoke few words." Netta knew not how to describe Mereck's gentle behavior, nor the heat that came from his body and flashed from his eyes. Shivers ran down her spine, remembering the feel of his beautiful hands on her arms. How would they feel should they smooth so gently over her body? Her breasts? That strange feeling she often had in his presence throbbed in the pit of her stomach.

She had no further time to think on it, for he joined them. He and Marcus talked together, their voices low. Why did Marcus stare at her? Every time she glanced at him he grinned like a lad with a secret. His silent mirth made her frown. What amused him? Mereck, on the other hand, glared at him.

While they waited for their meal, Mereck began to question Elise.

"Elise, you mentioned knowing Lynette of Wycliffe. Is the lady so plain of face and form her father couldna contract a suitable husband for her?"

"Plain, sir? Ne . . . , uhh, Lynette? Oh nay, she is far from plain."

"If not plain, are her eyes beady? Or do they cross at every opportunity?" He glanced at Netta. "Such as Netta's often do? Or perchance she is missing teeth?"

Netta gasped.

"Cross? I have never noticed such," she said, surprised. "Minstrels across the land have praised her eyes. They are a rare purplish-blue with flecks of gold. Nor are they beady, for they are oval shaped and beautiful." She twitched when Netta's elbow jabbed her side. "As for her teeth, they are white and even."

Netta squirmed and lowered her head. How did a person disguise their eyes? A puff of wind blew a leaf onto her lap. She studied it, clamping her lips together to keep from blurting denials.

"Does she lack hair? I have heard it said she is a pale Saxon with scrawny tresses. She must needs use the aid of a horsetail wig to cover her shiny dome."

Marcus strangled on a cough. He quieted, seeing Mereck's cold glare.

"Nay! That is not true," Elise blurted. "Her hair is thick and glossy with curls any woman would envy." She stopped, her curiosity aroused. "Wigs made from a horse's tail? I have never heard of such." She frowned at the men. "My friend has no need to alter her appearance. She is most beautiful."

Netta's hands twitched with the sudden urge to cover her head, but resisted it.

"Ah. Then her form causes men to turn away," Marcus declared. "I have heard she eats from dawn to dusk.

Mereck has heard the opposite. Be she plump as a fat sheep, or so thin a man fears her bones will prod him? Perchance she is too tall or too short?" Marcus' voice quivered, and his lips jerked.

What ailed the man? Netta glowered at him then lowered her head until her chin touched her chest.

"Fat? Thin?" Elise held up her hand. "Uh, how can bones prod? The goose girl at Ridley is very skinny, and she and the chandler often embraced behind his shop. He never looked to be in pain." She put a finger on her chin and raised her brow in question. "Now I think on it, he did moan a great deal."

Marcus coughed again but did not say whether the girl's sharp bones caused her swain's discomfort.

"Lynette is nigh perfect. She is a hand shorter than I. If she was not a great beauty, why do you think suitors have besieged her father demanding her hand?" Elise's face reddened with indignation.

Netta wanted to sit upright to appear taller, but she could not do so and keep her face lowered where they could not study it.

"Ahh, then your friend is a shrew who demands her way at all costs," Mereck said. "The lady will now be wed without her consent. They but need her presence before the priest."

"Lynette will never say the vows, sir. Her father tries to shackle her to a savage beast." Elise glared at them.

"Lady, she need not speak. Her betrothed will see she complies." Mereck rubbed his chin. "A bit of cloth in her mouth will stifle her protest. Add a hand behind her head to force a nod at each vow, and it will be all 'tis needed for an ambitious priest. What think you, Marcus?"

"Aye. It could be a new chapel, or a healthy stipend and

the promise of the baron's favor will be enough to prod the priest to sanctify the union. It has been done many times since the Conquest."

Elise's horrified gasp near sucked a leaf from the forest floor. Netta could stand it no longer. Her head snapped up. She glared at the two men. They wore surprised expressions as if to ask what had sparked her ire. She fisted her hands and bolted to her feet. It was most fortunate Angus called out the food was ready. She hurried to him.

"Simpletons. Dolts." Netta forced words through a throat tight with anger. "They think so little of my worth they would approve of forcing me to accept vows? Bob my head for me?"

Tears clouded her vision, for when Mereck had cleansed the blood off her arms, he drew her regard with the gentle way he treated her. She felt betrayed. Now she knew him to be no better than any of her hateful suitors.

"A woman is but a means to gain land and riches. They take all that was once ours, and then we must needs cater to them. Bow and scrape and have one babe after the other. Were we farther from Wycliffe and that despicable, loathsome savage, I would tell Mereck what a churl he is."

"Nay. Do not think to stoke Mereck's anger," Elise begged.

Netta eyed the trenchers of food Angus had served. She stepped aside to avoid a fallen branch and spied a cluster of worms on a leaf. She clinched her teeth. Seeing Angus' back was turned, she shuddered and picked up the leaf. Taking a prepared trencher, she shook two of the squirmy things on the food. They would be for Mereck.

Ha. This will give him extra meat with his meal. Wigs! If someone forced him to wed a toothless hag with warts on her nose, how would he like it? Let a woman want a fitting mate, and men become irate and carped like the meanest crone.

Glancing through her thick lashes, she watched Mereck tilt his head to the side. Did he listen to the sounds of insects? One worm started crawling atop a turnip. She placed a chunk of onion to cover it.

Elise's face turned every shade of green in the woods. She could not tear her gaze from Mereck's trencher.

"Do not stare at the food, Elise," Netta snapped. She grabbed a second trencher and stamped toward the men.

Taking two others, Elise followed.

Netta forced a smile to her lips when she handed Mereck his trencher then placed the other in front of Marcus. After Elise put their food where they were to sit, they went back to fetch cups of ale for the men and watered wine for themselves.

"Merciful saints," Elise gasped, almost skidding to a stop.

Netta could see nothing, for her tall friend blocked her view. As soon as they sat, Elise tugged on Netta's tunic sleeve.

"Elise, dinna disturb Netta while she eats," Mereck ordered, his voice ringing with authority. "She has worked hard to show what a conscientious servant she is. 'Tis a most admirable trait. She deserves to eat her food and enjoy the results of her labors."

Marcus choked on a mouthful of food. Mereck frowned and thumped him on the back.

Netta sniffed the delicious aroma from the stew as she dipped her fingers in her trencher and picked up a carrot. It was sweet and just tender enough.

"But—" Elise started.

Mereck frowned and raised his hand. "Silence."

Netta selected a juicy sliver of meat and savored it.

Elise gasped, rolled her eyes and made strange faces at her. What ailed her? Elise had not touched her food, but the men were eating with gusto. Netta grinned. Would Mereck notice aught strange about his meal?

Why did they watch her so intently? Marcus looked near to crying. His eyes watered, and he blinked to clear his vision. Did something in the forest cause his problem? Her father had the same happen when around weeds. Sometimes his eyes ran fountains.

She continued eating, scooping up a turnip with a bit of onion clinging to it. She brought it to her lips. Elise screeched and slapped the turnip from Netta's fingers then groaned and began to gag.

"Saints, Elise, what ails you? Are you in pain?" Netta leaned over to peer in her face.

"Do tell us. What causes your distress, lady?" Mereck's voice was soft as silk. "Was it too large a morsel for Netta's rotted teeth? Do you wish to exchange trenchers, for your meat is in smaller pieces?" He reached for their food.

Elise's face was a strange shade, neither yellow nor green. She clutched her trencher close to her body and swatted his hand away. Marcus roared with laughter.

"I just recalled, sir. Netta is prone to illness when she eats rabbit stew." Elise's voice was shrill. "She will break out in unsightly spots and her head will ache. In truth, I shall break out also if she eats another bite. For certs I will be sick and keep you all from your sleep this night."

"You do look green around the mouth, lady," Mereck agreed. "I will give your trenchers to Angus to take to the men on sentry duty. They will be pleased to exchange your stew for their rations of bannocks and dried beef." He stood and had to near wrestle their food from them.

"But, but—," Elise spluttered.

Mereck stared down, eyebrows raised, inviting her to finish her sentence. She looked from him to Netta and back again. It was a wonder she did not make herself dizzy with her head swiveling back and forth. When she did not continue, he turned and strolled over to Angus. He kept his back to them while he talked with the cook.

Netta raised her brows and tilted her head at Elise, who squirmed and glanced at Marcus. If he would withdraw his attention, mayhap Elise would speak. Rats! The man was not about to look away. He chuckled and acted like he could not take his eyes from them.

"This should be easier on your delicate stomachs." Mereck handed them bannocks and dried beef. "I insist you eat every crumb. I canna have you fainting from hunger on the morrow."

Netta's stomach growled. It was forever doing that of late. Although she was small and slender, she had the appetite of a much larger woman. She eyed Marcus' food, her mouth watering. Stew was one of her favorite meals. Why had Elise told such a story about her? Meanwhile, she avoided looking at Mereck's trencher.

The men ate with gusto. On occasion, Mereck hoisted a dripping piece of turnip or carrot and quirked his brows, questioning her. She shuddered and shook her head. Several times she peeked through her lashes and spied a pensive look on his face when he moved food around in his mouth. After his tongue finished its search, he shrugged and resumed chewing.

She had a sick feeling in her stomach, like when she peered over a steep ledge. Blinking rapidly, she stared at the ground. Why had she done it? Never before had she played such a mean prank. Guilt claimed her. She began to squirm. Mereck thought her a servant, yet he treated her more kindly than her father ever had. She could not fault him for insisting she serve them. After all, it was her duty since she posed as a servant. Shame filled her that she had let her hurt pride override her behavior as a lady. Remembering Elise's warning of Mereck's anger, she gulped, fearing he would discover her hateful prank.

She nibbled on the dry bannock, but the dratted thing was more than a day old. As hard as the bark on yonder trees. She dipped it in her watered wine, softening it. The dried meat was salty, but she was so hungry she devoured it.

"A most filling meal. What a shame you couldna share it." Mereck popped the last piece from the sopping trencher into his mouth.

Shame scorched Netta. She could not look at him.

"Aye. A man could have no better." Marcus sat back with a well-fed air. He thumped his chest, and burped. Leaning forward, he raised Netta's chin. She tried to draw back, but he held fast. He turned her face from one side to the other, then let her go.

"You are a wee bonnie lassie this day. Have you sipped a magic elixir?"

"Magic elixir? This day, sir? I am the same as any other." She paused and blushed when her stomach grumbled.

"What say you, Mereck? Dinna you agree?"

"Indeed. All for the better, I might add."

"What, sir? What is it you speak of?" Netta blinked at Marcus. Was the stain gone from her teeth?

"Your skin has not the red about it." Marcus eyed her. "What potion did you use to rid yourself of your strange flaw?"

Netta's hand flew to her face and neck. Her skin was smooth and soft. The sticky juice was gone. Then she remembered Mereck wiping her face with the wet cloth. She had to think of an explanation, for he peered straight into her eyes. His expression demanded she answer Marcus' question.

"Uh, the forest trees and flowers in the gardens of Ridley Castle trouble me. They have always caused me to react in such a way, have they not, Elise?"

"Aye, they did." Elise nodded with vigor.

"Your distancing yourself from Ridley made such a change for the better?" Mereck did not look like he believed her.

"It had to be the trees, sir. I am sure of it." Netta felt her cheek and pasted a pleased smiled on her lips.

"I dinna think it the true reason, lass."

Her heart lurched. He knew she lied. He had seen through her disguise.

"You are right, milord. It was not from the trees. When Lady Elise asked me to come to the Highlands with her, my aunt suggested if I was less comely, your men would leave me alone."

Making a sympathetic clucking sound with his tongue, Mereck shook his head.

"Have no fear of my men, Netta. You are under my care." He stared her in the eye as he added, "I will see to you myself. 'Tis time to be abed. You know where your pallet lies."

As he said those last words, a resonant sound like the purr of a giant cat rumbled from his chest.

Chill bumps scurried about Netta's back. She jumped to her feet, moving faster than she had in years as she headed for the tent.

"See to me himself, will he?" She turned to Elise after they entered the tent. "Not if I can help it. What was that blather about the food? I'm so hungry I could eat poor Lightning."

"While we were returning with the ale and wine, I saw

Mereck switch his trencher for yours." She shuddered and gagged again. "They watched us so closely, and he would not let me speak. I could not let you eat it, nor could I tell you why. Seeing you about to eat those worms, I was sickened." Her face looked like someone who spied a sumptuous feast, but was deprived of even the first bite. "I am hungry too."

Netta wanted to kick Mereck in the shins. The churls had been laughing at her the whole time! 'Twas no wonder Marcus near choked on each bite. She ground her teeth and fumed. Soon the humor of the situation struck them, and they rolled on the pallet, holding furs against their mouths to muffle their laughter.

Hearing Mereck's deep voice shout Netta's name, she gave him no cause to call her again. She hugged Elise, burst from the tent and dived under the plaid on her pallet in but scant seconds.

The farther from England they traveled, the more relaxed Netta became. She was glad she no longer had to wear the berry paste or the walnut stain on her teeth.

One day, as they traveled through the Central Lowlands of Scotland approaching the foot of the Grampian Mountains, they neared a small village. The peasants hurried from their cottages to stare at them. Mereck beckoned Netta to pull up alongside him.

"The trails are ever more steep. They are becoming difficult for your mounts," Mereck said, then turned to the villagers. "Does anyone have two Highland ponies to exchange for a fine farm animal?" He pointed to Lightning.

"Aye. I have what ye want." A man streaked with the dirt of many days of labor stepped forward. He near drooled as he gaped at Netta. "I see ye got a runt of a serving' lass. That one canna give a mon as brawny as ye a fittin' ride. I be willin' to take the puir thing off yer hands, and ye can keep the horse."

Mereck seemed to consider the man's words, for he nodded and waited to hear his bargain.

"I wud trade ye me strappin' Mollie here, too. Her tits be more than a mouthful." He leered at Mereck. "Her belly be soft and her hips plump eneuch to cush the grandest ballocks. She'll gie ye a ride ye'll no soon fergit." He reached behind him, grabbed hold of the woman standing pressed against his back and brought her forward.

Mereck's eyes widened. He ogled the woman, then glanced at Netta and frowned.

Netta gulped. A mouthful? She eyed the village woman's huge breasts. No mere mortal could possibly accomplish that feat. Why, you could balance two trenchers on the woman's obvious charms and still have ample room for more. Aye, for certs she was plump. No fear of her bones cutting a man.

Mereck's appreciative gaze roved over the woman, lingering overlong. After eyeing what he no doubt found interesting, Netta peered down at her own small breasts hardly tenting her tunic and shrugged. She scowled at Mereck's gawking men. A hoard of bare-arsed savages could spring upon them and nary a one of them would notice. Turned to pillars of salt, that's what they were, incapable of speech.

The slattern bent over to flick an imaginary insect off her leg, causing the freckled Ewen to gurgle some sort of exclamation and slide off his horse.

Huh! Netta scoffed. Little protection they offered, if it was so easy to distract them.

"I do need a lass with experience to ease me." Mereck

gave a gusty sigh and nodded at the codger. "The scrawny lass isna much to look upon, but in time she will learn to comfort my pain."

Hah! More than likely, she would give him a sturdy whack with a thick branch.

Mereck's hot green gaze returned to her, pinning her to the saddle as it raked over her body and stopped to linger on her hips. He leered at her as he leaned down to murmur in the old man's ear.

"I wud no hae guessed she wud do that," the villager chortled and slapped his thigh.

"Indeed, it is truth. Though I was rather surprised at the time," Mereck replied and nodded.

"Why you . . ." Netta spluttered and tried to scramble from Lightning.

Marcus grasped her shoulder, keeping her firmly in the saddle.

"He but wants to tease you." Marcus chuckled. "And 'tis a game he plays to win the villagers' goodwill."

He twisted in his saddle and motioned to Angus, who hoisted a huge sack of grain on his shoulder, struggled over and dropped it with a thump at the man's feet.

She watched the village men stare at the sack and smack their lips with obvious relish. Would they put the grain to good use to feed their families? Unfortunately, from their gleeful eyes and the way they drooled, they thought only of the ale they could make.

The old man's scrawny elbows prodded his son in the side. The boy ran and brought two Highland ponies forward. Marcus helped the women dismount and removed their saddles for the squires to place on the ponies.

To Netta's annoyance, when they led Lightning away, the traitorous horse near flew across the ground to reach the field. She frowned, insulted. The sway-backed beast preferred toiling in the fields to the task of carrying her. Marcus' squire, Fergus, put a lead on Elise's Buttercup. The mare followed docilely behind him when they started off.

Netta's new mount moved smooth and sure, and did not plod about jarring her with every step. She was soon grateful Mereck had the foresight to exchange Lightning for the smaller mount. That poor lumbering beast could not have climbed the steep paths.

The ground became narrow and dangerous. The men dismounted and led the horses. They rode close beside a steep drop, sending icy fingers of dread creeping over her body. Her arms became weak, her legs limp. Now, her heart raced and drummed in her ears. She trembled like she suffered an ague. Determinedly, she strangled her fear. She decided she was doing an excellent job hiding her dreaded fault from Mereck. Her father had ridiculed her weakness. Surely Mereck would humiliate her in the same way.

Mereck walked beside Netta, keeping a firm hand on the pony's reins. He heard her thoughts and noted the fear glittering in her eyes. Her face lost all color as she chanted prayer after prayer to every female saint he had heard of and some he had not. Was this trait common to frightened Saxon women? Elise had done the same when they attempted to leave Ridley.

"Oh! Blessed Saint Bride, protector of dairymaids. I know I have never tended a cow, but I do love their milk," Netta prayed.

The lass had never been close enough to a cow to ask it for milk, much less to touch it, Mereck decided. They moved slowly, and the path became even more narrow. Seeing her eyes widen in alarm, he patted her shoulder.

"Saint Martha, pray forgive me for not knowing how to cook. And for that little sin with the stew." She wrung her hands together.

"Are you hungry, Netta?" Mereck grinned at her. It was very likely life with Netta would be most interesting. For certs, she had amused him often in the past few days.

"Hungry? Why would I be hun . . . , oh, saints," she gasped and clutched the pony's mane. "What was it? Oh, aye. You complained of hunger. Did you not eat enough at our midday meal, sir?" Netta blinked and looked at him.

Oh my, it was a dreadful mistake, for they rode above the tops of the trees. The loch below looked like a small pond. Netta panted. Her eyes opened even wider. As they climbed higher, her mount's hooves slid, causing her to sway in the saddle.

"Yeew! Please, Saint Monica, protector of wives. Forgive me for not marrying the barbarian. But he was the worst of the lot Father tried to force on me." Netta's eyes were squeezed shut. She gasped moments later. "Bring me unharmed to flat ground," she added quickly, "and I vow I will marry the man you choose for me."

Mereck winked at Marcus and grinned. He would remind Netta of her promise. As for now, he kept up a steady stream of calming words and patted her shoulders in a comforting way.

His ballocks heated, remembering when he had soaped her arms after she tried to cook the hare in all its glorious coat. She had watched his hands move over her skin, his touch a soapy caress. Her startled eyes had showed surprise at her first stirring of passion. Feeling shivers spread over her body, desire had shot through him. Her skin had flushed, and he had cooled her face with the wet cloth, unmasking its flawless beauty.

The time would soon come when he would have her naked and in the bathing tub with him. He would lean her back against his chest, her lithe body cradled between his legs, exposed and available to him. His tarse heated and stirred beneath his plaid as he pictured his slippery hands caressing up over her arms, across her shoulders and down her perfect, small breasts. As they moved downward from there over her stomach, the painful fullness of his tarse reminded him the cliff's edge was too dangerous a place to distract his mind with pleasures yet to come.

At last they reached solid ground that held no fear of having a horse plunge over the cliffs. Mereck called a halt. It had been an arduous and exhausting walk for the men.

Mereck lifted her from the saddle and whispered in her ear. "I will see you honor your vow to Saint Monica, Netta." He held her closer than necessary to better breathe in her scent.

"Vow, sir? What vow?" Her brows rose, and her head tilted to the side.

"Your pledge that you would marry the man she chose for you, if she would see you unharmed to flat ground."

"I did no such thing," she gasped, astounded. "You are mistaken."

"Did you not? I heard you vow before everyone that you would honor the choice. What say you, Marcus?"

"You did shout it right loud, Netta." Marcus nodded briskly. "Every man to the end of the line heard your prayers."

"Aye," men hollered with enthusiasm. They smiled black-toothed smiles at her. Marcus grinned at her surprised expression.

"Your prayer to Saint Martha holds me curious, henny," Mereck continued, thoughtfully. "Something about cooking. Stew, wasna it? Would you care to enlighten me?"

"You should not listen in on a woman's prayers, sirs," Netta scolded. "They are private, sacred moments talking to God. He must be displeased with the lot of you."

"How could we cover our ears and lead the beasties, lady?" Marcus held up his hands and shrugged. "You shouted prayers loud enough for Cloud Dancer to hear as far distant as Blackthorn."

"Cloud Dancer? What manner of man has such a strange name?" Netta tilted her head and waited for his answer.

"Not a man but Lord Bleddyn's great eagle," Mereck explained. "They talk to each other in strange sounds. Cloud Dancer understands what he says."

"Sure he does," she scoffed. "Soon you will be telling us Lord Bleddyn has magic and knows what is to happen."

"Aye, he does. But it is not magic. Have you not sensed Caer Cadwell's overlord is a mystic?" Mereck's voice was soft.

"Of course, but he . . ."

Too late, she realized her error. Icy chills rolled like storm swept waves down her body.

Chapter 7

Netta swallowed great gulps of air. At first, her body felt as cold as if she burrowed beneath snow, then heat engulfed her. She opened her mouth. No words came, only a sound disgustingly resembling a whimper.

"I knew you to be Lynette of Wycliffe afore we left Ridley." Mereck's tone was soft and even.

His inscrutable face hid any clue to what he planned to do with her. Panic flashed through Netta. She grabbed his shirt and held on for dear life.

"I beseech you, Mereck, do not return me to Father. He would force me to wed a barbarian. A veritable savage. A giant!"

"A giant, lass? Though I have never met a man whose head was above those in mine own family, I have heard tales of men so tall and powerful they appeared to be giants. Having never seen one, I canna judge for myself." He rubbed his jaw and peered down at her. "Tell me more of this giant of a savage barbarian."

"His hair was as wild and tangled as his shaggy beard. Blue paint colored one side of his face, and wolf skins covered his shoulders. The wolf's head was still on the largest one. It had long, yellow teeth." She shuddered, remembering the sharp teeth.

Dafydd, standing beside them, snickered. Mereck turned but a moment to narrow his eyes at the young man, who hung his head and shuffled his feet.

Netta swallowed. "A hide tunic barely covered his nakedness. It left his body indecent to female eyes." She looked at his chest, avoiding his eyes. "He smelled. He likely never bathed."

The men had a strange sense of humor, for their chuckles turned to outright laughter.

"Nay! Ne'er bathed, you say? You were that close to the man?" Mereck's brows reached for his hairline.

Wanting him to envision the frightful man so he would not drag her back to her father, Netta hesitated. Though he had thought her only a maid, he had been far kinder to her than anyone in her family had ever been. Surely he would not refuse to protect her now.

"He chased me from my father's own hall, sir. Even as I ran from him, I could smell his unwashed body."

Mereck's right brow quirked.

"Did you hear her, man?" Marcus rolled his eyes. "The dastard giant smelled." Drawing close to Mereck, he wrinkled his nose and sniffed. He yelped when Mereck kicked his ankle.

"He cornered me in the stables and laid his beefy hands on me," she added. Blushing, she thought of his far from beefy hands gently squeezing her breasts as they searched for stolen goods.

"He had human skulls hanging from his saddle." Elise piped in, eager to help sway Mereck's decision.

Netta cringed. It was her fault. To correct the story now would be to call her friend a liar.

"Skulls, you say?" Marcus shook his head. "Well now, milady, 'tis a wonder the baron didna skewer the man."

The laughter grew louder. Mereck fixed his men with an icy stare, and they quieted.

Far from gaining sympathy, her distressing tale seemed to amuse them. "Father welcomed him into the castle. I did not stay for him to hand me over to the beastly man."

Her father's loathing for her was so great he would force her into the arms of such a one. Knowing it, a weight as heavy as an anvil settled on Netta's chest.

Mereck rubbed his chin, then nodded. "No young maiden should have to marry a giant. A savage. Or a barbarian. Especially one who smells and is so bestial he carries skulls on his mount."

Netta dared to hope. He patted her shoulder before he cupped her face in his large hands.

"I promised Baron Ridley I would see you safely to Blackthorn."

"You will not force me to return to my father, sir?" Her heart pounded, and her knees were ready to buckle at any moment.

"Nay, lady, I willna. I will do as I vowed and see to your safety and well-being." His eyes sparked through narrowed lids as he studied her. "E'en so, I intend you respect your own vows."

"Dinna fear, milady," Marcus assured her. "No bestial, smelly giant will claim you for his bride. Not with Mereck as your champion."

A rousing cheer from the warriors greeted his words. Moving to stand close to Mereck, Marcus reached up to measure the difference in their height. "Nay. Not even a giant would dare prick Mereck when he is wont to battle."

Netta's breath burst from her lips, surprising her that

she had held it. She smiled up at him and hugged herself, then stepped back.

"May Elise and I cleanse ourselves of the day's ride?"

At Mereck's curt nod, Dafydd led them to a spot where thick, beautiful elm trees stretched branches out over the water, adding privacy. It was close to the camp, and the squire promised to listen for their call when they were done.

"Oh, Netta, I have heard of Mereck's honor. They say he would rather die than break his word. He will demand you do the same on your vows today."

"I will have as husband the man Saint Monica sends to me. I will honor that vow for I made it," Netta reassured Elise. "But I made no promise to the beast Father would force on me. He cares not who I marry, as long as he is rid of me."

They bathed in silence. The woods became quiet. Too quiet. Instinct prickled Netta's skin. She stood hip deep in water and beckoned Elise to come to her. Her finger to her lips cautioned her silence. Her uneasy gaze searched the trees.

Warning her of trouble, hair tingled at the nape of her neck. Stealthy rustling came from the woods on their right. Someone or something watched and stalked them.

"Hurry, Elise. Don your clothes." Netta nudged her from the water and handed her clean clothing. Her eyes scanned the forest while she tugged a smock over her own wet body. Hearing a snarl and twigs cracking her heart thumped.

Elise screamed. A blood-chilling scream. Had it been autumn, its sheer volume would have tumbled the leaves from the trees.

"Wolves! The wolves Galan told me about. Quick, Netta. Get a knife. A stick."

She grabbed a hefty tree limb from the ground and thrust it into Netta's hand, then seized a rock.

From the woods facing them, a large beast hurtled through the trees toward them. Warriors screamed wild, warbling battle cries and pounded close behind in hot pursuit.

It was a man. At least Netta thought it was a man who burst into the open. She shrieked. Then froze. Unable to run, to move. Elise screamed and jumped behind Netta, then grabbed her around the waist. Elise's hand brandishing the rock quivered.

Slicing the air above his head, the man's great broadsword whistled. Wild, green eyes gleamed and probed, searching the area. Rage distorted his face. Like a wolf scenting prey, his nostrils quivered. Taut lips, ringed with white, drew back to bare his teeth, as an animal's roar burst from deep within his chest. He and the warriors raced toward them, their swords drawn.

He thudded to a stop. His wild gaze searched Netta's face, over her body, and the ground around her. The men spread in a semi-circle behind him. Bit by bit, his features eased, softened. His feral snarl relaxed. Full lips again covered strong, white teeth. The wild light in his eyes calmed. His nostrils lost their flair. He took a great gasp of air. His body shook as he fought for control and banished the last of his strangeness away.

She recognized Mereck.

When he stalked toward them, his face still taut, Netta gulped and fought to master her fear. Elise's rock thudded to the ground behind them.

"Saints above. They are demented," Netta whispered, shocked.

She tightened her hands on the branch, raised her arms and brandished it. "I know not what offended you, sir.

Even if you dislike my breaking Father's contract, I will not let you harm us. By the saints, but try it and I will bloody your nose."

Mereck's eyes widened. Netta's smock clung to her wet skin, the rosy hue of her nipples showing through. The dark triangle of hair shielding her woman's mound was evident, along with every sweet curve of her body. Though she held a belligerent stance, fear shone from her eyes. He saw no threat in the area around them. He did see the picture his soon-to-be wife presented to his men.

"Lucifer's fetid breath, lady. Have you no modesty?"

Mereck stormed forward, snatched her cloak from the ground and swirled it around her.

Netta, trembling still, shouted back. "Modesty? We had not the time to don our clothing." She stabbed the air with her finger. "Something watched and stalked us from behind that birch tree."

He unwrapped her fingers gripping the stick and threw it on the ground, then signaled his men to spread out on either side of the tree.

"Dinna move from this spot. Marcus, keep them here." He stalked to the tree and examined the ground and nearby bushes.

Marcus sheathed his sword. He picked up the end of Netta's cloak and bent over to peer at Elise. "Come, lady. You will stifle yourself under there, and you dinna want to injure your friend."

Elise, her gaze darting over his face, appeared. "I have heard of Mereck's temper, but why was he wroth with us?" Her voice quavered.

Marcus draped her cloak over her quivering shoulders and tied the laces under her chin. Before he answered, he also secured Netta's cloak. "With you? He wasna angry with you. When we heard your screams, he was afeared someone attacked you both. He came to do battle for you."

Netta's tense body began to relax. Though Mereck's terrible temper had frightened her, she realized he had fought to control it. He had not struck out at her. Though more frightening than her father or Roger at their most furious, Mereck had not laid a hand on her. *They* had.

Mereck studied the trampled grass and leaves. Something large had rested there. He spied the leavings of an animal. The tufts of fur and specks of blood worried him. They belonged to a wolf. From the amount of blood, a badly injured wolf.

"Come, lass." He gripped Netta's elbow, tightening his hold when she flinched away. He looked at Marcus and nodded his head toward Elise, then led them back to camp.

"What was it? Man or beast?" Netta forced a calm smile.

Mereck felt a pang of regret. Was she asking about him, or the creature under the tree? He preferred the latter.

Quietly so Elise would not hear, Mereck answered. "Wolf. By what we found, I expect he could no longer rule the pack, and they turned on him. We must find it and put it out of its misery."

He called his best hunters and pointed out the directions in which he wanted them to search. He swung back to Netta.

"You will both stay with Ewen. Dinna leave his side, lady, no matter what." He stared at her until she nodded, agreeing. He pulled a long, wicked-looking knife from his belt, turned and loped off into the woods.

* * *

Ewen gritted his teeth and rolled his eyes. He would rather face a ravenous wolf than one small Saxon with the tenacity of a badger. Elise was no problem. Her eyes sparkled with interest as she watched Netta demand he allow her to "take a stroll."

"Netta, I don't believe he will budge. You cannot push him either. He is much bigger than you. Have you thought of payment? Father always says you cannot get something for nothing. Surely some coins will sweeten his disposition?"

Ewen's temper exploded. "Bribe me, milady? Ye advise her to bribe me?" Ewen felt his face turn hot red.

Elise clamped her hand on her mouth and scooted back.

"Do not roar at her." Netta frowned at him. "You will frighten her again. Did you not hear me afore? I told you I give not a tinker's hoot what Mereck said. I have to leave this tent. I have to go. Now stand aside."

Why did the dratted man not understand? It seemed like much time had passed since Mereck and the hunters left. Wishing she had not drunk so much water with her noon meal, she groaned.

"Milady, I canna." Ewen's jaw jutted and his fists clenched at his waist.

"Move." Netta yelled so loud Ewen winced and stepped back.

Atop his commander's toes.

Saints! When had Mereck returned? He moved Ewen aside. Netta took one look at him and tried to pull Ewen back between them. Without a word, Mereck pried her hands from the warrior's arms and led her into the tent. Elise followed. The anger in his eyes and his set mouth made Netta more than a little uneasy.

"Have you no wits at all, lady? Do you have any idea

what could happen to you both? Though badly wounded, it took two men to kill the wolf. And you wished to roam the forests?"

When she opened her mouth to protest, he clamped his hand over it.

"Nay. Not another word." He barked his command. "As to Ewen. Never again will you seek to dissuade a warrior from his duties. Lady, when I put you someplace, you will stay until I give you leave to depart." He glared at her, his jaw set. "You will obey the men whom I charge to protect you." Threateningly, he towered over her, crowding her. "You will apologize to Ewen."

"Apologize? For what, sir? I did him no harm." Netta scowled and braced her fists against her hips. She had been very polite in the way she had handled Ewen, until she learned his sensibilities were as dense as a rock.

"I just told you why, woman. You tried to make him disobey my orders. Had he not ignored you, you could have caused him a lashing."

"Whip him? Because he let me go into the woods to tend something personal?" She was shocked. To cause someone to bear such a terrible punishment was unthinkable. "What kind of barbarian are you?"

"Something personal?" Mereck frowned at her.

Her face felt aflame. He had no more sensitivity than his men. Surely he did not expect her to elaborate. Did he?

"This has been about your need for, uh, privacy? Why did you not tell Ewen what you wanted?"

"Aye. You are a *crude* barbarian."

"Crude or no, barbarian or no, you should have made yourself clear."

"Blessed saints. I could not discuss that with him," she blurted.

Suspicious coughs sounded outside the tent.

"Am I to believe you have the same needs, Lady Elise?"

At the sound of her name, Elise groaned and nodded, her head in her hands.

"Follow me." The exasperation in his voice compelled Elise to follow Netta so quickly she stepped on Netta's left shoe, half pulling it off.

Hopping on one foot, Netta tugged it back on.

Outside the tent, she avoided looking at the men. After Mereck found a suitable spot in the woods, he admonished them to call out when they were ready. Netta glared at his retreating back as she moved a short distance from Elise.

Soon after, Elise called out to her.

"Netta, come see what I have found."

She hurried to find Elise crouched beneath an ancient oak tree, staring at the ground.

"Ick." Elise leaned back and made a face. "Look at the ugly thing crawling on this plant. He has green things atop of his head, like two extra eyes. Do you think he has four of them?"

"How fortunate, Elise." Netta leaned down for a closer look. "You found the Saint John's wort Brianna asked you to bring."

"A Sainted Wort bug?" Elise looked up, surprised. "I thought she wanted herbs."

"Not the bug. The plant the bug is on. She can dry the herb and flower tops to make tea, or soak them in oil for cuts and scrapes." Netta did not know how to cook a hare, but she did have some skill with herbs. Being careful not to crush them, she collected what she needed.

"Lucifer's teeth! Have you not finished?"

Mereck's irritated voice echoed through the forest. Startled, Netta fell back on her bottom, hitting a rock. She yelped. He charged through the woods and stopped when he spied her, sprawled on the ground, her lap full of flower tops and herbs.

"What are you doing?" Mereck eyed the cuttings.

"Picking herbs, of course." She grabbed the hem of her tunic and scrambled to her feet.

"Lady, you canna go afore the men with your clothing lifted to your knees." He took her arm, and attempted to dump the greenery.

"Leave off, sir." She pulled away from him. "Brianna will need every leaf we can find to make medicines. With all your scars, you men must be forever fighting. Here. You may carry them for me." Stooping, she grabbed the edge of his plaid and dropped the plants onto it.

Elise gasped behind her.

"Are you daft, woman?" He flapped his plaid. The cuttings flew back into Netta's arms.

Elise gurgled and covered her eyes.

"I willna go afore my men carrying weeds like a baker's wife with buns in her apron."

"Oh, rats and fleas. You are bruising them. Elise, lower your arms and help me." She placed half the plants in Elise's folded arms while she carried the rest. "Why do you fret about showing your knees?" she grumbled and hurried toward where they had entered the woods. "You show enough of yourself at other times."

He grabbed her shoulders to turn her in the opposite direction.

"Why do Saxon women not know where they are going? Brianna has the same problem. She canna find her way around her own castle." He jolted to a halt, recalling her last remark. "Have you been watching the woods when you shouldna?" His voice was incredulous. "Lady, you have no shame."

"I am not the shameless one. You men should select a tree ample enough to conceal you." Her conscience pricked her. 'Twas not entirely true.

He spluttered. She sauntered over to the tent. When she neared it, she looked up at him with an innocent look on her face.

"Thank you for your help, sir. I must tend the herbs now."

"Blessed saints, you willna speak to me in such a way."

"What way? Did I not say 'thank you?'"

"You thought to dismiss me, woman." He folded his arms across his chest and placed his feet wide apart. "Besides, you have not yet tendered Ewen an apology. You will both do so now."

She huffed and rolled her eyes, then carefully laid the clippings on the ground. She went to stand in front of Ewen. When he did not look at her, she nudged his boot.

He ignored her. Peering over her head at Elise, he nodded.

"I'm sorry for saying money would make you sweeter," Elise blurted. "It cannot. But truly, Father did say you should pay for favors and my father was never wrong."

"I ken, milady, and I accept yer apology." Ewen continued to stare over the top of Netta's head.

Netta nudged his boot harder and cleared her throat.

"It has come to my attention that when I tried to speak with you, I could have caused you a great deal of harm." She forced out the words from between clenched teeth. Determined, she kicked his boot until he looked at her.

"Speak, milady? What were ye trying' to say to me?"

"Oh, blessed saints. I told you oft enough that I *had to go out*. I could hardly make it more clear."

"Where would ye possibly go in the wilderness?"

Watching Netta struggle with her apology, Mereck wanted to put his arm around her in comfort. She was small and far more helpless than she realized. Her face reddened with shame. But he steeled himself.

For her own safety, this was an important lesson she must learn. When he told her to stay where she was, she must obey him. She could not wander about lacking an escort. Without male protection, a raider can easily seize a woman. It happened far too often in the Highlands. He shuddered at the thought Netta could unknowingly put herself in such danger.

"I did not wish to visit someone." Exasperation caused her voice to raise. "I needed to visit someplace. Now do you understand?"

"What place, milady? If ye needed somethin' from the packs, I would have sent a mon to fetch it. Ye didna want a bath, fer ye had already bathed. I canna think of another place ye would want to visit."

"Blessed Saint Martha. I had need of a privy place. Is that plain enough?" Her face felt on fire.

"Your apology, Netta," Mereck demanded.

"Oh, rats." Netta kicked the ground in frustration. "I'm sorry for near getting you punished, because you were too dense to understand a perfectly natural request. Are you satisfied now, Sir Mereck?"

She twirled around and gasped in dismay when she saw the men standing behind her. Lifting her nose in the air, she gave a disdainful sniff and disappeared into the tent as quickly as dignity would allow.

In Northumbria, the body of Baron Mortain lay on the table in the keep's great hall, awaiting burial. Roger's rage crackled in the air. The new baron had hated his sire with an intensity only equaled by the loathing he had earned from his father. Now Roger had more urgent business to attend than seeing to his father's remains.

"Your soul will linger until I return," Roger ordered the oh-so-still body. "I will have no masses said to speed your way, though 'tis to Hades Gates you will surely go."

With unseemly haste, he rifled through his late father's strongbox. It held gold and jewels, hoarded by generations of frugal Mortain barons. Buried in one corner, he found what he wanted, and made haste to Wycliffe Castle.

Months earlier, Baron Wycliffe had stoked his wrath when he rejected Roger's suit for his eldest daughter.

He had sneered that Roger had not the coins to buy her.

He did now.

Two days after his father's death, Roger slammed a small coffer stuffed with gold coins and jewels on the table at Wycliffe. It near struck George's eager nose.

"Summon Lynette!" Roger's fists rested on his hips, his legs widespread.

His scornful gaze swept over the baron's simpering younger daughters and ignored the baron's wife. Where was the girl hiding? When Wycliffe did not immediately beckon a servant to do his bidding, he leaned menacingly across the table, his nose almost touching the baron's quivering face.

"I must needs have a small amount of time," the baron stammered, greedily clutching an emerald many times larger than any he possessed.

"Time? How much time can it take to fetch the girl and call for the priest? We will wed at once." He swaggered toward the stairway that lead to the floor above.

"Lynette! Get you down and greet your husband."

When she did not appear, properly subdued by his mastery, Roger cursed and vowed she would pay for not obeying his command.

"She cannot hear you." Wycliffe's words spurted from his mouth, when Roger stalked back and reached for him. "Baresark, that wild savage, stormed through our gates less than a fortnight ago. He demanded Lynette to wive," he said all in one breath.

Seconds before Roger's hands could grab his plump neck, he bolted off his chair. "He left me no choice," he spluttered. "I feared for my very life. He forced me to sign the betrothal contract."

Wycliffe had given her to Baresark?

A savage. A barbarian. *A bastard.*

Roger's wrath exploded. Lynette belonged to him. His to bring home in triumph.

He bounded over the table, strewing gold-plated goblets recently filled with wine. Trenchers of greasy mutton toppled onto the rushes. Curses spewed from his mouth. His hands clamped around George's pudgy, sweating neck. He ignored the women's screeches and held the wriggling baron until three men-at-arms attached themselves to Roger like leeches.

Baron Wycliffe, shaking from head to toe, squeaked out a solution. "I vow I had no control over the berserker. Mayhap 'tis for the best. Surely you would prefer one of my lovely, dutiful daughters to replace that witch of a Lynette."

Priscilla and Elizabeth, tugged forward by their mother, cried and howled until their noses turned red.

They wanted husbands—but not this husband.

He chose neither. Both dowries combined did not compare to Caer Cadwell. Only after Wycliffe vowed to petition their overlord, Baron Hugh of Carswell, for aid did Roger finally stop frothing at the mouth. He pried the clasped emerald from the baron's greedy fist, replaced it in the chest and slammed the lid. Until Lynette was in

Roger's bed, Baron Wycliffe would not see the jewels or gold coins again.

When he returned to Mortain Castle and burst into the great hall, women scattered and disappeared. Grown men scurried from the room and tried to make themselves invisible to their new baron. He strode up to the table where his father's body lay.

"'Tis your fault, you stinking pile of bones," he hissed. "If you had released your coins, Lynette would be in my bed. The riches of Cadwell would be mine. I should long ago have rid you of breath."

He heard a gasp behind him and turned to find his father's old manservant. He did not spare a second thought. His fist cracked into the man's jaw, the blow slamming the man to the filthy rushes. Roger, ignoring the sickening sound of a skull meeting stone, began to pace.

"How dared the devil-eyed bitch." His words screeched like the voice of a raptor and sent even the rats scurrying. "She would not have *me?* She went happily with that *half-breed* animal?"

Roger had loved her, but she had betrayed him. The last time he had her in his grip, she had claimed she was not intact. If not for her guards, he would have done more than slap her disobedient face and beat her. He would have taken her. He did not doubt his manliness would get her with child. She would have wed him then. She would have had no choice. As she would not have when he found her.

For the past sennight, Mereck and his party had traveled on Morgan lands. They would reach Blackthorn afore the midday meal on the morrow. Netta planned to persuade Bleddyn, and he would convince her father to release her from the contract.

For certs she could attract her own suitors. Surely Saint Monica would send her a man superior to any her father had chosen for her. Hmm, perchance Mereck would court her? Her face heated. How would his beautiful hands feel on her body? Her nipples tingled at the thought.

Blessed saints! Whatever made her think that?

"Come, Elise, let us choose what we will wear on the morrow. You want to be beautiful. In case Lord Damron has chosen a mate for you."

"A mate?" Elise whispered, her sky-blue eyes wide with worry. "Do you think he has planned a nuptial without telling Father? Oh, heaven help me." She put her hands to her head and groaned. "He is even more stern than his cousin Connor."

"Lord Damron? Who is Connor?"

"Lord Damron's cousin. His first-in-command. I met him when he came with Damron to collect Brianna. He smiles often. Yet if I but do the slightest thing, he frowns and orders me about. Each time I looked up, he was watching. He barked at any man who came close to speak to me." She shuddered and with a tremulous smile asked, "Perchance you would care to beguile him?"

"Why would I wish to do such? He does not sound like someone who would allow me to do as I wish."

"Oh, but he is most handsome. He has beautiful brown eyes that sparkle and laugh." Her face took on a dreamy, wistful look. "His hair is brown and makes your fingers want to touch it. His lips are full and soft looking." She drew in a deep breath and released it on a sigh. "He is as big a man as Damron and Mereck, but far more comely."

Netta grinned. Did Elise not realize she favored the man she described? Hmm. It would be interesting to watch them together. If this Connor was not suitable for Elise's gentle soul, she vowed to protect her friend.

Sorting through the few ribbons and girdles they had brought with them, they finally selected their clothing for the next morn. Soon after they finished, Mereck appeared and ordered them to retire.

Chill bumps ran over her skin. Tonight would be the last they would sleep so close together. She blushed, for more than once she had awakened to find her head snuggled on his shoulder, her arm flung over his massive chest. To her shame, her fingers had clutched his plaid as she burrowed closer. For certs, she sought only his heat.

She hugged Elise and scurried out of the tent afore he must needs call a second time. He was unyielding when he gave an order. After they arrived at Blackthorn, he would have no right to demand her obedience. Her status as Lady Lynette of Wycliffe would cushion her from this dominating man.

Chapter 8

Netta awoke to the tantalizing scents of juniper and musk—along with thumping heartbeats beneath her ear. They came from the firm-as-a-tree-trunk, but oh, so delightfully warm body clutched in her arms. She gasped, then caught her breath as she moved as slow as a snail to lift herself off Mereck's chest and peek through her lashes.

Rats and fleas. His eyes were open.

Not only were they open, but their deep green hue made her more than aware something had prodded his emotions. And it was not anger. Blinking, she prayed he would look away.

He did not.

His steady regard made her shiver. His lips lifted in a wicked smile.

She pulled the plaid up high under her chin and glowered at him, accusing him for her own misdeed.

His smile widened.

"You will find our bedding arrangements at Blackthorn to be most satisfying, Netta," he whispered in a husky purr as he stroked her hair.

The deep rumble of his voice beneath her ear sent chill bumps coursing over her body. She tightened her grip.

"Undoubtedly, sir. I will likely share a room with Elise."

"For a time." He smiled again, this time pleased. His beautiful voice deepened. "Then you will have a most interesting bed partner."

She started to retort, but he stopped her.

"Milady, if you have ceased tempting me, I must rise."

Netta gasped and jerked away from him.

He chuckled and rose.

"When I have donned my clothing, wake Elise and make haste with your preparations. My men are eager to return to their families." He glanced down at her and ordered, "Close your eyes."

Puzzled, she closed them. Until her curiosity got the better of her. Mereck had always arisen before he woke her. She opened her lids the tiniest bit. It was more than enough. He was removing the plaid that kept him warm during the night.

He was a giant of a man. His body projected power. His neck was strong and firm, as was his jaw. Dark shadows showed he shaved each morn, afore she had even left her pallet. The breadth of his shoulders amazed her. She could not begin to circle them with her arms. Not that she planned to, of course.

His skin was golden all over and light brown hair dusted over his chest to narrow at his waist. The tartan lowered further. As it slithered past his waist, she followed the arrow of brown hair down to his . . . ! She had but a glimpse before she gasped and squeezed her eyelids shut.

Saints! Truly he is unnatural? With such an obstruction, how could he walk or ride a horse in any kind of comfort?

She heard the rustle of Mereck's clothing as he prepared himself for the day. She felt his movements when he sat down on the ground beside her.

"Rise, Netta, and wake Elise." Grasping a stocking, he worked it up over a tanned foot.

"Are you clothed, sir?" she whispered.

He grunted.

She gathered her covers around her and sat up.

Mereck straightened his right leg. His plaid covered his manly parts, but his left leg was bare to her view. Her gaze quickly traveled over a massive and hairy calf, and up to an even more impressive thigh. The sounds of warriors rising from their sleep distracted her. Glancing around, her eyes widened in utter disbelief.

She scrambled to her feet and made a frantic dash for the tent.

Mereck laughed and continued to dress.

"Wake up, Elise." Netta grabbed her friend's shoulder and jostled her. "Do you know I have been sleeping with all these men and they have been naked?"

"Naked? You have been sleeping with naked men?" Elise bounded upright, her eyes bright with interest.

"Not sleeping *with* them. But 'tis the same. They have been naked under their blankets. When I looked up, they were standing about. They did not deign to cover their secret parts." She blinked rapidly. "They scratched truly unspeakable places. Though they knew I slept close-by, none have worn even a scrap of cloth."

Elise dashed for the tent flap. She opened it enough to peer through. Her giggle made Netta join her. No sooner had she done so, than two very green eyes blocked their view and stared back at them. Elise backed up so quickly she threw Netta off balance. She landed on her bottom. A loud grunt sounded from the other side of the tent.

"Clothe yourselves and stop dawdling," Mereck's stern voice commanded.

They dressed as fast as their hands could snatch up their clothes and pull them on. Elise donned a dark blue tunic over an ice-blue smock and they wove blue ribbons through her braided hair. Netta wore a pale cream smock beneath an overdress of emerald green, the color of Mereck's eyes when he stared at her. They pulled a section of Netta's hair from each side of her face and secured it in back with dark green ribbons that mingled with her long, ebony curls.

Netta hesitated leaving the shelter of the tent after Mereck had caught them peeking. But when Fergus called, saying Mereck said they were to come immediately and break their fast or they would travel hungry, Netta grabbed Elise's hand. They sprinted toward Angus waiting with their steaming porridge.

The men seemed determined to force a greeting from them.

"Good morn, miladies," they called out as the women passed. Each time Netta was forced to look up and acknowledge the greeting, she saw a man who grinned laughingly at her—with blackened teeth. Oh, saints. Did they all know she and Elise had spied on them? Elise never raised her gaze from the ground. She whispered her own timid replies.

Mereck led them at a fast pace due north past Altnaharra. He had known Netta spied on him that morning. His body had felt it and reacted; his tarse had swelled and lifted in anticipation. He doubted anyone had instructed her in the ways of a man and woman and was glad for it. It would be his pleasure to initiate his little wife in the many delights they would bring to each other.

He shook his head and stopped his thoughts with a frown. Netta was creeping beneath his guard as surely as she had crept close in the night to fling her arm and leg over him as she slept. Though it was well and good to enjoy the lass, he must needs never allow his feelings to deepen.

A shudder racked him as he heard the cackling voice of old Beyahita. Her warning that a Baresark's destiny was to destroy any woman he was so foolish to love rang in his ears.

They forded a stream at the end of Loch Loyal, then entered the pass between Ben Loyal and Beinn Stumanadh, following Loch Loyal. Mereck called a halt at the northmost tip of the Loch, judging they were but two leagues from Blackthorn Castle. The women could refresh themselves with bannocks and watered wine.

The day had turned cold. After he helped Netta to the ground, he beckoned to Dafydd and made a quiet request. The squire hastened off to the pack horse that carried Mereck's clothing, and returned with his arms overloaded. On top was a plaid identical to the one Mereck wore.

Taking it, Mereck came over to Netta.

"You will wear this when we enter Blackthorn so our people will know who you are." He draped it around her waist and brought the ends up and over her left shoulder, pinning the plaid securely with a Morgan crest brooch like his. It pictured a hand holding erect a dagger fisted in its grip with *Manu Forti* engraved across the top of the circle. A bar ran diagonally across the whole. When done, he gripped her shoulders and studied her.

"Ah, sweetling, your lips would tempt a saint to sin."

His husky murmur made her shiver. He lowered his head and brushed his lips lightly against hers, surprising her.

And surprising himself.

When he lifted his head, Netta had the look of a woman who wanted more. Her eyes half closed, her lips parted slightly, and a flush stained her cheeks and neck.

He turned and strolled into the woods.

Netta drew a deep breath, then held it, unwilling to lose the scent that lingered from his skin. Her knees turned to weak porridge. She wished his lips had tarried longer. No one had ever kissed her like that.

Heaven help her. She shook herself. Of course no one had. She had no good memories of kisses. The few she had received were forced on her by men she thoroughly disliked.

After more than half of the warriors disappeared through the trees, she wondered where they had gone. When she and Elise finished their light repast, they decided to find a private area where they could rinse the honey from their fingertips. Dafydd must have been tending Mereck's needs, for Netta did not see him. She shrugged. She and Elise could find a spot of their own at the lake.

Following the direction the men had taken, they soon heard talking and laughter. Curious, they looked to see what the men found so enjoyable.

She soon wished they had waited for Dafydd.

She skidded to a halt. Elise bumped so hard against her back that Netta staggered and grabbed at a tree for support. Was her friend forming a habit of unbalancing her? Fortunately, one last stand of trees stood between them and the water.

"Umpfh. What happened?" Elise muttered. She needed no answer when she gaped over Netta's shoulder. "Blessed Saint Willibald. Why are they cavorting in the water like leaping fish?"

They did indeed jump and play around like madmen. Netta hushed Elise before the men could hear her.

No wonder some men strutted about like peacocks. They were all well-formed. Netta made a mental comparison. Not another man in the group could surpass Mereck's magnificent body. She gasped, for just as she thought of him, she spotted him waist deep in the water. He turned. Soap clung to his hair and shoulders. His frowning gaze searched the line of trees.

Had he seen them? How could it be? They were hidden behind a large elm. He ducked under the water to rinse himself. When he rose and took long strides toward land, Netta grabbed Elise by the hand and they raced back to camp. Ewen was there. She skidded to a halt and grasped his shoulder.

"Should anyone asks, please say we have been with you since we stopped," she pleaded. "'Tis but a game we play with milord Mereck." She put all she had into the request.

"Sure and ye were, lass." He chuckled and nodded.

He knew. His hair was wet. Saints. Had she seen him? She flushed all the hotter, for her gaze had not paid heed to faces.

Ewen offered them watered wine. They gratefully took it, for Elise was speechless and looked ready to slither to the ground.

To be honest, she herself was in dire need of encouragement. Netta gulped down her wine. When the men started to return through the woods, she stared at her lap.

The warriors quickly downed ale and laughed as they prepared for this last step of their journey. When done, they mounted and formed double rows. Dafydd and Fergus, Mereck and Marcus' squires, came to the women to help them into their saddles. When they had done so, they led them to the front of the line where Marcus waited alone.

He faced the men. Reaching out, he took the reins from Netta's grasp. Surprised, she looked at him, questioning him with her eyes. He smiled, but said not a word. No one spoke. Even the horses appeared to await something of import.

"What is amiss, Netta?" Elise's voice was so soft as to be almost unheard. "Why does no one speak?"

"I know not why. Mayhap we wait for Mereck. Where could he have gone?"

From the far end of the line came the sounds of men cheering and loudly thumping their swords on shields. Netta looked toward the clamor but could see nothing, for the file of men snaked around the trees. Soon, through the line of trees she saw two horses prance slowly toward them. When the horsemen came around the curve and into view, Netta shrieked. She tried to grab the reins from Marcus' fist. He held tight to them. He grasped her shoulder, supporting her, but keeping her seated.

The first horseman, a standard bearer, held a scarlet banner aloft. A single word, in large black satin letters, was sewn on it.

BARESARK.

The second horse was *M'Famhair.* Astride his back was the savage barbarian who had come to Wycliffe Castle.

Chapter 9

"Saints help me!"

Netta tried to pry Marcus' locked fingers from her horse's reins without success. Sickening waves of terror crashed over her as the fearsome rider came closer. She clutched Marcus' arm, her only security. Pride barely kept her from scrambling onto his mount with him.

The man riding toward her was a giant. Puffs of wind lifted light hair, golden mixed with brown, to fly about his face and shoulders. A Morgan plaid rode well above his knees as he straddled the back of *M'Famhair.* Wolf furs held by a huge brooch covered his massive bare chest and shoulders. Leather bands hugged his wrists and forearms. He used no saddle. Spread across the destrier's back was a blanket, not for the man's comfort, but to shelter the horse.

Blue paint covered one side of his face.

His eyes traveled over the men as he passed them; discipline and pride showed in their squared shoulders and erect backs. All wore the Morgan tartans. He nodded his approval.

Elise spied the barbarian sitting astride the huge

war horse and screamed, "Blessed Saint Agnes. Netta's barbarian found us."

With not a flicker of expression on his face, his back straight as a spear, he advanced toward Netta.

Icy chills crept over her back. Her teeth chattered together. She snapped them shut and lowered her chin to her chest, hugging herself, hoping he could not hear her shameful fear. But he would smell it, wouldn't he? The savage Baresark was as terrifying as if she were alone in the forest on a moonless midnight, hearing leaves rustling, twigs snapping and the deep, throaty snarl of a wolf.

Finally, he was close enough she saw his face. Light sea-green eyes studied her. She quaked as fearful images of being a possession of this man streaked through her mind. Waves of cold chills followed by heat washed over her.

"Greetings, *mo bean na bainnse,* my bride."

His voice was gentle, so like Mereck's voice.

"You cannot be here. I left you behind. What have you done to Mereck of Blackthorn?"

Netta gasped for air. Her tongue fought to form words in a mouth so dry she could not swallow. She shook Marcus' arm.

"Marcus, surely you know this man has followed us and slain your leader. Is he kin to Mereck? He poses as him. Are their faces so alike you do not see it?"

Netta cringed and tried to put as much distance as possible between herself and this barbaric man.

"Nay, milady. Our leader is afore you. *M'Famhair* would allow no other on his back but Mereck. Can you not see how content the steed is?" The war-horse nickered.

"B-But," she stuttered. "He's dressed like the savage."

"Sir Mereck seldom travels using Scottish clothing and trappings. For your comfort, he did so until now. He favors his Welsh ways"—he grinned wryly—"and is as you first saw him at Wycliffe."

The stable! Why had she not recognized it was Marcus who delivered the horse to her savage at Wycliffe? She swallowed hurriedly, for now her mouth filled with saliva. Oh, she was going to be ill. She put her hands over her lips and squeezed her eyes shut. Perchance if she closed them long enough the apparition would fade away and the demanding Mereck would reappear. Her shoulders shook. Soft moans escaped her clamped lips.

Gentle hands rested on her shoulders. She flinched.

"Come, lady. Dinna take on so. I am the same man whose pallet lay next to yours each night." His voice close to her ear was soft, coaxing. "The same man whose warmth you shared," he whispered.

Saints. Images flashed through her mind of the past mornings when she awoke snuggled tight to this man's side.

This *barbarian's* side.

She caught Mereck's familiar scent, causing that still unfamiliar tingling to streak from her breast to the pit of her stomach. She shuddered. Still, she refused to open her eyes.

"But you wear furs. Men do not dress in wolf skins."

"You must become accustomed to the sight. At Caer Cadwell, you will see many men garbed thus."

Netta peeped through cautious lids. His warriors chuckled over her fright. Dafydd and Fergus hurried to reassure her he was truly Mereck, and not strange in any way. This was the traditional way many Welshmen dressed. They likely thought her a frightened mouse to take on so. But they did not understand.

It was not only his clothing.

He was the man her father swore she would marry.

The man about whom her parents had told such gruesome tales.

The man from whom she ran.

Before she could worry further, the call of an eagle sounded high above. Her eyes widened when she heard the same sound come from close-by. Her savage had answered the call. He watched the sky, his face alight with pleasure. An eagle circled lower and lower until it was over their heads. Mereck's arm raised. With a soundless glide, the eagle landed on his leather-clad wrist.

"Cloud Dancer, I have seen you watch over us these last days. You come to escort us home, do you not?" He uttered soft chirps and warbles from deep in his throat, as he looked from the eagle to Netta. The raptor's gaze traveled from her face to his.

The eagle stared into her eyes seeming to study her. Soothing warmth seeped over her body, calming her. Surprising herself, she smiled at the beautiful face of the raptor.

Cloud Dancer ruffled the feathers on his great head and nodded. He walked sideways up Mereck's arm and perched on his shoulder, then gave a series of warbles, as if giving the man permission to continue his travels.

Her savage Welshman nodded, then motioned for Marcus to join him at the head of the line. Warriors closed in on both sides of Netta and Elise. Mereck gave her no time to fret, for he led them in a fast canter toward their goal.

"Hsst, Netta. Why did you not tell me Mereck was your barbarian? When he visited Ridley, he never dressed thus."

"Oh, Elise, I am so confused. Savage. Barbarian. Baresark. Mereck. I know not which man he is. But if he *is* my savage barbarian and has the marriage contract, what am I to do?"

"Bleddyn will help you. In Gwynedd, he is a nobleman. He is overlord over Caer Cadwell and controls all things there. 'Tis why your mother's legacy gives him final say as to the man who weds you."

They broke out of the deep woods, and Dafydd eagerly told them they rode on Blackthorn's ground. At the foot of the hill, the green forests ended. Ahead, the land rose in a gentle slope. A village surrounded by fields and lush pastures lay afore them.

The castle stood on the cleared span of land running north and south parallel to the bay's inlet. Tongue Bay cut into the eastern part of the ridge and formed river cliffs that protected the castle from attack. Curtain walls surrounded the huge area. On the west they followed the cliff's outline while the walls to the north, east and south rose behind a large moat. Sitting in the midst of a clearing was a massive rectangular keep, its formidable stones rising high in the air. It was built in the Norman way. Baileys surrounded by stone walls lay on either side of the castle.

Everyone halted to allow Netta to study the scene afore her. She startled when Mereck spoke.

"Lady, have no fear anyone will mistreat you in your new home. You and Elise will have ample female company. Connor's sister, Meghan, and Brianna are close of an age. Also, wives of the knights and castle members live with us." His gaze scanned her face. "Lady Phillipa oversees all."

"I do not fear such, sir. I would not allow it," she said with conviction.

It startled him, for her fragmented thoughts told a different story. *Savage temper—alone—defend Elise—who will champion me?* Pangs of regret struck him that she had seen his loss of control in the woods. He longed to reassure her he would never harm her. He would not—as long as he honored his vow never to love her. But no other man would hurt her. That he could promise with confidence.

As they rode closer, people hurried from the fields and buildings of the village. Men astride short Highland ponies raced on either side of them, shouting and welcoming the men back home. They slowed as they rode through the village, and the comforting aroma of food cooking in the huts drifted to them.

The villagers must have become used to having a Sassenach as their laird's wife, for the women smiled and waved as they passed. She returned their greetings. If Bleddyn refused to help her, she would make plans to escape Blackthorn and mayhap find someone here who would give her aid. To even think on it was foolish. She was at the farthest tip of Scotland's mainland, surrounded by the fiercest warriors in the country.

The exciting skirl of bagpipes called to them. She spied two pipers high atop the barbican. A fascinating figure stood beside them. Even from this distance she could see a man wearing a brilliant hued cloak about his shoulders. Long, shaggy black hair whipped around his face.

Cloud Dancer screeched his greeting. Careful not to harm Mereck, the bird moved from his shoulder back down to his raised wrist. With a slow sweep of his wings, the eagle lifted into the air without ruffling a hair on Mereck's head.

Netta watched, fascinated, as it soared above them to the man waiting beside the pipers. After landing on his left shoulder, Cloud Dancer's right wing moved like a caress over the human's head.

"Do you see, Netta? 'Tis our Bleddyn. You may not remember him clearly. Baron Wycliffe sent you to us these last five years when he expected Bleddyn to visit. Bleddyn was a great favorite with my Sinclair cousins. Brianna and her sister Abbess Alana are his special loves. He has always seen to their protection. The same way Father says he has looked after you and Caer Cadwell."

"I remember him. Does he bear a terrible scar that starts from the right side of his forehead and across the eyelid to end at his lip?"

"Aye. When he paints it red and the opposite side of his face blue, he frightens men who are as big as yonder steed." She pointed at *M'Famhair* with a nervous giggle.

As the sounds of the pipes swirled around them, they rode up the steep trail to the castle entrance. The closer they came to the massive portcullis, the clearer Netta saw the second piper was a woman. The entrance through the curtain was an arch, with an elaborate outer gatehouse behind. A round tower stood to the right of it, another at the end corner of the curtain wall.

The battlement walkways above the gatehouse swarmed with men on each sides of the pipers. The young woman pulled the instrument from her lips and let loose a signal cry so powerful they heard it above the wail of the other bagpipe.

Mereck's gaze lifted, and he echoed the sound back to her. She waved and turned to race down the steps to the bailey.

They clattered over the wooden bridge and through the confining entrance to the gatehouse. Netta studied the archers' slits and the murder holes on the ceiling above. This was a massive fortress, nothing like her father's castle. As they rode across the bailey toward the entrance to the keep, people gathered to await them at the steps.

Netta flinched when Mereck lifted her from the mount. His familiar scent comforted her, though she tried to pull away from his possessive hand on her waist. He would not allow it.

Before they could step forward, Elise's shout halted her.

"Netta. Tell him to go away. I told you of him. You vowed you would protect me."

Netta turned. Elise, atop her mount, scowled down at a very large man. She refused to allow him to aid her and held tight to the horse's mane. The hair on its poor neck looked like she was likely to pull it out afore she would release it.

The man's laughing brown eyes looked up at Elise, his mouth stretched wide in a smile. He was as tall and muscular as Mereck. Was the Highlands a land of giants? From Elise's description of him earlier, Netta recognized Connor, Mereck's cousin. He did not appear a villain to her.

"Come, little mouse. I vow not to eat you afore dinner," Connor coaxed. He pried Elise's fingers from the pony's mane and lifted her to the ground before she had time to utter a word. She bolted straight to Netta and clung to her arm.

"Connor, shame on ye, scarin' the puir lassie."

The tall girl who played the pipes had spoken. Her hair was long, and as deep brown as Connor's. Light green eyes sparkled beneath a broad forehead, and her mouth was as wide and generous as his. Were her eyes brown instead of green, she would have looked to be his twin. She wore breeches and a long open-necked shirt with a leather belt around her waist. A sheathed dagger hung from it and rested against her hip. When she approached Connor and shoved his shoulder, she surprised Netta.

Then she remembered Elise speaking of a young woman called the Warrior Woman of Blackthorn. It was her.

"Keep yer grimy paws off the lass, brother, at least 'till she has rested. Greetings, Mereck."

Mereck solemnly bent and kissed her cheek. Laughing up at him, she hugged his waist before coming to Netta and Elise.

"I am Meghan." A broad smile lit her face. "I see this lumberin' beastie brought somethin' besides smelly men back with him. Connor has paced the battlements fer hours. We have been expectin' ye, Elise." Meghan hugged Elise, then turned to Netta and studied her. "Bleddyn told us ye wud be comin', Lynette. Welcome to Blackthorn. Do ye prefer Netta, as Elise calls ye?"

As Netta nodded, Meghan engulfed her in a warm hug. Other than Elise, no one had ever hugged her. It felt wonderful.

"Enough, Meg. Netta has not yet met the laird."

Mereck led Netta to the foot of the steps where a man, as much of a giant as he, stood waiting. The men looked near alike, except for the laird's neatly trimmed black hair that hung to below his shoulder. Had his many responsibilities as laird caused his stern expression? When they drew close, his dark green eyes studied the brooch holding the tartan at her shoulder. He stepped forward to greet her, a pleased smile softening his face.

"Bleddyn told us Mereck would bring two beautiful young women to live with us." He leaned forward, put gentle hands on her shoulders and lightly kissed her cheek. "I am Damron. This wild man's brither."

"Laird, this is Lynette of Wycliffe. She is under my protection," Mereck said with an enigmatic smile. He turned to the beautiful older woman waiting beside Damron. "Netta, I wish you to meet Lady Phillipa,

Damron's mother. She is responsible for making me a civilized man."

Netta could not hold back a disbelieving huff at the word "civilized." Saints. If Lady Phillipa had softened him, he would be a fiend without it. She politely curtsied, and when she rose, found herself clasped in another embrace.

"Welcome, Netta. I am so very pleased Mereck has chosen you." Phillipa patted the brooch on Netta's shoulder and gave her another quick squeeze before releasing her.

"Connor, leave off tormenting Elise," Laird Damron demanded. "Mother and I wish to greet her properly."

Connor grasped Elise's arm and led her to where Damron and Lady Phillipa smiled and waited. The laird studied her pretty face and spoke gently to her. They had met at Ridley where Elise had followed Brianna like a timid shadow.

"Welcome, Elise." Damron frowned when her frightened eyes met his. His frown made him look ferocious; she looked even more timid. He patted her shoulder to reassure her. She fell back against Connor, who righted her. Damron looked puzzled, obviously unaware of the forbidding sight he presented.

"You have no cause for alarm, Elise. As my ward, you are entitled to my protection." Damron introduced her to Lady Phillipa, who greeted her warmly, saying she was delighted to have the young women added to her household.

"Come, we must not tarry. You are not accustomed to the brisk wind that comes off the bay." Damron motioned them forward. "My Brianna will be eager to see you both, once you have refreshed yourselves." A proud sound of possession rang from his voice.

Lady Phillipa led them up the wooden stairs to the

keep's entrance above the ground floor. Netta studied the building as she climbed the creaky stairs. Unlike Wycliffe, the ground floor had no window openings. She realized it was for protection. The keep's defenders could burn the stairway, should an enemy breach the inner bailey.

Entering massive doors, they turned left into a great hall twice as large as her father's. The display of weapons and armor that adorned the walls was impressive. Colorful banners hung from the ceiling, and trestle tables stood about the room. At the far end, the stately laird's table was on a dais. The room smelled fresh and clean.

The men seated Lady Phillipa and the women in chairs grouped in front of the fireplace. Servants brought wine, ale and cheeses. After Laird Damron downed a cup of ale and nibbled a piece of cheese, he left to check on his beloved wife.

Netta had planned to throw herself at Bleddyn's feet and plead her case. That was afore she met the Morgans of Blackthorn. Now, finding so much dignity in the room, she discarded the thought.

Conversation flowed easily. But why did everyone stare at her brooch, then smile? They even grinned at Mereck and raised their brows. He shook his head at them. She frowned. He kept close to her, as though branding her as his possession.

A warm breeze drifted over her, and she looked up, surprised. Lord Bleddyn, wearing a cloak of brilliantly colored feathers, stood in the doorway. He bore the eagle on his shoulder. Shaggy hair framed Bleddyn's face, and the left side of that face held the same blue paint as Mereck's.

"He honors you by painting his face in the old ways, Netta."

Mereck's whisper rustled the hair at her ear. She shivered.

As Bleddyn approached, he spoke to Cloud Dancer, and the eagle flew over to perch on a window opening. Bleddyn's dark eyes studying Netta's face felt like a comforting caress. Relief flowed through her, for she knew she could trust this man with her life.

"Little Lynette, your mother is most happy you have come to us." A strange smile lit his face.

Her eyes widened. Her mother? Why had he spoken as if he knew what her mother would have felt? Before she could ask, he stilled her with a fingertip to her lips.

"Tomorrow we will meet. Mereck and Damron will join us. For now, relax and enjoy learning about your new home."

He placed a kiss on her forehead, spreading peace through her. Savoring it, she closed her eyes. How had he known she wanted to meet with him? When she opened her eyes, he was nowhere to be seen.

Everyone kept the travelers busy answering questions about their journey. Mereck surprised Netta when he allowed her to talk without interfering, something her father had never permitted. Elise soon had them laughing, telling about her fright over meeting a "Heeland coo."

"The Heeland coos are great shaggy beasts, with hair swaying in the breeze as they walk. Their tongues seemed as long as my arm, when they licked out and over their faces. No one would tell me what manner of beasts they are. They laughed each time I ran from them. Are Heeland coos not ferocious beasts?"

"Elise, love, your 'ferocious beast' is a cow. A Highland cow." Connor grinned at her. "When you had milk with your porridge, did you not wonder where they got it?"

"Well, blessed saints. Why did they not tell me it was a cow?" She scowled at him as if the fault was his.

"Could it be because watching you leap and dart away from the gentle creatures was amusing, Mousie?" He stood beside her chair, his hand resting possessively on its back.

Meghan's feet shifted beside Lady Phillipa's chair.

"Aye, Meghan, you may leave and take the ladies to Brianna. I know she is waiting impatiently." Lady Phillipa turned to Mereck and shook her head. He released his hold on Netta's shoulder.

Meghan sprang forward with all the energy of a pup. "Come, Brianna awaits ye. The bairn didna sleep well last night, and she is cuddlin' the wee one."

When they entered the solar, the beauty of the scene struck Netta. A petite woman sat in front of a window opening. The golden sunlight flowing over her added to her fragile beauty.

Laird Damron knelt at her side. Anyone seeing them knew the lady's husband would defy the world and even heaven for her. His tender expression was near painful to see. He stroked his wife's chestnut curls and watched as she nursed the bairn. So much love flowed between them that Netta caught her breath. Would any man ever look at her with such gentleness? Brianna glanced up, a sweet smile lifting her full lips at the corners.

"Elise, love. It seems forever since I've seen you. Come. Give me a big hug, and meet our little Serena." Her chin went up with this last, the gesture defensive.

Her husband rose to his feet. He smiled down at Brianna, and caressed her cheek with the backs of his fingers. He turned toward them. Sadness lurked in his eyes, afore he masked his expression and left the room.

Elise flew across the room, near tripping in her eagerness to reach her cousin. Netta felt drawn to follow. Brianna lifted the sleeping child to her shoulder, and she hugged and kissed Elise. When Brianna's brown gaze met Netta's, mystery and barely suppressed sorrow lingered there.

"This must be Mereck's Lynette my Nathaniel spoke about."

Her musical voice had an accent Netta could not place. Not French, Saxon or Scottish. Its inflection was unfamiliar to her. She listened closely and soon became used to the soft, drawn-out sound of the words.

"I hope you do not mind another woman on your hands, Lady Brianna. I left Wycliffe to be with Elise. We had not time to seek your permission."

"We are very happy you are here. We did expect you, you know. My Nathaniel told us of your plight."

"Nathaniel? How could this Nathaniel have known?"

"She speaks of Bleddyn, Netta," Meghan said. "'Tis her special name for him. He knows happenin's ahead of time. E'en that Damron would wed Brianna and bring her here. Damron was leagues away in England, but Bleddyn knew of the king's message. He journeyed from Wales to go with Brianna and Damron. To watch o'er her."

Elise spoke up. "He has always been close to her sister Alana. He was at Sinclair Castle when Brianna was born. He looks after them, and keeps them from harm."

Netta watched Brianna place the sleeping babe in the nearby cradle. The nursemaid sat close-by, fierce protectiveness on her face.

Netta listened and watched the unusual Brianna, and she hoped someday to hear her story. She laughed, watching Elise flit from Serena's cradle to Brianna, and back again.

"Mousie, you will wear a path in the floor running

betwixt them," Connor's deep voice said from the doorway. "If 'tis a bairn you wish, Damron will gladly hasten the quest for a man to husband you."

Elise stopped in her tracks and plunked down on the floor between Netta and Brianna's chairs. She kept her head lowered and refused to look at Connor's grinning face.

At the mention of finding a husband, Netta wondered how to thwart Mereck and her father. Well, rats and fleas. Thinking of the man had drawn him to the room. He had discarded the wolf skins for a shirt and breeches.

Mereck bent and kissed Brianna's forehead, then went to stand over Serena. His beautiful hand gently stroked over the babe's head. Netta's heart skipped a beat. He then lightly drew the backs of his fingers across the soft baby cheek.

"The wean is thrivin', Brianna. She has grown much in my absence. Does she still greet if ye are from her sight?"

Netta looked at him, surprised at the brogue in his speech. His voice was husky, and she could not believe the change in his face. All the harsh angles disappeared, softened by tenderness and love. Yearning shone from his eyes when he looked at the child and Brianna. Would he love his own wife as deeply?

"Serena's always hungry. Fortunately, I've more than enough milk for her. If she cannot see me, her cries are not as frantic as they were when you left. She's feeling safer every day. I can now leave her for longer periods."

A sad expression lurked on her face. She must have seen Netta's questioning look, for she spoke to her.

"Soon after I lost my own bairn, our little Serena came into the world. When her witch of a mother found she had birthed a girl, she abandoned her. The little darling would not accept any wet nurse, until dear Johanna brought her to us." She flashed a wide smile at the woman guarding the cradle.

"And me braw brither?" Mereck asked. "Is he still hidin' his love for ye? Or has his heart taken over his head?"

"You should be proud of my Lord Demon, Mereck. He is either trying to stuff food in my mouth, or packing me between blankets and insisting I sleep. I begin to fear my skin will grow to the sheets. Every time I open my eyes, I spy him. He lurks over the bed, worrying whether I'm breathing too slowly or too rapidly." She flushed and laughed, a shy expression on her face. "He has finally relented and allowed me out of bed this week."

"Speakin' of restin', love, if ye would dine with us, ye must have yer nap," Damron ordered as he strolled into the room. "Meghan and the girls will visit Father, whilst ye get yer rest." He looked pointedly at Meghan as he bent over his little wife.

Lifting Brianna into his arms as easily as if he picked up a child, he hugged her tight to his heart and kissed the top of her head. "Mereck, will ye take o'er the men while I see our wee Brianna does not stint her nap?" He did not wait for Mereck's nod afore he left the room. The nursemaid followed, with a servant who carried the cradle.

"Come, ye must be meetin' Granda, fer he felt a mite poor in the stomach this morn and couldna greet ye properly." Meghan jumped up and waved her arms for them to follow her. She fairly ran to the end of the hallway, and up the winding stone steps there. Laird Douglas' room stood next to the stairwell on the third floor.

"Ye will be sharin' a room with me three doors down. Connor and Mereck's room is close-by," she added.

She threw open the door. "Granda, I bring two lovely lassies to brighten yer day." Her long legs swiftly carried her over to the great bed against the wall. Her grandfather, the old laird of Clan Morgan, rested against a mound of pillows.

His was the kindest face Netta had ever seen. Streaks of white flashed in his long, shaggy brown hair and short beard. Keen golden brown eyes studied both young women. He smiled and beckoned for them to sit on the bed beside him. He tugged Elise's tunic, urging her closer.

"Come, lass. I would see our new ward." Old Laird Douglas' gaze studied her. "Think ye, Meghan, the wolf must needs guard her from her suitors?"

Elise blanched white as a full moon on a clear night.

"Oh, blessed saints, sir. Do not say such." Netta patted Elise's shoulder. "She fears Scotland's wolves plan to have her for their next meal."

"Ah. Ye must be Mereck's Lynette. Bleddyn said yer beautiful eyes would turn a man's heart to puddin'." He smiled at her.

"My lord, I am not Mereck's Lynette, but simply Lynette of Wycliffe." Well, rats. Had Mereck already branded her with his possessive attitude? "I came to Scotland to keep Elise company."

"Ock, Meghan." Laird Douglas chuckled. "I ken Bleddyn has summoned another lovely Sassenach who fights her destiny."

Chapter 10

Netta started to question Laird Douglas' words, but the clicking sound of an animal's nails on the floor distracted her. The beast padded around the foot of the bed and came to a halt beside them. A large, furry head jostled Elise's legs. She jumped and jerked them away. Scrambling onto her hands and knees, she peered over the side of the bed.

"Blessed Saint Eustace," she yelled. "Mereck failed to kill the beast. The wolf has tracked us to Blackthorn." Searching for balance, she thrashed her arms about. It didn't help. The pallet heaved and jiggled on its rope supports. She tilted over and bumped Netta, tumbling her off the edge of the bed.

Netta landed atop the biggest, hairiest creature she had ever seen within castle walls. Sliding off its broad back, she hit the floor with a thud. Before she could protect her face, a very wet tongue licked her cheek. A huge friendly wolf appeared to grin on seeing her startled expression. She burst into laughter at the idea.

"Ah. I see you and Guardian have met, lady." Mereck lounged against the doorframe watching her.

The sight of his laughing bride sprawled on the floor,

skirts baring her legs near up to her thighs, prodded his shaft to beg for attention. Although his gaze focused on her intriguing eyes, he noted every enticing inch of visible flesh.

She was not mindful of her disarrayed clothing.

He was not about to tell her.

"Do you often play with beasties? You have a way with him."

"Nay, sir. Never have I had a pet. Father said to feed an animal which did not perform a service was a foolish expense. He had his hunting dogs, his horses and his falcons." Her voice became strained. "I befriended the barn cat, but he would not allow me to feed her. He said starving cats made better mousers."

Mereck studied the stricken look in her lovely eyes. Having seen for himself Baron Wycliffe's harsh behavior, he had no need to hear her thoughts. No doubt, the cruel man destroyed any animal she befriended.

Netta thumped the great wolf on his sides. The beast licked her knee, bringing her bare legs to her attention. She blushed and scrambled to her feet. Guardian was not helpful. He demanded attention and near nudged her to the floor again.

Connor joined Mereck, and when he spied the rumpled bed, he padded over to tower above Elise. His brown eyes crinkled in amusement.

Laird Douglas put a protective arm around her.

"Are you the cause of this mayhem, Elise?" Connor's slow, appraising glance caused Elise to blush and stare down at her hands. "Mereck told me of the mischief you both caused on your journey. I see I must needs keep watch o'er you."

"Mischief, sir? We did not engage in mischief." Her

timid gaze lifted, and her forehead wrinkled with worry. "Did we Netta?"

Connor's brows waggled upward. "What? You dinna believe aiding Netta to deceive Mereck, helping her put worms in his stew, and enticing a wounded wolf to stalk you wasna mischief?"

"Did you tell one and all every mishap, sir?" Netta, her hands on her hips, glared violet fire at Mereck.

"Uh, come to think on it"—Mereck rubbed vigorously at his jaw—"I failed to mention Elise suggested you bribe your guard to shirk his duty. If Damron learns of it, he will likely lecture you both. And, aye, I didna tell anyone how you spied on the men hoping to see something you should not. Hmm . . ." His brows wriggled. He whispered loud enough for all to hear. "Or how you tried to seduce me as I slept."

Netta's mouth dropped open. She turned pleading eyes to Meghan and Laird Douglas and blurted her denials. "I never tried to seduce him. I became cold in the night and slept too close. And I did not spy on the men. I could not help it if they were careless. They should wear nappies and not expose themselves at every opportunity."

Meghan's throaty laughter filled the room. Her eyes sparkled with humor. "Aye, ye have the right of it Netta. But then they could not display their wares fer all to see. It be how a woman selects her partner fer the night. He with the longest prick dips his wick the sooner."

"Haud yer wheesht, Meg," Connor bellowed and put his hands over Elise's ears—too late.

Her curious "What is a pr . . ." burst out before Connor's hand flew from her ears to cover her mouth.

"I think Damron should find a stern husband for Meghan afore he looks to Elise." Mereck's tone was harsh but belied it when he winked at his grandfather.

"One who will thrash her regularly whene'er she spouts such things." With a clamp-your-mouth-shut look, Connor glared at his sister. "I'll search for an older man. One who will think nothing of taking a switch to her at eventide, in case he missed chastising a fault that day."

"Hmpf." Netta gave Connor a scorching scowl and moved to stand between him and her new friend. "That is a vile notion, sir. Why can men say any horrid thing they please, but when a woman dares open her mouth, you stifle her?"

"Because we are your masters, and you are but foolish women, of course." Mereck's voice was so close behind her, it stirred the hair behind her ear. "Women will speak in the way we instruct them, and act how we decree."

Netta whirled about, her eyes spitting fire. That she was angry and would stand up for herself and her friends pleased Mereck. He spoke again, before she could.

"If women were given the same freedoms as men, family structure would collapse. You would not have time to tend our comforts."

Meghan snorted and raised her hand at him, her third finger aimed upward. A most strange gesture.

Connor needed an extra pair of hands. He tried to cover Elise's eyes but was not quick enough.

"What does that . . ." Elise could say no more afore he interrupted her.

"So help me, Meghan, if ye e'er do such a vulgar thing again, I will have Damron take the flat of his hand to yer arse."

Netta blinked in surprise.

"Fat lot of guid it would do him," Meghan scoffed. "Damron kens I will be a lady when I wish. Quit yer slabberin' over Elise, brother. Canna ye see ye upset the poor lass slappin' yer paws from one part of her face to the other? Now that we have livened Granda's rest, we had best freshen up."

Meghan glared at her brother's hands still lingering on Elise's shoulder. When he released her, Elise bolted off the bed and detoured around him.

Mereck moved aside for both her and Meghan. Before Netta could leave, he shifted, partially blocking the doorway. She tried to scoot past. Her breasts brushed his chest, sending hot flashes of pleasure straight to his tarse. When her hand grazed his suffering sex, he snapped his jaw tight. Wide-eyed, she glanced down, blushed and jerked her arm back. She bolted after Meghan.

Netta gazed around Meghan's room, pleased by the way it reflected Meghan's brisk personality. Sprigs of pink and purple heather spilled from a wicker basket setting beside the door, their fresh scent drifting on the air.

She crossed to the opposite wall, and peered out a large window slit. It overlooked a steep slope into the valley. The sun's rays entered to brighten the leaf-green bed curtains tied to the posts of a large bed. Someone had neatly folded their few belongings atop the forest green cover. Alongside their clothing lay several colorful tunics and smocks.

"Ye are close to my height." Meghan selected a tunic and held it up to Elise's shoulders. "I chose some of my own garments for ye. I ne'er wear skirts if I can help it. Why should a man have the comfort of breeches, when we must drag a mountain of cloth about our legs?" Meghan's eyes sparkled with humor. "Not to mention it hinders carryin' a blade."

Three wooden chests, one with a sword atop it, sat

beneath colorful tapestries on each side of the room. Netta picked up the sword to study it. "Ah, the sword is your own? 'Tis beautiful. Was it crafted for you?" A small crystal sat low on the handle. The sword's blade, engraved with Celtic designs, reflected the room's colors.

"Aye." Meghan nodded. "Damron gifted me with it on my sixteenth name day." She threw the door open and called for servants to bring a tub and buckets of water for bathing.

In a far corner of the room, the bath was soon set up beside a washstand holding a pitcher, basin and cloths. A privacy screen shielded it. After the door closed behind the servants, Elise insisted Netta should be first to use it.

"Meghan, what is a prick? Is it the same as a tarse?" Netta's voice was only loud enough to hear above the sounds of her bathing.

"Aye. Their member has many names. If it be long, they do like to call it a tarse, a rod or shaft; if hard and strong it becomes a ram, a dabbler or weapon. Sometimes it be small and pitiful afore it grows, and prick or pintle seems more apt. A man does hate to have his weapon called a prick." Hearing Netta's bark of laughter and Elise's surprised giggles, Meghan grinned and rolled her eyes.

"Father would never let me attend male visitors." Netta grimaced, realizing her own naivete. "I thought they were like those on little boys. Until I started watching our escorts. The wind was most helpful."

Meghan chuckled. "So Mereck didna lie about yer lookin' at the men? Did ye really try to seduce him while he slept?" The bed ropes squeaked when she sat on the pallet.

"I never did!" Netta sprang from the tub in such haste water sloshed onto the floor. Hugging a drying clothing about her, she rushed from behind the screen.

"He insisted on sleeping so close to my pallet, that in my sleep, I thought he was part of it. I did wake to find my bedding warm as fresh baked bannocks. Instead of bread, I found my head on his chest, his heartbeat beneath my ear. Its pounding awakened me."

Thinking about Mereck reminded her to ask about Meghan's unusual gesture. Surely it meant something men disliked intensely, else Connor would not be so offended.

"What was that sign you made? Connor was so aggrieved I thought he would thrash you."

Netta picked up a stool and moved it to where the sun's rays streamed through the window slit. She sat and combed the tangles from her hair while Elise bathed.

"Huh. He can try." Meghan shrugged. "As a young girl, I had a frightenin' experience. After it, I persuaded Granda to allow me to train with the boys. Years later, when my skills equaled theirs, they dubbed me the Warrior Woman of Blackthorn. Connor knows I can hold my own with him.

"The gesture was somethin' Brianna used one day, when we women dunked rose-scented, soapy water o'er the men. The dirty auld sheep lovers canna bear to cleanse their bodies. They believe water will shrivel their male parts. When Damron ordered Brianna to stop, she threw him what she called 'the finger.' She said it was common in the strange far away land where she was born. It means a man should swive himself."

Netta thought that would be an unusual event, for she did not know how one would swive to begin with.

"Does Damron not mind that Mereck loves Brianna? I watched him with her and the babe. He turned soft as gruel around them." Nettta felt a sharp twinge. Surely not jealousy?

"Aye, Mereck loves Brianna. But as a sister. Sincc he

was but seven winters old, he has vowed ne'er to love a woman as wife. He has led a strange life. After our parents and Damron's father were murdered, Damron and Connor fostered for six months of each year with King William's family in Normandy. Aunt Phillipa took me with her."

"Did not Mereck go?" Elise asked as she splashed a tide of water under the screen.

"Nay. For a reason. Afore Damron was born, his Da captured a Welsh woman in a raid. She fell deeply in love with him. She died when Mereck was born. Earlier that same hour, Aunt Phillipa had birthed Damron. She refused wet nurses and insisted on nursing Mereck along with Damron. She would have kept Mereck with us when we went to Normandy, but Granda wouldna allow it.

"Because he feared for him. When still a youth, Mereck learned he was called the last Baresark in Wales. The wild blood of the Welsh strengthened the fighting blood of the Scots in Mereck. My cousin ne'er speaks overmuch, but his temper is legendary. The first man in Normandy to call him a by-blow would have found himself with Mereck's great weight on his chest, his short sword at his neck. Any clan would be honored to call him their own. He is the finest warrior in Scotland."

Netta felt a pang of sympathy. Mereck must have always felt like an outcast. What a terrible burden for anyone to bear.

"How does that explain the closeness between Mereck and Brianna?"

"Why, because of Damron's French leman. 'Twas unfortunate she was already increasin' when Damron brought Brianna to Blackthorn. The leman swore 'twas Damron's doin'. Our Brianna's bairn was stillborn.

"The leman birthed a girl and ordered Johanna to kill

it, then disappeared. Johanna protected the bairn, but the little one refused to nurse. When Brianna heard her pitiful cries, she demanded they bring the child to her. The bairn latched onto Brianna's breast and still wails pitifully if she canna see or hear her new mother.

"Ye ken, Brianna did for Serena what Aunt Phillipa did for Mereck? Mereck loves her for it."

Elise bobbed her head as she came from behind the screen. "Saints preserve us, Netta. I do not want to wed a Highland giant who has those leman creatures hanging about. Father would rather I died a shriveled old lady, he would."

"Damron has oft tried to find a man with a 'firm hand' to wed me. I soon discourage them." Meghan laughed.

"How have you gone about it?" Netta fought to control her ebony curls with a silver circlet around her brow. "I have not found men easy to turn away. At times, I acted like they had an unpleasant smell to insult them. If it did not, I crossed my eyes whenever the suitor was around. Too often, I could not keep it up." She looked up and grinned. "If the man was fastidious about his person, I did not bathe and spilled food down my clothing. I even sprinkled dirt around my neck. It made nasty little mud balls when I began to sweat. I wore the same tunic until the suitor left in disgust."

Meghan laughed as she combed her own hair.

"Aunt Phillipa watches me too closely for those tricks, but I ha'e my own ways to upset the churls."

"What do you do? My eyes don't cross easily, and I hate dirt." Elise looked surprised when they laughed. "What? Why do you laugh?"

"I have known ye for but half a day, and yer eyes cross every time Connor comes near. Have ye not noticed?"

Elise put her hands on her cheeks, hiding her blush. Meghan hugged her shoulders.

"If the unwanted man plays the pipes," Meghan said, "I invite him to a contest. I can out-pipe the best of them. If he thinks himself a great swordsman, I demand we meet in the practice field. They fall o'er their feet afeared to draw a drop of my blood. They worried for naught, for I can compete with most men. If neither of these ideas works, I aim my dirk at a spot on the bench."

"Why would that stop them?" Netta could not think why Meghan's solution would scare a man away.

"It will. If the spot is betwixt their hairy thighs." In a flash, Meghan's arm raised and a blade flashed across the room and thudded into the door.

Her skill was so great, Netta had not even seen her draw the blade from the sheath at her thigh.

"Damnation, Meg, cease," Connor yelled from the corridor.

He eased the door open and scowled at Meghan, then stood aside.

Brianna's maid servant entered carrying an armful of bright clothing, saying her mistress wanted Netta to have them. They were of the same small stature. On the morrow, the ladies of the castle would help sew the young women new outfits.

Connor's entrance kept Netta from asking Meghan if she had found a particular man to her liking. When she had spoken about her suitors, her eyes had filled with sadness.

"Have you not noted how late it becomes? Granda is enjoying a nip with Mereck." Connor looked down at Netta, his eyes twinkling. "Lady, Mereck declares you are to present yourself at once, or he will change his mind."

"Change his mind, sir? About what?" Netta reached up to sweep an unruly curl from her face.

"He didna say." Connor pivoted on his heels and left.

Upon entering the great hall, Netta did not see Mereck for all the people milling about. They made their way toward the group standing around the fireplace. She spied him deep in conversation with Damron. He lounged with casual grace, one shoulder braced against the heavy wood of the mantel. As if to anchor himself, he had spread his muscular legs slightly apart. A large basket sat beside his feet.

"Blessed Saint Cuthbert," Netta blurted. "He wears a wee lambkin about his shoulders."

The large bundle of white around Mereck's neck stiffened and jiggled about precariously. A very fat tail flapped back and forth, swatting his face. Netta could only glimpse his startled green eyes as the tail attacked. A head rose to press close to Mereck's cheek. It squinted gleaming, yellow eyes at her.

"Saints! It still lives." The creature's yowl of displeasure at rudely being interrupted from a well-earned nap made Netta skid to a halt.

The fur piece scrambled, stretched and dug its claws into Mereck's chest. Reaching up with soothing hands, he murmured in Gaelic and gathered the animal in his arms. Fascinated, Netta watched him stroke from the top of its head to the end of a long fluffy tail, comforting the animal. How odd that Scotland's most feared warrior looked so gentle.

She felt a fool. Why, it was no small lamb, but the largest white cat she had ever seen. Mereck had imposing shoulders, yet the animal had more than covered their breadth and down the sides of his arms. Surely anyone would have mistaken it?

"Now that you have disturbed Mither's much needed rest, lady, I can see nothing for it but that you soothe the savage beasties." He nodded at the basket, no longer setting quietly but swaying and creaking at her feet.

Inside was the biggest litter of kittens Netta had ever seen. They were all different colors. Had the cat mated with every tom in the barn? Nay, that could not be the reason. They were also different sizes. She looked up at Mereck, puzzled.

"They are as you see them. She feeds not only her own get, but the bairns of mothers who became food for a sneaky fox."

Little kitten faces peered up at them, their mouths agape. Tiny white teeth and pink tongues showed as they set up a mewling racket begging sustenance. Without thinking, Netta plunked down on the floor beside the basket and folded her legs beneath her tunic.

Which one should she pet first? The littlest with eyes not fully open? Or the larger kittens that acted like they were starving? She solved it by lining the four smallest on her arm and cuddling them to her chest. After scooping several other babes onto her lap, she soon ran out of room.

"Oh, I cannot comfort them all." Distress streaked through her when the other kittens looked up at her and seemed to beg for the same attention.

Elise joined her, taking over the remaining kittens. Netta's heart beat happily. She had never had so many small ones to pet and hold. When they crawled up her clothing to nuzzle at her neck, she giggled and shivered when rough little tongues licked her skin and tried to find a teat to nurse.

Mereck's gaze roved over Netta. He feigned but mild interest in what he saw. Netta was beautiful enjoying the little balls of fur. He recalled her happy face in Granda's room when she petted Guardian. Though not born a bastard, her father truly earned the epithet by his deeds.

Wycliffe had thought to rule Netta, to force her to his will. One did not master such a spirit as hers by harshness. He would seek her compliance by other means.

He would woo her with what her father denied her. First was her desire to have something to love and call her own.

His gaze fell to her sweet neck. His bride squirmed as a kitten's tongue tickled her beneath her ear. Would she squirm when his tongue lapped over her, his mouth suckled her skin? Her innocent face was soft and yearning.

Sweet Christ, let it soon be for him she yearned. One look at Netta jolted his body to respond. His ballocks ached, his tarse hardened and stirred. Never had a woman caused him to stay in such a ready state of arousal.

He had neglected his needs far too long afore he met her. Ne'er did he share his favors for long with a lass whose company he enjoyed. If he felt his regard soften, he was always on guard, fearful it would turn to love. Now, he didna feel right swiving another, for Netta was all but his wife.

"Ye had best settle the beasties, Mereck, afore ye burst."

Meghan's lips fought a grin. When she nodded at his bulging sex, he realized what was evident to all in the room. His desire for Netta. Muttering curses in Gaelic, he knelt beside the two young women.

"Come, Mither. Yer bairns are demandin' their bellies be filled." He put the cat in the empty basket and plucked the smallest kittens off Netta. He helped each latch onto one of Mither's teats.

His knuckles brushed against Netta's breast when he pried a kitten's claws from her clothing. His ballocks throbbed with need. How sweet she would taste when he drew that same nipple into his mouth. Her breast would swell, the nipple would harden and the areola would pebble with passion. He stifled a groan.

Netta's gaze darted to his face. What she saw there must have startled her, for she gasped and plucked the next hungry creature from her chest and put it in his hands. Her face flushed. He watched her pulse pounding in her tempting neck.

His resolve hardened thinking about the marriage contract. She would fight it. But not for long. He would not allow it. If she refused to say her vows afore the priest, he would force her to nod her head in agreement. He would not give up Caer Cadwell.

Netta shivered again. Something in his face, nay, not something. A look of wildness was there that reminded her of the day he hurtled from the woods, his sword drawn and a snarl on his lips.

Now, smoldering flames burned in the depths of his darkened eyes. His face looked hungry. Lean. His expression sent tremors through her stomach. Everywhere his gaze touched, heat seared her flesh.

How could he cause such strange feelings with but a look? She lowered her eyes and placed the last kitten in the basket.

Mereck gripped her elbow and helped her rise. She didn't dare pull away. Her legs would not support her. It must be exhaustion from the long journey. Aye. That's what this is about, the reason for these strange feelings.

How had they crossed the great hall to the high table so quickly? Shaking her head to clear her thoughts, she saw he watched her. His eyes brimmed with amused pleasure.

"He asked ye twice, Netta"—Meghan's voice floated to her senses—"which of the wee beasties ye wud like?"

"Like? I may have a kitten of my own?" She could not keep the surprise from her voice, nor the worry from her soul. Would he be like her father and later take delight in destroying something she loved?

"Ye seemed to coddle the runt of the litters, lady, but the wee one is not verra strong," Mereck said, his voice hoarse.

"Is it the little white one with the black tip on his nose and chin that you call the runt? How can you give a sweet little creature such an ugly name, sir?"

She stared at his mouth. The tip of her tongue darted out to moisten her lips; his lips softened and pursed slightly.

"Aye, such a sweet little creature." His finger under her chin tilted her face up to him. His warm lips brushed hers.

She blinked. Could he have guessed she was curious how his lips would feel against her own? The mewling kittens drew her attention back to them.

"I may truly have a kitten?" She fought to keep the pleading note from her voice.

"Ye may. But it must stay with Mither until strong enough to live apart. Ye should oft check its feeding so it does not get pushed from its food. I keep the basket in the kitchens so the young ones will be warm."

"I will do everything you tell me to do, and take very good care of it." A happy grin spread across her face. How strange to feel so. Elise tugged lightly at Netta's sleeve, but before she could respond, Connor interrupted.

"I suppose you want a bairn also, Elise?" He sighed and draped an arm around her shoulders. "If you ask nicely, I may beg Mereck to part with another of his prized younglings. A most difficult task, for he is selfish with Mither's charges."

Elise peered up at him, frowning worriedly as she tried to pull away. When she turned to plead with Mereck, Connor made a face at him and grinned.

"Well now, I am right possessive of the kits." Mereck gazed at her and rubbed his jaw.

Elise swallowed and looked undecided whether to duck from under Connor's arm or stay put. She stayed put.

"Do you think you can ask him to let me have a kitten, sir?" she whispered to Connor. "I will take very good care of it. I won't let anything hurt it or take it away. Not even the wolf." She shuddered and squared her shoulders.

"If you gave me a wee kiss, mayhap I could brave coaxing Mereck into partin' with another wee bairn." He sighed.

Meghan thumped him on his back. He lurched forward.

"Stop teasin' the lassie. Ye have no need to ask me brither, Elise. Mereck will gladly give ye a little beastie."

"Stop baitin' the lassies and seat yourselves," Lord Douglas commanded. "Brianna has arrived and canna linger all evenin'."

Damron sat at the head of the table, Brianna on his right, his grandfather and Lady Phillipa on his left. They all took seats, including several women whom Meghan introduced as widows of knights killed during clan raids.

A table along the right side of the hall served the castle knights and their wives, and on the opposite side of the huge area was a long table for the unmarried knights and women of the castle. Men-at-arms and other warriors, who made up the defense of the castle, sat at lower tables. All wore a variety of clothing and hair styles that puzzled Netta.

"The long-haired warriors are Saxons who came with Brianna," Mereck explained softly. "The men who wear their hair cropped short were with Damron in Normandy.

They insisted on staying with him when he returned to Scotland. Of course, Scots make up the greatest number of warriors."

Damron rose and lifted his hand to quiet the room.

"Elise of Ridley, cousin to Brianna, has become my ward. As ye know, England lacks eligible men from whom to select a husband for her. I have promised her father I will take the utmost care in choosing her mate."

"Damron, for God's love, you are not auctioning the prettiest mare at a village fair," Brianna scolded. "Don't you think they would have figured it out for themselves without you announcing her eligibility?"

"Well, now, it isnae like I am tryin' to sell the lassie," Damron blustered. "They canna ken she is more than a visitor if I dinna tell them." He turned back to the room. "Come forward and speak yer names, for I would know who is interested."

He ignored Brianna as she sighed and threw up her hands. Pandemonium broke out in the room as men jostled each other.

"Halt yer blather," Damron bellowed. "Stand quiet, and I will call each man in turn." He beckoned to the first man.

"Oh, Netta, they are much like Galan's friends told us when we were little," Elise whispered, then groaned. "Mayhap these are the ones who stole English girls and fed them to wolves."

A huge man swaggered up to the table. Every bit as tall as the three Morgan men, his hair was long and wild. A black beard and bushy eyebrows framed a face twice the size of Netta's own. His ham-like fists rested on his hips. His gaze raked over Elise. When he met her eyes, he licked his lips, exaggerating the gesture. A rumble of satisfaction welled from his chest. Grasping the staff

Damron handed him, he raised it knee-high then slammed the end on the floor with a loud thunk.

"Ye be a most tempting morsel, Saxon, sweet to the taste. Yer hair is the color of blackberries." Elise gasped when a beefy fist grasped a black lock to slide through his fingers. "Yer eyes like blueberries, and a mouth plump and sweet lookin' as the softest cherry." He turned his gaze to glare at Connor and bellow, "Ha'e ye sampled this little dessert, laddie?"

Elise looked ready to faint. Connor put his arm around her shoulders and drew her to his side. He glared at the man.

"Lady Elise, this is Uncle Angus MacLaren of Argyll. Uncle, dinna scare the wee Mousie. She thinks we are wild men and fears she will flavor someone's stew. She heard tales that we Scotsmen are savages and not the timid, civilized people she sees today." His lips twitched.

"Enough, the two of you," Lord Douglas scolded them. "You have the lassie proper affrighted. Is this how Lady Phillipa trained you to treat such gentle women?"

Now that he had intervened, Elise shoved Connor to loosen his grip. She lifted her chin.

"I am no one's dessert, sir. If any man tried to eat me, I am certain he would find himself poisoned from the taste."

When the waiting males roared with laughter and licked their lips, her eyes widened. Connor glared at them to hold their pestering.

Damron called one warrior after another to come to the table. Each picked up the staff and thudded it on the floor until the room echoed with the sound. He then announced his name and family, and whether or not he had bairns in need of mothering.

All shapes and sizes of men begged introductions. More than a few would interest a young woman. Connor scowled at these men, keeping hold of Elise's hand all the while.

Netta noted he did not spare his cousin from his distemper either. Each time Damron motioned another person forward, Connor glared all the harder until his eyes were mere slits conveying his displeasure. After Damron had introduced everyone and sent them back to their tables, Netta sighed with relief.

Brianna signaled for the cook's helpers to bring in the food. The aroma drifting from large platters of lamb, trout, baked fowl and grouse made Netta's mouth water. Bowls of steaming vegetables came next, then tempting hot breads.

Mereck selected bits of each offering onto the trencher they were to share. Netta's favorite carrots and peas were among the vegetables he loaded beside the poultry and mutton.

Mereck raised a succulent morsel of chicken to her lips. She hesitated. A shudder rippled through her. Since her disgusting fiasco with a former suitor and his filthy fingers, she had been leery of sharing a trencher with anyone other than her family. Mereck watched her, waiting.

She shook herself and stared at his strong fingers. They were scrupulously clean. Her heart thumped, as it often did whenever she saw his hands. Daintily, she took the food with her lips and sighed with relief.

The rest of the meal passed pleasantly. She enjoyed the lively conversations between the family. Mereck listened, but did not join in the teasing between Meghan and Connor. Soon they served everyone fruit and candied sweets.

It would not be so hard to fit in, Netta decided. Several men seemed the pleasant sort. Not hard on the eye, either. Mayhap, when she knew them better, she would accept an offer from one of them. As she thought that, a man stood and cleared his throat until he had Damron's attention.

"Laird, ye ha'e introduced yer lovely ward, but there's another lassie sittin' at yer table. I see no ring o' possession on her finger."

"Lucifer's spawn!" Mereck snarled, the sound bestial. He exploded to his feet.

Chapter 11

Sparks of tension radiated from Mereck like miniature lightning strikes. The room fell still.

"The lady is my betrothed. The ring will band her finger directly after Laird Damron grants leave for the ceremony." Mereck's voice, soft as a kitten's purr, belied a menacing smile and eyes colder than a loch on All Soul's Day.

Defying him, Netta wriggled from beneath his hand clamped on her shoulder to keep her seated. Though instinct told her to heed him, she swallowed and stood on shaking legs. Dwarfed by his imposing height, she stiffened her spine and strove to give the illusion of height and fearless determination.

"Laird Damron, Father signed the contract without my consent. I would choose mine own husband." Well, rats and fleas. Her knees quaked. She grasped hold of the table to steady herself and groaned. Where had she come up with such foolish nerve? From too much watered wine, that's where. Only a dolt would believe any man would allow her such freedom.

"Oh? The way ye chose a mate from the many who courted ye?" Mereck bristled with irritation. "Baron

Wycliffe spoke of yer plots to dissuade suitors. I signed the contract after I allowed ye to flee to Ridley. Had ye not acted as a headstrong lass, yer signature would have been on it."

"Your father gave you no choice in a husband, Lynette?" Sympathy flashed in Brianna's eyes.

"She had many choices. Her father declared she found each man who wooed her had a flaw too vile for her *delicate nature.*"

"Delicate nature?" Netta's voice spluttered. "Do you think a suitor older than mine own sire should have caused me to leap for joy? Or do you refer to the man who came afore him? He was not old, but his great weight forced us to provide a special, sturdy stool to sit upon. No castle bench could hold him."

"Granted they were not suitable for a dainty flower like yerself, lady." Mereck's lips curled in a snarl. "What did ye find distasteful about Sir Cecil, Sir Kenneth or Sir Robert? All young and worthy knights? Yer father listed at least ten and two ye scorned."

"Oh, oh!" Coherent thought flew from Netta's mind. She spied the soggy trencher beside her hand and thought to drape it across his head. She hesitated. He was too tall. Instead, she reached for the goblet of watered wine. Her hand never grasped it. He captured it in his own.

"Enough. Both of ye," Damron ordered. "This is not the place fer this discussion. Ye will come to me after we break our fast on the morrow."

Mereck jerked his head in agreement. Netta did not respond until he squeezed her hand.

"Aye, my lord." It sounded weak to her ears. To make up for it, she held her head high.

Something tugged hard at her skirt and caused her to lose her balance. She grabbed Mereck's arm to steady herself. The wolf Guardian wished her attention; his patience seemed at an end. He looked up at her eyes, uttered a soft growl, then turned toward the fireplace. The kittens' basket was in danger of toppling. Servants bustled about, too busy to note they had bumped it very near the flames when they tended the tables.

Netta dashed toward it. The basket overturned and kittens spilled out onto the stone. The smallest landed a hands width from the hot coals. Guardian streaked past her, his great jaws agape.

"Eewww. He will eat the babe. Quick, give him a bone." Elise grabbed Connor's shirt and yanked on it.

"Me? Give that great beast a bone? If he decides my arm to be a choicer morsel, lady, will you wed me?" His face looked comically hopeful as he blinked down at Elise.

"Leave off yer teasin', brither." Meghan patted Elise's shoulder. "He is not goin' to eat the babes, Elise. He but plans to keep the little ones from the fire,"

Guardian stood waiting, his jaws grasping a creature by the scruff of its neck. When Netta held out her palm, he placed the wee kitten in it then licked it from head to tail, before sinking back on his haunches.

"What a great father you would be. What a shame you have no babes of your own." Netta ruffled the fur behind his ears.

"Babes? Of his own? A litter of wolves? Oh, Netta, do not give the beast such thoughts. They will soon overrun the castle. We will have to stay abed with our doors barred."

Connor tickled the hair on Elise's nape and chuckled when she jumped. "An excellent idea, Elise. Surely you will wish me there to defend you. I must needs seek a good breeding mate for Guardian."

Elise's lips rounded in alarm. Finally, she and Netta gathered the kittens and returned them to the basket.

"God's teeth, Brianna. I told ye all yer lovin' on Guardian would ruin him." Damron snorted with disgust. He slapped his hand on the table. "Look at the great beastie. Not e'en a mark on the wee un. Some protection he has been. He hasna e'en bit the pants off a man fer days."

"I have not ruined him, husband. He's but gentled about the edges." Brianna huffed. "Guardian will still tear a man to shreds if he threatens one of us." She patted Damron's arm. "A little love will ruin neither man nor beast."

"Where is that foolish Mither?" Netta scolded the absent cat. "She should not have left them alone."

"I suspect she had to tend her own needs, or else soil the beddin'." Mereck reached around her and took the heavy basket. "Come, I'll show ye where they spend their time in the kitchen. If ye would keep it, it is there ye will see yer kit properly nurses. Elise, ye may choose your babe."

Meghan went with them to the kitchens, and they sat on a rug close to the cooking hearth, the basket of kits in front of them. Mereck left to return to Damron, and Netta seized the opportunity to question Meghan.

"Meghan, why do your men change their way of speaking?"

"Ye mean the brogue, do ye not?" At Netta's nod, she continued. "We all speak Norman French, Gaelic, Saxon English and other languages. Damron converses in at least six, German bein' his favorite for singin' to his Brianna. If upset, angry or amorous, they revert to their Scots brogue. 'Tis the language we started with as babes and springs most readily to our tongues."

"You do it too," Elise exclaimed.

"Aye. I prefer the brogue. I use the others if I wish to 'put off' a man who seeks to become too familiar. It makes them verra uneasy." She laughed. "Now. I'll show ye how to assure yer little one gets her fill."

"How do you know a girl from a boy?" How could Meghan tell the differences in them? Netta had seen their little furry undersides when she played with them, and they all looked alike to her. She turned the littlest on its back and stared at it.

"Alike? Nay, can ye not see the difference?" Meghan plucked the precious little runt from her hands, along with another kitten, and held them both upside down.

"They look alike. Are they not both girls?" She and Elise brought their heads closer to the kittens until their three heads near banged together.

"Are ye searchin' fer fleas, ladies?" Connor's curious voice rumbled through the room.

Netta jerked back; her face heated.

"Dratted man. Do you never announce yourself afore you burst into a room?" Elise's face wrinkled as she glared up at him.

"In the kitchen? Ye want me to declare myself? As you wish, milady." Stepping back until he was in the doorway, he drew himself up to all of his formidable height.

"'Tis I, Sir Connor of Blackthorn. I am about to enter this room and wish all within to know of my august presence." He grinned at their laughing faces. "Be that better?"

"Ye are a great pain in the arse, brother, and well ye know it." Meghan smiled, shooing him away with her hand. "Begone. Ye scare these little kits with yer noisy presence."

Meghan watched to make sure he had gone, then

showed them the differences in the sexes. Netta also learned how to place the runt on Mither's fullest teat, and to protect it from being forced off by a more aggressive kitten. When the babes had all been fed properly, the women made their way to Meghan's room. They undressed and were asleep as soon as they climbed into bed.

Cloud Dancer, perched on the arm of Bleddyn's chair, chirped. Bleddyn obligingly stroked the eagle's regal head while he explained life at Wycliffe to Mereck and Damron.

"Baron Wycliffe married the widow Barkly and started a new family. His wife used Lynette as her girls' companion and maid. When they were full grown, she could not wait to rid herself of Netta. It was she who urged the baron to accept Hexham, Mortain, and later Durham, as a husband for Netta."

"Hmm." Damron's fingertips drummed on the table. "I ken Welsh raiders met Hexham. They say the leader rode a giant of a horse, and he struck so swiftly Hexham's men bolted." He stared first at Mereck and then Bleddyn. Both rode giant destriers. "Mereck, ye were in the area reinforcing Brianna's Stonecrest Castle."

"I didna do the deed. Not that I wouldna. At the time, Lynette of Wycliffe was naught but a name Bleddyn mentioned when he spoke of Caer Cadwell."

Damron's gaze probed the mystic's face. Bleddyn smiled without comment. They knew. He had seen to freeing Netta.

"I examined the betrothal contract with care. All is in order. When do ye wish the ceremony?" Damron leaned forward to refill their goblets with ale cooled in the well. He awaited an answer.

"Netta plans to enlist your aid." Mereck braced his arms on his knees. "She will entreat you to compel her father to overset the betrothal contract. Father Matthew will soon return from the MacLaren's. We'll wed then. I dinna feel it wise to give her many days to dwell on it."

For the first time since he had come to grips with his Baresark legacy, Mereck felt unsure. Vulnerable. He hesitated a moment. "Do you approve of me as Netta's husband?"

Bleddyn quirked his scarred brow at him. "If I did not, would I have sent you to Wycliffe, knowing what you would find there? Netta lived her life under the harsh control of a man who despises her. When he sought a husband for her, she knew she would go from one ruthless, restraining hand to another. She needs a breath of freedom."

"Aye, a breath. But not o'ermuch. As my wife, she'll have the liberty she can handle—appropriate for her own protection, but not so much she will cause herself or others harm."

"Those few days on your journey were the only carefree times she has ever had. She gloried in it." Bleddyn smiled.

Rare laughter burst from Mereck. "Gloried is the right word. You should have seen her face the day she believed she had fed me wormy stew. It was almost gleeful, until I pretended something moved in my mouth. She turned greener than the pines in the forest. Her hand twitched and started to rise and stop me, but she didna."

He rubbed the back of his neck, hesitated, then frowned at Damron. "Brother, I dinna want to give her the time you gave your own wee wife. Yet I also dinna want her frightened and unwilling.

"Never has she had something to love and call her own.

That is why I gave her the kitten. Bleddyn, if you will allow Cloud Dancer to aid me, we'll search for a young kestrel. If she trains an eyas fresh from the nest, it will teach her independence comes with discipline. Though the raptor flies free, it returns to the falconer for its main food supply."

"Aye. On the morrow, I'll send Cloud Dancer to search. Once he has found what we seek, he will lead you to it." Mischief tilted Bleddyn's lips at the corners. "Even now Netta dreams of you. Do you wish me to ensure her dreams are favorable?"

"Nay. Dinna. I want her to come to me on her own, not by another's will."

His answer pleased Bleddyn. The mystic would not have offered, had he believed Mereck would stoop to such tactics.

Mereck crossed his arms beneath his head and stared at the ceiling over his bed. He thought of his bride. When he had made known the betrothal contract, he noted the fear in her eyes. He didna wish her to come to him looking such.

Her face, as she watched Mither and her brood, had jolted his senses. As if begging for a kiss, her lips softened and pursed. Her eyes were dreamy. He wanted that expression for himself. His tarse awoke and stirred like a sleeping beast. As he imagined kissing those lips until she clutched his shoulders and cried out his name, his tarse bucked.

"Christ's blood, Mereck." Connor's laugh sounded sleepy. "Cease thrashing about on your pallet and go to sleep. Tell Netta on the morrow that, if she would be a virgin the night she weds, she had best see the vows are soon spoken. Do ye take my drift?"

"I would not force her, and well you know it."

"Aye. But does she?"

Flap! Slap! Netta's flying arms struck her bed partners.

"Ow, Netta." Elise winced and grabbed the arm that had cracked her across her chest.

"By the saints, lass. Do ye always awaken yer bed mates with bruises?" Meghan removed the elbow pressed against her throat and sat upright. "When ye wed Mereck, ye must needs be more careful of where yer fists fly. After enjoyin' a night of ridin', he would not take kindly to yer pummelin' his manly parts.

"I'm sorry, Meghan. I forgot to warn you. When Netta sleeps, she flops around like a fish on dry ground. If you are not careful, you will find yourself on the floor come sunrise."

"Hmm. No wonder Mereck claims she accosted him."

Netta did not need the sun's rise to know she grinned. It was there in her voice.

"We should put her on the edge, not the middle of the bed. Then she can bruise only one of us," Meghan decided.

"Forgive me. Now I have woken you. I'll dress and see to the little ones." Netta scrambled to the foot of the bed. Her feet hit the cold floor, and she hastened to grab her clothes and leap back onto the bed. Meghan and Elise bounced around as she dressed. Once she pulled on her stockings and shoes, she leapt down again.

Drawing the plaid Mereck had given her around her shoulders, she pinned it with the brooch. She sniffed and savored her breath, for it held his heady scent. The material's warmth amazed her. It was far more comfortable than a cloak for wearing indoors.

She found Mither feeding her brood. The stronger babes pushed the littlest away. Netta sat on the floor and placed her kit at the teat closest to Mither's front legs. The little one was kept warmer there, for the mother cat snuggled it close while it drank its fill.

The smell of baking bread started Netta's stomach rumbling like approaching thunder. A rotund helper turned, looking around to search out the sound. When Netta's stomach again protested, the woman laughed and placed a cold cup of milk near her hand.

"Here ye be, lass. If'n yer guts bark any louder, Mither will attack ye, thinkin' ye be a dangerous beastie." She slathered a hot scone with honey and handed it to Netta.

Netta blushed. "The sound is most unseemly. I can never stop the dreadful noise. You would think I had not eaten in days."

Meghan and Elise joined her, and both regaled the servants on how Netta had near knocked them out of bed. Elise saw her kitten fed, and when Netta returned her kit to Mither's care, they went into the great hall to break their fast. Mereck was nowhere in sight. She prayed he had forgotten the impending meeting. She should have saved her prayers. She was finishing her porridge when he and Connor sauntered into the room, exuding satisfaction from every pore. Their tunics were damp. So were their faces and hair.

"Broadswords? Battle axes? Which, brither?" Meghan pushed a milk pitcher close to Mereck's steaming bowl of porridge.

"Mereck was spoiling for exercise. Damron obliged with the battle-ax, I with the broadsword." Connor grimaced. "I'm not such a fool to be near Mereck when he grips an ax."

"Do you not practice with wooden weapons, sirs?" Elise eyed them, clearly looking for wounds.

"Wood?" Connor nudged Meghan so he could sit beside Elise. "Nay, lady. Not since we were nine summers old. If 'twas wood, we would soon grow careless. A nick now and again is a good reminder to keep eyes and mind on the weapons."

Never having witnessed warriors at their practice, Netta was about to ask Meghan if they might watch them. Before she could, the laird's squire arrived to tell Mereck that Damron was becoming impatient.

"Come, wife. Damron's temper doesna improve with waiting." Mereck gently grasped her elbow to help her rise.

Netta's chin lifted. She spoke slowly and distinctly. "Do not call me wife."

"You became my wife from the time your father and I signed the contract, and wife you will remain." His jaws snapped together.

"Aye, Netta. You wear his badge. All who see it know you belong to him." Connor ignored Mereck's cold glare that clearly bid him to shut his mouth.

"What do you mean?" Twisting her head, she studied the brooch on her shoulder, but still didn't understand. Except for the single bar dividing it, it was the same as Connor's.

"'Tis the bar that proclaims you Mereck's. When we were but halfin's, young boys," Connor explained, seeing her questioning look, "still training with wooden weapons, he insisted his shield be divided. He declared himself part Scot, part Welsh. When we saw you wearing it, we knew he claimed you for his own."

"Haud yer wheesht if ye dinna want yer pretty face out

o' shape," Mereck ordered, giving Connor a baleful look. It did not intimidate his cousin.

Mereck seized Netta's wrist and tugged her from the room. She dashed two steps to each of his one, with an occasional skip to catch up.

"Rats, sir. Must you run?" Breathless, she hauled back on her hand.

"If you dinna wish me to throttle the gowk, the fool, you willna mind a little hastening."

Mereck grimaced. Connor's teasing could muddle things more with Netta. She wouldna take kindly to knowing he had set his mark on her, declaring her his possession. He sighed. A fortnight should be ample time for her to adjust to becoming his bride.

During that time, he would rein in her quest for independence, for therein would lie disaster. The Highlands was a harsh place, filled with men who would think nothing of plucking away a woman who strayed but a few steps from protection.

At the door of Damron's solar, he spied the stubborn tilt of Netta's jaw. She aimed to defy him. He would have to be merciless, else she would attempt to get the upper hand.

Netta greeted the laird, Brianna and Bleddyn. She pulled from Mereck and marched over to Bleddyn.

"Lord Bleddyn, please tell Mereck my father's contract does not bind me to him. Father neither asked my consent, nor did I sign that I promised to marry this man."

"The document states you were unavailable at the time. Your stepmother signed in your stead. The family priest and the castle steward witnessed it. Since you are reluctant to accept Mereck of Blackthorn, I would hear your objections. Did he force you to come with him?"

He leaned back, and his gaze pierced hers. It was compelling. Magnetic. He fixed her mind solely on him.

"Nay, he did not."

"During your travels, did he mistreat or threaten you in any way?"

He had not. Other than having her ride the swaybacked Lightning, he had treated her well. Even his insistence she tend to her duties as a maid had been done politely.

"Nay." Her voice dropped lower.

"Ah, then. While under his protection, he took advantage of you?"

"Nay!" Her voice rose. He had forced her to sleep on a pallet close to his side, but he had not taken advantage of her person. Remembering the mornings she had awakened to find her arm or her head snuggled against his warm and wonderfully scented skin, she blinked. Why, one dark night she had thrown her leg across him. Fortunately, he knew nothing about it, for he had continued to snore.

She blinked. Her face heated. Why, she had taken advantage of him!

Of his warmth, of course.

"So. Mereck has neither forced, mistreated nor taken advantage of you. Then 'tis his appearance that revolts you?"

Blessed saints! Surprise swept her. How could any woman object to his appearance? He was by far the most comely man she had ever seen. His forehead was strong, with well-defined expressive eyebrows arched above eyes that fascinated her with the way they changed from the faintest green to dark emerald. His cheekbones were high and prominent, beside a nose set just right above his lips. His beautiful lips, she amended, sighing.

And his form? His massive shoulders and chest rippled with muscles, his stomach a hard slab. She recalled his hardness. She had likened his body to a tree trunk. His hips were lean, and his legs long and muscled. He had just the right amount of enticing hair over all to make her want to trail her fingers through it.

The only reason a woman could object to his body was his size. Though it no longer alarmed her. She had become used to it.

She could not protest that she wanted to do the choosing. Although she had oft used that reason, she knew a woman had not the right. Saints! She remembered a most valid objection.

"Baresark. He is Baresark," she near shouted. "I would feel unsafe to dispute the smallest point with a man deserving of such a name."

"In your travels, did you say or do anything to stoke his anger? Did he unleash his temper on you?"

Netta scuffed the toe of her shoe on the fur rug. She had called him "sirrah" the first day on leaving Ridley. He had not struck out but calmly rested his back against a tree. Why, Roger of Mortain would have backhanded her face for the disrespect. She plucked at the girdle around her waist. She thought of her mean prank with Mereck's food. Any other man would have upended the stew on her head.

Bleddyn smiled and nodded.

Her chin bobbed against her chest, and she studied the tips of her shoes that peeked beneath the hem of her yellow tunic. If Bleddyn approved of Mereck, she knew of no truthful reason to refuse him.

She studied Bleddyn, noting the contrast between his physical and inner being. He was large and powerful like Mereck and Damron. Black and shaggy hair framed his disfigured face. He had nearly lost his eye from the sword that caused the horrific scar that stretched from his forehead down across his right eye, ending at his lip. Even so, his face was beautiful. Men kept their distance from this strange man who caused a mixture of fear and awe. Fear of his savage being. Awe of his mystic powers.

He wanted Mereck for her husband. Perchance he had known her father would give her to Mereck. The same as Meghan had hinted Bleddyn had known about Damron before they had ever met.

"Nay, Lord Bleddyn." She sighed and looked at his compelling dark eyes. "Mereck has neither done nor said naught to me I did not deserve. I would learn more of him, for I know not who his mother was, only that she was Welsh." She listened closely.

"You should know more about the man you are to marry. Before I placed your mother's family in Caer Cadwell, Mereck's mother, Aeneid, and her husband, Rhys, resided there. She was the great-granddaughter of Gruffyd ap Tewdwr, and the only daughter of Aenias and Kyrie.

"Men from across their northern border raided where Aeneid, Rhys and her parents were traveling. They killed her husband and family and took her into the Gunn family territory. Donald Morgan and his men came that evening to take back cattle the Gunns had raided from them. After the skirmish, he found Aeneid bound to a tree and brought her back to Blackthorn. Mereck is the son of Aeneid and Donald Morgan. Both are honorable families.

Remembering all the tales her father and stepmother had woven about Mereck's ancestors, new waves of panic swept over her. Though he had been gentle with her, might he be as they predicted if she should anger him?

She clapped her hands over her mouth to keep from crying out. Her shoulders began to quake.

"Your father should not have repeated the foolish legends about the ap Tewdwr wives," Bleddyn said softly. "The first wife, Elgin, became despondent after birthing her child. Losing touch with reality sometimes happens in such cases. Both Fallon and Lienid died because they refused the aid of an old midwife, claiming she was too ugly and scared them. They preferred a young woman who knew nothing of cleanliness during childbirth.

"Mereck's mother, Aeneid, though having far better care, had a different tragedy. She deeply loved Donald of Blackthorn, but she had become a very close friend to Lady Phillipa. I believe Aeneid grieved over their situation, and she succumbed from a broken heart."

"But what of the ap Tewdwr gift?" Of a sudden, she gasped, wary now. "I forgot. You also are an ap Tewdwr."

"Do you feel any harm has come to you from my knowing your thoughts?" His melodious voice soothed her.

She mulled over his question. Her mind flew from one remembrance to another, when Bleddyn had been at Wycliffe. She could not note any elements missing. Surely if he had stolen them, she would note the gap? She sighed and shook her head. Feeling overwhelmed, she sank down into the chair Mereck brought over to her. She had forgotten he and the laird were in the room.

"Well now that we have the problem settled, what say ye to speakin' the vows in a sennight?" Damron walked over and leaned his hip against the table, his arms folded. "Bleddyn tells me Cloud Dancer has spotted Father Matthew leavin' the MacLaren's. He will be here in plenty of time."

Brianna laughed. "Blessed saints, love. Give the lass a

while to learn all our names. A sennight? It will take her longer than that to find her way around this drafty place. And the ladies must have time to sew proper clothing for her."

"What is the matter with what she has on? She looks finely attired to me." Damron's gaze scanned Netta. He nodded his approval. "She wears the Morgan tartan. And Mereck's badge."

"A lady cannot be married with naught but the clothes on her back. Now, you must show Netta the contract her father and Mereck signed."

"Why, my heart? 'Tis a wedding contract like all others. It states Netta no longer belongs to Baron Wycliffe. He has turned over his authority to Mereck of Blackthorn."

Brianna rolled her eyes at him. "For the same reason I wanted to read our own, you great ox. Why must men treat women like so much money and property?"

Brianna's eyes flashed fire at Damron. Mereck hooked his thumbs in his massive belt and spread his legs for balance and comfort, knowing they were in for one of his brother and his lady wife's rousing arguments.

"Aye? Do ye not come with dowries and lands? If ye had none, we would ha'e no cause to marry ye." Laughter lurked in Damron's eyes.

Connor was not the only Morgan who liked to tease.

"No cause to marry us?" Brianna spluttered, slapped her hands on his chest and tried to shove him. He didn't budge. "If men did not marry, who would care for them and oversee their castles."

"Why, our stewards and a vast array of servants. Not to mention squires who see to our personal belongin's."

"Heirs. What of sons to carry on your name?" Of a sudden, her face crumbled. It must have struck her that she had provided no heir for Damron.

"Oh, my love, I was but 'pullin' yer leg' as ye are so wont to accuse me. I would marry ye again and again, fer I could not live without yer sweet self. And well ye know it." Damron ignored everyone but his wife. He scooped her up in his arms and sat on a chair with her. He kissed her soundly and rubbed her back. She gave an exasperated snort. Finally, she smiled back at him.

"Nathaniel, what do you think of the contract?" Brianna's gaze switched to Bleddyn.

"Everything is as it should be. Netta's mother, Kyrie, and I drew it up after Kyrie's marriage to Baron Wycliffe. I kept it at Caer Cadwell until Netta reached an age to wed."

"Now that everyone else knows what is in the papers, do you not think I should have the same knowledge?" Netta began to think she was invisible the way conversation flowed around her.

"You can read?" Damron asked skeptically.

"Nay, I cannot. I hoped Lord Bleddyn would read it to me."

Mereck's heavy hand fell on her shoulder. She felt displeasure radiating from it. She looked up at him and tried to pull away.

"Release me. You do not have to have a snizzy-fit about my learning the terms of the contracts."

"Snizzy-fit? What is this snizzy thing?" Damron asked. "Wife, is it one o' yer strange words ye have taught the girl?" Damron's frown became gigantic. "Dinna tell me 'tis like that 'patoot' word ye used last Beltane." He looked appalled.

"Don't jump to conclusions, Damron. I haven't been alone with Netta. I'm sure she means Mereck doesn't need to get his bowels in an uproar about a little request," Brianna scolded him and winked at Netta.

"Now ye have Mereck's bowels in a roar? Ye ne'er explained that one to me either, and now ye are warnin' Mereck?" Damron nearly dumped his wife onto the floor.

Mereck laughed and watched his half brother's disgruntled expressions. Ever since Damron had brought his Sassenach wife to Scotland, she puzzled everyone with her odd vocabulary. Only Damron, Connor, Meghan and himself knew that Bleddyn had called Brianna's reincarnated soul back from far in the future to relive this life. Damron was in constant fear the Brianna he loved would someday be taken from him.

Mereck led Netta to stand beside Bleddyn. He unrolled the parchments on the table and put weights on the corners to keep it flat. Though he could also read, he deferred to Bleddyn. It did not take the Welshman long to decipher it for her, for the wording was short and to the point. It stated that Caer Cadwell passed from Lady Kyrie to the eldest of any daughters she birthed. Along with it was a sizeable amount of properties surrounding Cadwell, and a more than adequate fortune to maintain them. The future husband had authority over all said lands.

It closed with two stipulations. The first was that Bleddyn ap Tewdwr, Lord of Gwynedd, must approve the selection of a husband for Kyrie's daughter. The second stated that until Bleddyn knew they were happily married for the length of one full year, the couple were not allowed to live at Caer Cadwell.

"I don't understand. If you had control over selecting my husband, why did you not stop Father's betrothing me to James of Hexham and then lastly to Baron Durham?"

Netta looked up in time to see knowing looks pass among the three men. Recalling the tale about the Welsh raiders, she realized who had protected her from Hexham. But what of Durham?

"Baron Durham could not have withstood the rigors of

even the humblest wedding," Bleddyn said. "He would not live to his wedding night. As you found, you were never in danger from him."

"Aye, but after Father decided I would marry the first man who came to the castle, how could you leave the selection of a husband to him?"

"Hmm," he murmured. "After your father's decree, was Mereck not the first man to appear at Wycliffe?"

A smile of sheer beauty lit his face.

Chapter 12

One lone tear spilled from Netta's eye. She turned to stare out the window opening and brushed the moisture away with the back of her hand. Mereck hardened his heart at the sight of her distress. His lips tightened. Even so, he lengthened Damron's suggested sennight for the wedding.

"A fortnight will be best."

Knowing she didna trust him pierced his pride. In time, she would learn he was not the savage she believed him and become reconciled to being his bride.

Connor charged into the solar, his forehead creased with worry. "I am sorry to interrupt, Mereck, but a messenger arrived from our western borders."

"And?" Damron spread his legs and clasped his hands behind his back. One brow hiked in question.

With an almost imperceptible tilt of his head, Connor glanced at the women. Damron motioned with his hand for the men to follow him to the farthest corner of the room.

Connor sighed and raked his fingers through his hair. "The MacDhaidh of Rimsdale raided o'er our border this past sennight. He lifts cattle but hasna harmed the villagers."

"There is more?" Damron prodded.

"Aye. At each croft, he left the same message." An explosion of air passed Connor's lips, before he read it aloud. "'Ye destroyed that which I loved most. Look to yer own.'" He handed Damron the scrap of parchment.

"The MacDhaidh still believes you responsible for his wife's death." Mereck grimaced and rubbed his chin.

"Aye. Ye ken Rolf's mistake." Connor nodded.

Damron tensed, his temper a barely banked fire.

Mereck well understood why. Damron blamed himself. While he and Connor were bringing Brianna to Blackthorn, it was Damron's leman who stole a tunic and helm from Connor's war chest to give to a Morgan rival. After painting the Morgan crest on their shields, the man and his band went on that fatal raid.

Connor clasped Damron's shoulder, giving him a little shake. "'Tis not your fault." He nodded his head toward the women. "Meghan must not learn of this. Her feelin's for Rolf MacDhaidh is the reason she willna wed another."

Mereck nodded. "I will see the gate keepers know no lass is to leave the castle grounds. Especially Meghan."

"Add extra patrols at eventide, Mereck. And nay, Connor. You willna ride with them." Connor started to protest, but Damron's gimlet stare and stern voice stopped him. "Dinna argue."

Connor, lips pressed tight, nodded and left the room.

Mereck went to Netta and placed a finger beneath her chin to tilt her face up to his. He lowered his lips. He hesitated. Would she reject his kiss?

She did. She turned her face aside. He drew back, stroked her soft cheek with the backs of his fingers and followed Connor.

* * *

Netta stared at her pewter mug. Her trembling hands near sloshed hot tea on her lap.

Brianna's lilting voice disrupted her gloomy thoughts. "Men have no notion how women feel, do they Netta? I planned to wed another, but King William had his way. For that matter, Damron didn't have a choice either."

"When my father paraded me afore every unwed man in Northumberland, I truly was not being over proud," Netta whispered. "Half my suitors had children near as old as I. The other half may have been the proper age but were loathsome in some way. Is it foolish to want an intelligent man? One who can read, write and do sums—who can converse with reason?"

"Nay, 'tis not, Netta," Meghan's lilting brogue answered as she came into the solar with Elise. "Ye now have a man who trips the heart with his physical beauty. Tho his face isnae as pretty as Damron's, a lass wouldna soon forget it."

"You don't find his face comely?" How strange. She found him more pleasing to the eye than his brother. Their bodies were near of a size and power. Though Damron's hair was black and Mereck's shades of gold and brown, one could not mistake they were siblings.

"I think him most handsome," Brianna agreed. "The first time I saw Mereck, I knew right away he was Damron's brother."

"Did ye ken Mereck tutored with Damron and Connor, Netta?" Meghan's lips fought a smile. "He has a keen gift for languages. He also writes a fine hand and does sums in his head. When we were in Normandy, Granda saw to it Mereck kept busy honing his mind and body. He is most intelligent."

Was that amusement in Meghan's voice? Netta studied her, but spied only an earnest expression on her face.

"At Ridley, we looked forward to Mereck's visits." Elise took two hot scones from a serving tray. "He sang duets with Galan. Women forever rivaled for his eye. They would do the most peculiar things." She stopped to lick honey from her fingers. "Mother told Father that Lady Edith stalked Mereck like hunting dogs do a hare. She said Edith backed him into an alcove, and rubbed herself all over him. But he was too polite to complain."

"Why would she do that?" Netta's brows rose. "When I bumped against him, I found him hard and solid as a tree. I should think it would be most uncomfortable."

Brianna coughed, and Netta glanced up at her.

Elise handed Netta a honeyed scone. "Mother rescued him. Poor Edith told her she couldn't help it. She said it was because she had a terrible itch only Mereck could soothe."

"Why did she not scratch it herself?" Netta bit into the delicious quick bread, licked honey from her lips and frowned. "Perchance she could not reach?"

Meghan laughed and sprang from her seat.

"Come. We must leave. Mari has come to see Brianna rests. I will show ye the grounds. Mayhap we can find somethin' to keep yer mind busy."

Meghan led them out of the great doors. Netta was thankful for the distraction from worry. Before she went down the wooden steps, she scanned the inner bailey and watched people going about their business. It was a rare dry day with few clouds in the sky. A haze of dust drifted above a spacious area at the far end of the outer walls. Curious, she asked Meghan about it and learned it was the men's special practice area. It piqued her interest.

They visited the huts built along the inside wall of the bailey where blacksmiths worked on shoeing or making weapons, a bowyer made bows and a fletcher made arrows. In one hut, a cooper made barrels which, if not for storing ale, Meghan explained, they would use them for cleaning chain mail. The rusty links would gleam like new after squires rolled them in a barrel filled with sand. Armorers worked in close touch with the smiths, the archers and the bowmen. The loud clanging of the smith forging a new sword made Netta clasp her hands over her ears.

Sitting on a stool outside his doorway, the cobbler sewed on supple leather. Why did many warriors leave their feet bare when they could avail themselves of his fine leather brogans?

Of most interest, though, was a large section behind the castle where warriors and squires honed their skills. Bowmen practiced with targets so far distant she could barely see them. Meghan explained that Damron favored using the Welsh longbows, for they carried an arrow a much longer distance.

"They are brainsick!" Elise's shout made Netta jump. "Look. At that fenced area. The man tried to spear the dummy, but a sack thumped his back and knocked him senseless."

"It be a quintain." Meghan laughed and walked over to prop her arms on the fence. "If a man is not fast and agile enough when he strikes the target, the bag of sand will hurl around and toss him from his horse. Trying to outsmart it is fun."

"You have tried this?" Netta blinked. How could a woman perform such a strenuous feat?

"Only when Connor and Damron are not around."

The next area was filled with young men throwing knives at a straw target shaped like a man. The old warrior instructing them spied Meghan, and he called her over and asked that she display her skills. Meghan obliged. She landed one blade after the other in the red circle painted on the dummy's chest. She moved so fast the knives whistled through the air after leaving her hand.

"Could you teach me to do that?" Netta envied Meghan's freedom to learn to protect herself. When Meghan grinned and motioned for them to follow her, Netta's spirits lifted.

"Come, ye will need proper clothin' fer the learnin'. I ken where to find it."

They hurried back into the keep and up to the second floor. Netta hoped Mereck would not appear, for surely he would not allow her the activity. Meghan glanced in both directions before leading them into Connor and Mereck's room.

"What are you thinking? You don't intend to steal Connor's clothes, do you?" Elise whispered. "Merciful saints. If he finds his breeches missing, he will beat us all. Surely he will."

"He will ne'er miss what I take," Meghan assured her. "Stay afore the stairwell. Call out if anyone approaches." At the bottom of her brother's oldest chest, she found the first real knife he had used after he mastered a wooden blade. She also found clothing to fit Netta and Elise and rolled them into tight balls to stick under their tunics.

She left the room and coaxed Guardian, who padded out of the old laird's room, to follow them to the castle roof. Netta chose a spot as far as possible from the edge. Even looking off into the empty distance made her stomach queasy.

Guardian sprawled within the circle of their outstretched legs. Each time a guard passed close, they petted and crooned to him. Still afraid of the big beastie, Elise tucked her legs beneath her. A dark section of hair circled Guardian's neck, and as they clipped bits of this hair, they hid it in their pockets.

"Why are we doing this?" Elise's brows raised.

"To disguise ourselves as squires." Netta picked up a tuft of hair, held it beneath her nose and grinned. "I will learn to throw knives like a squire in training."

"Oh, Netta. Do you think to murder Mereck?" With her artless eyes mirroring her terror, Elise put a hand to her chest. "Damron and Connor will be duty-bound to kill you and feed your body to the wolves." She rocked back and forth, her face scrunched up like a newborn babe. "Oh, what can y-you be thinking w-with all the b-blood that will surely f-flow?"

"You goose. We don't plan to harm anyone. 'Tis for protection if we are caught alone with no other recourse."

They returned to their room and near threw on the clothes pilfered from Connor's chest. To aid their disguise, they smeared sticky pine resin on their eyebrows, then added Guardian's hair clippings to bush them out.

"Fer now, ye must wear the wee shaft on yer belt like a squire. After, ye must secure it on yer thigh where no one will see it." Meghan showed Netta how to strap on Connor's blade.

As they left, they pulled their cloaks' hoods low over their foreheads. Satisfied no one would recognize them, Meghan affected an arrogant pose. "Walk like ye are king of the world. Pretend ye be a man, burstin' with pride and confident ye have somethin' no other man can rival." Her arrogant stride carried her from the room.

Netta mimicked her example, but the Scotswoman's legs were longer than her own. Netta soon fell behind. "Hsst, Meghan. Slow your pace. If someone spies me springing across the bailey, they will query us."

Meghan, a case of knives used for practice tucked

under her arm, led them to a quiet corner. A post stood there, a wooden replica of a man nailed to it. She showed Netta how to hold the knife and flick her wrist as she threw it.

Netta squinted at the target and attempted to imitate her.

"Well, rats. It went way wild of the mark," Netta mumbled.

After a lengthy time, Meghan sighed and stopped her.

"I am sorry, love, but I ken ye will cause more damage to the trees, sheep, dogs and anythin' else in the area rather than yon target." She patted Netta's shoulder. "Ye had best forget throwin' the wee blade to protect ye, Netta, unless ye persuade the man to stand close enough fer ye to skewer him. Come. We must return afore Sir David orders everyone to the barracks and he learns who we are."

She motioned for them to precede her. After a few steps, she sauntered up to Elise. "God's bluid, lass. Stop swishin' yer hips and huggin' yerself, or someone may pull ye behind the next bush."

"Whatever for?" Elise's eyes stretched wide.

"I'll explain later. By all that's holy, lower yer voice."

Guardian followed, nosing Elise's heels. She hopped after each nip, but as they went up the steps, he gave up the sport. Once they entered their room, Netta hid their garments at the bottom of her clothing chest.

Meghan settled back on the bed, her hands behind her head. A smile lit her face. "I know the perfect weapon. Swords."

"Swords?" Elise's word echoed in the room. "Oh, Lord in heaven. Can Netta not elbow someone's ribs, or ram her head into their stomach? Swords? Swords spill even more blood." She moaned and rocked back and forth on the bed.

"Nay. Not a real sword. Do ye think me dafty to put a proper blade in her hand? Wooden swords. I'll give ye the one I used when I was yer size, Netta. I had several till they deemed me skilled enough for a real blade."

Shouts beneath their window drew them to it to seek the cause. An irate Scotsman hauled a screaming woman by the arm, cursing and threatening to beat her within an inch of her life. Another man stood nearby, shamefaced. He adjusted his tartan over his still rampant sex.

"Well, now. She is in for it this time," Meghan muttered.

"What happened? What is he bellowing about?" Netta scowled at the man's back.

"'Tis the cobbler's daughter and her promised husband, the ale maker. She's been samplin' other shafts than his. He will beat her soundly afore he swives her till he knows she willna be craven' another man soon."

"Beat her?" Elise whispered, her naive eyes as round as cook's buttered scones. "I won't marry a woman-beating Highlander. I'll make them think I'm not good enough for them."

Meghan shrugged. "The woman should have known he wouldna share after he declared for her. Do Sassenach men not care if their women stray?"

"I'm sure they do, but I suppose they never let others see their rage." Netta felt a stab of understanding. "Oh. One dreadful night, I awoke to hear Elizabeth screeching. I tried to go to her, but found my door latched tight. Mary, my maid, came to tell me that Father beat Elizabeth, because she was 'sampling' a bit. I knew not what she meant. It was at the time your father"—she nodded at Elise—"sent a message to tell us Lord Damron had arrived at Ridley with his men. Mary said we dared not go, for new 'male meat' would be too much temptation for Elizabeth." Her face heated. "No wonder Father hastened to marry me off. He must needs find a mate for Elizabeth."

"Did your father ever beat you?" Meghan asked, curious.

"He did," Netta confessed. "The worst was after I spurned Percy, Baron Beaufort's son."

"Why did you refuse him, Netta?" Elise asked. "He smells of flowers, and he dresses with the utmost care. Father said Percy could not be prettier if he were a king's woman."

"That was one of the reasons. I tried to tell Father I did not want a husband whose male friends glared at me if I brushed his arm. Percy did not favor my touch, either. He drew back as if I had pinched him. Father said Percy had a problem, and after I provided him an heir, he would go his own way. The next time Percy came to call, I hid until he left. Father was furious." She hunched her shoulders, still feeling the blows of his walking stick. "He beat me for thwarting his plans."

"Ye didna know what Percy's 'problem' was, Netta?" Laughing, Meghan fell back on the bed.

"Father never said. Percy did not appear feverish or sickly. His hands were always cold and limp. He did have a slight lisp. Do you think it likely he has a problem with his throat?"

Meghan broke into another round of laughter. Before Netta could ask what amused her, servants arrived with their baths. In their hurry to prepare for the evening, the matter slipped her mind.

Mereck awaited at the entrance to the great hall. Netta could not help comparing him with Percy. He had neither a delicate face like her former suitor, nor a slight body. Mereck was twice Percy's size. His beautiful hand gripped hers, and its warmth spread up her arm. Men also looked at him, but with respect and gruff greetings. They threw no glares her way for allowing him to put her hand in his.

But Percy had one great advantage. He could not steal her mind, or drain her thoughts. Mayhap she had been wrong to shun him?

As everyone settled at their respected places, she started to apologize for being tardy. Mereck's long slender fingers touched her lips, silencing her.

She inhaled his scent. Her stomach fluttered.

"'Tis well worth the waiting to have you at my side, Netta." He filled their trencher with choice bits of mutton, pork and salmon. He added peas and cabbage beside them. "How spent you the day?"

The delightful aroma of the food distracted her, making it hard for her to think of something to tell him.

"We were busy talking."

"Talking? Did Meghan not show you around the grounds?" He offered her a bit of pork and quirked a brow at her.

Could he know what they did today? Netta worried, uneasy. Was he listening to her thoughts? If so, how could one protect oneself from an ap Tewdwr man? Perchance, if she hummed, he could not hear them? She started to hum.

Mereck enjoyed the expressions flitting through Netta's lovely eyes. Hesitation was there, making him curious. He didna oft release his mind to hear thoughts. At an early age, his grandfather had taught him to respect other people's privacy. He used his "gift" only when needful. Or when someone intrigued him, as did Netta. He found that, far from being painful, her thoughts were as a light summer's breeze soothing his mind.

He had spent hours in the far practice area honing the men's fighting skills, but he knew Netta had been up to something. He studied her face. The longer he did, the more she revealed.

"We took Guardian to the roof and sat in the sun for a time," she ventured. She hummed a little stronger. They had cut his hair for their brows, but she could not tell him of it.

His eyes narrowed. So, they used hair clipped from the wolf to disguise themselves? He would have to ensure they did not come to harm. "Did the wolf enjoy the attention?"

"Oh aye. He likes to have his neck scratched." The tune she hummed became disjointed.

"Did you stay on the roof all the while, or were you also in the bailey?"

"We did go down into the bailey. Meghan took us to each hut and explained their purpose."

Mereck plied her with food between questions. She started to eat in earnest. He did not doubt her appetite, for she seemed to enjoy her meals. It was also apparent she did not want to reveal more of her day. He coaxed her again.

"Where else did you go in the bailey?"

"Uh, we watched young men practice with knives." Meghan had made it look so easy to hit the target, but she herself had never even nicked it.

He placed a juicy bit of pork at her lips.

Netta couldn't resist it. She chewed and remembered the surprise on the young man's face when the sand-filled bag knocked him off his horse.

"Hmm." Mereck rubbed his hand over his mouth. "If ever you are near the quintain, stay behind the fence. A horse sometimes becomes wild when the sandbag unseats its rider. It may bolt from the area."

Netta's eyes widened. Her gaze darted down to stare at the food on the trencher. Had he been stealing her thoughts? She recalled her whole day from start to finish. Nothing seemed to be missing in her memory, for she could account for each stage of the sun. Possibly his was a gentle stealing? Did he but borrow her thoughts and then return them?

Servants brought cheeses, cakes, apples and pears to the table. Meghan suggested the women would enjoy a round of songs by the men, for it had been a long time since they had done so. Mereck was reluctant, but Brianna had but to smile at Damron, and he agreed.

Meghan picked up her pipes from beside the hearth, Bleddyn brought forth his bodhran, and Fergus, Marcus' squire, produced Elise's small harp he had protected on their journey. After they coaxed her to join them, they played through the melody once for her to learn the tune. That was all Elise needed.

Mereck, Damron and Bleddyn's voices began to fill the hall.

Without taking his gaze from Elise, Connor slid into the seat beside Netta. "Mereck rarely sings for our benefit. 'Tis an honor he does you, lady." He tilted his head to the side, a slight frown flitted across his face. "Truth be told, the last time he did such was for Brianna. When Damron snatched her from under Sir Galan's nose, her lost love composed a most poignant and beautiful love song. Mereck sang it to her. It made Damron furious." With a rueful expression, he grinned at her.

Mereck and Damron started a rousing duet in French then switched to English for the next. On the third, Mereck sang in Gaelic. Alone. His heated gaze flowed over Netta.

Mereck's sensuous baritone stroked her skin much as if his fingers stroked her. She shivered. Her nipples prickled. She pretended to check for stains as she eased the tunic away from them. Was it the material that chafed her breasts and caused such sensitivity?

She groaned. Well, rats. So much for hoping no one noted.

Mereck had. Why else would his smoldering eyes mock her?

At the end of the melody, Bleddyn's voice soared about the room in a wild Welsh ballad that had everyone stamping their feet.

On their last song, another duet with Damron, Mereck again kept his gaze on Netta as their voices filled the great hall. They sang in German, but she knew it to be a love song. Who could not know, when Damron looked at his Brianna the way a starving man eyed a trencher heaped with succulent boar?

"One dreary evening, Damron sang this melody to his bride," Connor whispered. "All in the keep knew he sang his way into her heart. A blind man would know Damron's heart was in his voice. It helped persuade Brianna to fall in love with him." Crossing his arms, he sat back with a satisfied look on his face, as if he alone had caused Damron's good fortune.

Mereck's voice filled Netta with sensuous yearnings. The ties of his white shirt slid open, baring the hard planes of his chest. She stared as his powerful muscles flexed with his movements. Her pulse quickened. Would his bare skin feel hot to her hands? Would the hair on his chest tickle her palms? The room seemed hot. She sipped her watered wine. It helped not a whit. When her woman's flesh pulsed, she squeezed her thighs together.

While singing the last notes, Damron strolled over and put his arm around his Brianna. Their love flashed bright as lightning on an overcast day. Before the notes faded, he hurried her from the room. The obvious bulge of his rampant tarse beneath his plaid spurred ribald calls of encouragement from the men.

* * *

At Castle Mortain in Northumbria, Roger's sharp nose twitched. His lips thinned to a taut line. He circled the men holding the drunk varlet upright, and his nostrils flared at the stench wafting from the filthy lout. He motioned for a servant to throw a bucket of water over the drooping head.

"Gor! No needs ter drown me," the man spluttered.

A guard grabbed the churl by the neck and shook him like a wet chicken.

"Are my orders firmly planted in your brainless skull? Repeat them." Roger's voice snapped with irritation.

"I am ter spy out and ketch the devil-eyed bitch and brung 'er to ye."

"And?"

"Wot do ye mean 'and'? Ain't thet . . ." A backhand to his mouth stopped his question.

"And you are not to . . .?" Roger tapped his foot.

"Look or tech 'er. But 'ow am I ter git the right'un if'n I don't look, melord? Gots to tech 'er too."

"Fool. Find the Wycliffe bitch and bring her to me."

He should not have to put himself out in such a way. From the first time he saw her, Lynette belonged to him. He wanted her. No, not merely want. He *had* to have her.

With Lynette as his wife, no great house in England would be closed to him. For certs, King William would request their presence at court.

He ordered two men to go with the lout and wait at the Morgan border. Once he delivered Lynette to them, they knew what to do. Gold? The brainsick fool believes he will give him even one of his hard-earned coins?

Aye. Roger would see to his payment.

He would get what he deserved.

Chapter 13

It was a beautiful early morn. Netta passed through the keep's massive doorway to lean against the rough wood of the railing, the better to study the outer bailey. She squinted her eyes not only against the sun but in puzzlement. "Why must they practice so distant from the keep, Meghan?"

"To avoid distractions." Meghan shrugged and grinned. "'Tho they still have it. Every lass able to sneak past watchful eyes will be hangin' on the fence and droolin'."

"Drooling? Why? Over sweat-soaked men brandishing broadswords and getting filthy?"

"Come. Ye'll soon see for yerself. We canna hang on the fence, for I dinna doubt Mereck would forbid it. A lean-to stands at the left end of the field. The men sometimes take shelter there. We can peer between the slats without their seein' us."

Netta didn't ask any more questions. Meghan and Elise were already far ahead of her. As they eased through the shadows along the walls, she felt a delicious sense of forbidden adventure. Before they were close enough to see what happened there, the clang of weapons and the men's blasphemous oaths created a deafening noise.

They slipped up behind the shelter. Netta's ears rang with the clamor. She clasped her hands over them, quieting the din to a soft roar. If there was such a thing. Near thirty men brandished broadswords and shields. Her curiosity got the best of her. She sought an opening between the boards, and she and Elise peered through it. Scant inches away, a man hefted a massive shield and countered his opponent's blade. His arm flashed up to swing his own weapon. Broad, sweaty shoulders blocked their view. She moved farther down to the next opening.

"Blessed Saint . . ." She didn't know what saint to call upon. In front of her loomed a man's back.

A hairy back.

A hairy all-the-way-down-to-the-legs back.

Elise also realized the men were nude. Meghan clamped a hand over Elise's lips to stifle her gasps.

A frisky wind fluttered skirts, drawing Netta's attention to the wooden rail fence opposite them. With arms crossed over the top of it, women watched with avid eyes.

Even from this distance, she noted their interest. They drooled. What fascinated them? She followed their gaze; she found out. Her fists clenched. Anger heated her face.

They lusted over a man. A man who wore his hair braided at the sides, and tied back to keep it from his eyes.

She'd blacken their eyes, she would!

He was not just any man. He was supposed to be hers.

Mereck.

He and his opponent battled, his face tight, his eyes narrowed. Well-matched in body and skills, they must have fought for a goodly time, for sweat ran down Mereck's face and dripped off his chin. His opponent's naked back faced them. She recognized Connor's thick brown hair falling past his sweating shoulders. It was the only thing she recognized. He aimed high for his cousin's arm. Mereck lifted his shield to block the blow.

Netta blinked. Mereck's gaze darted toward the shadows. A man-hawk searching its prey. Elise gurgled. She plunked down on the dirt, her eyes squinted shut.

"Come. Mereck senses us," Meghan whispered. "Hurry if we dinna want to get caught."

They grabbed Elise's arms and sprinted—like deer afeared of the cook's bowman—from the area. Netta's heart raced faster than her feet. Finally, they reached the inner bailey. She took a deep, calming breath.

A small orchard grew behind the cook's vegetable garden. With bright green leaves rustling from a light breeze, a pear tree offered shelter from the sun. Magpies, upset for they were no longer alone to fill their beaks with fruit, cried their displeasure and left. When Netta looked at Elise, she wondered if her own face flamed as red. Meghan's throaty laughter assured her it did.

"Now ye know why Morgan men have lasses pantin' after them."

"I don't think anyone would say the Morgan men have, um, what did you call those little ones—a prick?" Netta giggled.

"Not since they grew from halfin's, young boys."

"How do they keep their minds on their swords when their, er, parts, are unprotected? Do you not think it would distract them?" Netta asked.

"Aye. 'Twould seem so." Meghan grinned and shrugged. "Clothin' restricts their movements. In olden days, ancient Celts fought bare-arsed. Damron says it makes for valuable trainin', for they dare not let their minds stray. In battle, bogs and trees hinder the horses, so they do their battlin' on the ground. But with loincloths to cover their nether parts."

"Barearse! I'll ne'er think of him as Baresark again." Hearing Elise start to mutter, she turned to her. "What is it?"

"I keep seeing them. How can they be so different from each other?" Elise's face flamed. "Do you think Connor has a handsome trio, or by chance it is repulsive?" She shuddered.

"Well, now. From what I've heard of my strappin' brother, the wenches seem to think all of him is handsome. They say he ne'er tires and kens how to *take care* of a lassie. If ye get my drift." Meghan fell back on the grass and chuckled when Elise opened her eyes with a weak grin.

Mereck felt someone watched him. Lasses who could sneak away from their duties lined the rails, but he had grown used to their stares. Allowing himself a quick glance, he spied a flash of yellow in the shadows.

Ah. He knew.

This sudden knowledge lowered his guard. Connor cursed at the same time as Mereck felt a sharp sting on his arm.

"Bluidy Lucifer. What are ye doin', Mereck?" Connor shouted. "'Tis nae like ye to forget ye are facin' a sharp blade." Worry that he had near seriously injured his cousin fanned his anger.

Mereck nodded toward the shadows along the walls. Connor's eyes widened.

"Father Matthew had best not tarry. The sooner Netta is wed to ye the better."

"What of a husband for Elise? Are you eager for Damron to choose her mate? Afore he broke his fast, two hot-eyed youths met with him in his solar." Seeing Connor scowl, Mereck laughed. "He had best hurry with his selecting. Netta did not appear alone. She and Meghan drug Elise away by her arms. She seemed reluctant to stop gaping at her petitioners."

Connor shouted for their squires and clothing. They found the three women beneath a pear tree in the orchard. Meghan lay on her back laughing. None heard Mereck and Connor's approach.

The shadows deepened like clouds blocking the sun. The back of Netta's neck tingled. She peeked over her shoulder.

Her nose bumped a hairy leg. Swallowing, she allowed her gaze to raise above sturdy knees, a carelessly donned plaid and a sweaty bare chest. When she got past an unyielding jaw, she saw Mereck studied her through narrowed eyes.

Connor stood by his side.

Neither man appeared happy. Or amused. She gulped.

Elise, hands still covering her eyes, giggled afore she spoke. "I saw two of the men who thumped the staff when Lord Damron announced he sought a husband for me."

"Uh, Elise. Open your eyes," Netta begged.

"Nay. If I do, I'll see all those . . ."

She did not finish. Netta grabbed her arm and pulled her hands away. Just then, Connor bumped his legs into Elise's back.

"Holy Mother. We are done for," she yelped and scrambled to her knees. She turned and edged between Netta and Meghan.

Meghan scowled at the men. "If ye e'er want her to couple without a blindfold, brither, stop scarin' the lass."

"What have you been teaching them, Meg? If I catch you showing them something they should not see, I'll have Damron whip you properly."

"We took a walk in the sun, that is all. We could not

help that everything was there afore our eyes." Netta sought to defend Meghan. She could not meet either man's gaze but studied Connor's chin instead. Something warm fell on her arm, drawing her attention.

Blood! Her gaze flew up. Rivulets of blood ran down Mereck's right arm and dripped off his fingertips.

"Blessed Saint George! A fine patron saint you are," she scolded the heavens above the cloudy sky. "You don't take very good care of your warriors." She leaped up and turned an accusing glare on Connor. "For shame. You have hacked your cousin. Do you not know he could well bleed to death? Or suffer a killing wound from your dirty sword? Why do you stand like statues? Hurry. We must find Bleddyn." With both hands, she grabbed Mereck's left arm.

Beside the chapel stood a building which Damron had set aside for the mystic and his herbal room. She tried to tug him toward it. He did not budge.

"Cease, Netta. I need no stitches. 'Tis but a scratch. It will soon stop. Have you ne'er seen bloodied men?"

"My father's men are not foolish. They practice with armor."

Oh my. She could not meet his eyes. Why had she admitted she knew he trained without protection? She huffed. Protection? Well, rats. He had not even worn a scrap of cloth to cover him. She cast a desperate look at Meghan.

"Were ye no watchin' Connor's blade, Mereck?" Meghan sprang to her feet. "I think ye need a lesson from Damron on the hazards of gettin' distracted."

"Aye," he replied. "And you need a lesson from Damron on the hazards of being where you should not."

"Oh, they are all going to fight, I know it," Elise whispered. She crouched at the women's feet.

"No one is going to fight, Mousie." Connor bent and clasped her elbow to lift her to her feet. Elise flushed even more and refused to meet his gaze. "Do as I say, and you need have no fear of me. I want to take care of you."

Elise blanched. She darted glances at the front of Connor's plaid. She must have recalled Meghan saying he knew how to take care of a lassie.

It was one sure way not to soothe her friend.

She tried to judge Mereck's anger. He did not deign to talk as he and Connor led them into the great hall. Though his face was taut, he did not seem enraged. After the men saw them to their seats, they reached for ale to refresh themselves afore they returned to their training. Damron's squire came to Mereck with a message. He excused himself and, when he returned, Netta saw Bleddyn had cleaned and bound his wound.

Why would the dratted man not go to Bleddyn when she tried to take him there? Huh! It was naught but foolish male pride.

She stared at it and sniffed. His eyes narrowed to mere slits. She clamped her mouth shut.

Connor leaned close to whisper in her ear.

"When we came through the doorway, Damron spied Mereck and knew he would think nothing of the gash. I warrant he ordered him to report to Bleddyn. Since the Welshman has bided with us, we dinna have wounds become foul."

While they talked, Elise regally motioned Sir Marcus over to the table. On their first night at Blackthorn, Marcus had stated his interest in the tall Saxon, declaring he prized her company on their journey.

Leaning close, he bent his head to hear Elise's whisper.

"When you ride your horse, do you not squash your bannocks, Sir Marcus?" Elise asked.

"Bannocks? What bannocks, Lady Elise?" Marcus tilted his head, puzzled.

Afore she could reply, Connor shoved a wedge of cheese between her lips.

"She refers to the bannocks we carry in our sporrans when we travel. Is it not so, lady?" Connor's glare and the curt nod of his head squelched any attempt from Elise to defy him.

She plucked the cheese from her mouth and muttered, "Of course, that was what I meant." She stuck the cheese back.

She had not fooled Marcus. He excused himself and all but ran out the doorway of the hall. No sooner had he disappeared into the corridor than they heard shouts of laughter.

"Why did you not let me finish, Sir Connor?" Elise grumbled. "I must dissuade these men, so they will not seek to marry me. I cannot if you stop me from insulting them."

"Ne'er again speak such to a man, lady, or I will take steps to stop you." Connor's words hissed through his teeth.

Elise scooted as far away as possible without sitting in Meghan's lap.

The men were so tense, Netta felt like two stone pillars hemmed her in. Connor glared at Meghan. Blaming her. Thankfully it was bannocks and not ballocks that Elise said. Still, what benefit was it since Marcus knew her meaning? It did not raise his ire either. Not when his eyes had sparkled with humor. And they had all heard his hearty laughter in the corridor.

For truth, Elise's plan did have merit. Netta would try it herself if she thought it would be of benefit. Such would not deter Mereck. Likely he would explain the differences between the words.

In great detail.

"Did you not hear what I said, Netta?"

She jumped and looked at him, then shook her head.

"I told you Cloud Dancer has found a young kestrel, an eyas fresh from the nest. Its mother perished and it needs care. Bleddyn brought it to Simon, the head falconer. He is tending the wee thing today. Mayhap you would like a raptor of your own?"

"Oh aye, Mereck." Netta sparked with enthusiasm. She started to rise, hoping to run to the mews right away. His hand on her shoulder forestalled her.

"The eyas must become accustomed to his new home and to you. After the next sun rises, you will talk to him and let him smell your breath afore you touch him." He moved his head close to hers, his lips almost brushing her own.

His breath smelled sweetly of wine. Her scalp tingled.

"You will caress him and repeat his name while you tell him how lovely he is. Much as a man gentles a woman to his touch."

His warm hand caressed from her nape down over her shoulders and up again. "Ah, Netta, you are a feast to my eyes," he whispered.

A shiver streaked down her spine.

"You will sip water into your mouth and dribble it in his beak as his mother would." He took a sip of wine and leaned closer yet. Powerless to move, his pursed lips brushed hers and his thumb gently pulled down on her chin.

Warm wine trickled over her tongue.

A whimper escaped her.

"Once he takes it, you must give him the raw meat he will learn to crave."

That broke the spell.

"Can I not cook it a little?"

"A kestrel's favorite foods are the smallest creatures of the woods. They dinna hunt in Cook's kitchen." Mereck chuckled. "You canna train him to eat wild boar. Even a peregrine would not be so reckless as to attack a large creature. After you have seen him, you must name him. When you ask Rory to bring him to you, you canna call him 'birdie.'"

"I have never named a pet before."

"'Tis true? I would not have guessed it." His eyes opened wide in pretended surprise. "You must needs also name the wee kitten. If you dinna, each time you call Kit, a string of cats will follow you."

"I will bid Meghan and Elise to help me."

"Heaven help the kestrel. Meghan will have you name him eejit, or goup for fool." At Netta's puzzled look, he explained. "She calls her own sparrowhawk Simple, though rightly so."

Damron entered the room, interrupting him.

"Have ye men grown soft as lassies then? Ye have dawdled enough." Damron frowned at Mereck. "Come, brither. Ye will work with me fer the rest of this day. By the time we are done, ye will remember to keep yer eyes on the blade. I will not have ye gettin' yerself killed o'er lassies admirin' yer comely arse."

Mereck glared at him and cursed in Gaelic.

Netta thought it was Gaelic. It could have been Welsh.

Netta and Elise dressed in their squire's clothing and bushed out their eyebrows. They followed Meghan below, where Meghan staked out a corner of the practice area. She showed Netta the basic moves with a sword. Elise sat on the grass. Each time Meghan delivered a stinging slap across Netta's thighs with the wooden sword, Elise gasped.

A dozen times in a row, Meghan knocked the sword

from Netta's hand. She soon learned to hold on with all her might. Sweat tickled its way between her breasts with the strain. When they paused, she patted her eyebrows, afeared they would slip. She would look frightful if they rimmed her jaw instead of her brow.

After they stopped to refresh themselves with cold water at the well, they made their way to a more secluded corner.

"I'll show ye how to protect yerselves if a man becomes too forward. Elise, grab me around the shoulders and try to hang on." When she did so, Meghan went limp, slid under Elise's loosened grip and twirled around to land her foot softly at the juncture of Elise's thighs. "When ye do it, strike with all yer weight behind the blow. 'Tis positive I am ye will get away."

"What if I do it and his 'thing' withers into one of those wee little prickly ones?" Elise worried. "Will he not try to kill me for it?"

"If ye're afrighted about damagin' his family jewels, aim higher and knock the wind from his stomach," Meghan replied.

"Family jewels?" Netta asked.

"Aye. 'Tis what Brianna calls them. She has the right of it, for men do polish and rub them til they fairly gleam."

Netta's nape prickled a warning. She glanced behind her to see who watched them.

Mereck stood beneath a tree, legs spread wide and arms folded across his chest.

Waiting.

Chapter 14

"Hmpf! I see you neglect today's mace training." Mereck scowled, his eyes mere slits, hiding his amusement. He jerked his hand to beckon them forward. "Soft as lassies, all of you. Come. By the looks of your puny forms, you have hid overlong from hearty exercise."

The women tucked their heads down and studied the dirt path as they followed him to the stables.

"These two spindly boys are to clean stalls." Mereck pushed Elise and Meghan toward the stable master. "The runt will spread hay." Mereck near laughed aloud at Netta's outraged huff. He cleared his throat, pivoted on his heel and left them to the stable master's mercy. Now and again, he returned to the stable door to scowl at them, assuring they didna shirk their duties.

As the day wore on, he saw by the looks of their sweating faces and sagging shoulders, they had learned their lesson.

"Puny." He shook his head and sucked his teeth. "Not a solid man's muscle betwixt you. Shirk your duties again, and I will set you to train with the warriors in the farthest field. Mayhap your clothing hinders your movements?

The warriors would soon have it off you." He kept his mouth grim as he glowered at them.

Netta clutched her clothing tight to her neck as if it was already in danger. He wrinkled his nose. "Begone from my sight. Your stench near makes me sick. Cleanse your filthy hides. How could you get more muck on your clothing than what you carted away?" He swatted Netta's bottom and pointed to the barn door.

She yelped and lurched forward. Her shovel clattered to the ground. Before its noise quieted, she fled, kicking up swirls of dust in her wake.

Mereck clasped Netta's elbow and led her to sit beside him for the evening meal. Her gaze darted to his face to judge his mood. His features looked sculpted in stone, for no expression showed there. What if he asked how she passed the day? She prayed he would not. If he learned she was one of the three squires he scolded earlier and forced to spread hay and shovel buckets of revolting filth, would he unleash his bestial temper? Her worry eased, hearing his polite request for her meal choices.

"The salmon, sir. And possibly a little lamb and honeyed chicken?" Rats. Her voice sounded timid. 'Twas shameful.

He filled the left side of their trencher with juicy, generous portions. Her mouth watered. He nodded toward a large platter of vegetables. His brow lifted and his green eyes sparked his question.

She sat taller and squared her shoulders, then forced confidence in her voice. "Carrots and beets. If you please."

The delightful aroma of baked bread drew her gaze to a basket, a pot of warm honey sitting alongside it. Smiling, he speared a loaf and poured honey into a small bowl between them.

The main table was unusually quiet. Though Mereck was courteous, tension radiated like sparks between them. He knew. She felt it. Saints! Of a sudden her hunger fled. Never had it done that afore, not even when her father had bellowed and raved and locked her in her room. The worst part of her sire's punishment had been the meager array of food he allowed her maid to bring her. This was different.

If Mereck was to let his temper fly, would it not be best here? With his family to protect her? She could not stand the waiting.

"We did not go to the practice area to spy on men."

She sucked in her breath. Was it her lips that just blurted those foolish words?

"Then for what purpose did you go, lady?"

She sneaked a peek at him. The line of his mouth tightened. His eyes were like misty green stones.

"'Twas a lark."

"Ah? A lark? How do you deem espying naked men at their practice a lark?"

She blinked and started to hum. What gremlin led her to mention it? She began to fidget.

"We did not go there apurpose to see men unclothed. We were seeking a breath of air when we stumbled upon it."

"After you stumbled upon us, were you gratified by what you saw? You need not have been so hasty. You will soon be free to study a naked man at a much closer range."

She flushed and lowered her head. Heat radiated from her chest. No doubt if she could see it, it would be fiery red.

"Ah. You have no wish to answer, Netta," he murmured. "By chance you will find it easier to tell me why you dressed as a squire this day? Did you plan to explore the barracks when the men returned to cleanse themselves?"

"Nay. We would not do such." Oh, rats. Why had her voice decided to burst out in near a shout? Elise kicked her leg. "You knew it was us? Yet you bade us clean those filthy stalls?"

"I could hardly greet you and kiss your brow. Do you think warriors take kindly to women who pose as boys? Well now, if not to spy on them, for what purpose did you don men's clothing?"

"To learn how it feels to wear clothing which does not hamper our legs."

His left brow flashed up then settled in place. He leaned back and studied her, a lopsided smile on his face. She hesitated. He did not favor that answer. She hummed a tune while she scrambled for another reply. If she told him she wished to learn the use of weapons like Meghan, for certs he would forbid it.

"After you found men's clothing to be of more comfort than your own, did you then seek manly pursuits?"

"Manly pursuits?" Startled, she forgot to hum. Did someone spy them yester morn while Meghan showed her how to throw knives? Or this day with their wooden swords?

"Aye. Were you curious about weapons? Or by chance the quintain drew your interest?"

"Weapons?" Netta's voice squeaked.

He nodded, his face a solemn mask.

"When I saw Meghan toss a knife and it stuck in the door across the room, I thought 'twould be a skill useful to women as well as men. I wish to learn the how of it."

"Did you have success with the trying?"

"Nay. I could not strike the target until I moved close." She scowled and honestly added, "Very close." Surely the youngest of Blackthorn's squires did better than she. "This morn, Meghan deemed a sword more suitable."

"Eh? Why so?"

Netta huffed at his surprise. "I would be closer to the enemy."

"This day wasna the first that you ventured out dressed as a squire." A statement, not a question. "How fared you with a sword? I trust she didna allow a blade in your hand?"

"For certs not." How could he think his cousin so unwise? "We used wooden swords."

"You willna attempt to learn any form of weaponry with Meghan, Netta, unless I agree." Mereck's voice was cold, stern. "You will also stay far from the quintain. E'en experienced warriors have suffered injury when in the area. Do I make myself clear?" With green eyes cold as glaciers, he stared at her, awaiting her reply.

"Aye, sir. I do not ken why you dislike my wish for the skills to defend myself." She grumbled and stared back.

"Your wish for skill in wielding a weapon is not the problem. You should have asked me afore going to another. On the morrow, after I have shown you how to care for the kestrel, I will begin training you in the use of a sword. Make no mistake. You willna find me as gentle as Meghan.

"Scotland is harder for a lass in more ways than our harsh climate. Women are prime targets for ransom. If the saints smile on them and the captor returns them, it isna always in the same condition as when they stole them."

Netta swallowed and nodded her understanding. An old man shuffled over to sit in front of the fireplace when servants brought in cheese, fruits and pastries. His fingers lured soothing notes from a lute while they finished their meal.

"Do you sing, Netta, or play an instrument?" Brianna smiled over at Netta.

"I have never been able to carry a tune, and I cannot play an instrument any better than the rudest peasant." Netta lowered her gaze to the table. "Our castle bard told Father I had no ear for music, and if a tune was a snail, I could chase it for the rest of my life and ne'er catch it."

"I'm sure you have many talents other than music." Brianna reached over to pat Netta's arm.

"My wife has a vivid imagination for tellin' stories which frighten not only pages but squires too." Pride rang in Damron's voice. "'Tis likely one rainy evenin' she will tell another. She has e'en invented a war cry we now combine with our own to frighten the enemy."

"I have no doubt I will soon uncover your many hidden talents." Mereck's voice was deep and arousing in Netta's ear.

The hungry look in his eyes held her motionless. Was this how a deer felt when eyed by the wolf?

Mereck collected a wayward curl and brought it behind her ear. Warm fingers stole beneath her hair to caress her nape. Her gaze was drawn to his lips. They softened and pursed.

His teasing fingertips traced over her jaw, then lingered to cup her cheek in his warm palm. Juniper and musk tantalized her senses. Why was the room so very hot? Her tongue darted out to moisten her dry lips. He would not kiss her in front of everyone. Would he? She caught her breath.

He would. He did.

The kiss was not the brief brushing of lips as afore. This was like no other kiss she had ever had. Thomas of Durham had once forced his cold, wet mouth on hers. She shuddered. It made her sick to remember it.

Mereck tasted faintly of wine and honey. Though firm and demanding, his warm lips did not hurt her own. He nibbled and played with the corners of her mouth, sending shivers sweeping through her. She sighed. Her lips parted.

Had he awaited this?

His silken tongue slid between her teeth to explore and swirl around her own, then retreated. Had he found her distasteful? She had her answer when it returned to deepen the kiss. Mingled with the pounding of her heartbeat were soft mewling sounds. Had a kitten strayed from Mither? Mereck also heard it. He eased his lips from hers and showered soothing kisses over her cheeks and eyes. She sensed his reluctance when he drew back. Had they been elsewhere, he would not have stopped.

Connor and Meghan regarded her with amusement, and Elise eyed her with curious interest. Netta cleared her throat and pretended nothing had happened. She'd turn their attention elsewhere.

"One of the kits is crying. We must find the wee thing afore someone tramples it."

"'Twas no kitten, Netta." Connor grinned at Mereck.

"Aye, it was. Did you not hear it?"

"What ye heard were yer own sounds of need, love," Mereck murmured in her ear.

His soft breath tickled, making her shiver. "Truly, you did not hear aright. I did not make those sounds."

When he nuzzled her ear with his lips, she trembled.

When his tongue stroked the opening, she shuddered.

When she heard the soft sounds she could not suppress, she believed him.

Heaven help her. How could she have such feelings over a man who might someday throttle the life from her?

* * *

Heavy rain fell throughout the night but stilled at the first rays of dawn. Netta was taking her last spoonful of porridge when Dafydd raced through the great hall's doorway and skidded to a stop before her.

"Lady Netta. Sir Mereck bids you await him here. He will come for you after he sees the men started on their daily practice." He bobbed at the waist, grabbed a scone and dashed back out the door before Netta could take her second breath.

She waited. Impatient. Each time someone entered, she expected the man whose presence sent her pulse racing. Most times from uneasiness, but sometimes of late from other reasons. An image of him in the practice field stole into her memory.

Naked. The mat of hair on his chest glistening when the morning sun hit it. His massive body moist with effort.

Um, Bareass. It was a much more fitting name than Baresark.

Far more fitting. And interesting.

Mither stalked through the doorway, head high and tail twitching. How strange. The cat was never alone. She was either caring for the kittens or stalking Mereck, waiting for him to carry her about on his broad shoulders.

Why must she await him in the great hall? She was eager to see the kestrel. He would know she had gone ahead to the mews if he found she was not here. She hurried through the doorway. The sun's rays nearly blinded her, until a great shadow blocked the light.

She blinked, then blinked again. Mereck's stern face stared down at her. Having seen Mither, she should have known he was close-by. Wet hair dripped onto his collarbone. Fascinating rivulets of water rambled and wove through the blond hair matting the hard wall of muscles that was his chest. He had stopped to wash at the well.

"Did Dafydd not tell you to await me in the great hall?"

Saints! He was displeased. His brown brows near met over his nose. She gulped.

"He did. I thought you had forgotten."

"I ne'er forget. And I ne'er go back on my word. You must learn to obey my wishes." His voice was harsh as he grasped her elbow. "See you remember, wife."

Mayhap it would be wise to keep her mouth shut.

A young, red-haired page awaited in front of the mews' door. He held a bit of raw meat in one hand, and his arm cradled a small pewter cup of whiskey and one of water against his thin chest. Attempting to lift the overlarge plaid trailing in the dust, he stretched his narrow shoulders near as high as his ears.

Netta smiled at the boy, but eyed the meat with distaste as Mereck took it and the cups from him.

"Come, Netta, 'tis the kestrel's favorite food," he coaxed.

Bracing herself with a smile, she motioned him to lead the way. Her nostrils flared, expecting the stench of Wycliffe's mews. The room's fresh smell surprised her. Simon stood by Cloud Dancer's perch. On seeing them, the raptors called for attention.

"Each raptor has its own time of day for free flight. They return when Simon raises his wrist and whistles." Mereck stopped by each bird, quieting them with his voice. Their heads swivelled to follow his progress.

"Will they not fly away and not return?"

"Nay. They know where they are assured of a good treat—from the falconer's gauntlet." Mereck looked down at her and smiled. "Have you a name for your kestrel?"

"Aye. Tuan. When I was a youngling, my nursemaid

told me the myth of Tuan mac Carill. He lived for generations in different forms. One as an eagle. She said any creature given the name would have a long and happy life." She peeked aside at Mereck. Would he think her foolish to credit such stories?

"Sprite is my kit's name. What think you?" she added.

He nodded, his face serious. "The name is most apt." His hand on the back of her waist urged her toward Cloud Dancer's perch.

The eagle trilled a tune, which he promptly answered. "You must learn to whistle for Tuan. He will hear you and obey when he flies free."

Netta worried her lip with her teeth. Could she learn to whistle a tune when she could not sing one? Hearing a chirping sound, her gaze followed it to spy a small nest next to Cloud Dancer. Cuddled within was the most uncomely bird she had ever seen. Her heart ached for the motherless eyas. She lifted the nest to bring it close.

Mereck had no need to tell Netta how to gain Tuan's love, for she crooned to the little one. She raised the nest to place her lips close to the tiny head. "Ohh, how sweet you are, my Tuan. We will be together always."

Her lips played over Tuan's head and back, then her cheeks did the same, while she whispered to him. As she crooned, it was as if she was loving each raptor in the room. Even Cloud Dancer preened and swayed back and forth.

"Pick him up gently in both hands. I will bring the cup to your lips so you may water him." His voice was rough, almost husky.

He shifted, restless. How would Netta's lips feel if she caressed his head and back in the same way? At the thought, shivers tickled the nape of his neck. He flexed his shoulders. All the while she lifted the little life into her soft hands, sipped the water from the cup and offered her lips to dribble it into the tiny beak, he did not take his gaze from her.

"Did it taste sweet, love?" She kept her lips close to Tuan's beak, letting him learn the scent of her breath. After she again sipped and offered water to Tuan, she whispered softly about how beautiful was her little love.

Mereck watched her pursed lips, so like a lover about to kiss her mate. At the thought of them on his bare flesh, his skin burned and his thigh muscles tensed. Blood surged in his veins and pooled betwixt his legs. His ballocks grew heavy and ached. He selected a sliver of meat and offered it to Netta. When she took it between her dainty teeth, his fingers lingered on the softness of her lips.

Each time Tuan took the proffered morsel, Netta praised him for being such a smart little raptor. When done, she remembered to compliment him on his great beauty, though at the moment the nestling was far from such. Mereck held the small cup of whiskey to Netta's lips.

"Cleanse your mouth well, wife, but dinna swallow." His voice rasped with need.

She did as he told her. Netta held the small body close against her breasts, guarding it. He could not draw his gaze away.

He imagined her cuddling his face against those twin treasures. His tarse bucked and strained against the tight confines of his breeches.

Vivid dreams of Netta tormented his nights. Dreams so real he awoke feeling her hips meeting his as she had urged him deeper into her moist, hot body. Did she sleep alone, he would have already claimed her. From the time he had signed the contracts with her father, she was his as much as she would be after a priest heard their vows.

Father Matthew had best soon return, for he feared his

lack of rest would take its toll on his temper. As fearful of him as she was, he did not want to chance losing control afore her.

Mereck reached into his pocket for the gauntlet he had bidden the tanner make for Netta. This past night, he had etched designs on the soft leather and had sewn on a silver hook to secure Tuan's jesses. Silver bells chimed from the jesses, sounding like an angel's tinkling laughter. Netta chuckled, her voice as sweet as music.

"Oh, 'tis beautiful, Mereck."

She leaned forward and tugged the braid at his temple, then rose on her tiptoes to kiss his cheek.

"Thank you. Never have I had such a wondrous gift."

A strange feeling filled his chest, one ne'er felt afore. He wanted this marriage with Netta for Caer Cadwell, and the holdings she would bring to it. He was e'er conscious that by no other means could he gain such wealth. But the castle, lands and holdings were not the only advantages from this marriage.

He would have a wife that amused him at every turn. A mate he could surely train to be a passionate partner in bedsport. If she lost her fear of him, mayhap he would also have her love. He need not return it. Dared not.

Upon reentering the great hall, they discovered a visitor standing beside Damron. The man was busy teasing Connor, who seemed flushed, his body tense.

"Oh, Netta, he's another one of those giants," Elise whispered close to her ear. "Do you think he is another kin? His hair is as light as Mereck's, and he smiles like Connor."

"Cease, or I will take a sword to your flabby arse." Connor cuffed the man on the shoulder.

"Blessed saints. 'Tis a fight they start," Elise shouted.

The men turned in surprise. The stranger sauntered

over to Elise, captured her hand in his and bent to kiss it. Scowling at him, she promptly snatched it back and held it behind her.

"Eric of the MacLaren's, beautiful lass. I be kissing kin to the Morgans. If you willna suffer me to kiss your hand, perchance your cheek will do?" He gripped her shoulders, lifted her off her feet and kissed her on the cheek. Her feet kicked out at him, but he was agile in evading them.

"You are no kissing kin to Elise. Keep your fat lips off her." Connor grabbed Elise out of Eric's arms and stood her on the floor.

Damron moved between them and ordered everyone to take their seats. "Eneuch. Both of ye. Canna ye see ye scare the lass with yer rough manners?" Before Damron escorted Brianna to the table, he lifted Serena from her arms, kissed the babe's forehead and handed her to her nursemaid.

Connor and Eric jostled each other until Mereck's hand gripped the back of Eric's sturdy neck. That ended the matter. Connor escorted Elise to the table, but the sneer he gave Eric didn't last for long.

Eric took the seat opposite Elise.

"Lass, you are far too bonny to waste on an uncouth Morgan." Eric's admiring gaze roved over Elise. "Did Damron not tell you I must needs wed again for me puir son? You will find a MacLaren far more pleasurable than the scruffy lad at your side." His eyes twinkled with mischief.

"If Connor doesna kill him, Elizabeth might." Mereck chuckled, and spoke softly to Netta. "She hasna married. Whenever suitors ask for her hand, she flies into a lather, throws tankards of ale at them and tells them to be gone if they want no further bodily harm."

Netta watched, fascinated, when Eric winked and

made kissing noises with his mouth to Elizabeth Neilson, the steward's daughter.

"Why does she not want any of her suitors?"

"Perchance for the same reasons you scorned your suitors. The fellow was either too tall, too short, had bad teeth or did not bathe frequently. Likely she found they thought her to be dutiful. Who knows why a lass will forego such goodly offers?"

Did he tease her? Eric distracted her when he spoke.

"Laird, might I meet with you directly after the meal?" Eric's grin was huge when Damron nodded assent.

"Ow," he soon yelped. Connor had kicked him under the table.

Netta gulped. Would they fight now? After a hard glare from Damron, the men quieted. She relaxed.

"We were all forever rivals as growing boys. We could ne'er let another best us, whether on the practice field or with the lassies," Mereck murmured.

"Who won most often?" Netta turned to study his face.

"Well now, on the practice field 'twas even between Damron and me, and between Connor and Eric. We all went wanting with the lassies when Eric came to visit. It seems they canna resist his grin. Connor had best look to secure his dreams afore someone snatches them from under his nose," he murmured.

Eric kept everybody on their toes with his wit. A flush never left Elise's face, for he flirted with her outrageously. Connor's scowl lasted throughout the meal. When they stood to leave the table, Eric waggled his brows at him and put his arm across Damron's shoulder as they left the room.

"Come. If you would wish your first lesson with the sword, change to one of your riding outfits and join me beneath the tree in the outer bailey." Mereck stood and helped Netta to rise.

"Can I not wear . . . ?"

He cut her off. "You willna dress as a squire again, Netta. Obey me in this, or risk my anger." Mereck scowled. His stern voice warned her not to object.

She thrust her chin in the air and hurried from the room.

When she arrived for her lesson, Elise and Meghan trailed behind her. Elise carried a blanket. All they needed was food. Mereck shook his head and rolled his eyes. Lasses could turn even a serious lesson into a family gathering. He carefully examined the wooden sword Meghan had given her. It would do.

"Where is your wooden sword, sir?" Netta's forehead creased when she eyed his short sword.

"I have no need of wood swords, wife. I have long since learned to control my weapon." When Meghan snorted with laughter, he glared at her. Turning back to Netta, he handed her a shield and moved behind her. He used his foot to widen her stance. "The sword is a heavy weapon. You must balance yourself well."

Her hips pressed against his thighs did naught to ease his eager tarse. He snaked an arm around her and showed her how to position her shield to protect her body when her weapon could not. He released her and picked up his sword. Her eyes were huge as she watched his blade.

"I am pleased you are afeared. If I were to use wood, you wouldna be as careful as you now are. No matter what happens, dinna take your eyes from your opponent's weapon. Remember this." He nodded for emphasis.

He worked using slow movements until Netta learned to move the shield in place, before he showed her how to deflect his blade. Her hair escaped its ties. Her flushed face was sweetly serious, and her mouth pursed with concentration. He longed to hold her and kiss those sweet lips, to sink his tongue into her mouth. He ached to have her in his bed, naked and panting beneath him. Father Matthew could not arrive soon enough to suit him.

He eyed her breasts pushing against her tunic and pictured their soft roundness and pink nipples. He wet his lips as if he were ready to suckle there. His blood surged and his tarse rose to attention.

"Hah. Ye have control o'er yer weapon, do ye Mereck?" Meghan taunted. Her husky laughter floated on the air.

He couldna let Netta see his aroused state. Bad enough that Meghan would surely delight in telling her later. Netta's gaze darted to Meghan. His blade flashed to slit the ribbons at the neck of her tunic. The gown drooped at her shoulders and bared the tops of her lush breasts. She looked like a woman about to make love. He groaned aloud.

Netta yelped and dropped her shield to grab the tunic opening.

"I warned you to keep your eyes on your opponent's weapon. You could be dead now." Mereck's long arm shot out. Turning his blade to the side, he tapped her across her delightful bottom. Though he thought he had done so softly, Netta lost her balance and sprawled face first on the ground.

Mereck sprang forward. He dropped to his knees and turned her over and to sit upright. Gently, so as not to chafe her delicate skin, he brushed the dirt from her face. His hands near shook when he cleaned the tops of those soft orbs he coveted overlong. Netta smacked at his hands, sputtered and made huffing noises trying to rid her lips of grass and dirt.

"Blessed Saint George. You did not have to hit me."

"Saint George? Is he the saint o'er women who fight as men by chance? Or is he a saint who protects a lass who canna concentrate?"

"He sees to the welfare of warriors, of course. Who else would I call on with a sword in my hand?" She shifted away from him. "Ow." She grabbed her bottom.

"I know how to ease the hurt, wife," he murmured.

"What could possibly heal a bruise but heartbeats old?"

"Come with me to the loch," he whispered in her ear. "We will take off our clothes, and you will float in my arms while I kiss your stinging flesh."

Mereck nuzzled his lips against her neck, and trailed his tongue up to the tip of her dainty ear.

"Hmm. I am wonderin' why you have your bride sprawled afore others?" Eric's laughing voice asked. "If you canna wait for the weddin', handfastin' will do the job." He moved to stand close to Elise.

"Leave off, Eric. I tapped her sweet arse a mite hard and knocked her off her feet." He shot him a warning look as he helped Netta to rise.

Connor edged himself between Eric and Elise, ignoring her attempts to push him away. "Well now. If Netta hasna the strength to skewer you with a blade, wouldna a bow and arrow do the trick?"

"Ye may be right, brither. I had not thought of it." Meghan laughed.

"Hmm, does the lovely Elise also wish to best her suitors?" Eric's eyes twinkled at the lady in question.

Netta's hand rose to caution her friend.

Chapter 15

Elise eyed Netta's upraised hand and fidgeted from one foot to the other. She took a deep breath, shoved Connor aside and confronted Eric.

"Sir Eric, might I have a word with you?" She beckoned him closer and smiled up at him. "I heard you fostered with Laird Damron and his family?"

Eric nodded, his eyes puzzled.

Connor scowled. Even as his angry "Elise, dinna" rang out, she huffed and ignored him. She put her hand on Eric's arm, and her words blurted from her lips.

"Have you, uh, swiveled any ladies today, sir?" With trembling lips, she smiled sweetly at him.

Eric touched his lips with his forefinger and cleared his throat, a serious expression on his face. "I believe the word you sought was swived, my lady. Though it pains me, I must answer no. Did you by chance have someone in mind?"

Elise's knees wobbled so badly it was a wonder she still stood by the time Connor grabbed her shoulders. Eric held up a hand and leaned close to waggle his brows and grin.

"Let her speak, Connor. Her words are most curious."

"I meant not to draw your interest. By Saint Martha's sweet hair. Do you not know when someone insults you?" She stamped her foot, but soon her eyes brightened. "You are even more of a prick than Sir Connor. There. That should draw your ire." She released her breath in a gusty sigh.

Mereck beckoned to Eric and grabbed a livid Connor by the shoulder. He chuckled as he led them toward the practice field. Before they reached there, Damron joined them. Spying Connor's countenance, he frowned.

"What has upset ye, cousin? Yer face is the color of an overripe plum."

Since Connor was still spluttering half words, Mereck answered for him. "The fair Elise has found a curious way to remain unwed. She hopes to discourage suitors by shocking them." When asked to explain, he made light of the incident.

Damron sighed and shook his head.

"I will have words with her on the morrow." He eyed Connor and Mereck. "If ye have any thoughts on how to curb her, I will hear of them then."

Meghan watched until the men were out of hearing distance before she cautioned Elise.

"Dinna be too swift with yer insults Elise, or ye may find Damron weds ye to a man ye have angered unduly. Now come. Let us visit Netta's Tuan."

Simon watched with an indulgent smile as Netta fed and watered the little eyas. Tuan, his stomach filled, was soon tucked in his nest. Meghan coaxed her sparrowhawk, Simple, onto her gauntlet, and they went out into the bailey so she could show Netta how she exercised the bird.

"What caused you to name a lovely creature such an

ugsome name?" Netta admired the elegant hawk as she stroked its back.

"Because she is right glaikit, of course." When Netta frowned, Meghan explained, "Glaikit means silly or foolish. I could have called her Gowk. For certs she be a great fool when she hunts, gettin' excited and not lookin' where she is goin'. The first thing in her path knocks her to the ground."

Meghan removed the green leather hood from Simple's head and raised her wrist for the impatient bird to take flight. Simple soared upward while Meghan tied a chicken neck on the end of a slender line. She whirled it in the air in sweeping circles that coaxed Simple to dive and attack. Then she shifted the arc of her swing to make the sparrowhawk work for her treat.

Meghan next offered a chicken head. Instead of tying it to the line, she cast it high into the air. Simple screeched and swooped after it. When she caught it, she plunged to land and enjoy her catch. True to Meghan's word, the hawk took no note of a sentry patrolling the walkway. The hawk crashed into the warrior's shoulder, making the warrior lurch. Dazed, Simple flopped at the man's feet.

"Meghan, lass, didna I tell ye to draw this'un a map?" he shouted and righted the raptor.

Wobbling on shaky legs, Simple squawked and watched the man nudge the dropped reward toward her. Wisely, she ate it afore taking flight when Meghan whistled.

After they returned the hawk to her perch, Meghan coached Netta to whistle a three-note tune to call Tuan. Netta pursed her lips, huffed and puffed until she drew forth a whistle close to the notes she was to use.

The afternoon had turned cold. Back in their room, they sat on brown fur rugs close to a large brazier of coals. Netta felt restless. She couldn't stop picturing what Mereck had said he would do to her in the loch. Had he known that all the while he talked, she had felt that rigid heat of him pressed against her side?

"Ye look worried, Netta. Are ye thinkin' of Mereck?"

"Does it turn red?" Netta blurted in a wobbly voice.

"Did yer mother never tell ye about men?"

"She died birthing me. Father's new wife said I was sinful to wish knowing anything afore my husband tutored me in the marriage bed."

"Scots are more open about teachin' a lass what to expect. If by it ye mean his shaft, I'm told the tip darkens somewhat. Not the rest of it. What made ye think so?"

"He pressed against me, and I felt hard, fiery heat. It changes too. Is it normal for it to change shapes?" From the glimpses she had seen of the men at the practice area, they did not look like what she had felt.

"Not all the time." Meghan laughed. "Only when he is near ye and thinkin' lusty thoughts."

"Do they not dangle all the time?" Elise's blue eyes lit with curiosity.

"Ha, only if they are pursuin' their other favorite sports—eatin' and fightin'." Meghan snorted.

Before Netta could pose her next questions, their bath water arrived. It was just as well. She already had enough new knowledge to ponder.

At the end of the evening meal, Mereck fed Netta pastries filled with wild berries. His finger rubbed juice over her lower lip. She ran the tip of her tongue to lap it up.

"You didna get this spot, love," he murmured.

Mereck's head lowered. His beautiful mouth came close. She held her breath. When she did not draw back, a growl rumbled low in his throat as he nibbled and feathered kisses on her lips.

She should stop him. She did not. His gentle handling turned her thoughts of him to the impressive Barearse, rather than the fearsome Baresark. She forgot she didn't want to marry her barbarian.

Far from it. He tempted her with his soft love play. She longed to taste his enticing lower lip, to draw it into her own mouth. If she were to be so bold, what would he do?

Eric interrupted her exciting thoughts when he asked if Brianna would tell one of her famous stories. Servants hurried to clear tables and arrange benches opposite the great hearth. Mereck draped Netta's cloak about her shoulders and sat close beside her.

"Why are Brianna's stories famous? The only teller of tales we had at Castle Wycliffe was an old, grizzled warrior. His tales were not very interesting."

Mereck's answer surprised her.

"Brianna began telling them on her travels here. Damron at last had to forbid her to tell any others while crossing the forests. The squires and even some warriors were, eh, worried by them." He winked. "We are a superstitious lot. Many Scots believe in faery people, witches and shape changers."

Soon after Brianna's unusual voice started the tale, Netta knew why Damron had stopped his wife.

"Once upon a very long time ago, in a country close to this, a strange beast terrorized small mountain towns," Brianna began. "The nights of the full moon, all the residents in this cursed hamlet locked themselves in their homes before dusk fell. The sun no sooner set than terrible groans and screams, the sounds of a man in anguish, rent the air. After what seemed eternity, the screams deepened. Growls and howls like the triumphant calls of a giant wolf echoed in the dark night."

"Yech," Elise shouted and edged closer to Connor.

Brianna wove the tale of the shape changer who became a werewolf. Netta noted several stalwart warriors glancing over their shoulders. Were they afeared the creature would appear in the pitch-dark hallways? Dafydd hurdled into her back, near knocking her from the bench in his bid to be near Mereck's stalwart protection.

Mereck moved close to put his arm around her shoulder. Netta didn't mind. She was grateful for his presence.

When his arm moved from her shoulder to her waist, she didn't protest. Brianna's story so engrossed her that she paid little note to his large hand stealing ever lower to cuddle her stomach.

When his long fingers roamed lower, she shivered.

But, when he pinched her thigh and nibbled her neck, that got her attention.

She yelped and near jumped out of her seat, but for his restraining arm.

Damron shook his head and looked up at the rafters. Elise hunched forward, her face buried on her knees, her arms over her head. Connor touched her shoulder in inquiry. Her arms flew out and her outstretched hand struck his mouth. A shriek came from her lips, muffled curses from his. Between their noise and Spencer's frightened howls, they barely heard the laird's growled commands.

"Eneuch." Damron turned to Brianna. "'Tis too frightenin' a tale to finish. Wife, ye should save yer voice for singin', not for scarin'."

Not even Meghan scoffed at the men's offer to escort them to their room. Connor kept Elise at his side and shouldered Eric away whenever he sauntered close.

The women spent a goodly portion of the next morn in Brianna's solar visiting her and the old laird. Meghan had told them Brianna called Damron's grandfather "Poppa Dougie," much to Damron's chagrin. Brianna explained she never knew her own grandparents, but if she had, she would have been as familiar with them as she was to Lord Douglas.

Netta looked with longing at the old man cuddling little Serena in his arm. His was an impressive face framed with shaggy brown hair streaked with white, a short beard, and golden brown eyes.

Though he could shout and command even Damron into submission, Meghan claimed her grandfather was not the hard man he portrayed. Most times his ranting was bluster. When Guardian entered the room, Elise, wary after the previous night's werewolf story, near crawled into the old man's lap.

The ferocious-looking wolf gave her a haughty look, padded over to Brianna and rolled onto his back for her to scratch his chest. Netta laughed. Would her fierce Mereck one day sprawl before her and pant for her to run her fingers through the crisp mat of blond hair she glimpsed on his torso? Heaviness pulsed at the joining of her legs when she thought about the hair that narrowed down his abdomen to the place which stoked her curiosity.

She may not want to wed and be a man's possession, but she began to believe she would revel in the physical parts of marriage. Whatever they were.

"What causes yer frown, granddaughter?" Lord Douglas' voice had a rich dark tone.

Netta glanced at Brianna, awaiting her answer. Brianna smiled back and motioned toward her Poppa Dougie. Why, he had called her, Netta, granddaughter. She now had a grandfather. Happiness surged through her. She looked at him and saw he watched her with compassionate eyes.

Never at Wycliffe had any man looked at her thus. She swallowed. Could she speak her mind?

He motioned for her to sit on the rug beside him, then patted her head much as Brianna stroked Guardian. She couldn't stop the current of words which sprang forth.

"Since I have been at Blackthorn, I have had more freedom than ever before in my life. I come and go about the castle and bailey as I wish, and I have Sprite and Tuan to love. I don't want to marry. After we wed, I'll lose what little I have gained. Mereck holds no love for me. He will be like Father. If I displease him . . ." She shuddered. "He is much larger than my father and his temper . . ." Again her voice trailed off. Her eyes blurred. She hunched her shoulders, making herself a smaller target.

Lord Douglas cradled the sleeping Serena high on his shoulder. His hand stroked Netta's hair and soothed her as he would a frightened child.

"Like Father, he will demand I obey his every wish. To sew and do wifely things. Everyone will know how unworthy I am." She hesitated, but went on when his nod encouraged her.

"My stepsisters were never easy to be with like Meghan and Elise. I may never learn to properly toss a knife or use a sword, but I'm able to try. Mereck told me Fletch, your master archer, is making a bow and arrows for me." Why did he grin at her?

"Do ye not hear yerself, granddaughter?"

"What mean you, Lord Douglas?"

"Call me Granda as Meghan does." He smoothed a stray curl from her forehead and nodded. "Think on what ye have told us. Who saw to it ye had Sprite and Tuan?" He tilted his head and waited.

"Mereck, of course."

"Who took over when he learned ye wished to master

a weapon? I know it didna go well with the swords. Did ye not just tell me he had a bow fashioned for ye?"

"Aye, he did. But when he is my husband, he will change. He will command my every moment."

"From the time Mereck signed the betrothal contract, he had the right to govern ye as if ye were already wed. Yer freedom since leaving Wycliffe, these special privileges ye enjoy, are they not ones he has granted ye? Ask Brianna, and she will tell ye how lightly Mereck treats ye."

"I was much like you," Brianna said softly. "When Damron brought me here, he knew my every move. If he could not be near, he assigned guards to shadow me and made David their captain. I no longer notice someone is forever close-by." At Netta's wide-eyed look, she explained. "I've all the freedom any woman could want. Damron has a terrible fear something will happen to me when he's not by my side to prevent it. I don't mind the guards, for I know it's a sign of his great love for me."

Netta saw the truth of it moments later when Brianna rose. The morning had tired her, for her face was pale.

"Poppa Dougie, I think it is time for our morning rest."

Brianna gently took Serena from his arms, then kissed his cheek and told him she loved him. She had not taken two steps afore a young warrior stood close-by, proving her point. Brianna smiled, and he puffed up his chest as if she had given him the greatest courtesy of his life. Lord Douglas accepted the guard's help as they left the room.

"Damron fears for Brianna. We all do." Meghan nodded at them. "On bringin' her from England as his bride, knaves abducted her. When Damron gained on them, their swinish leader tossed her from his horse. But not afore he bit her so she'd ne'er forget him. 'Tis the crescent scars ye see on her jaw. Later, other attacks occurred. Damron's leman was behind them. He ne'er ceases fearin' he will lose Brianna."

Netta knew Brianna to be different. Mystery lurked in her eyes, and her words and tone of speech were unusual. Brianna radiated such love and compassion. How could Damron have been so foolish to have a leman for even a day after they wed?

It was common practice for men to keep a lover. Did Mereck? Could one of the women who drooled over him at his battle practice also be his leman? Anger rolled through her.

During the noon meal, she watched to see if Mereck gazed overlong at any woman. He kissed Brianna's cheek. But it was his habit when he saw her for the first time each day. He patted Elise's head and nodded at Elizabeth Neilson. Hmm, Elizabeth. She was beautiful with straight, red hair and large sky-blue eyes. She oft glanced at Eric, who teased Elise most when Elizabeth appeared nearby.

The rogue sought to make Elizabeth jealous. A cruel ploy. Had he not already spoken to Damron, offering for Elise?

"Come, Netta. Fletch crafted the finest bow in either Scotland or England. He waits to gift you with it." Mereck grasped her elbow and urged her to rise.

Fletch awaited them near a man's replica fastened to a post. He beamed when he showed her the bow made from supple wood. It weighed less than was usual for a woman. He had also crafted a quiver filled with arrows. Each arrow, identical in size and weight, bore the initial "L." After she thanked him and told him how lovely they were, he left to attend his duties, a grin lighting his face.

Mereck showed her how to aim and release the arrow and explained the reasons behind each motion. He had her heft the bow several times to grow accustomed to the weight. When ready, she notched an arrow with his guidance. Her first attempt to loose the arrow was weak. It fell to the ground a short space away. She laughed up at him.

"I pray no curious worms are about."

"At least ye pointed at yon target," Meghan said with a chuckle.

Mereck smiled and handed Netta another arrow. "I will help you this time."

He moved behind her, his hot, muscled body molded against her back. His hands covered hers, the hair-roughed skin of his arms teased her own. She inhaled his scent, enjoying the tingling it evoked in her. Being held within his strong arms, his body surrounding her, she could not stop the shivers his touch created.

His breath ruffled the hair on her neck; her breathing became rapid.

By the time the arrow sped toward the target and struck firmly in the heart painted on the target, she panted.

Once they loosed several arrows, she was in danger of melting into the ground.

"May I try the next one on my own, Mereck?" Hearing her unsteady voice, she flushed and hoped he did not notice her reaction to him.

He stepped back with a knowing smile. Rats. He noticed.

Netta aimed her next arrow at the straw man and repeated what he had shown her. Pleased, she watched the arrow whiz through the air a good distance. It went left and wide of its mark.

"Humph." She held her hand out for another, tried again, and this time sighted a bit right of the target. The arrow struck low on the base.

"Blessed Saint Wistan, did you see it?" Netta crowed and grinned with delight.

"Saint Wistan? Did ye make him up?" Meghan huffed out a breath. "I vow ye sneak in saints no one has e'er heard of."

"Nay. She did not." Elise defended Netta. "Saint Wistan lived until the year of our Lord, 850. June is his own month."

"Ladies, enough quibbling. Netta must keep her mind on her training," Mereck ordered. "Raise your sight on this next arrow, wife. Allow for its weight."

Why must he call her "wife"? He knew she did not favor it. She started to protest, but he brushed a stray curl from her eyes. She took a deep breath. His hand held his arousing scent. His smoldering eyes meet hers and made her forget what she had thought to say. He continued handing her arrows until her arms and back quivered from strain. He praised each effort.

"I believe ye are much more apt with the bow than at knife throwin'." Meghan punched her fist high in a salute and yelled a battle cry.

Netta beamed with pride.

Soon after, Spencer arrived with a summons for Mereck.

"Rest a bit while Dafydd gathers your arrows." Mereck patted her shoulder and motioned his squire to stay with her. "When you are ready, Meghan will guide your practice."

Connor clasped Elise's hand, and Mereck moved to her other side. Netta's eyes widened in surprise. Had they chosen a husband for Elise? She started forward. Mereck frowned, and held up a hand to motion her back.

"Nay. Damron wishes to speak with Elise. She will rejoin you soon."

Netta had promised to protect her friend. When the

men turned and led a reluctant Elise back to the keep, she stubbornly followed.

Mereck glanced back and scowled. "Obey me. Stay with Meghan. I'll protect your friend."

Meghan's hand on her arm stopped her.

"Ye must listen to him, Netta. Mereck willna permit anyone to thwart his orders."

Chapter 16

Elise tried to pull from Connor's demanding grip. He frowned and tightened his fingers.

"Dinna fear, Elise, you willna come to harm," Mereck murmured.

"Meghan's bound to stick her nose in where it isna wanted." Damron closed and latched the solar door. He ambled to the fireplace and beckoned Elise to come to him. She stood before him, but had not the courage to look at him. She studied the tips of her shoes and fidgeted with the pocket on her tunic. He sighed.

"Ye will look at me, Elise, while I instruct ye." Her gaze moved from her shoes to the tip of his black boots. "Look at me. Not my boots; not my knees." As her eyes meandered up his body, he grunted and added, "And not my chest."

Mereck noted she twitched when her eyes passed over Damron's plaid. By Lucifer's toes, were all Saxon virgins so frightened of a man's sex? At first he feared he had spoken aloud, but since she did not shriek or faint, he knew he had not.

"My face, lady, my face. I dinna ken what has come over ye." Damron threw up his arms. "Did ye hear yerself speakin' words ye shouldna be privy to? Ye spoke of men's body parts. Until ye met Meghan, I'm sure ye ne'er thought o' such. How am I to find a suitable husband to rule ye if ye get a reputation for bein' ill-bred?"

Elise's glassy-eyed stare had returned to his boots. Damron shifted and waited. At last, she noticed the quiet. Her chin raised and her voice quavered.

"What?"

"What? What do ye mean what? Were you no' listenin' to me?"

"I was. When you came to a 'suitable husband to rule' me, I got stuck on it. What do you mean rule? If it means do I want a husband to tell me all the things I cannot do, then I will learn something disgusting every hour to keep him away." She stared at Damron's chin.

Connor's snort drew her attention.

"Prick! That should remove your interest, Connor." She glared at him. "I'm sure Meghan will supply me with enough new words to repulse every Scotsman for leagues around."

Mereck would never have thought timid Elise would become braw enough to defy a man. He approved of her new-found courage. He kept his face impassive, but Connor's chin near dropped to his chest. Damron tilted Elise's face up so she had to look at him.

"Did ye not listen to a thing I have told ye?" His voice thickened with disbelief. "Ye willna speak about vile words with Meghan."

"If they are vile, my lord, why did you speak such when we were present in the hall? We overheard you and Connor refer to men's body parts."

Damron's brows hiked up to meet his hair.

"Every word used to describe your wild doings was clear when you boasted among yourselves while talking with Sir Eric." She frowned, took a deep breath, then near shouted, "Why, Father and Sir Galan never used such words around Mother and me." She cleared her throat and whispered, "We knew when Galan had a, ah, willing partner for the evening. But he never discussed her in our hearing."

"She willna stop until she insults every man she thinks might seek her marriage bed." Connor huffed and slapped his thigh.

"Aye. She is makin' a good start." Mereck grinned. No wonder the women oft had their heads together whispering.

"Do you agree her beautiful lips spoke the words?" Connor asked. "They are the source of her misconduct and therefore deserve the punishment."

Damron nodded. Mereck saw where he led.

"Do you plan to wash my mouth with soap?" Elise's chin thrust out. "Well, let me tell you, my lords high and mighty. Mother did so more than once. If you want me to spew all over those skirts you wear and ruin your best boots, go ahead." Her shoulders squared in an fitting imitation of Brianna.

Mereck swallowed a laugh.

"Nay, Elise. There's a more pleasant way to still your unruly lips should you decide to belittle a man."

Elise eyes squinted, eying Connor. He did not hold soap. Nor did he remove his belt. She backed away until he caught her and tugged her to him. His eyes roved down her face to her rosy lips.

He stared; she swallowed.

He wrapped his arms around her and molded his lips to hers in a thorough kiss. When he drew back, she was stiff with surprise, her eyes wide with shock. Connor drew a deep breath, steadied her and turned to Damron.

"That takes care of the word prick to me. But the lady

aggrieved both Eric and Marcus." He looked loath to have another exact such a penalty.

"I think we should assign you the task of correcting the lady." Mereck looked at Damron for confirmation. At his brother's nod, he continued. "We wouldna want her to become acquainted with the lips of every man with whom she comes into contact."

Elise edged toward the door. She reached the latch and tugged. Connor caught her.

He clamped her arms to her sides before he raised her chin to look into her eyes.

She gasped. He groaned low in his throat.

She began to struggle in earnest. Someone banged on the door, creating a din as he again captured her lips. No soft kiss this. His tongue invaded her sweet mouth and stabbed deep. She whimpered. It softened and swept over hers, caressing her. Long steaming heartbeats later, he lifted his head and inhaled with shuddering breaths.

"That was for Marcus' ballocks and Eric's swiving," he whispered, his voice hoarse as an old codger's.

Tears streamed from Elise's eyes. She shoved at him until he released her.

When Damron unlatched the door, Netta and Meghan burst into the room. Netta spied Elise's swollen lips and rushed to put her arms around her.

"What have ye done to the little one?" Meghan shouted. "Dinna tell me ye have hit her and caused her mouth to swell. Shame on ye that ye wud batter such an innocent." Her glare rounded on the men.

Connor's body was obviously in urgent need of release. Meghan stared at his soft, puffy lips, and the lust lingering in his eyes. Before he guessed her intent, she struck him square in the stomach; hard enough that air burst from his lips.

Connor doubled over clutching his belly.

"Satan's pointy tail, Meg. I kissed her for punishment. I have done her no harm."

"How do ye know what harm ye have done? She is gently reared and hasna been around men such as ye. Ye have all tupped every doxy betwixt here and Edinburgh. What harm? How do ye know if ye have set a craving she will satisfy with another? What great foolish lumps men be."

Meghan's scornful gaze took in Damron and Mereck. Mereck knew she ached to hit them too. His gimlet stare warned her. She replied with a defiant look, then turned on her heels to follow Netta and Elise back to their room.

"What have they done, sweetheart?" Netta wrapped Elise in her arms and cuddled her head against her breasts as they sat on the bed. Elise bawled and clutched her so tightly Netta could barely breathe.

"Oh, Netta," Elise wailed. "I d-dreamed of kissing C-Connor some day, but not like that. He has been g-gentle and laughing, but t-today he was all hard and unyielding." She took a deep, ragged breath.

"What part did Mereck play in this?" Disappointment in him was like cold water flowing over her.

"N-Nothing. He but nodded to Connor. At first, I thought they meant to wash my mouth with soap. I threatened to spew on them. Perchance that is why Connor did it?" Her voice sounded hopeful. "He didn't want me to splatter his clothes and boots? How c-could he stick his tongue in my mouth? Surely it is an evil thing to do? Now Father Matthew will have to give me special penances," she ended in a wail.

"You have done nothing which needs a penance. Father Matthew may ask you to govern your words, but I'm sure God isn't upset with you. Shh, love. A girl's first kiss should not be this way. A kiss should be beautiful. But, sometimes it can be a vile touch. When Roger came to Wycliffe, he often tried to force his attentions thusly." Netta shuddered, thinking of the cruel man.

"What did ye do?" Meghan cocked her head.

"Why, I bit his tongue, of course. He couldn't eat for days."

"Did he not try to punish ye?" Meghan asked, surprised.

"Aye. But I ran much faster than he. It was fortunate Father heard his ranting, even with Roger's tongue swelling and like to burst from his mouth. Father put a stop to it and sent me to my room."

"Was it after your father betrothed you to James of Hexham? Was he as disgusting as old Baron Durham?" Listening to the dreadful things that had happened to Netta, Elise began to calm.

"Nay. James came first. He was another matter. Though he was grossly burdened with fat, I could not outrun him." She shuddered. "His hands were filthy, his fingers thick as sausages with dirt-encrusted nails. He forced food into my mouth and tried to make me suck his finger. I bit him, too, but didn't get away as easily." She swallowed remembered fear.

"He lurked in the darkest part of the keep and grabbed me in his arms. He bruised me with pinches, and he tore hair from my head trying to force his kisses on me." She near gagged at the memory. "He bruised me badly a day before Lord Bleddyn came to visit. Father locked me in my room. He told him I was visiting you, Elise.

"Later on, I learned James and his knights had been set upon. Unhorsed and badly overweight, he wallowed like a giant turtle on its back. He couldn't get up from the ground." She shuddered. "His great weight was his downfall."

Mereck, outside the partly opened door, heard her stories. Lord Hexham had been no challenge for Bleddyn. No wonder Netta was loath to have a man feed her.

Wishing the news he brought her was at a better time, he worried how she would take it. He retreated several steps and returned, walking heavily. His boots striking the floor warned them before he called out and asked for entrance.

At Netta's "Come," Mereck entered. The women sat in the middle of the bed. He studied Elise and saw she had come to no real harm. When she wed, she would soon accustom herself to the ways of men. Netta looked impatient. If she knew what he intended to say, she would not be eager to hear him out.

"Bleddyn left to meet Father Matthew. They will soon be here to perform two weddings."

"Two weddings?" Netta asked. Her face blanched, but she did not protest.

"Aye, two. Our own, and Damron has selected the man to husband Elise. He speaks to him now."

Elise's voice squeaked. "Did I not disgrace myself enough there will be no wedding? How could he marry me to someone when they know the things I said and what Connor did to me? I will tell the man, that's what I'll do. Then he won't want to marry me." She looked hopeful.

"Dinna count on it, Elise." Connor appeared beside Mereck. "You'll be sadly aggrieved."

"Hmpf! Why should you care?" Her puffy, red-rimmed eyes lit with hope. "You should be afeared the man will beat you within a breath of your nasty life. I will beg him to avenge me." She started to scramble off the bed.

"Start begging." Connor put his fists on his hips and widened his stance. Laughter sparked from his eyes.

"What?" Elise asked, uncertain.

"You must beg most earnestly, and convince me why I should beat myself within a breath of my nasty life. Though it may prove a most irksome chore. What think you, Mereck?" He rubbed his jaw. "Would fists against my shadow do the deed?" He fisted his right hand and jabbed the air in front of his face. "Or by chance a broadsword would be best?"

Elise gasped and scrambled behind Netta. Mereck was pleased to see the color return to his own bride's face while she listened to Connor's teasing. What took women so long to realize their desires? A strong attraction pulsed between Elise and Connor. Netta realized it. Did Elise not know her eyes followed Connor whene'er he was within her sight?

And Netta. Her gaze heated and roved over his own body whene'er he came near. If he touched her, her eyes dilated, and her breath quickened. If his face came close to her, she dampened her lips, readying them for his kisses. Did her woman's flesh betwixt her thighs grow hot and weeping? She showed every sign of being a passionate woman.

He pictured her naked and writhing beneath him, the sheets tangled and pillows tossed to the floor. He imagined her voice as she begged him to drive deeper into her. His body tensed. His heated blood pounded through his veins. Swallowing, he hooded his eyes to mask the lust flaming there.

"I have arranged for the noon meal to be brought here to you." He looked the women over. "I thought perchance you needed time to accustom yourselves to the idea and do whate'er it is women do to prepare for their weddings." Sad yearning struck his chest like a fist. He turned and left the room.

Elise peeked at Connor over the tip of the pillow

hugged to her chest. Amusement flickered in his eyes. He blew her a kiss and followed on his cousin's heels.

The afternoon passed quickly. When their meal arrived, Netta saw all of the things she liked best. Roasted chicken, small boiled carrots and greens cooked with salted pork. The smell was heavenly. Wine arrived with the food, not watered as usual, but rich and full. She was grateful for its calming effect.

After they finished eating, Brianna and three of the castle widows came to the door. They carried bolts of cloth of every type and color. Brianna waved a square of parchment on which she had sketched pictures of several tunics.

It struck Netta that one of the differences about Brianna was her clothing. Not all of her tunics had the round or square necklines which were common. Some had vee necks cut in the front and back. Others had a flap of material which started at the shoulders and lay open at the chest. Brianna called it a "lapel." When she grew cold of an evening, she pulled it across beneath her neck and secured it with a pin.

If anything made Netta restless, it was selecting cloth and colors for gowns. Content with the tunics Brianna had lent her, she asked if her new clothing could be modeled after them. Her thoughts brightened when the women agreed.

Later when they went to the great hall to listen to a traveling jongleur, she was more than a little nervous. She looked at Mereck in a new light. He waited, Mither draped across his broad shoulders. The huge cat purred loudly while he scratched her behind her ears. How could a man look like a pagan one day, be charming and courteous on the next then turn into a forbidding warrior at the drop of a pence?

"Come now, Mither, you neglect your kits," he admonished the cat as he removed her from her perch. When he put her on the stone floor, she rubbed against his bare calves and turned her head to run her raspy tongue over his skin. Satisfied that she had groomed him properly, she uttered a hoarse meow, stabbed her tail high and regally made her way from the room.

"*Mo bean na bainnse*, my bride." Mereck kissed her cheek and murmured, "I have missed you. Soon we will have long, cold nights to while away exploring each other's secrets."

Netta swallowed. Hard. His scent drew her to him. It never failed to make that secret place between her legs hot and sensitive. Long nights together? He would have the right to sleep next to her. Well rats and fleas. What secrets did he seek?

"I have no secrets, sir. You need only ask, and I'll tell you what you want to know."

He bent to whisper in her ear.

"Which will pleasure you most, little bride? My lips on your throat?"

His hot, open mouth moved to follow the curve of her throat. His tongue licked her skin; his teeth nipped her gently.

"Or my body when it covers yours?"

He moved until he pressed against her from her head to her toes. His heat seared through her clothing.

Oh my. She felt more than his heat. She moved back like he had scalded her.

"You need not act as a cover, my lord. We have ample blankets." She forced herself to look up at him and was sorry. His heated gaze promised something. She knew not what. It made her squirm. That intriguing area began to throb and dampen. The nipples on her breasts tingled and hardened to strain against her clothing. Swallowing, she folded her arms across her chest in a bid to soothe them.

What had she been about to say? She remembered.

"Blankets. They make them here at the castle. Did you know Brianna has a weaver's hut where five women and one man work? They make the plaids as well. She thinks to add two women to keep up with the need." She began to ramble as much as Elise sometimes did, but she could not stop herself. "Why do you suppose there are not more men skilled at weaving?"

"Could women keep the skill a mystery?" His eyes crinkled at the corners, and his mouth twitched.

Hmm, what about his secrets? Would she finally satisfy her curiosity about those parts she had glimpsed? Her mouth went dry at the thought of those things being in the same bed with her. Perhaps he slept in braies, those loose-fitting drawstring pants she had helped to mend. The idea calmed her. She decided, to be on the safe side, she would make sure she had many heavy nightdresses.

After they took their seats, Netta spied a wooden perch waiting there.

"Tuan will soon be ready to spend more time out of the mews." Mereck smiled as he spoke. "I fastened a nest to the crosspiece, for he canna stand for long. Do you like it?"

Netta took in the trees, flowers, birds and scenes of the forest and lakes he had engraved on the upright post, all painted in vivid colors.

"How did you find time to do such intricate work?" She was delighted with the gift. "It is beautiful. Thank you, Mereck." She blinked when he leaned down, his face close to her lips. It took her a while to understand he requested a kiss for his efforts. Flushing, she bestowed the kiss. The rough feel of the hair grown there during the day surprised her. She tested it with her fingertips. She liked the feel of it. Sighing, she started to relax.

Until Damron rose and announced the upcoming weddings.

Chapter 17

Netta felt Mereck's light grip on her elbow and gulped. Though her knees wobbled, she feigned calm and rose without protest.

Elise clung to her seat. Connor snaked an arm around her waist to lift her to her feet—no easy task. She released the chair, only to have it crash backward with such force, a gust of laughter filled the hall.

"Could I not send for my father? Mayhap he has changed his mind?" Netta asked Mereck as casually as she could manage.

Mereck stiffened. "Nay, little bride. We willna be waiting. A promise must ne'er be broken."

Though Mereck's tone was firm, she tried again.

"What promise?" She hoped he didn't refer to her frightened plea on the mountain. His next words proved he did.

"You well know what promise, Netta. Your pledge to Saint Monica to marry the man she chose was loud enough for every creature of the forest to hear. Both Bleddyn and Damron agree I am that man. Ne'er vow what you dinna plan to keep."

His face hardened. He looked down his nose at her

with a frigid stare. When her father wore the same expression, she soon found herself banished to her room. She studied him from the corner of her eye. He made no move to do the same.

Relief flooded her when Dafydd brought Tuan's food. She fed and watered the little raptor, then placed the sleeping bundle of feathers back in his nest.

"Yech! Netta, you have bird droppings on your clothing. Someone bring hot water and soap. Lots of soap. Lots of water," Elise yelled to no one in particular.

Netta glanced at her hands and her chest where Tuan had made herself at home. She grinned at Elise. "Have you never changed a baby's bindings?" Lazy nursemaids had oft disappeared when her stepsisters were babes and their bindings needed changing.

A page balancing a sloshing, too-full basin of hot water slid careful feet across the floor, his tongue peeking between his lips in concentration. Another followed with soap and linens.

"The water is too hot for your hands, Netta." Mereck turned her so her back was to the room. He dipped a cloth in the water and wrung it out. He smiled as he smoothed it over her neck, then cleansed her tunic down to the soft tops of her breasts.

His gaze held her own, daring her to move while he attended her. The feel of his hands brought an unwelcome blush to heat her face. She stared at his tanned fingers against her pink skin and shivered, picturing them on her naked breast.

Did she imagine sparks in the air between them? Mereck's nostrils flared, his eyes glinted. His fingers darted through the opening of her gown, caressed her nipples and withdrew. How had she forgotten to hum? Of late, his dreaded gift slipped her mind. His smoldering gaze traveled over her breasts, stopped to stare at her nipples thrusting against her tunic, then up past her chin to meet her eyes. Lust heated his sea-green eyes to the green of a forest at dusk. Ever so gentle, he cupped her breasts and squeezed.

"Nay." She tried to push him away, but he captured her wrists, dunked her hands in the cooled water and washed them. After he finished and dried her, he turned her chair back to the table.

Why did the widowed ladies smile so knowingly? When Meghan grinned and patted her chest, Netta glanced down.

Wet handprints marked her tunic. She started to rise and race from the room. His speed amazed her. His right hand gathered her wrists, and he went on to fill their trencher with his left. His eyes warned her to stay seated. The damage was done. Leaving the table would cause an unwelcome scene.

Netta's days passed swiftly as she helped cut and sew her wedding outfit in Brianna's solar. It was a hated chore. As Mereck's wife, would he insist she spend her days sewing as so many women did? At the thought, she pricked her finger for the third time. She scowled and stuck it in her mouth.

"Go, Netta, afore you drip so much blood on the cloth it will seem the whole of it is red." Elise reached over and rescued the shift Netta had attempted to hem.

"But you have your own to do."

"I'm done with this day's garment." Elise grinned and gave Netta's shoulder a light push.

Glad to escape the solar, Netta didn't need any more

encouragement. She hugged Elise's shoulders and jumped up.

In the bailey, Netta searched for Meghan. She learned Meg had Simple out on a short hunt, escorted by the castle huntsman and his helpers. Netta played with Sprite and worked with Tuan, but she still felt restless.

She shaded her eyes to study the archer's area. No one awaited a turn. Mereck had not mentioned a lesson for today. Could she not practice by herself? Women shouldn't be alone in the practice fields, so she would wear Connor's old clothing. In her mind, she heard Mereck's stern voice forbidding her to don them again or risk his displeasure. She hesitated, then shrugged. For certs, he but meant to intimidate her.

She changed her clothing and hurried to the bailey with her bow and quiver of arrows. Two young men called to her when she passed by the quintain. She waved and pretended she hurried on an important mission to the stable where the head groom worked on a giant warhorse. Thankfully, 'twas not Mereck's *M'Famhair.*

She got no farther.

Rough calloused fingers grabbed her collar and swung her toward the stable door. She held her breath. She had not even loosed the first arrow and Mereck already found her out. She exhaled in a rush on hearing the groom's gruff voice.

"Fetch the brush from Angel's stall, lad. His be the second from last. Go on now. There be a knot in his mane what needs fixin'." He shoved her into the dim stable. She hurried down the aisle, until she heard strange sounds coming from within a nearby stall. She skidded to a stop. Moans. Someone was hurt and in need of tending. Why did they not call out? Before she ran for help, she looked over the top of the rails to see how much aid they required.

Her eyes snapped open. The moans came not only from a man, but also from a buxom young woman. A naked, buxom young woman. She knelt with her hands on the floor, her heavy breasts dangling beneath her. An equally naked but far from buxom man knelt behind her. He bumped against her buttocks while he squeezed and played with her breasts.

His head reared up. He moaned, his face taut with pain. She gasped. Heavenly saints. She spied Sir Marcus' profile. What she didn't recognize was Sir Marcus' bare arse, the muscles flexing then relaxing as he bounced away. What did he do to her? If it pained him, why did he not stop? She turned and scurried back out the door. She tried to race around the groom. He scowled and shoved her back through the entrance.

"Fetch the bluidy brush and be quick aboot it."

She gulped, took a deep breath and called out, "I be going to fetch the brush what's back in the far stall."

"O' course 'tis in the far stall. I told ye so." The groom sucked his teeth, disgusted with the simple-minded boy.

Netta went a short distance. "The groom wants Angel's brush right away, 'tis what he wants," she hollered. She stomped around, making as much noise as possible. When near her destination, she yelled again. "That's what I be aimin' to do. Get the brush and make the master proud, I will. If'n I don't find it soon, I'm afeared he won't be happy."

She kicked a bucket standing beside a rusted shovel. It made a terrible din. Enough to make horses stick their heads up and gaze at her. Marcus' head poked out the entrance to the stall. He blinked, then a wide grin split his face.

Oh, saints. He recognized her.

Her face heated. She bobbed her head and dashed into the next area. After a hasty search, she grabbed the brush and raced out so fast not even Guardian could have caught her.

Netta dropped the brush at the groom's feet and bolted away before he could make another request. Her heart didn't slow its racing until she was well away from the stable. She lost her desire to practice. Before she got into any more trouble, she'd best return to the keep.

Sewing was a safer pastime.

Not two steps farther, a young man slung his arm around her shoulder.

"Come, lad. You dinna seem to have duties, and I have need of you."

What was it with Highlanders? Did they always grab unsuspecting people to do their bidding? She recognized him. He had challenged Meghan but a day before. He steered her to where the quintain creaked and groaned.

Hoping to sound manly, she ducked her head and deepened her voice. "I be sorry, but I canna reach the posts."

"Douglas left the nag he used. I must needs have you ready the crossbar." He pointed at the old horse standing beside him.

Before Netta knew what to expect, he picked her up and dumped her onto the saddle. She scrambled about and tried to seat herself. Impatient, he took her right leg and threw it over the saddle. His friend Douglas must have been short, for the stirrups were the right length for her.

She blinked and clutched the reins.

"Seize the end of the crossbar by the dummy, and start it around. Mind you, keep out of its way," he added.

It sounded simple enough, for the bar moved easily.

She did a rather good job. She congratulated herself a mite too soon. Something heavy thumped her shoulder. She lurched forward. Her bow and quiver of arrows fell to the ground. A most unmanly cry burst from her lips. She grabbed the horse around its neck. Her hat landed in the dirt, and her dark curls tumbled over her face.

"Satan's horns. The commander's bride! He'll thrash us for sure." The young man threw his lance down and stomped toward her. "He be planning to watch my progress when he comes from the field."

She knew he meant her no harm, but he was not the problem. From her added height on the horse, she saw Mereck in the distance. If she did not hurry away, he would catch her not only dressed as a boy but inside the quintain enclosure. She groaned. Two forbidden pursuits.

"I'm sorry. I have to go. I'll return the horse soon." Netta grabbed the reins and kicked the startled nag into fast motion before the young man could reach her.

Where in the world was she to go? She made her way to the opposite side of the bailey. Milling people, horses and carts were everywhere. The laundress with a barrow full of soiled sheets crossed in front of her. Netta held back on the horse to let her pass. A peasant bearing a stout rod across his shoulders, fowls trussed and hanging from each end, hurried toward the cookhouse. Destined for the ax, their cackle and fuss sounded like they knew their fate.

Netta winced. Her own fate didn't look much more promising.

The barbican loomed before her. On her left, fishermen with their catch strung on sturdy lines crossed the drawbridge. The gamekeeper, with a loaded cart, made his way behind them. Peasants with produce tied into large bundles slung over their shoulders pushed around her right side. She tried to edge past as a line of warriors left the castle, but they hemmed her in, taking her with them.

Sweat trickled down her neck. She peered back and glimpsed the young man heading toward Mereck. Did some code of chivalry demand a squire confess if he caused a damsel to be struck on the shoulder?

She would find Meghan. Together they would think of a way to get her back inside the castle before her soon-to-be husband found her out. Surely other women in the castle had the same color of hair? Saints help her. Mereck had warned the women not to leave the castle grounds without ample protection. She could almost feel the hot depth of his anger if he learned she had done so. She nudged the old horse to go faster.

Netta found the path into the woods and sighed with relief. Meghan would soon return. She would hide inside the first lines of trees and await her. Her sigh turned into a shriek, for the sharp point of a sword pricked her back.

"Shut yer trap, else me fist will shut it fer ye," a surly voice growled. "Right stupid of ye to fall into me 'ands, and making me job easy. Keep riding and 'ead to that knoll, else I gut ye 'ere and now." He uttered a menacing growl.

Netta's stomach knotted as he continued to give directions in the lower-class accent from the east end of London. What was he doing in the Highlands? He took her deeper into the woods on a track too overgrown to be in current use. There was no chance Meghan would come upon them.

Fearful images flashed in her mind. She hauled back on the reins and attempted to turn the horse. If the churl meant to ravish her, he would have to do it here and now. If they didn't get farther away from Blackthorn Castle, at least she would have a better chance for someone to hear her screams.

"I didn't tell ye to stop." He cuffed the back of her head.

Netta cried out and dropped the reins. He growled at her to get moving. She didn't start fast enough to please him, for he jabbed the nag's rump with the tip of his sword.

The horse screamed and shot forward. Netta grabbed for the reins, but they flew free before she could catch them. Frantic, she grasped the horse's mane and held on for dear life. The animal, who looked too old to trot, galloped like he trained for knightly battles. Horses were a puzzle. Lightning could not outpace a worm until he saw the open field. Now this four-legged snail tried to race.

A shiver of panic swept her. A short distance ahead a tree lay across the road. She doubted the beast knew anything about jumping. The horse saw the tree and tried valiantly to clear it.

Blessed saints. Maybe he did know what he was doing. For certs, she sure as Lucifer didn't. His front hooves cleared the tree. When they again met the earth, she catapulted off his back. The scream had not quite cleared her lips, before the hard earth rose to meet her.

Mereck's head jerked up. His body stopped in midmotion. Fearful prickles coursed down his spine. He searched the crowd in the bailey. Netta is hurt. He knew it with as much certainty as he knew where he stood. He ran, sounds of distress bursting from his lips. A young man tried to stop him. Mereck started to shove him out of the way but stopped on hearing the word bride.

"What did you say?" His fingers dug into the man's shoulder.

"I didn't know it was your bride. The sack knocked her and she near fell. It was her cap coming off and her hair spilling free that warned me." Kenneth's voice wavered.

"The Lady Lynette, where is she? Is she hurt? Did you seek aid for her?" He searched the squire's ashen face.

"Not hurt. I came to meet you, for she took off into the outer bailey. She tried to make her way back, but the crowd carried her out of the castle walls. I lost track of her."

"Get Sir Connor and twelve men. Send them behind me. Hurry!"

Kenneth ran to do his bidding. Mereck readied *M'Famhair* and finished in lightning speed, for he had no need of a saddle. Rider and horse soon crossed the drawbridge and headed into the woods. Connor and his men followed not far behind.

Mereck scanned the cleared countryside around the high curtain walls. His bride wasna among the people who came and went. On entering the path in the woods, he slowed his pace. He inspected the ground and trees and listened, but he heard only forest sounds.

When he found Netta, he would impress on her the dangers of being out and alone. Lucifer's crooked nose! This is not the English countryside. She defied him to again dress as a squire and enter the quintain enclosure. He remembered his promise of swift consequences if she did so. His mouth set in a grim line.

After the first knowledge she had been hurt, he felt no other sense of her. His body tensed. Was he too late? Connor and the men caught up with him, and they spread out to search the surrounding woods. After several leagues, Mereck stiffened.

Fear.

He felt her fear as surely as if it was his own. He would use it to find her.

* * *

Ohh, her head ached. Every inch of her felt bruised. Damp musty earth cradled her chin. Grass and leaves tickled the skin of her face. Mercy sakes. A busy ant crawled across her cheek, headed for her ear. She stirred and tried to lift her hand to swat it. She did not get far. The man threw her onto her back much like a sack of grain.

Her eyes widened. She opened her mouth to yell her lungs out. Before the first cry burst through her lips, a grimy and foully odorous hand clamped over them. When she took her next breath, she gagged from the taste and smell. With the face too close to her own, she blinked and tried to uncross her eyes.

Surely his was the most disgusting face in the world. Strings of greasy black hair fell over a narrow forehead. Warts covered a gourd-like nose, and hair protruded from his nostrils and ears. The nose dominated the man's face. Bulging, brown eyes rivaled it for prominence.

She closed her eyes and wished the horrid face would go away. It didn't. He removed his hand, only to replace it with cloth torn from her shirt. She knew it was from her clothing, for it was clean. From the sight and smell of him, the man couldn't have a clean thing on him.

"Stupid girl," he hissed. "Yer 'orse ran. Now ye'll 'ave ter come up with me." He bound her hands behind her and slung her up on his horse. Seconds later, he mounted and clamped an arm around her to haul her tight against him.

Her skin couldn't crawl with revulsion any harder, or it would strip away from her bones. She tried to pull away from him. He cursed and held her all the tighter, wedging her hands against his sex. His breath became hard and ragged, so foul and strong it defied the brisk wind to waft beneath her nose. Something moved against her hands.

She clenched her fingers; she tried not to touch him. Feeling his limp male flesh heat and squirm against her wrist, she shuddered.

Mereck. Why had she not listened to him? He would save her if he could. What if he failed to learn she was missing until too late, and she was long gone from here?

They rode farther into the woods and came to a small clearing near overtaken by the forest. She stared at the jumble of growth and spied an abandoned bothy in the center of it. From the looks of it, many years had passed since anyone used the shelter. Part of the thatched roof had long since rotted and fallen inside. The door hung by one strap.

He seemed surprisingly agile when he dismounted and pulled her off his horse's back. Holding her neck in a cruel grip, he forced her toward the hut. He shoved the door out of the way and thrust her into the dim room. She tripped and fell on the hard dirt floor and rolled on her back as fast as possible. As fearful as he looked, not seeing him was more terrifying. She wouldn't know what he planned to do.

"Well, now. Ye be a pretty one. God in 'eaven. Ye 'ave the devil eye 'e told me of. I wud a knowed ye from 'is describing, I would." He hunkered down and pulled the gag from her mouth. "Ye must be a bit queerie wearing pants. Ye wants to be a boy? The gent did not say ye be odd." Stubby fingers felt over her face and chin. He grasped her jaw to yank down on it.

Netta gritted her teeth together and refused to open her mouth. What did he seek to find? If she had all her teeth?

He untied her hands and jerked her to her feet. She backed up until she collided against the sagging wall behind her.

"Take off yer clothes. I wants to see wot all the fuss be about. Ye must 'ave something worth pawing, or the bloke wud not 'ave paid 'ighly fer ye." He scowled, for Netta made no attempt to obey but clasped her arms across her chest.

"If you value your life, you will leave this place as fast as your horse can carry you." Netta forced confidence into her voice. "My husband, Lord Mereck of Blackthorn, saw us leave. He must be but a short distance away. All of Scotland knows he is a knight never bested by another."

"Take off yer clothes. Yer 'igh and mighty knight won't find us. Ye'd best not displease me. We'll be 'ere long enough fer me to see the prize I be 'anding over.

When Netta still ignored his orders, his hands shot out. He whipped the short tunic over her head, careful not to tear it. "Don't want the wealthy bloke to know I sampled 'is treasure," he muttered. He didn't take the same care with her shirt. He tore it from her in his haste to see the wealth hidden beneath it.

His gaze raked over her breasts. She tried to bolt around him. He grabbed her. His hands bruised her shoulders and arms. Like a demented woman, she fought him. She screeched and scratched at his eyes. Spinning her around, he twisted her arms behind her back. A hand groped at her waist and untied her leggings. They fell to the floor to tangle around her ankles.

She kicked out at him and almost fell. He ran a hard, calloused hand over her back and down to squeeze her bare buttocks. Frantic, she jerked away. He slapped her bottom with a hard, stinging blow. He forced her to lean over, and he cursed at her to be still as he thrust and bumped his groin against her inflamed flesh.

Netta cried out. She lurched forward. Her twisted leggings tripped her. He let go of her wrists. With avid glee, he watched as her naked body hit the ground. When she tried to pull her clothing back up, he stamped his foot on them. Chortling, he pulled her shoes free and yanked the leggings away. Netta scurried backward and wedged herself into a corner. Seeing the straining bulge in his breeches, she sobbed, terrified.

"The 'igh and mighty lord what hired me will ne'er know I sampled 'is dove. I'll tell 'im I stole ye from the stable where ye rutted with yer Mereck of Blackthorn." He leaned down and reached for her, tearing at the dirty rope securing his own clothing.

Netta was close. Mereck felt her.

"Do you hear her?" Connor asked.

Mereck held up his hand. In his mind he saw the abandoned bothy. And he saw Netta being shoved through the doorway. She fell to the ground. Wrath flooded him, changing him. His soul hardened, became ruthless. Curses rang from his lips as he guided *M'Famhair* to find a seldom-used path. He urged the great horse faster. When they neared the clearing, his hand lifted, signaling Connor to dismount.

For what the lout was doing to Netta, he longed to crush his filthy neck within his grasp. Swift and silent, he ran down the path to the shelter.

Netta's frightened scream overwhelmed his mind.

Mereck roared with rage. He seized the sagging door and tore it from its last hinge.

'Twas Baresark who hurled it to the ground.

Chapter 18

The brutish creature's filth-encrusted nails tore at the stubborn knot in his breeches. He grunted and cursed, sending spittle flying from his lips while he fought to free his sex.

Netta retched and choked from the stench of his urine-soaked clothing. She hunched in a ball to protect her naked flesh. She could go nowhere. If she tried to kick him again, he would seize her ankle and have her on her back afore she could escape him.

"Take yer 'ands away, devil girl. I wants to see yer pretty nippies get 'ard and eager-like when ye sees me cock." He paused to yank her hands from her breasts and force her arms to her sides. He stared, drool running from the corners of thick, purple lips. His tongue, covered with a thick yellowish coat, licked it away. Frustrated with his efforts to unknot the ties, he drew his knife.

He meant to slit her throat! Netta screamed. The sound no sooner left her lips than the door tore from its last hinge and hurtled to the ground. A huge shape lunged through the doorway, blocking the light. It was impossible to see who stood there.

Mereck's gaze tracked Netta's whimpers. He spied his little bride. Naked on the floor with her back pressed into a corner, she had brought her legs close to her body, hiding her female secrets. She clutched her arms over her chest, shielding her breasts. Throaty, bestial snarls filled the room.

Kill the bastard!

Erupting with rage, Mereck leaped across the room. A man crouched opposite Netta, his knees touching her. He jerked up, a knife in his hand, and swung around. Had Mereck cared, he would have been wary of the steel. The man lunged at him, sweeping the blade from left to right and back again, leaving streaks of blood across Mereck's chest, arms and face. Mereck ignored them. He pivoted and struck the blackguard's wrist with his booted foot. The knife fell to the ground.

Mereck's big hands fisted. He put all his strength behind a smashing blow to the hated face. Teeth gave way under his knuckles. He struck again. His opponent lashed out, clouting Mereck on the mouth and eye. Mereck didn't flinch but drove repeated blows to the man's stomach and ribs. He then aimed for the huge nose. He grunted with satisfaction. The cartilage gave way, followed by a steady flow of blood. He shifted to the left, bringing his left fist from low on his hip. With his weight behind the blow, he aimed for his antagonist's jaw. The man lifted off the ground and hurtled across the room to land against the wall. Like the snake he was, he slithered to the floor.

Lightning fast, Mereck pounced on him. This creature had hurt his Netta, had bruised and terrified her. Knowing how quickly foul men violated their victims, feral growls ripped from his throat. Blood roared in his ears. His hands closed around the hated throat. Voices shouted at him. The words sounded like gibberish. Hands grappled with his arms. He ignored them. He squinted his eyes and watched the loathsome face turn purple, the eyes bulge from their sockets.

Mereck finally paid heed to Netta. Only her terrified cries reached him. He shook his head; his eyes cleared. Connor's voice came through. Surprised, he found Connor and Marcus clinging to his arms like leeches. He fought to calm the great gasps of air he drew into his lungs. He nodded his head to let them know he understood. Finger by finger, he released his grip and dropped the odious head to the floor.

He stood. The muscles in his legs twitched, trying to control their need to kick at the still body. He lurched to Netta. She stared, as terrified of him as of her abductor. He struggled to quiet his shaking voice.

"Be not afeard. He will ne'er hurt you again." He reached to take her in his arms, but she screamed and recoiled. Her dilated eyes fixed on his blood-soaked hands.

Netta knew this must be the man who paid for her abduction. This face, so filled with rage and blood lust, was strange to her. She had seen the men battle. Had watched in horror each blood splattering blow. When her abductor's face had turned purple, his eyes bulged and his tongue protruded, she had vomited til nothing was left in her stomach.

"Mo gradh, my love. He canna hurt you now. Come, let me hold you."

Mereck's voice spoke from the strange face. He reached for her. She saw only the blood on his hands and patterned across his bare chest and plaid. It dripped from cuts on his face. The face that belonged to the savage. Baresark! Where were his furs? The bands on his arms?

"Nay, nay. Do not."

Her cries of fear shamed her. She cringed away from him, and longed to become one with the wall. Frantic, she tried to hide her body. Hysterical tears flowed down her cheeks.

"Please. Do not beat me. I did not run away."

"Netta, love, I would ne'er beat you. You canna believe I would do such a thing."

She couldn't understand his words for the roaring in her ears.

Mereck was sick with regret. Netta had seen him at his worst. He always kept a tight rein on his temper. But when he witnessed cruelty to the helpless, he couldna and fought blindly, nothing in his mind but killing. He knew if they had not stopped him, he would have savaged the man until not an inch of flesh was left unmarked.

Netta stared at him with such fear and loathing. And then she fainted. He stood and fumbled with his plaid. He would cover her nakedness.

"Nay, mon. Too bluidy." Connor put his arm around Mereck and squeezed his shoulder. Mereck's pale stricken face showed how badly it hurt for his bride to have seen him lose control. "Marcus found her clothin'. Ye should dress her while she doesna know of it."

Mereck took Netta's clothes and knelt, while both men turned their backs to the woman on the floor. He slipped her arms through the sleeves of the torn shirt without much difficulty. The drawstring breeches were another matter. Who would have thought such small, limp legs would be so hard to manage?

The ugly bruises and scratches on her tender skin sickened him. He wanted to resurrect the man. To kill him again. The icy fear bound around his heart eased, for he saw no sign of blood on her thighs. He closed his eyes. Tilting his face heavenward, he uttered a prayer of thanks for sparing his Netta. He no sooner slid the short tunic over her head than she stirred.

Remorse was a physical pain on hearing her cry out when she saw him. His touch frightened her. Helpless, he jerked back. His eyes pleaded with Connor.

"Netta, 'tis I, Connor." Connor inched closer to her.

She looked at him. She recognized Connor and reached frantic hands for him. He went down on his knees, and she wrapped trembling arms around his neck. Her tears soaked his shirt. He soothed and stroked her in a brotherly way, until her stiff body began to relax. At last, her eyes focused on him. She looked at neither Mereck nor the body on the floor.

Moving out of her sight, Mereck unwrapped his plaid and wiped blood from his face and body with the ends of it. Reversing it, he again put it on. He would hide as much of his torn flesh as he could. He glanced at the sprawled body on the floor and moved to block the sight from Netta. When he finished belting his plaid, they were ready to leave.

"Take her up with you, Connor. Marcus, round up the men and bring that foul body back to Blackthorn. Mayhap someone will recognize him."

Connor passed Netta to Marcus until he mounted. Mereck watched to see his cousin settled her safely with him. She hid her face against Connor's shoulder. Her crying slowed to whimpers.

The ride back to Blackthorn took forever. Netta's body ached. She kept seeing Mereck's face while he had fought. His eyes had narrowed to slits. Hate and fury flashed like jolts of lightning from them. Inhuman snarls tore from his throat, and his teeth bared like a wolf ready to rip into the flesh of a kill. The veins stood out on his neck and the backs of his hands. His fingers had squeezed the man's throat until the face became a thing of nightmares. Those beautiful fingers, which had caused her to shiver and secretly dream of them exploring her body, now caused her to shudder at the thought.

They clattered over the drawbridge and up to the keep's

entrance. Everyone seemed to be awaiting there. Elise and Meghan raced to meet them; Damron and Brianna hurried to follow. The laird studied his half brother's battered face.

When Damron's gaze turned to Netta, her fear increased. She saw the hard expression on his face. She felt impaled by his steady green gaze. With a guilty pang, it hit her.

All that had happened was her fault.

She should not have dressed as a squire, and she should not have gone down to practice alone. Worst of all, when she found herself outside the gates, she should have returned and faced Mereck.

"Ohh, Netta, where have you been?" Elise hopped up and down, trying to see her friend's face. "Connor, let her down from there this instant."

Mereck jerked his head at Damron. He came forward to take Netta from Connor. When she murmured she would walk, Damron helped her to stand. Everyone outside the barbican could have heard Elise's loud cry.

"Saints preserve us! Your face is swollen like a squirrel with a cheek full of nuts. How did you get that bruise?" She rounded on Connor and Mereck. Fury flashed from her blue eyes. Her hands clenched at her waist. "Did you do this? I will have my father thrash you. And Bleddyn will run you through. What has happened to my Netta?"

The men blinked at her sudden change from a meek, frightened girl to an avenging angel.

"They had no hand in this," Netta whispered. "I fell from my horse." She was so unclean. So shamed. Not only had the horrible man seen her naked, but so had Mereck and the others.

"Please, may I go to my room?"

She heard Mereck ask Brianna for a bath to be brought

up to her. She could not look at him to thank him, but bobbed her head.

"Come, little one." Meghan's voice was brisk. Masking her help in a friendly gesture, she put her arm around Netta's waist to lead her up the stairs. "Ye have the looks of a lass who needs pamperin'. Do ye not? A guid hot bath for ye, and Elise and I will have ye to rights in no time. That we will." She nodded to Brianna, letting her know she would look after Netta.

Damron took Brianna's arm and motioned the men to come to his solar. By the time she cleansed and treated Mereck's battered face and body, the warriors returned from the forest.

"What?" Mereck roared with rage. "How could a man who looked to be dead get on a horse and ride?"

"We tracked him into the mountains, then his trail disappeared. He vanished like he had been picked up on wings and carried away." Marcus raked his hair with frustration. "From the blood that soaked the dirt of the bothy, he canna last the night. He'll become faint and guide his horse off a cliff."

In the women's room, Meghan acted like Netta had just returned from an outing. Netta was grateful.

Elise clucked over her as they undressed her for her bath. "Did you fall on a pile of rocks? Blessed saints, even your breasts have bruises. Why were you outside the curtain walls, Netta?" She propped her hands on her hips and frowned.

"I thought to meet Meghan returning from the hunt. Neither I nor the nag I borrowed was skilled at jumping. A tree lay across the path. The horse went up. I went down. Smack into a pile of rocks, just like you said."

Netta no sooner finished soothing Elise than Brianna came to ask Elise for her help with Serena. Brianna nodded at Meghan as she drew Elise from the room.

"Ye were smart not to scare yer friend with the truth." Meghan's no-nonsense voice was soft. "Dinna think I will fall fer the same fib. Many a long year has passed since Mereck wore that mask of self-loathing. And I saw the look on me brither's face. I canna believe Mereck did this to ye. Yet ye would not look at the mon. Set my mind to rest. Tell me the happenin's."

"Oh, Meghan. I'm so ashamed. They saw me naked. And Mereck went berserk with blood all over him, and his eyes and tongue bulged from his face and blood poured from his nose and mouth." Netta gasped for breath.

"Mereck's eyes and tongue bulged?" Meghan cocked her head to the left and frowned. "I saw his battered face, but I didna think it wud cause bluid to gush."

"Not Mereck's. That horrid man's blood. Now I can't look at Mereck and his beautiful hands because they made his horrible tongue come out."

"Slow down, henny. Take a deep breath. Begin with the reason ye dressed as ye were."

"'Tis all my fault." Netta began to sob. "He forbade me to dress in Connor's old clothes, but I did it anyway." She took a deep breath and tried to calm her speech to recount her dreadful experience. It was hard to remain coherent when so many conflicting fears tore at her.

Fear of discovery when she saw Mereck coming through the bailey changed to horror of her revolting kidnapper. When Mereck become the nightmarish Baresark before her eyes, terror had filled her soul.

Now, when Damron's hard gaze had swept her from head to toe, she had the dreadful knowledge she was not worthy to be a part of his family.

She was soiled.

Laird Damron would send her back to her father in disgrace.

Chapter 19

Netta squeezed her eyes tight, denying the room's blackness was lightening to gray, for it foretold dawn. She longed to hide in the room, but she could not. Her thoughts turned as gloomy as the Highland day was sure to be.

She was thankful Meghan was with her when the sun rose high and Spencer arrived to request her presence in the laird's solar. Her stomach churned. Inside the solar, it took all her courage to look at the laird. Damron's face was not forbidding as she expected.

"Good morn, Netta." His voice was soft, his eyes gentle. "Ye look verra tired. Did ye not sleep at all last night?"

"I could not, milord. I have disgraced myself." The words flew out of Netta's mouth. "I understand why I'm unfit, and you wish to send me back to Father. Mereck thinks me unclean. Despoiled. Truly, I didn't know the horrible man lurked about. I even caused Mereck to turn into a raving beast." Her breath caught on a sob. "Now Father will surely marry me to a swineherd."

She clenched her teeth to keep from blurting out another thought. Oh, God in heaven. Without thinking, she had rattled on saying everything that came to her mind, just one thing after the other, and goodness she even did it in her thoughts. It must be the wine Meghan made her drink before coming here.

"Why do ye think my brither believes ye despoiled?"

Netta stared at the tips of Damron's boots. A curl slipped over her brow, and he brushed it back from her bruised face.

"Why? Because." She blinked, trying to ward off tears of shame. "That is why."

"Because of what, Netta?"

"He tore my clothes off." She swallowed and kept her voice low. Only he would hear her.

"Me brither?" Damron's voice rose in surprise.

"Nay. That foul man. He touched me and bumped me and ruined me, and everybody saw me naked." Her last words trailed off. She swiped away the tears wending their way to her jaw, and felt further shame when she hiccupped.

Damron patted the top of her head. Before he drew Mereck and Connor to the far end of the room, he eyed Meghan and tilted his head at Netta.

Meghan moved close to smooth the ebony curls back from Netta's damp cheeks. "Henny, because the man mistreated ye doesna mean ye are unclean or soiled. Did he hurt ye in any other way ye didn't tell me of?"

"That filthy man bumped me." She hiccupped again, then looked suspiciously at Mereck. She pulled Meghan between them to safeguard her thoughts. "He didn't sound like it hurt him the way Marcus had in the stable, but he bumped me and moaned and beat my bare bottom when I tried to get away."

"Bumped ye?"

"Aye."

Meghan sounded more than a little confused to Netta.

She looked it, too. Why, her not knowing about bumping was strange.

"Tell me about this 'bumping' and Marcus. Why do ye think it makes ye unclean?"

Netta blushed and described what she saw Marcus doing in the stable. She told her how the vile man had kept bumping his horrible sex against her arse while he fought to free his tarse. Meghan chuckled. Netta didn't think it was one bit funny. Meghan hugged her and told her the "bumping" forced on her was nothing like what Marcus had done, for the man had not uncovered his sex.

"Blessed saints. He didn't despoil me? I am only unclean?"

"Nay. Ye're not unclean either. I had me doubts ye would have any skin left on yer hide the way ye scrubbed it last eve."

Netta was woozy with relief. Or was it the wine again? She wished they had waited one more day to question her, for every bone in her body ached.

Reassuring warmth, like a warm breeze blowing across the room, flowed from her head to her toes. On a dreary Highland day? Puzzled, she peeked around Meghan in the direction it seemed to come from, and met Mereck's gaze. She could not believe the warmth and gentleness there, so at odds with his battered face. So very at odds with the Baresark she had seen.

He came toward her, his voice as soft as his look. "Netta, lass. You are neither unclean nor despoiled. Not one thing that another could do to you would e'er make you unworthy. E'en if the worst had happened, you would remain pure in my eyes."

He lifted his once beautiful hands to touch her face. She flinched and drew back. His battered knuckles were split and swollen now. The blackguard's dirty nails had dug long bloody gashes in their backs when he fought to free his wretched neck from their grasp.

Mereck dropped his hands and stepped away, his movements stiff and painful.

Wary still, she studied him. She noted the cuts on his face, on his arms. White bindings swathed his chest. Merciful heavens. The swelling on his left cheekbone almost closed his eye. His split lower lip looked likely to bleed if he smiled. Her stomach sank. She had caused this.

Brianna called out Damron's name and entered the room. Netta was grateful for the respite. The changes in Damron's face whenever his wife was nearby still surprised her. Why, that huge man near turned to mush. Elise trailed behind her, her eyes wide with surprise.

"Cloud Dancer flew right to the window opening of Brianna's solar. He had a parchment bound to his leg." Elise's voice squeaked with excitement. "Look. Bleddyn rolled and sealed it with wax. Like a regular missive." She was so interested she ignored Connor's arm around her shoulders, and even that he drew her against his side.

"He is but a day away. Father Matthew is with him." Brianna handed her husband the Welshman's message.

"What say ye to a wedding Sunday, two days hence, lass?"

Damron strolled over to sit on the edge of the table he used to keep his accounts. He handed the small missive to Mereck.

Netta hoped he was speaking to Elise. He was not. He looked at her, waiting for an answer. She blanched. How could she stand in front of the world and God and vow to be a wife? She was woefully ignorant on matters between a man and woman. What if he didn't like the way she bumped? She would sooner spend her life in a nunnery than chance angering Mereck.

"Should we not wait until Spring? We do not know each other well. Lord Bleddyn wouldn't want us to be hasty." Seeing Damron's brows raise, she added, "Surely he would not."

Mereck came to stand toe to toe with her.

"Netta, Bleddyn himself suggested we hold the ceremony on his arrival." His forefinger under her chin lifted her face. He did not let her flinch away. "You may go to your room and rest, but you must attend the evening meal. We will announce our plans then."

She thought to protest; he frowned and shook his head.

"You will be there," he commanded and released her. He kept his gaze on hers, showing her his resolve.

Well, rats. Hundreds of fleas, too. He was doing his mind thing again. She had a hard time tearing her gaze from his. When she did, she turned and bounded from the room. Elise was hot on her heels.

"I suspected the same as Bleddyn has written," Mereck told the others after she left. "It was no random assault, and no paid kidnapping for ransom. It had the flavor of revenge." In his concern over Netta's distress, he forgot Meghan was in the room. "I believed it was the MacDhaidh, but Bleddyn suggests otherwise." Hearing Meghan's alarmed thoughts, Mereck rubbed his hand over his face, winced and drew it away.

"Let me see the note." Meghan snatched it from Damron's hand and scanned it quickly. "Saxon men are eejits."

"Aye. They are passing strange." Mereck flexed his shoulders to ward off the stiffness settling in. "Baron Wycliffe has a problem I couldna wish on a more despicable father. The fool insists Netta's a changeling, though Bleddyn confirms she looks markedly like her mother."

"He must be havin' a time of it, what with five of her

former suitors threatenin' war." Damron strolled over and sat on a chair. He patted his lap while looking at Brianna. She soon settled against him with a sigh.

"They believe he betrayed them. When they heard Wycliffe betrothed her by his infamous decree, they must have been furious since they previously offered their suits. An immediate wedding is wise." Brianna wriggled on her husband's lap. He growled deep in his throat; she giggled and cuddled closer. "That wily old bastard will take the biggest bribe to break your contract."

"We will have the wedding. I canna promise the bedding."

Mereck's face was rueful as he sprawled in a chair next to Damron's. He raked his fingers through his hair, messing it.

"Oh?" Damron's voice rose in surprise.

"Don't you understand, husband?" Brianna prodded him with a sharp elbow. "I doubt that doughy old Wycliffe ever lifted a sword in his life. He never exposed Netta to warriors. Not only did her abductor frighten her near witless, but she saw a man being strangled by her betrothed's hands. Mereck will have a hard time getting those hands on her any day soon."

Damron pinched her as a warning to still her wriggling against his already turgid rod. "Well now, brither. I seem to remember yer great laugh at my expense when ye learned I didna have my weddin' night fer sennights."

"Aye, but that was different. Your bride was mad as Hades at you. Netta is afeared I'll drain her very sanity from her. Now she's terrified I'll go berserk and strangle her. How did you fake your, uhh, husbandly duties?" Mereck's smile was bleak.

"Hah. Your ever diligent brother near cut his arm off over the sheets. Thinking he skewered me in haste, my poor aunts were so upset." Brianna scowled at Damron while waiting for them to stop laughing. She used her name for him when she continued. "It's not funny, milord Demon. You didn't have to accept those jars of healing salve and wonder why everyone was so worried."

"If ye do not stop yer wrigglin', wife, ye will have need of those jars afore the day passes." His eyes twinkled when her hand flew up to cover his mouth.

To Netta's thinking, the hours passing were far too swift. She dressed in a light green chemise with a deep green tunic, and a silver girdle hung low on her hips. Elise combed and arranged Netta's black, silky curls to sweep down her forehead to hide the bruises on her face.

Netta explored one excuse after another to avoid going to the hall. She finally hid one of her shoes in the bed-covers.

"I must needs send Mereck a message that I cannot attend the evening meal. He would not want me to appear wearing naught but stockings." She pretended a diligent search for the missing shoe.

"Do you think that great wolf took your shoe?" Elise's eyes grew huge with the thought. "Maybe he ate it thinking it a part of you."

"Guardian wouldna do such. He likes his meat raw. The shoe is leather." Meghan grinned at her. "How can ye lose one shoe, Netta? The other is here where ye left it before yer bath." She stopped her own search to watch the Saxon girls.

"You could have lost it when we hurried up here. Perchance you left it outside the door."

Elise cracked open the door and peeked out. When she found nothing that even resembled the missing shoe, she searched the room. When she came to the bed, she knelt to thrust her head beneath the bed ropes. She drew back, sneezed and rubbed her eyes, declaring it far too dark to see. She marched over to Netta's trunk and lifted the lid, then near stood on her head while she searched through the few things there.

She must have made herself dizzy between the kneeling and leaning over, for she wobbled her way to the bed and threw herself face down.

"Youch!" She jumped up, rubbed her breast and scowled.

Meghan pulled back the cover and found the missing shoe. She turned to Netta and shook her head.

"Ye willna get off so easily. If ye dinna hurry, Mereck will be demandin' ye come to the meal."

"Aye, shoeless or not, you will come. Without delay." Mereck braced his shoulder against the doorframe and crossed his arms over his chest.

Netta groaned. How long had he been there?

"Wife, put on your shoes." His voice softened to a husky purr. "If you dinna, I must carry you down. I wouldna want the stones to injure your feet."

Stiff from bruised and injured areas she could not see, he moved toward her without his usual grace.

Netta's heart slammed against her ribs. She shivered at the thought of him carrying her anywhere. He was so big he filled the doorway. She didn't think she was a coward. Any woman would be leery of such a giant. His eyes, the color of a new leaf, stared at her. They didn't soften.

She grabbed the shoe from the floor and leaned against the bedpost to slide it on. After she snatched the second from atop the covers, she hopped in a circle trying to slip it on her foot. A sigh, sounding like a strong gust of wind, should have warned her. It ruffled the hair on her head. She gasped when he lifted her, sat on the bed and settled her on his lap. She sucked in a full breath, capturing his scent.

"Be still," Mereck's deep voice cautioned. He slid the remaining shoe on her foot and laced both shoes around her ankles. When done, he lifted her like a child and stood her in front of him. His gaze scanned over her to see if she had missed putting on anything else. Satisfied, he turned her toward the door and gave her a light shove.

She startled. He may have meant it as a command to get her moving, but she thought it was more an excuse to touch her arse with his big hand. She did what he expected—she bolted. Before she remembered she didn't want to go down to the hall, she was halfway down the stairs.

On the last step, she halted. Memory of her disgrace flooded back on seeing the crowded hall. She backed up a step. Mereck's hard body, but one step above hers, pressed against her. The back of her head was against his lower ribs, her shoulders against his corded stomach.

Saints help her. Something hot and hard jutted against her back. When she realized what it must be, she flew down the remaining steps. Connor, who stood at the foot of the stairs, took her arm to steady her. She scowled at him when he laughed. He didn't release her until Mereck took possession of her arm.

Damron sauntered over to thunk a pewter tankard hard on the high table, getting everyone's attention.

"We will have a weddin' on Sunday, just two days hence. Mereck and Lynette will be joined as man and wife. We have much to prepare in so short of time, and I expect yer help."

By the rowdy response, Netta expected the men looked forward to the diversion. Mereck seated her and selected the choicest morsels of the foods she enjoyed. When her stomach rumbled, she realized how hungry she was. He waited, patient, not eating himself. Did his lips and jaw hurt too much to attempt it?

His belabored face made her stomach lurch with guilt. It was her fault the horrible man abducted her. And if she had not worn male apparel, he might not have wondered what lay beneath her clothing. She was to blame for Mereck's rage when he found her naked to the man's eyes. Her fault, too, that he had turned into Baresark before her eyes.

She was the cause of his split lips and swollen face. She cringed, thinking of the blood that had streaked across his chest from the foul man's knife. If she had not been so selfish in wanting to practice alone, that hateful man wouldn't have injured him. She glanced up at his beautiful eyes, then dropped her gaze to her clasped hands.

"Mereck. I am so very sorry."

Her whispered voice barely carried to him. He tilted his head. What he didn't hear with his ears, he heard with his heart and mind.

"Ah, little wife, 'tis not your fault the man stole you away. 'Twas mine. I should have better protected you. The blame was not yours that I did not keep a rein on my temper. You did not cause my rage."

Noting her puzzled expression, he tried to explain.

"Seeing what he had done to you, I wanted to break every bone in his hateful body. 'Twas not because Connor or Marcus saw you unclothed, but because he dared to strike you and tear your clothes from your body. No one should e'er cause you pain, whether of the body, or of the mind. No person has the right to treat you in that way. Not me. Not your father. Not anyone.

"Come now. Eat and regain your strength. You have been through a terrible ordeal."

Her face relaxed. He smiled and coaxed laughter from her when he related escapades he and the other men had gotten into as young lads.

All through the night Netta tossed and turned, no longer sure how she felt about Mereck. His voice, his beautiful hands, the way he looked at her so tenderly made her heartbeat quicken. When she thought of his scent, of his hot skin and graceful body, she sighed. However, she was still frightened of the unknown. At last she fell into a restless sleep.

On going down to the hall to break her fast at dawn, she found Bleddyn sat at the table with Mereck and Damron. Blue paint covered the left side of his face, and red outlined the long ragged scar on the right side. He dressed much as Mereck did at Wycliffe, but instead of wolf skins across his shoulders he wore his beautiful cape.

His black eyes glanced at Mereck and Damron. Both left without a word. Well, rats. Did everyone in this blasted keep read thoughts? Mayhap Mereck had signaled Damron in some other way, she decided, trying to calm herself.

"Mereck told me of your horror when you witnessed the fight, Netta. Fearing conflict is natural for you. Wycliffe was isolated, and you never saw a castle besieged. While your father did his share of killing in his time, they have not called him to war since he injured his leg. You were but a babe at the time. He has paid scutage since, and sent knights in lieu of his own service to the king."

Netta nodded. "I don't think I should marry Mereck until we know each other better. He will surely find we do not suit. Then what will happen?" She didn't give him time to reply. "Why, he will be unhappy every time I think ugly things about the dreadful gift he possesses. He might even be angry enough he would never allow me to again have another sensible thought." She shuddered.

"Do you believe him to be so cruel?" Bleddyn's black eyes crinkled at the corners. "Mereck has long since learned to control his gift."

"Then how did he know when I was where I should not be the other day? Also, how did he find me in that horrible abandoned bothy?" Her frown deepened.

"That day you went out to the warrior's practice field with Elise and Meghan, he heard your surprise at what you saw. In the bothy, your mind cried out for him to save you. These were unusual conditions, where you could not help sending him your thoughts."

"Oh, saints alive," she groaned, resting her elbows on the table and putting her chin in her hands. How could she go through life without any surprises? Would she have to think only dull, ordinary thoughts? She'd rather go to bed and not get up again. Her eyes brightened. Could she plead an illness?

"Netta, do not think to delay your wedding." His smile was kind.

She threw up her arms and muttered, "I'll never think near you both again, just see if I do."

"I should tell you that several of your former suitors attempt to force your father to break your betrothal contract. If the baron will not agree, they plan to seek the king's aid. Do you favor one of these men over Mereck? Tell me your choice, and I will consider it. If you prefer none to Mereck, you had best wed on the morrow. Your father will attempt to give you to the man with the most influence at court. If you have wed, the matter is closed."

Did she favor another? Ugh. Not Edward of Chester, who shoved her in alcoves and tried to suck her earlobes. William of Hampstead was not too awful. Except that he said she would have to defer to his mother in all things. The hateful woman would ruin her disposition in a day's time. She grew nauseous thinking of Charles and placed her hand over her nose. His rotted teeth had caused her to hold her breath every time he spoke. Hmpf! Several other were not suitable either, because of their attitudes. They thought of her as chattel, nothing more.

Not one of them would allow her to have a bow and arrows. She was sure of it. In fact, she could not recall a single man who would trouble to teach her to use a sword. Except for Mereck. Nor would they be kind enough to allow her a pet. Or her own raptor.

She sighed. Never before had she felt the strange yearning that filled her when Mereck came near. Nor did she recall feeling heat in the center of her body when any other man touched her arm. She felt it with Mereck. Not only the heat, but other more curious sensations. Just a look from him, for that matter, and her body tingled and throbbed in alarming places.

She sighed again. Still in deep thought, she stood and left the room.

Mereck was hers. She was going to keep him.

Chapter 20

"Hurry, Netta, hurry. 'Tis late. The sun is already high."

Elise's burst of excited chatter awoke Netta the next morn. She swallowed, scrunched her eyes tight, and tried to hide beneath the covers. What foolish reasoning befuddled her brain into keeping Mereck? Saints help her! She must wed him today. Panic sizzled through her veins. Her stomach lurched like she rode the waves crashing against the cliffs below.

Elise darted around the room with the servant Bran following her from one side of the room to the other, trying to slip Elise's shift on her. Meghan sat on the bed laughing at them both.

"Do you want to eat first, or take your bath? Meghan ordered your bath, and Bran brought our food so we need not go down to the hall. You can have mine. I'm too excited to eat. You must keep up your strength though."

Elise skidded to a halt. Bran seized the moment to pull the tunic over her head.

"Bran said you must eat for energy because sleeping with a man is strenuous. Why?" She looked expectantly at Bran.

Bran grinned, but kept her reasons to herself.

Elise frowned and drew her own conclusions. "Of course! It is because they snore and flop around on the bed. That is why Bran is so stiff this morn. She said her husband was restless last night."

"I dinna think his floppin' caused it. What say ye, Bran?" Meghan's eyes twinkled; laughter was in her voice.

"He ne'er flops. At least not fer long. He be more the rammin' kind." Bran rolled her eyes and sighed.

Netta looked at Elise and shrugged. What were they talking about? Mayhap eating would fill that falling sensation in the pit of her stomach. A bad decision. Ugh! The porridge clung to her mouth like a lump of rising dough.

"Ye must eat, Netta, else that bear grumblin' in yer stomach will frighten Father Matthew when ye say yer vows." Meghan chuckled and handed her a hot scone slathered with honey and a goblet of milk.

Never had she taken so long to eat so little. She couldn't swallow without a gulp of milk to wash it down. After several bites, she hid the scone under a linen cloth.

"Ye'll not get away with such. Eat now, or ye will faint when ye see yer handsome husband awaitin' below." Meghan raised a brow and swiped the cloth off.

Brianna slipped into the room, a beautiful smile on her face.

"Netta, I've never seen Mereck at such loose ends. I doubt he slept a wink. In the wee hours of morning, Damron heard swords clashing on the practice field. He found Mereck and Bleddyn happily grunting and slashing at each other, as happy as two dogs with a yard full of bones." She smoothed Netta's wedding dress out on the bed and grinned at her. "He'll want to retire early tonight and get a good night's sleep."

That sounded like a good idea to Netta. After the

wedding banquet, she would suggest he looked weary and should hie himself off to bed. With any luck at all, he would be fast asleep afore she joined him. She sighed with relief and got into her waiting bath.

Below in the men's bathing room, two oversized wooden tubs sat in the center of the room opposite a fireplace, a naked man in each. Buckets of steaming rinse water awaited nearby. Drying cloths, large enough to wrap around a warrior's body, rested atop a crude pine table. A long gutter ran from beside the tubs and ended at a narrow opening that emptied the water into the moat.

Mereck's lips quirked in a smile as he stared up at the ceiling.

Damron threw a glob of soap, striking him on the shoulder.

"Stop listenin', brither. Let the lass keep her thoughts private on her weddin' day."

Mereck waited in the hall with Father Matthew, Damron at his side. He watched the stairway, uneasy that Netta might still balk at marrying him. He couldna let her. Not only because of what she brought to him—Caer Cadwell, its holdings and great wealth—things he, a bastard, had never dared dream about. More important was the greatest gift. Netta. He watched her coming down the grooved granite stairs, her hand clutching Bleddyn's arm.

She was the most beautiful bride a man could dream of. When he looked at her, his body's response was as powerful as if he hadna had a woman in many years. He kept a close rein on his thoughts, for he didna want to send her scrambling from the room if she noted how she aroused him.

An ice-blue smock, topped with a deep violet tunic the

color of her eyes, hid her graceful curves beneath it. The women had embroidered Celtic dragons on the square neckline of her overdress. More silver embroidery circled the full sleeves at her elbows; a silver filigree girdle rode low on her slender waist. A circlet of woven blue and violet ribbons banded her forehead and streamed down the back over her flowing black curls.

His fingers longed to comb through the silky hair falling past her waist; his lips longed to taste her slender neck. Meeting his gaze, she flushed and lifted her chin.

Netta mightily pleased him. Not for her appearance. Beauty is something with which a person is born. Her courage pleased him. Though she trembled, her eyes stayed bravely on his. He did not allow himself to hear her thoughts.

He knew she feared him.

He did not want to know he repulsed her.

To Netta, Mereck looked larger and more threatening than he had last eve. Blessed Saint Monica. Was the man growing? Or was it because he stood so still, watching her? With each downward step, she studied him.

He had braided his tawny hair on either side of his temples. His eyes were the light green of the sea on a calm day. He wore a creamy white shirt tucked beneath a finely woven green, black and blue plaid belted around his trim waist and draped over his shoulder.

Etched pewter decorated his sporran. What design was on it? She flushed, hoping he did not think she stared at anything other than the fur pouch. She had never seen the beautiful sword strapped to his side, its hilt encased with many jewels. Long white stockings covered from his feet up over muscular calves, black garters holding them just below his knees. Black leather shoes covered his feet.

"The sword you admire long ago belonged to his Welsh

great-great-grandfather Gruffyd," Bleddyn murmured. "Mereck's father, Donald, took it from the battlefield afore he found Aeneid, Mereck's mother."

Mereck's gaze engulfed her as she stood before him. Glancing up at his somber face, she blinked. She avoided his eyes in favor of his high cheekbones and strong nose. The bruises on his face were not as vivid. When she came to his full sensual lips, she decided he was a wolfishly handsome man.

"Come, the priest awaits." Mereck kept his voice gentle.

He smiled and offered his left hand, palm up and non-threatening. He watched her swallow and allow Bleddyn to place her hand in his. It felt like a small, quivering bird nestled there.

During the ceremony, he gently squeezed her fingers to remind her to respond to the vows. He was prepared to be resolute, if she offered resistence, for only he could protect her. Any man forced on her by her father would not be gentle, but would quickly kill her spirit.

"Mo fear bean, my little wife," he whispered.

"Are we married, then? 'Tis over?"

"Aye, we are wed. But until the night is through, 'tis not over." Not wanting to give her time to worry, he brushed a kiss on her lips. He intended only a light kiss, favoring his still sore lip, but found he could not separate from her sweetness. His arms enfolded her, molding her soft body to his. Gentle still, his lips moved over hers to nibble her lower lip. He drew its lush fullness between his teeth and sucked, arousing his male needs. A growl formed low in his throat when he released her,

He longed to taste all of her.

Netta studied his handsome face. She stared at his moist lips. They had tasted of mint. Her cheeks heated wishing he would kiss her again. Her mouth felt puffy. Would anyone notice? Well, rats, of course they would. They stood in the great hall, didn't they? When Mereck released her, her knees buckled. She was thankful he slipped his arm around her shoulders and held her close to his side.

"Dinna break her bones, brither," Damron cautioned, then kissed Netta on the forehead. "Welcome, wee sister."

"Ha, you call that a kiss of welcome?" Connor jostled Damron aside, took Netta's flushed cheeks between warm hands and kissed her soundly on the lips.

"Ouch!"

Mereck slammed his foot on Connor's toes. When a dainty foot kicked his leg, Connor's eyes widened in surprise. He glanced over his shoulder to find Elise scowling at him.

"What was that about, Mousie?"

"You're not supposed to kiss the bride that way." Her voice sounded stern.

"Oh? I didna know there is a special way to kiss a bride. Will you show me how to do it right? I dinna want to disgrace myself again." He pulled her into his arms and started to lower his lips to hers. She shoved him away.

"Horrid man. Keep your puckered lips to yourself."

Netta giggled and relaxed her stiff spine. The hall was fair to bursting with everyone at Blackthorn. One by one, knights and warriors offered their tributes. By the time they finished, the men had kissed every inch of her face. The younger men, who had hoped to win her hand, took their one opportunity to kiss her lips. As they drew back, Mereck spoke.

"Dawn. The far field after you break your fast. Be there." Each time he said it, his eyes became more stern, his expression more forbidding.

"It was well worth it," claimed one man.

"Can I have another and meet you twice?" another offered.

"Why are you asking them to meet you, husband?"

"Since they dinna work this day, they must practice harder the next."

"Ha. He speaks an untruth, Netta. He means to make them pay fer slabberin' on ye." Meghan chuckled and hugged Netta.

"Pay? You do not mean to punish them, do you Mereck?" She frowned at her new husband.

"Punish? I wouldna dream of it." He patted her shoulder and switched to Gaelic to say, "Nay. Not punish, but I sure as Lucifer's blood-speckled eyes plan to reshape some noses."

She started to ask Meghan what he said, but Eric stepped forward. He kissed her hand. Catching him wink at Mereck, she decided he did not want to deal with her husband at dawn.

Netta felt the weight of a ring on her finger. When had Mereck placed it there? She peeked and saw a silver band. Encircling the ring, the silversmith had engraved hearts connected with lovers' knots. In the center of the largest heart lay a glistening sea-green stone.

"Thank you for the beautiful token, Mereck." Feeling shy, she whispered.

"You are welcome. The band is a *mo cridhe,* a 'my heart' wedding ring. 'Tis the custom to place a jewel the color of the husband's eyes in the center heart. The other hearts are for children yet to be born."

"Hear me. Take yer seats so we may toast my brither's good fortune," Damron bellowed from the center of the room.

Netta sighed, relieved. Servants had covered the trestle tables with fine white linen, and at the head table stood silver trenchers and carved wooden spoons, along with silver chalices engraved with wolves and deers. She blinked at the chalice's size. How many toasts did they expect her and Mereck to honor?

No sooner did one toast finish afore another began.

Mayhap it was a good thing. If she could get her new husband to take a hearty swallow with each toast, he could not help but fall asleep as soon as he went to bed. As the toasting wore on, she relaxed. She was doing a fine job of hiding her fear of him.

Cook, with the aid of a score of servants, brought food to the tables. They had decorated the foods with violets, rose buds and marigolds. The aroma of roasted boar stuffed with mushrooms and large platters of beef, venison, veal, and oysters cooked with almonds and ginger made her mouth water. Bowls of beets, turnips, lettuce, and wild carrots in honey sat aside the meats. Brianna insisted on vegetables with each meal. Loaves of ale-flavored bread rounded out the meal.

Whenever Mereck offered her the wine chalice, she kept her eyes on his hands. By the time they served the puddings and pastries, she felt soft as butter. In fact, she felt downright boneless.

It took a mighty effort to keep her spine straight.

Much later, after the jugglers, mimes, acrobats and jongleurs finished entertaining, the clan piper Angus announced a contest to find the most agile sword dancer. Eager warriors scattered crossed swords on the floor in the center of the room until they covered every available spot.

"Merciful heavens, Netta. They are brainsick." Elise bolted up from her seat and pointed. "They have tippled so much they can hardly walk, yet they plan to dance around a bunch of sharp swords? Blood will be all over the place. Yes it will." She nodded so fast it was a wonder she did not make herself dizzy.

Before the words left her mouth, Connor vaulted over the table and joined the laughing men. Damron and Mereck refused to participate. Netta decided they did not because they were the most skillful and would ruin the other's chances. She thought it a most considerate thing to do.

Also sensible. Before the pipers began to increase the rhythm of the tune, several men limped from the floor. Netta found it a most interesting dance. When the music became livelier, so did the dancers.

Their knees lifted high; their plaids lifted higher.

"Could I have more wine, husband? 'Tis quite hot." Netta fanned her flaming face and avoided looking at the dancers. When she glanced sideways and saw Elise peeking between her fingers, she giggled. Mereck lifted a chalice to her lips. Cool water from the well. She looked at him, wondering.

"You dinna want to be sick on your wedding night, *mo cridhe,* my heart." He nuzzled the soft skin behind her ear.

"Nay." Why did her voice squeak like a mouse?

"Nay? Nay what, *mo bean,* my wife." His warm lips moved down the side of her neck and pressed a kiss on the hollow there.

"Nay, I do not wish to be sick, of course."

The music ended with Connor and Eric equally taking the honors. A strange little man came over to the table carrying a gaily painted jug. He spoke in Gaelic. Why did everyone cheer?

"Dougal has brought a gift of wedding mead," Mereck explained. "We will drink it each night for the next fortnight to assure a son will be born afore the year is out."

Netta's eyes widened at the mention of a son. "Merciful saints. I forgot about babes."

"Dinna you want children, wife?"

Though his voice was soft, she heard worry in it. She nodded, but how could she tell him it was the one thing that made her think this marriage would work. She had always wanted a babe. Now that they would be bumping, surely they would make one of their own. He smiled back at her with sleepy eyes.

"Would you like to seek your bed now, husband?" She hoped he would. If he didn't, they would stay here until he couldn't keep his eyes open.

"It has been a long day." His eyelids drooped even farther. He patted a yawn.

Why was Connor laughing? Mereck glared at him from near-closed lids. When her husband yawned again, Connor choked and put his hand over his mouth.

Concerned, Elise pounded his back. At least Netta thought it was Elise. Her eyes tended to see double. She rubbed them and blinked, until only one Elise appeared in her view.

"'Tis off to bed then. Mereck, give us a small while afore ye come bargin' up the stairs." Meghan took Netta by the elbow, Brianna smiled and stood, and Elise bounded off her bench to follow them.

Unfailingly polite, Netta thanked Damron, Lady Phillipa, Lord Douglas, Brianna, Elise, Connor, Meghan, the widows and even the four squires. Did she miss anyone? She frowned and looked for Marcus and Eric. Meghan tugged her forward.

"Do ye think to dawdle the evenin' away?" Meghan's smile broadened as she made sure Netta did not trip on the first step.

"Nay. I'm trying to wait until Mereck is near asleep."

Netta's whisper was more of a soft bellow. When she heard laughter, it surprised her. "They are all sotted," she explained to the women accompanying her. When the laugher grew, she craned her head and looked for the entertainer. "For truth, Scots are passing strange."

It was good she kept her head about her, for when they reached the third floor, the women bypassed Meghan's bedroom.

"You have forgotten where I sleep."

"Ye dinna sleep with us any longer. Mereck has taken the room next to Damron's. Bran has moved yer things to it and will serve as yer maid." Meghan grinned at her.

Netta skidded to a halt and dug in her heels.

"Mereck is your husband, love. You'll share his room from now on." Brianna put her arm around Netta and hugged her. "He'll keep you cozy and warm on our cold Scottish nights."

What a fine idea. She was inclined to be cold at night. Her feet moved on their own again, and before she knew it, she was in a new room.

To the left of the door, a fireplace cast a warm glow over the room. She hurried toward its warmth and stood on the thick fur rug. She enjoyed the heat while she looked around her. Two chairs stood near the hearth. A massive chest sat to the right of the doorway, a battered sword hung on the wall above it. When someone scratched on his door, did he greet them with his sword?

A tapestry picturing a castle high atop a hill covered much of the wall across from her. Someone had placed her clothing chest there. A brace of candles illuminated a huge bed with forest green bed curtains. Closed shutters blocked the night air from windows on either side of the bed.

Her body cooled and she glanced down. She wore only

her ice-blue smock. When did the women remove her wedding finery? Brianna asked her to lift her arms and keep them there for just a moment. The smock disappeared, and a lovely white sleeping garment replaced it. She sat in a tapestry-covered chair while Elise brushed her hair. A commotion outside the door startled her to her feet.

"Fair Netta, your husband is eager for your company," Connor shouted before the door burst open. He and Damron escorted Mereck into the room. Eric and Marcus crowded in behind them, silly grins on their faces as they slammed the door shut.

Mereck spied his lovely bride in front of the bright flames and glared a warning at the men. They grinned back. As he put the wedding mead on the small bedside table holding a platter and two silver goblets, Eric winked boldly at her, drawing Mereck's ire.

"Come, we keep them from their bedsport. Dinna forget to do what is necessary." Damron nodded at the eating knife tucked in Mereck's belt.

"Come, now, the hour grows late." Brianna kissed Netta's cheek and whispered, "Relax, love. Mereck will show you the way of it." She made sure everyone left before she followed them.

Mereck stared at Netta. The heat from his eyes warmed her front like the fireplace did her back. She swallowed. What should she do with her hands? Cover her chest, she decided. The women had cut the bodice dreadfully low on the sleeping garment. Why, her breasts showed above the neckline. 'Twas indecent.

Chapter 21

Lord in heaven! Mereck wanted Netta. The soft glow from the fireplace outlined her beautiful body. Though she thought she covered them, her breasts glowed beneath the gossamer gown, their pink tips inviting him. He indulged his senses, letting his gaze rove over her. He should no' have. Her softly rounded hips, and the black curls at the juncture of her thighs, stirred the need to touch her near beyond his control.

His heart hurtled blood through his veins straight to his manhood, making his ballocks painfully heavy. He willed his turgid shaft into obedience, for he tormented himself if he thought he could take his bride this night. Netta's wide-eyed gaze darted from his face to his hands. When they made love, he wanted her soft and yearning, not stiff and frightened.

"You are lovelier, my heart, than sun sparkling on dew-wet heather." Far from looking happy at the compliment, she seemed more uneasy. He was pleased she didn't place a high value on her beauty. He strolled to his war chest beside the door, unstrapped his sword and laid it and his belt atop it. When he again faced her, she took a step back, her eyes wary.

"Did you know Granda likened your bravery to that of Brianna when Damron first brought her to Blackthorn? I didna witness it myself. I was in Northumberland overseeing the rebuilding of Stonecrest Castle, her family home." Reaching up, he flicked open the ties of his shirt, exposing his strong, brown neck. "You and Brianna have much in common. She was at Saint Anne's Abbey with her sister Alana. When she learned Damron was on his way to fetch her, she also escaped to Ridley Castle." He shrugged and smiled. "We Morgan men are ill-fated to have the wedding before the wooing." He sat on the edge of the bed to remove his boots.

Netta eyed Mereck. Her forehead wrinkled. He didn't look sleepy anymore. He looked hungry. Perhaps she'd better feed him and ply him with more wine. That is, after she figured out how to do that deed and keep her chest covered. She couldn't stop blinking and wanting to yawn. Why are his eyes alert now? Is he no longer sotted? If she coaxed him to drink more wine, would he become drunkener again? She giggled. It didn't sound like the right word. Surely, there was one for that condition?

He removed his stockings. Blessed saints. He had beautiful calves. They were strong and muscled, with thick tawny hair covering them. It looked soft. She started to make a wide detour around an outstretched leg, but yearned to swerve close to brush against them. She caught herself in time. If she touched him, he might think she wanted to bump. She hiccupped.

Mereck stood, unpinned the large brooch holding the Morgan plaid and tugged his shirt free. Seeing his head disappear beneath it, she darted past to grab a wedge of cheese off the platter. If she could appease his hunger and coax him to drink the wine, he would surely fall asleep before he thought to remove the plaid belted about his waist.

"You look hungry, my lord." Netta thrust the cheese toward him and misjudged the distance. She gaped at the yellow smudge on his chest. How interesting. The muscles on the left side of his broad chest tightened and jumped upward. Did the wounds healing there cause it? She blinked and looked at the right to see if that side was also defective. For truth, it moved in the same manner. His warm hand gripped her wrist, interrupting her staring. She watched, fascinated as he lifted her hand and nibbled at the cheese. Her gaze darted to his face; his eyes crinkled at the corners. Suspicious, she glanced down to find both sides of his chest moving. She shoved the cheese into his hand and pulled back.

"How can a man laugh when beset with such a condition?" she muttered while searching for the wine. There wasn't any. Only the wedding mead. It would have to do. She poured the wedding goblet half full, debated a moment, then filled it to the top. She used both hands to lift it, and turned around. Mereck had disappeared. What happened to him? He was beside the bed a moment ago.

"Over here, Netta."

His velvety baritone sent shivers rippling down her back. She found him seated in a tapestried chair beside the fire. She took a deep breath, then took care with each step. For certs, the floor had faults in it. The wood was uneven and tended to sway.

Watching Netta scowl and make her way to him, Mereck's lips twitched. He took pity on her and rose to rescue the overfull vessel. He set it on the floor beside the chair and before she could resist, he lifted her in his arms and sat back down, holding her on his lap.

"I believe it will increase our enjoyment to drink it this way." He anchored her with his right arm across her legs while he stroked his left hand down her tense back. Several strokes later, her muscles softened. He picked up the goblet and pretended to take a hearty swallow. After, he held it to her lips. She took a dainty sip while eying him with suspicion.

"Dinna be afeared, little wife. Afore we seek our bed, we will enjoy the mead and the fire's warmth." Her muscles stiffened when he mentioned bed. She looked at the goblet in his hand, scowled up at him and then stared pointedly at it.

He cocked his head at her. "Do you think we should save the rest for later?"

She near jumped off his lap in alarm. "Now. We should drink it now, my lord." She grabbed his wrist and coaxed him to put the cup to his lips, tilting the bottom so quickly mead splashed down his chin.

He righted the goblet before the rest of him became awash in mead.

Netta's spellbound gaze followed the wet stream creeping to the hollow at the base of his neck. When it overflowed there, her eyes widened. She watched it ramble down his chest. The hair curling there diverted it into tiny rivers.

"Did you know you are clumsy? Almost as clumsy as my sister Prissy. She also spills her drinks." Netta grabbed the end of the plaid wrapped around his waist and patted the sticky liquid from his face and neck. She took great care around his injuries.

He forced his face to remain impassive. The raspy sound she heard while dabbing his cheeks puzzled her, for she leaned forward, squinted her eyes and stared at his chin. One lone finger came up and rubbed against it. When she felt the stubble there, she gave a pleased smile, looking like she had solved a great mystery. It must have made her thirsty, because she craned her neck toward the cup of mead.

"I would have a sip now, Mereck."

Her sip was a mouthful. He allowed her but one.

Emboldened, she patted and cleaned him, paying attention to the smudged cheese. Drawing back, she inspected her handiwork, but scowled when she saw the hair on his chest flattened to his skin. She dropped his plaid, took both hands and combed her fingers through the hair there, fluffing it.

"You shouldn't be so greedy about your drinking, husband."

When she hiccupped, she looked surprised. She squinted her eyes at him, as if the sound came from him. He could hardly contain the grin tugging at his lips.

"Thank you for instructing me, love. We have been wed less than a day, and already you have worked hard to improve my manners." He put the goblet on the floor and snuggled her closer against his chest. She looked pleased over his praise.

He tilted her chin so his lips could nuzzle her neck and kept his hands gentle. It was sweet torment feeling her velvet skin. Warm spring roses and heather teased his senses, and he could not resist the urge to taste her.

The tip of his tongue traced a path up her neck to her jaw. His hands soothed the chill bumps that formed on her arms. Before she could draw back, he rested his lips on hers. He kissed her, plying his mouth across hers until she began to respond. Cautiously, he moved back a wee distance. Her lips followed, delighting him. He lifted his head and smiled at her.

"Do you think we may go to bed now, wife? I am sorely tired and so very sleepy, but I didna want to disappoint you this night."

Mereck leaned his head back and covered his mouth, while he expanded his chest for a huge yawn. His arm tightened around her waist to keep from dumping her on the floor. His little bride's yawn was nigh as hearty as his own. Her eyes drooped.

"I'm most tired also, husband. Sleepy, too. But I'm never disappointed when I'm sleepy." She smiled and nodded her head.

When he carried her to the bed, Netta didn't seem to notice. She was too busy yawning and patting his chest. He held her against him with one arm while he pulled off the bed cover and blankets and dumped them on the floor. He easily stripped her gown from her and placed her on the bed before she thought to protest. Fast as a fox, he pulled the sheet up to her chin and tucked it around her.

He pinched out the candles, then kept his back to her while he undressed. He joined her in the bed, but didn't move for a short while. Finally, he eased on his side to face her. He saw the gleam of her eyes watching him.

"Rest well, little wife." He stroked her hair and kissed her forehead. She began to shiver from the cold. He smothered a grin. He knew he should be ashamed for pushing the warm blankets to the floor. But he was not.

"Come. Share my warmth," he murmured. He moved closer to her, and when he rolled her to her side and snuggled her back against his hot body, he thought she would bolt from the bed. Gritting his teeth, he willed his raging tarse to obedience.

Netta tried to edge her soft bottom away from him. He pulled her closer. He couldn't stop the groan that rumbled from his throat at the sweet torment.

"Are we bumping then, my lord?" Her whisper was near inaudible.

"Aye, wife, we are bumping." He could imagine how wide her eyes must be when his hot tarse came in contact with her warm skin. He rocked his hips against her soft, sweet arse until his breath rasped from his throat. He gritted his teeth, but kept up his gentle bumping. Surely he must be daft to torture himself so? At last, he moaned again and went still. She rewarded him for his efforts with a sigh of sympathy.

"I'm sorry for your pain, husband. Meghan says it gets better with time," she whispered. When he made a strangled noise, she made comforting sounds and gingerly patted his thigh.

His sweet, daft wife was asleep in seconds. He snuggled his pillow against her back, then got out of bed. He padded across the room to fetch his eating knife, then did what was necessary. Satisfied with the result, he went to the basin and pitcher of water atop the corner table. When he returned to bed, he retrieved the blankets from the floor, removed his warm pillow from her back and snuggled his Netta against him.

She gave a gusty sigh, grasped his hand and held it close between soft, warm breasts.

He gave an equally gusty groan that ruffled the hair on the back of her neck.

Connor snared Elise's wrist. "God's blood, lass, come away. You heard Mereck say Netta needed sleep so she can recover from last night. If you dinna come forthwith, I will punish you." Connor's voice was stern.

"I don't have to listen to you. You are not my husband." Elise defied him as she raced across the room.

"Yet. I am not your husband yet, Elise, but I soon will be. You must learn to obey me."

Netta sat up quickly. Ugh! She was sorry she had. Her head was three sizes too big for her neck. And little pixies banged miniature maces against it. She pressed her temples and moaned.

When she could focus her eyes and saw Connor stood there, she knew it was worse than a dreadful mistake. But why did he look so surprised? She followed his gaze down, then grabbed the sheet and jerked it up to her neck. Even though she was now an experienced married woman, she blushed.

"Devil take it, brither," Meghan scolded as she entered the room. "Ye should not be botherin' Netta with yer and Elise's squabbles." She put her hands against his chest and shoved him back through the doorway. He laughed and walked away.

Brianna breezed in, leading servants carrying a tub and hot water. After preparing the bath, the servants left.

"Come, Netta. After you've had a good soak, you'll feel much better." She put a robe around Netta and smiled in sympathy at the young woman.

As they led her to the tub, Netta craned her neck to look over her shoulder at the bed. Puzzled, she stared at the bottom sheet. After seeing her settled, Brianna drew a privacy screen around the tub and opened the door.

Mereck, Bleddyn, Damron and Father Matthew silently entered and watched Brianna strip the sheets from the bed. Seeing bloodstains on the sheet, Elise's eyes widened, her face blanched. Nodding toward the privacy screen, Bleddyn handed Meghan a cup. Quietly, Brianna and the men left the room and shut the door.

"As laird o' clan Morgan, I declare the union between Mereck of Blackthorn and Lynette of Wycliffe duly consummated. What say ye, Bleddyn?"

"As Lady Lynette's overlord, I believe her to be a true wife to Mereck. And you, Father?"

"I am satisfied." Father Matthew grinned wryly at them. "I will affix a note to the signed wedding contract that I witnessed the stripping of the sheet from their nuptial bed. We have enough witnesses that I think we need not fear any man can contest the marriage."

Satisfied that his wife would now be safe from her father's hatred, Mereck smiled.

Inside the room, Netta felt much better. After she drank the potion Bleddyn had sent her, her head began to stop clanging. Did all brides have such terrible headaches from bumping? She sighed and felt pleased with herself. She was a woman now.

"Was it dreadfully painful?" Elise's whisper was so low Netta strained to hear her.

"I don't remember any pain from the bumping. But it was painful for my husband." She said the word with prideful possession. "He moaned somewhat fierce. You saw the stains on the sheet. I would know how he fares this morn, but I don't wish to embarrass him by asking. I believe men must be sensitive to such queries." She nodded and tried to look wise. Hearing a choking cough, she glanced at Meghan and saw her face was red and tears streamed from her eyes. What ailed the woman?

Netta raised her eyebrows at her, but the Scotswoman shook her head and caught her breath.

"Dinna ask," she said.

Meghan's voice sounded husky. She wheezed too. And what did she mean? Do not ask her? Or, do not ask Mereck? She wished she could read her mind. Read her mind! She gasped.

"I can't believe I disremembered that nasty gift of Mereck's last eventime."

"Mereck gave you a nasty gift? Well, were I you, I would give it right back to him. The man was being hateful!" Elise's indignation turned her face red. "Whatever possessed him to do such?"

"I meant the gift of his hearing thoughts." Netta blinked, startled, when an idea struck her. "Do you think my head pounds this morn because he pulled my thoughts from me while I slept?" Meghan's laugh reassured her.

"I think yer discomfort was from the wine ye drank with the toasts. We have lived our life with the man and ne'er had a wee problem with his gift. Only the family knows of it. For certs, he didna need special skills to know the thoughts of the men who kissed yer lips last eve. They are right sorry fer it today, to be sure."

Before Netta could ask why, a maid summoned them for the noon meal. Netta was famished. She was too nervous the day before to eat more than a few bites. As if to verify the fact, her stomach grumbled an appeal.

"I could hear your hunger before I reached the room, wife."

Mereck's large body filled the doorway. She blushed when his warm gaze traveled over her and came back to rest on her face. "Is your headache much trouble this day? Bleddyn assured me his potion would aid it."

"How did you know I would suffer from that affliction? Do you think not eating has caused it? Meghan said she thought I honored too many toasts." She looked at him, hoping he would prove the Scotswoman wrong. She would be dreadfully embarrassed to learn she was a sot.

"I believe you needed to eat more, wife. You have a healthy appetite, but with all the turmoil, you ate barely enough to sustain Tuan. I was the one who drank too heavily."

She beamed at him. This matter of having a husband to defend you was delightful. Her heart fell, remembering the sheets. Did he suffer any ill effects from their bumping? He didn't seem to walk with any difficulty. She was pleased she was so knowledgeable about mating. She needn't worry about any more stained sheets, for she understood it only happened the first time. But why was a man of Mereck's advanced years not more experienced at coupling? Like Marcus? The thought that he was not pleased her.

Mereck made another strange sound. Her poor husband. He had a terrible cough. He must have caught it from Meghan, for he had his hand over his mouth and sounded as if he were choking the same as Meghan had earlier. She would ask Bleddyn to prepare potions for both of them.

When they sat at the table in the great hall, Mereck turned to her with a smile.

"My heart, you have pleased me mightily. I would have all the world know it." He removed a square of blue silk from a tunic pocket. When he laid it on the table to unwrap it, she watched his beautiful hands. The salve Bleddyn had rubbed into Mereck's injuries had done a wondrous job. In another day or two, no one would even guess he had been in such a terrible fight.

Mereck picked up his morning-after gift and held it up for his bride to see. Hanging from a chain of gold links was a lovely pendant, also done in gold. It was a gryphon, the fabulous beast with the head and wings of an eagle and the body of a lion. One also vividly adorned Mereck's war shield. The eye of the beast was set with the same sea-green as was in her wedding band. She reached out a tentative hand to touch it. It was much heavier than it appeared. Mereck had gifted her with two beautiful offerings in as many days. Her ring and now this. These gifts were more than she had ever received before. What a generous man she had married.

She ducked her head for him to slide the chain over it, and when his hands brushed her nape to lift her hair free, she shivered. As the warm pendant settled between her breasts, she folded her hand around it. She gave him a worried look.

"I do not deserve such a splendid gift, husband." She stretched up to whisper for his ears alone. "Father always said no man would bestow anything upon me until I learned to be as dutiful as my sisters."

"Your father was wrong. You deserve many lovely things for your courage. I know the great effort it took for you to be my bride. The whole world should know of my pride in you."

On hearing his praise, she beamed at him. Mereck cupped her face in his hands and waited. To his delight, she didn't flinch from them. He covered her mouth with his and swept his tongue across her lips. He coaxed and teased, and when his hand moved up to press down on her chin, her lips parted. Such sweetness. Honey. And the taste of Netta herself.

Had there not been the sound of someone running into the room, Mereck would have kept on kissing her. When one of the MacLaren's knights came up to him, he drew back and stood. The man looked like he had ridden hard.

"Mereck, sir, the MacLaren sends you words of greatest urgency."

When he gave a slight jerk of his head toward Netta, Damron suggested they leave the great room. Mereck nodded for the warrior to follow them, and once inside Damron's solar, the man relayed his message.

"Laird MacLaren sent me to warn you that one of the Lady Lynette's former suitors, Baron Mortain, is on his way to Blackthorn. He has come with his overlord, Baron Carswell, and forty warriors. My laird refused to give so many men leave to cross his territory, and he forced Mortain to leave all but five men on MacLaren land. He said to tell you he would keep them well occupied until they returned across the border." He took a hearty swallow of ale from the mug Damron handed him.

Mereck clenched his fists. "Do you have any other message for me?"

"Aye. Angus MacLaren rides with them. He is taking them o'er the highest peaks to delay their arrival. He said you were to 'get the deed done speedily afore he arrives.'"

"How many days behind you are they?" Mereck's voice was calm, his eyes hard as steel.

"The MacLaren delayed their departure a day. The longer route will put them four days behind me."

Damron bade the messenger return to the hall for something to eat. He would stay at Blackthorn until MacLaren arrived.

The bitch will pay for this added insult. She will be sorry she scorned me when I deal with her. As he walked toward the fire MacLaren's men had built, Roger of Mortain fought to keep a grimace from his face. He was unused to riding for hours on end. His thighs felt rubbed raw. His ballocks ached even more than his thighs, causing his disposition to become fouler by the second. Overlarge for his body, his ballocks were always a source of pride for him, but the constant pressure of the day's ride was taking its toll.

It will soon be her sex that screams. Her thighs that ache from being spread.

He waited, impatient, for his squire to untangle the knots in the drawstring of his breeches. He would not handle this menial job for himself. When the clumsy hands did not free his tarse fast enough, urine seeped and ran down his leg. His fist lashed out and struck the boy's jaw.

Bloody Lucifer! His knuckle's hurt. He rubbed them on his breeches while a cold smile twisted his thin lips.

Netta would atone for this discomfort also.

Chapter 22

"Hsst, hurry Netta, but don't let anyone follow you. I must ask you something." Elise darted out of the hall.

The way she was acting, everyone in the castle would know she was up to something. She scooted ahead, every few feet peering over her shoulder and wriggling her fingers at Netta. Why did she not just shout, "Follow me?"

Elise disappeared around a corner. Netta hurried past an alcove, and gasped when a hand reached out and jerked her into its darkness. Elise fidgeted with her tunic but did not speak.

"What is it? Why do we hide here?" Netta whispered.

"Now you are married and have experience, I must ask you something. I did not want to ask Meghan. She would learn how woefully lacking Mother was, and Mother said when the time came she would tell me, but how can she tell me when she is not here? Do you understand?" Elise gasped and waited, wide-eyed.

"Ask me what?" Netta rubbed the chill from her arms and leaned closer.

"Well, blessed Saint Agnes. Must I say it?" Elise's voice rose. "The sheets. Is the pain dreadful? How does one do *it?* I will surely displease Connor if I don't know how to do it properly. He threatens to show me soon."

Netta gasped and shook her head. "Never be alone with him. If he should find you unaware, be sure you don't go down on your hands and knees in front of him. I saw Marcus doing it this way in the stables. I believe that position must hurt men the most. His moans were much louder than any of Mereck's last eve."

"There is more than one way to do it?"

"Oh, yes." It pleased Netta to impart her knowledge to soothe her friend's fears. "We were on our sides last eve. Mereck did not heave and bump as frantic as Marcus looked to be doing. Nor did his moans sound as painful."

She frowned and nodded. "Be sensitive to Connor's feelings when he is done. I believe they feel shamed when they are unable to stifle their cries."

"Netta, love. Are you there?" Mereck called nearby.

Netta held a finger to her lips, then poked her head into the hallway.

"There you are, my sweet. You disappeared. I was worried about you." The corner of Mereck's lips twitched as he lifted her hand to nuzzle a warm kiss on her palm. "I thought by chance you would like to practice archery today? 'Tis unfortunate I canna be with you, but Meghan will take my place. Will this please you?"

Meghan, sporting a wide grin, stood beside him.

"Thank you, husband." Netta avoided meeting his eyes. Had he overheard her instructing Elise? She hoped not. She would dislike embarrassing him further about their bedsport last eve.

"You may wear Connor's old shirt o'er your tunic, but not his leggings." He leaned forward and tilted his head close to her face. With a long elegant finger, he tapped his chin.

Netta stared at him. What did he want? She twisted her head to look at Meghan for a clue.

"He wants ye to kiss him." Meghan winked at her.

Netta rose on her tiptoes and pressed her lips to his chin. The skin there already bristled. Why, he must needs scrape away his beard more than once a day. She closed her eyes and inhaled, enjoying the excitement his scent caused. Her lips hovered just above his skin. Would he mind if she kissed his mouth? She went ahead. His lips played softly over hers. His tongue begged entry, but she clamped her teeth together. He gripped the back of her head and kissed her senseless. When her body melted against his, he drew away.

"Thank you, wife. 'Tis custom that Saxon wives kiss their Highland husbands when they part. Have you not noted Brianna doing such?"

She looked at him, suspicious. Damron did as much of the kissing as Brianna. Was that laughter in his eyes? Before she could decide, he spun around and was gone.

Meghan was a hard taskmaster, not relenting until Netta's arrows hit the target five times in a row. Meghan's pleased laughter filled the air.

"I believe ye have a natural talent fer the bow."

"My wife has a natural talent for many things," Mereck's sensuous baritone declared.

Heat spread from Netta's brows down to the top of her tunic. Meghan's praise warmed her, but Mereck's words made her proud. She vowed to practice twice as hard and prove him right. She gazed into his intense, emerald eyes, and his thickly lashed lids drifted lower. What was he thinking?

Mereck winked at Netta. He had but a few days to make her wholly his. If someone learned she was still innocent, he couldna ignore the chance that money might buy the king's favor. Recalling his wedding night, he stilled the smile threatening his lips. If Damron or Connor e'er discovered his performance, he would ne'er live it down. A sennight ago, he would have declared any man daft who suggested his bride would still be chaste the morn after their vows. He felt great sympathy for what Damron must have endured in the first months of his marriage.

When he had returned from bathing in the river, he had watched Netta from a distance. Every time she notched an arrow and drew the bow taught, her breasts strained against Connor's old shirt. Now, his gaze slid over her creamy neck to her breasts. As he lingered there, her nipples hardened and jutted against the material. He wet his lips. He could almost taste her sweet flesh. The persistent anticipation was near unbearable. Thankfully, he wore his plaid and not breeches, for his tarse throbbed with rampant need. This night would be too soon. But mayhap tomorrow . . .

A cadre of warriors galloped across the drawbridge into the outer bailey, drawing his attention. Damron had sent the men to call the clan together for Connor and Elise's wedding four days hence. Elise's family would soon arrive. Netta would not guard her speech around her friend's mother, adding an increased urgency for Mereck to make Netta his.

Mereck escorted the women back to the inner bailey, and he didn't see Netta again until he went to their room afore the evening meal. Expecting to find her resting, he eased open the door. The bed was empty. Water splashed, and he turned to see Netta sitting cross-legged bathing, the tub ample for her small body. She ran a soapy cloth over an outstretched arm. Her breast skimmed the top of the water. He slid the door closed and enjoyed the sight of his bride.

Netta had gathered her black curls in a twist atop her head, and ringlets had escaped to rest along her cheeks and down her nape. He ached with longing but forced himself not to go to her and kiss that delightful spot.

Netta sensed his presence. She spun around and screamed. Her eyes wide and dilated, she tried to scramble from the tub.

"Netta. Look at me." It was a stern command. "'Tis Mereck, your husband, not Durham who stands here." He waited. Indecision lurked in her eyes. "You are safe with me." He spaced each word evenly.

Netta blinked and her panicky look slowly eased.

He motioned for Bran to leave her mistress to him. Nodding, she placed a large drying towel in his hand and left the room.

"I told Damron how you please me with your progress in archery. His Brianna tried to learn the skill. No matter how close she stood, she ne'er hit the target. He claims she canna see past the nose on her face." He smiled, his voice soft and soothing as he ambled over to his bride.

Shy of her nakedness, she crossed her arms over her breasts. As he drew near, one hand snaked down to nudge a bathing cloth across the joining of her legs, shielding her sex from his gaze.

"Come, love, you grow cold." He held the big towel up in front of him, high enough to hide his face and make her secure from his eyes. The water splashed as she stood.

"I am here, husband." Her lilting voice sounded shy.

Bundled in the towel, Mereck carried her to a chair close to the fireplace. He snuggled her close and rubbed his hands over the towel drying her, talking all the while.

"Elise's family arrives in two days' time. We will have

another wedding. Do you think she and Connor will stop their quibbling once they are wed?" He felt her heart slow its wild beat against his arm.

"They do seem to be at odds most of the time. But do you know something, husband? I have seen the way she watches Connor when he speaks with other women." She tilted her head up at him now, more confident. "Elise glares at the ladies till they leave his side. When he goes to her, she frowns and turns her nose in the air at him. Do you not think it passing strange?"

"I do." He hugged her closer. "I have noted the way he watches her. If she but blinks at Marcus or any other man, Connor is ready to throttle them. Is this not also strange?"

Netta was warm and dry now, but he did not release her. She leaned against him, unaware that she played with the mat of hair on his chest. Mereck knew it though. She seemed fascinated with the swirls of hair around his nipples. When her dainty finger traced around them, he broke out in a sweat. The nipples hardened and the skin around them puckered. She stopped, looked surprised and stared at them. Peeking up at him through thick lashes, she eased her hand down to her lap.

His brow knotted, and he pretended to mull over the other couple's problem.

"I believe they have strong feelings for each other." She looked expectantly at him. "What think you, husband?"

"You have solved the puzzle, my wise little wife. Why didna I think of it before?" He bent his head and kissed her brow.

"Men are not as observant as women about another's feelings." She smiled and patted his cheek. "My father was never aware that his thoughtless words hurt."

Mereck hugged her close, hiding his anger. He yearned to strangle Baron George.

"Up with you now, or we will be late to the table. Do you wish help dressing?" After seeing a quick shake of her head, he stood and slid her soft body down his own hard length until her feet touched the floor. He patted her bottom before he turned his back so she could dress in privacy.

Mereck strolled over to the corner wash stand and filled the basin with hot water. He soaped his face and peered into a polished metal square hanging on the wall there. He scraped his face smooth with a small knife honed to a keen edge. When he saw the image of his wife drop the towel and lift her arms to don her chemise, he nicked his upper lip. That was bad enough, but when his demented tarse started another merry dance on seeing the nest of curls guarding her sex, he near cut his throat.

Later that evening in the great hall, they sat in front of the hearth listening to the castle bard recite verses about battles fought by the old laird. When he finished telling the story of the terrible raid that left Damron and Mereck without a father, and Connor and Meghan without parents, Netta's eyes filled with tears. She didn't relax until Damron recounted mischief Brianna and Meghan created when his wife first arrived at Blackthorn.

Whenever Elise and Connor squabbled, Netta leaned close and whispered to Mereck. After Connor nibbled on Elise's ear, Netta giggled, for Elise pinched her husband-to-be.

"Would you pinch your husband for the same offense?" Mereck's tongue traced the shell-like opening of Netta's ear, and when he puffed little bursts of hot breath there, he felt her shivers. Drawing the dainty lobe between his lips, he nibbled before he suckled it.

She didn't pinch him.

His mouth moved to kiss the tender skin behind her ear and stroked wet kisses down her neck. He nuzzled her face and groaned low with pleasure.

Netta's eyelids flew wide. She shifted to face him, and he did not hide his heated desire for her. He read her confusion.

"Dinna let my sounds distress you. They come from pleasure and need. You will soon learn to ken them."

"You are not in pain, then? It is a good thing?"

"Oh aye, wife. 'Tis a verra good thing." Her relieved expression delighted him. His gentle wife worried that she caused him pain. She did cause him pain, but not in the way she thought.

As the women and married couples began leaving the hall to seek their beds, he studied Netta. When he helped her rise, and he put his arm around her shoulders, she did not appear threatened. She called to everyone to enjoy their dreams and went trustingly with him.

Bran helped her mistress, and Mereck turned his back to them while he removed his sword and boots. After she settled Netta on the bed and left the room, he pinched out the candles and stripped by the dim glow from the fireplace. He removed his long shirt, folded it and laid it atop his chest. When she spoke, he knew she watched him.

"You are most considerate, Mereck. Father threw his clothes on the floor, even when they didn't need washing. The maids said he trod over them apurpose to cause them more work. Do you suppose this was so?"

"By chance he wanted to be sure they earned their keep? What think you?" He truly thought George Wycliffe spiteful.

Musing over his question, she was silent for a time.

"I believe both you and the maids must be right. He did

leave boot marks on the shirts. And he was also very tight with his coins. But I think he was spiteful to cause them more work."

When he smiled and nodded in agreement, she looked pleased. He removed the belt and held on to the gathered plaid as it slid from his body. Turning from her, he rolled his belt and folded the plaid over the back of a chair. Knowing she could see his naked body from the fire's glow, he sought to keep his movements slow and nonthreatening. When he strolled toward the bed, she glanced up at him and then down to the snowy white linens. She seemed drawn to look, for she did not keep her gaze lowered for long. After several darting glances, she blinked and slid deeper beneath the covers.

"Is Elise pleased her family will soon arrive?" He eased into bed and propped his back against the headboard. He drew her up close against him, and she did not pull away. Shy still, she rested her head on his shoulder.

"Oh, aye, she is." Her head bobbed against his chin. "I hope Sir Galan will come. He is like a brother to Elise. He was but a young boy when he came to foster with them. Did you know Brianna had at first hoped to marry him?"

"I did. I spent several days with Galan. After compline each night, he went to the highest point of Ridley Castle, faced toward Scotland and sang a melody he wrote for Brianna." He tilted his head and looked at her. "Would you like to hear it?"

"Aye," Netta whispered and snuggled closer while he sang the poignant verses. She sighed and smoothed her hand over his chest.

When he finished the melody, he nuzzled the top of her head. Lord in Heaven, she smelled like fresh summer flowers. He trailed kisses across her forehead and took his time traveling down to her soft lips. His heart surged on reaching them for, soft and pliant, they awaited him. When his tongue first slid between her teeth, she startled, near biting down on it. His tongue flirted lightly and danced around her own until she tried to anticipate its next move. When he stilled for a second, she tentatively stroked her own against it.

Her response pleased him. He continued his sensual assault until her body softened against him. While his hand slid down her waist and hip, he occupied her mind with his kisses. He cupped the rounded curves of her buttocks and turned her toward him. When his hand moved back up and over her hips and continued to the side of her breast, she squirmed. Gently he cupped her breast in his warm hand and fondled it. All the while, his tongue thrust deep into her mouth.

He whispered while his thumb rubbed over the hardening nipple, "Do you like this, *mo gradh,* my love?" Netta gasped with budding desire and clutched his arms. He rolled her onto her back and moved his body to cover her. Careful to keep his weight rested on his arms, he continued to caress her. He eased a hand between her thighs to coax them open for a moment, then allowed his hard sex to nestle there. He stroked, up and down, and kept a tight curb on his desires as his tarse teased her.

"And this, *mo cridhe,* my heart?" Her whimper as she dug her fingers into his shoulders answered for her. Soon he felt her nether curls dampened with dew. Sweat beaded his forehead. When he could stand no more of this self-inflicted torture, he gave one final, deep kiss. For this night's lesson, it was enough.

Tomorrow would be another matter.

During the night, Netta awoke pressed close against Mereck's side. She felt protected in his arms, and knowing he was asleep, she nuzzled her cheek against the soft mat of hair covering his chest. His heartbeat was strong against her ear. She liked the sound of it. Before she reached her fingertips to feel over his face, she lifted her head to reassure herself he slept.

His strong forehead and straight nose pleased her. His lips in sleep were as soft as a rose petal. Her hand explored his cheeks and jaw, and she enjoyed the raspy feel against her fingertips. Thinking of how that hard part of him had touched her, she grew hot and moist between her thighs. She squeezed her legs together, but it made the pulsing worse. The heat coming from his body intensified the feeling, and she inched away. A short while later, she felt normal again.

Satisfied, she turned back to him and threw her arm over his chest. As if he were her favorite pillow, she tried to mold him tighter against her. Soon, she fell fast asleep and dreamed she was a loved and cherished wife.

It was late afternoon. With Simon's guidance, Netta had Tuan on a lead training him to fly for his daily rations. Tuan's lead had been short to begin with, but as the kestrel became adept at its lessons, they extended the length of the lead. Soon it would fly on its own and attack the lure as it would do its prey.

"Simon, is not Tuan the smartest raptor you have ever seen?" Netta turned her head to peer at the falconer. "Except for Cloud Dancer, of course. An eagle is much larger. Surely their brain is also. I think Cloud Dancer does the training, not us." She looked over and smiled at the raptor.

Cloud Dancer always stayed close to the little raptor. When Tuan was first attached to the lead, the eagle flew beside him as if to reassure him. Now the great eagle watched from a stoop, sometimes nodding. Was it in approval? At other times, he swooped off into the air, scolding the kestrel in a loud voice.

"Aye," Simon agreed. "He has been doing some teaching. Of an evening they yatter like two ole women. The way he behaves is most amazing. We could trust no other great bird to be free. It would soon make a feast of all others in the mews."

Netta grinned and whistled for Tuan to come to her gauntleted hand and laughed with delight when the kestrel obeyed. She turned Tuan over to Simon, thanked him and left.

The day was sunny and crisp, with not a hint of rain. Netta strolled through the baileys having ample time before the evening meal. After leaving the mews, she stopped for a brief visit at the hut where the candle makers had finished for the day. She asked the chandler to send a week's supply to their room and felt a sense of pride at this wifely duty.

The sounds of horses racing in the side paddock, the shrill whinny of a mare and the loud trumpet of a stallion drew her attention. Her father had told her you did not turn a mare and a stallion out in the same field. He never explained why. She took off as fast as she could run, intending to find the stable master to tell him someone had made a mistake.

When she approached the paddock, Netta jolted to a halt. Her eyes widened in disbelief. Brianna's mare Sweetpea raced from one side of the enclosure to the other with Angel, Damron's white destrier, in pursuit. In a flash, Angel maneuvered Sweetpea into a corner where she could not elude him. He threw back his head and shrilled his triumph.

Why, he was trying to climb atop the trembling mare.

Horrified, Netta turned to a pillar of salt. At the mare's scream of protest, Angel bit down on her long, curved neck, holding her still for his purpose. Both horses panted. Surely the mare would fall under the weight of the great destrier?

Netta's salt melted when she spied Damron, Bleddyn and Marcus calmly watching.

"Make him release her," she bellowed in outrage. "How can you stand by while that huge warhorse is almost crushing her? Can you not see she needs help?" She whacked Damron on the shoulder with her fist to get his attention. He didn't move, but looked at her like he thought her deranged. "If you do not get in there and pull him off, he will kill your wife's horse."

A hand on her shoulder startled her. Mereck was there, looking like he had been running. He would put a stop to this budding tragedy.

"Husband, tell your brother Brianna is not going to be happy when she wants to go riding and finds he let that great warhorse cripple Sweetpea. Why, all that weight on her back could break her legs." Now she understood the rules about mares and stallions not being together. They fight.

"Shh, love. You will lose your voice, and I'll lose my hearing if you dinna stop bellowing. Dinna upset yourself so." Mereck saw the amused looks from the men. They eagerly awaited his explanation to his bride. "They are not fighting, Netta. Sweetpea is ready to carry a foal." Seeing her blank expression, he added, "A baby horse. Angel is giving her one."

Fortunately for Mereck, while Netta wasn't looking, Angel completed his chore, gave a last trumpet and pulled away. Angel nuzzled Sweetpea's neck as if to soothe it.

Netta looked over her shoulder, pointed to the horses and scowled. "Do you see Angel giving her anything, husband?"

"He planted the seed for one, love. 'Tis the way to make bairns."

"Nay. You cannot be serious." Reaching up, she yanked the braid at his temple until his ear was close. "I changed my mind about wanting a bairn, Mereck."

"Why, wife? I thought all women wanted bairns."

"I don't wish you to chase me about the room, and I don't want you to bite my neck. Is there some other way to plant the seed?" She prayed there was.

"Dinna worry, love. I promise. You will enjoy it."

Netta let go of his hair. Before she agreed she would enjoy it, she would insist he explain it to her.

As they walked and talked to the horses to soothe them, Damron and Bleddyn hid their amusement. The laird ran his hands down and across Sweetpea's head, neck and body and spoke lovingly to her, telling her what a beautiful mare she was and what fine colts she would bear.

Netta decided Sweetpea looked pleased with the compliments. She gulped and shivered when Mereck whispered his own loving words in her ear.

"Tonight, my heart. Tonight we will make our own bairn."

Chapter 23

Mereck suggested they seek their bed; Netta suggested they take a walk. A long walk. A *very* long walk.

She wished to tire him before they went to their rooms and he started with the chasing. Saints help her. She wasn't the fastest runner in her family. Her legs were too short. Netta shuddered, remembering the most frightening time she'd needed speed and came up lacking. On her eighteenth birthday, her father presented his gift to her.

A suitor.

Roger was a tall, thin man with pale blue eyes so small they looked as if he had squinted them into shrinking. His lips were near nonexistent, too. What there was of them looked mean.

She rubbed her arms, feeling the pinches and bruises he put there when she refused to allow him a kiss. The day she lied and told him she was no longer a virgin and was barren, he flew into a rage. She thought he would withdraw his attentions. He didn't. He cornered her in the formal gardens of her father's castle.

His venom-laced voice rang in her ears as she struggled against him.

"Yield, little bitch." He had hissed the words at her, spewing a disgusting trail of spittle on her cheek.

He was amazingly strong for such a thin man, for only hard muscle covered his lanky bones. Gripping her with one hand, he hiked up her skirts with the other. Cold, hurtful fingers clawed at her thighs while his lips crushed hers.

She seized the opportunity and bit his tongue.

He screeched curses. His grip slackened. She shoved him off balance and dashed through the maze entrance.

"Return fer yer punishment, stupid girl, or I will take the skin from yer back fer yer disobedience." Roger shouted what else he would do to her when he caught her, most of which she was thankful she didn't understand. She screamed and raised such a ruckus her stepsisters said they thought he was slaughtering her. Finally, he caught her and raised a stout branch torn from a tree at the maze entrance. If arriving men-at-arms hadn't grasped it and held tight, he would have beat her across her head and shoulders with it.

Castle knights escorted him outside the castle gates. She thought her father valued her, because he had refused Roger's suit. It was not so. Prissy told her a messenger had arrived that very hour and informed him Roger's finances were in desperate straits. It was then she learned her father demanded a large bride price for her.

"Netta?"

Blessed saints. She hummed and stared at Mereck. What if she was too late and he had already stolen her thoughts about her disgrace? Merciful heavens. Another horrific thought occurred. She stopped humming.

"Did you pay my father a great deal of money for me?"

"Your father didna ask it of me, but had he, I would

have paid my entire fortune for the privilege of having such a worthy wife."

Little tingles of desire filled her at his words. She studied his face to see if he mocked her. His expression showed admiration. She decided to accept the compliment. Her thoughts kept her so occupied she didn't realize they had finished their walk and stood afore their bedroom door. He embraced her shoulders and guided her inside.

While Bran helped her prepare for bed, Mereck disappeared behind the privacy screen. On emerging, he wore a soft green chamber robe belted at his waist. His bare feet and ankles drew her attention. Feet are not usually an appealing part of a person's body, but Mereck's were truly different. Could you call feet pretty? Probably not, but surely they were handsome? Bran helped her tie her robe when Netta's hands couldn't seem to handle the job. Mayhap she could think of a reason to delay Bran's leaving? She would ask her about her family.

Mereck did not give her the chance.

"Thank you, Bran. Your mistress has no further need of you."

Well, rats and fleas. Netta hummed again as the servant left the room.

Mereck drew her to him, making soft soothing circles with his hands over the tense muscles of her back. His lips lowered to float light as a butterfly's wing against hers. They hovered over the corners of her mouth, and the tip of his tongue teased her there. He followed the rim of her lips and returned to dampen the seam with a subtle increase of pressure.

"Open to me, my love." His husky voice surprised her. She did not heed him. He doubled his efforts until she opened the smallest bit. His tongue slid beyond her teeth and explored hers.

Merreck's thudding heartbeat against her breasts made her sigh. When he drew back, she was disappointed. Ha. That was putting it mildly. He might be inexperienced at bumping, but not kissing. She never wanted his kisses to stop. He lowered his mouth to her shoulders.

"Tell me what you know of mating between a man and woman, my heart," he murmured.

"Whenever I asked my father's wife about the subject, she said my husband would teach me all I needed to know."

Embarrassed, she squirmed against him. "She said it is painful and scolded that I was not to scream and ruin my husband's pleasure. Um. Was she not confused, husband?"

He smiled. "I will give you no reason to scream, Netta. The first time is sometimes painful for a woman, but the pain is soon gone and pleasure replaces it."

"Blessed saints. Now *you* are confused." She reached up to whisper in his ear, "The man is the one who suffers."

Not wanting to remind him of his groans at night, she clamped her lips and thought about hearing Marcus and the serving girl in the stable. She forgot to hum.

"What we did before was very pleasant." He stopped to nuzzle her neck. "However, I didna plant my seed in your body."

"There is another way?" Her eyes felt like they bulged from their sockets. When he took her face between his hands and his gaze clung to hers, her face felt hot. She hummed, loud, then lowered her lids to shield her from his piercing gaze. He picked her up in his arms and went to sit on the bed, an arm around her waist.

She stared at those beautiful hands, those elegant fingers that looked to have a will of their own. The white lines of scars proved they had many stories to tell of where they had been and what they had done. She hesitated, then ran her fingertips over them. Curious, she turned his hand over to study his palm. Calluses from wielding weapons had hardened his skin. One long scar crossed from his left wrist to the base of his fingers.

Such strength was in his hands—how was it possible they were so gentle when they touched her? Thinking of the way he would plant his seed, she shuddered. He had said they could do the deed another way? Hopefully, it didn't include a bite on her neck.

"Netta, in these past nights you have seen the differences in our bodies."

She knew he was not referring to the greater abundance of hair on his. He was not reminding her of the affliction in his chest, either. Tonight, the muscles in his chest were not moving against her shoulders. That left what she had seen of naked men on the practice field and glimpsed here in their room. She swallowed and nodded.

"Your body is different from mine in the same area." When she stiffened, he smoothed her hair and murmured soothing sounds. "You have an opening where my shaft will enter to plant the seeds for a bairn deep inside your body."

He took her hand and guided it to his hot, engorged member jutting high beneath his robe. She jerked her hand away. If his arms had not held her, she would have bounded from his lap.

"I think we will wait, husband." She could barely lift her voice above a whisper. "I have decided I'm not yet ready for a bairn. Mayhap in a fortnight or two, you will not be so swollen? You must have done yourself an injury."

"'Tis no injury, sweet, but my need for you."

Those words did not reassure her. He stretched out on the bed with her resting atop his length. He did nothing more threatening than rub her back and stroke her arms. When he kissed the top of her head, she could not stop herself from squirming closer to his face so he could reach her mouth.

She craved his kisses.

His lips wandered across her brow, down to the tip of her nose and back over her eyelids, leaving soft kisses along the way. Her cheeks were next. The silky feel of his warm lips on her skin delighted her. When he finally obliged her impatient, pursed lips, she sighed. He whispered soft words and endearments.

He kissed her witless.

Had he not, she would have known when he removed her robe.

And she was no longer atop him.

His body covered hers, his weight balanced on his arms. Her hair spilled across the pillow, where he combed his fingers through the curls and lowered his face to smell its fragrance.

She, too, inhaled deeply, her pulse quickened. The urge to taste him near overpowered her. Where in the world had that thought come from? She tried to disguise her goal with an openmouthed kiss against the side of his neck. Her tongue peeked out to explore his skin.

Netta didna hear the soft sounds she made deep in her throat. Mereck did. His tongue outlined her ear, and his teeth tugged the lobe. Feeling her shivers, he pressed the tip of his tongue into the small opening. He whispered into the dampness, telling her how good she felt while settling his lower body against her.

Netta wriggled her hips beneath him. He delighted in a moan that escaped her, and when his heavy arousal pulsed at the joining of her thighs, she rocked her legs to cradle him. The need to feel her bare skin against his own almost swept away the shield he had built around his desire. He stilled, fearing his rampant need might affright her.

His kisses caressed a trail down her neck, and back up to her mouth, to wage another tender assault. His tongue plunged, distracting her with its slow rhythm. He shrugged out of his robe. His fingers stole between them to open the ties of her night garment and slide the thin silk to her waist. His hands explored over the velvet skin of her waist, her hips. She gasped when he rubbed his hair-roughened chest against her breasts.

Her nipples hardened and puckered. She grasped the thick hair at his nape to pull his face close. His tongue slid between her lips, and she suckled lightly. He nudged his tarse against her. She raked her fingernails through his hair and across his shoulders. Her heartbeat thudded against him. After several more thrusts of his tongue, he slipped his hand between her thighs.

Before she knew what he was about, he eased a finger in her tight center and imitated the motion of his tongue. After her first jerk of surprise, he enveloped her in the pleasure of it. When he gently added another to stretch her, she stiffened and started to protest.

"Shh, my heart," he soothed. Slowly, her muscles loosened around him. He became more demanding. Shudders racked her as her passion awakened. He dampened and suckled each pink nipple, building her tension. Gasping for breath, she clutched his arms.

"I think you had best stop now, husband." Netta pulled his hair.

The tumult of emotions his loving caused had frightened her.

"Shh, love. Dinna fear the pleasures I bring you."

She squirmed. With a tortured growl, he drew and tugged a nipple, nipping ever so lightly with his teeth. When he moved to the other breast to do the same, she near pulled the hair from his head. Not to pull him away, but to pull him tighter to her. He slid his fingers from her heat. His throbbing shaft rubbed against the weeping, downy triangle between her legs as he suckled her breast deeply into his mouth.

Her body vibrated. He spread her legs wide with his knees and nudged his tarse closer. She stilled. A groan rumbled from his chest, feeling her wet heat. Taking great gasps of air, he dropped his head to bury his face in her neck.

To cool his lust, he tried to distract his mind with thoughts of battle. It didna work.

He conjured scenes that should cause his manhood to shrivel.

It didna.

He stilled his body atop hers.

"Is it done then, husband?" Her voice was hopeful.

His shaft rested against her opening, and while he tried to school his voice from quivering, she wriggled against him. He gasped when the tip entered between her sweet nether lips.

"But a little more, dear heart, and we will plant my seed." His voice was a hoarse croak. It disgusted him.

Reaching between them, he sent a litany of thanks heavenward on finding hot, wet curls there. He ran a finger around the sides of his shaft where it entered her, and she gasped when he teased her hidden nub.

He seated himself farther. She shoved against his shoulders.

"Release your seed now, Mereck." It was a breathless demand.

He almost complied. She dug her heels into the sheet and tried to scoot away, but he held her shoulders in a firm grip.

"Put your arms around me, love, and hold tight. 'Twill sting at first, but soon the pain will be gone. Kiss me, sweetling."

His open mouth, blatantly hungry and cajoling, covered hers as he teased a nipple with his thumb until she again writhed beneath him. He kept up a steady thrusting of his tongue. When she started to arch her hips against his, he drew back and thrust into her.

Her maidenhead gave way without a struggle.

Netta didn't. She bit his lip.

She released him quickly though, so she could take a deep breath and howl. It near deafened him. However, at the moment, he wasn't concerned about his hearing. He stopped moving but stayed imbedded in her heat.

"Shh, sweetling. The hurt will soon be gone." He groaned when she squirmed again and drove him deeper. "Please dinna move or you will undo me." He clamped his teeth together and called on all his strength to not shout and ram himself into his bride. Her heart pounded against his chest.

"I am sorry, love. Never again will our loving hurt you," he murmured. His lips coaxed hers, his tongue stroked and teased until her muscles begin to ease around him. Taking a grateful breath, he eased back and entered again. She did not protest. He began a steady rhythm. Soon she sighed and stopped tearing his back to shreds.

Although thinking it unlikely she would find full satisfaction in this first joining, he continued to caress and soothe her, knowing he stretched her body and made it easier for their next mating. Her fingers dug into his shoulders. She moaned and arched her hips to him. He thrust faster.

Surprise crossed her face. She stiffened and panted now. She gripped her lower lip between her teeth and strained against him. He felt the spasms of her first orgasm squeezing his shaft.

It proved his undoing.

He tensed and arched against her. She yelled and clamped him with her legs when he exploded, releasing his seed into her depths. Burying his face in her neck, he cried out his triumphant male possession in sweet agony.

"Ah, sweetling." He gasped for breath. "You please me mightily."

Netta struggled to regain her senses. She let go of her fierce grip on his hair, and gave him soft pats over his heart. When he withdrew and moved to her side, her leg muscles screamed their protest.

She pinched him. Though he arched his brows at her, she didn't bother to explain.

"We have made a bairn, then?" she asked, breathless. The look she gave him warned his answer should be what she wanted.

"God willing, we may have made a babe."

"May? What is this 'may,' husband? Either we did or we did not. Did you not do it right?"

"Sometimes it takes one time to make a bairn. Then again, it may take many." She scowled. "God made us this way, Netta. You dinna want to argue with Him, do you?"

She mulled the question over and shook her head. She didn't want to anger God. Besides, it had been most pleasurable. Only the part when she thought he would split her asunder had been disagreeable.

Mereck kissed her forehead, got out of bed and brought the basin and pitcher of warmed water to the bed table. He coaxed her to let him wash her there, telling her it was the custom for a husband to do such. She squeezed her eyes tight.

The heated cloth felt good against her tender parts. She clamped her legs together to keep it there. When she realized she had also trapped his hand, she blushed and relaxed her muscles. While he was occupied soothing her, she glanced down at his body.

She gasped and jerked upright while she stared at his manhood.

"Of merciful saints. I squeezed it to death!"

When he gave a strangled sound and very near squashed the breath out of her, she deemed it was in retaliation.

"You did me no injury, love. What you see is how a man's rod normally looks. My tarse only becomes swollen and hard from my wanting you."

She didn't know whether to believe him. That is, until he took her hand and placed it on his flaccid member. When it stirred and started to swell, she snatched her hand away.

Mereck stretched out beside her and wrapped her in his arms. He kissed the tip of her nose and brought her close, guiding her head to his shoulder. "Sleep now, little wife."

She patted his chest, liking the comfort of his steady heartbeat. She sighed. She had too many things to think about to go to sleep. After she mulled over this business of mating and made sense of it, she would heed him.

Her eyes drifted closed. By the time he had counted to ten, she snored in little puffing bursts.

Before dawn, Mereck tucked the covers around Netta and drew the bed drapes closed. He left orders below stairs that no one disturb her.

When the sun had risen high in the sky, a sentry came to tell him the MacLaren men and the visitors would soon arrive. At Damron's questioning look, Mereck nodded. Since his room was next to theirs, he knew his brother and Brianna must have heard Netta's shout when he took her maidenhead.

"Spencer," Damron called to his squire. "Please ask Lady Brianna to come to me." The young man was off like a flash and back with the laird's wife before too many heartbeats.

"My sweet, the man who covets our Netta approaches. Until we learn his intent, would ye keep the women above stairs?" He beckoned her close to whisper in her ear. She nodded.

"Don't worry, love. I will see to her safety." Brianna kissed Damron's forehead and hurried from the room.

"Dinna turn your back on Mortain," Connor warned Mereck. "He plans to stop a wedding. After he finds his prize has slipped from him, he will be overwrought."

Mereck stood, feet braced wide apart, his face a cold mask. One hand rested on his sword, the other on the hilt of a lethal-looking dagger.

Any man foolish enough to cross him would have to have a death wish.

Chapter 24

Roger of Mortain passed through Blackthorn's barbican, his eyes studying his surroundings for any weaknesses in the castle defenses. Sentries stood five paces apart, covering the battlement walkways. He ground his teeth in frustration, for Blackthorn displayed more hardened warriors than most fortresses.

High atop the castle, stiff gusts whipped and cracked a glaring white flag below the Morgan standard. His eyes narrowed. The wind teased the edges, sailing it out for all to see. Curses spewed from his lips. Hatred clenched his heart. A sheet hung there for all to bear witness a deflowering had occurred.

Mereck of Blackthorn would pay for this. The bitch who had spread her legs for Baresark would watch her lover die.

Netta scrunched her face, thinking of a way to tell Elise she had been mistaken about the bumping. She had not a chance, for someone was forever by her side. Thinking how she had so proudly educated her friend on mating, she cringed. Secretly, she was relieved not to have the chance to admit her own ignorance.

The sun had started its decline when Mereck and Connor came to escort the women to the great hall. Mereck placed a possessive hand on her neck. His strong thumb rubbed gentle circles in the downy hair at her nape. It reminded her of the way his fingers had circled her nipples—and other places. She flushed. Her female place heated at the memory. When next they went to bed, could she coax him to touch her there again?

Had he picked up Mither? She heard the sounds of a giant cat purring and peeked up at him. No, he had not. Oh, saints. He's listening again. She hummed and occupied her thoughts recalling names of saints with birth dates on the next two months. Until she saw Eric blocked their path, she did not realize they had reached the stone steps into the hall.

Eric cleared his throat. Not for the first time, if the laughter in his eyes was a clue. "Mereck, I have heard it said your bride's hums wake the beasts in yonder forest."

"Hums? I didna ken she was humming."

"How could you not notice?"

"Why, I believed her stomach protested its lack of food. I was polite and didna mention the matter. She has a hearty appetite, you see." His conspiratorial whisper as he guided her to the high table was almost as loud as her humming had been.

Netta scowled and poked his ribs with her elbow. It was a healthy jab, but he didn't flinch. She started to pinch him too, but realized they had halted afore Damron and the visitors who stood beside the fireplace. She remembered her manners and curtsied while Mereck introduced her as his wife. A hand as smooth and white as the underbelly of a fish extended to assist her. Manners decreed she accept the offer. Rising, her eyes skimmed long skinny shanks in tight breeches.

When cold fingers clamped painfully on hers, she winced.

When wet lips touched her skin, she shuddered.

"Roger of Mortain and his overlord, Baron Hugh of Carswell, wish to offer their congratulations on our marriage, Netta. Is this not so, Mortain?" Mereck ignored the man's title. Tapping the baron's wrist with a firm finger, he reminded him to unhand his wife.

Fiery streaks of alarm jolted Netta. Her gaze flew to the hawkish face in front of her. She could not still a gasp. Roger's satisfied smirk sickened her.

She nodded her head, then tugged back her hand to rub the palm against her skirts. His cold eyes registered the gesture. Grasping for Mereck to tug him close, her hand brushed against his sex. She grabbed his belt, and had he not been ken to a giant, she would have toppled him in her haste.

Baron Carswell cleared his throat, drawing her attention. He was nothing like his vassal. His smile was open and friendly, and he was at ease with Damron and Mereck. He studied her face, and when he bent to kiss her hand, he frowned at the angry red marks before gently kissing them.

Later when they sat for their meal, though Mereck piled their trencher with all of the things she especially liked, Netta hardly ate. Every time she sought to put food in her mouth, that cold blue stare impaled her. She sighed with relief when the meal and entertainment ended and Mereck escorted her from the room.

She bolted into their room, and after Mereck shut the door, she checked to see he had latched it tight.

"Bran, please bring a tray of bread, cheese and a

pitcher of wine." While he waited for her to return, he stoked the fire.

Netta need not worry that Mereck would steal thoughts from her mind while he untied the back laces of her tunic. Her musings were not worthy. Far from it. They were cowardly, saints help her.

"Netta, you do me a disservice when you fear that nithing of a man. Do you doubt my skills to protect you?"

Mereck's voice sounded angry, mean even. Her mouth gaped. So much for his not pilfering chickenhearted thoughts. When he spun her around and scowled down at her, he would have scared a woman less brave than she.

He did not simply look mean. He looked furious.

Heaven help her. She had displeased him.

"'Tis not that I think you lacking in skills, husband. He is such a vile man." Revulsion swept her on thinking of Roger's hands on her body the way Mereck had done last eve. She rubbed Roger's imagined touch from her arms. "When he gazed at me, I felt forewarned something terrible was about to happen. Did he mention he sought to wed me? Father refused his offer. What brings him here?"

"He went to Wycliffe to demand your father honor his suit. He has a signed missive from Baron Wycliffe stating if you were not honorably married, or the union unconsummated, Damron was to turn you over to him." Mereck scowled.

"Mortain claims he sought to protect you. He brought Carswell with him to force Laird Damron's hand." His lips hardened to a thin line. "He sought to return you to Wycliffe, to spare you from 'being another Morgan leman,' as he put it."

Netta gripped his ears and tugged his face close. "Don't let him take me, husband. I'll not stand for it."

"Enough. You insult me." He grasped her wrists to let her know she was to release him.

"You will not let him," she ordered and gave his ears another healthy pull before she relaxed her fingers.

"Wife, I ken you are affrighted, but you will stop your foolish fear of him. He is but a man. Not much of one at that."

"I know. Truly I do. But he is such a weasel of a man. Please do not turn your back on him." She was glad when Bran returned with the food. Mereck wouldn't chastise her with the woman present. Until his anger faded, she would keep Bran close.

She asked Bran to brush her hair.

Without speaking, he took the brush from the maid's hand.

She asked Bran to help her change into her night garment.

Still silent, he took Netta's robe and nodded pointedly at the door.

Bran left.

Mereck stood in the center of the room and beckoned with one finger. Netta stared at it as if not understanding his meaning.

She knew, all right. She couldn't help it if she was distracted on recalling what those commanding hands had done to her body. Oh, rats and fleas. She squelched her thoughts, tore her gaze away and hummed a disjointed tune.

With effort, Mereck kept his face impassive, for he also remembered the satiny feel of his wife's body. He sighed and undressed. While he donned his robe, he watched her pretend he had not bid her come to him. At the rate she hummed and flitted like a hummingbird from one part of the room to another, it would be time for Matins at dawn afore she obeyed him.

Instead, he went to her. He talked to her about the people who would begin to arrive for Connor and Elise's wedding. While he occupied her mind, he removed her chemise and wrapped her in her robe.

He picked up a cushion from one chair and placed it on the floor in front of the other. He tugged her hand and sat, gesturing for her to sit on the cushion. When she eyed him from the corner of her eyes and settled herself, he took long, even strokes of the brush through her raven curls.

Her head bobbed lightly with each sweep of the brush, and he kept up the soothing motion until her shoulders relaxed. He enjoyed playing with her curls. Never had he known hair could hold such warmth. He stretched a hank of hair straight, then smiled when it coiled back around his fingers.

He did not intrude on her thoughts. Once he sensed they were serene, he put down the brush, gripped her waist and stood her between his legs as easily as if he lifted a child.

Turning her to face him, he slid the ribbon free at her waist. The robe slithered open, baring her body from her neck to the lush, ebony curls guarding her sex. His breath caught. He placed his hands on her slender hips and smoothed them in a long caress down to her thighs. He nudged her robe wider to cup her pert bottom. The tips of his fingers caressed her silky skin and teased the hidden area between her legs.

Netta pushed at his wrists. He ignored her. She would soon grow accustomed to his touch. A rosy blush wandered from her face to her breasts. He pulled her close and nuzzled his face in her perfect stomach. His tongue teased the hollow of her navel; his teeth playfully nipped her skin. With a will of their own, his hands made their way to the sides of her breasts. Drawing back, he admired the sight.

She stared at his hands. Had she noticed the stark contrast between his tanned skin and her creamy flesh? He watched her while his thumbs traced the pink areola of her breasts. The skin puckered, and a soft sigh escaped her. When he teased a now erect nipple, she shivered. Blushing even more, she again grasped his wrists and tried to pull them away.

"We should not do this, Mereck. Someone could see us." She tugged harder. "We should blow out the candles, draw the bed curtains and get beneath the covers."

"Who will see, wife? We are alone. I have latched the door."

While he watched her trying to think of another excuse, he hid a smile. When she found one, he knew, for her eyes lit.

"God." She nodded emphatically.

"God? You are afraid God will see me make love to my wife?"

"Not only God. Our guardian angels too. And what about all the spirits who must abide in the castle? These stones have seen many lives come and go. They can all see us."

"I believe God and the spirits are much too busy to spend time spying on our bedsport, wife."

When he removed his thumbs and nuzzled his face at the warm skin between her breasts, she sighed with relief. His hot, moist tongue traced circles around a nipple, evoking a moan. One hand splayed across her lower back while he molded and stroked her other breast. When his mouth closed around her nipple and suckled, she turned to liquid fire.

His hand left her back to roam over her hips and between her legs. His searching fingers found burning heat and wetness seeping there. She was swiftly learning to respond to his touch. He sucked in a deep breath as his eager finger entered her. His heart raced feeling her muscles squeeze it, searing him with her heat.

Breathing heavy and ragged, he spread his robe wide and rose to slide his naked body up over hers. As his turgid sex caressed her, her eyes closed, and she tilted her head back and sighed with pleasure. He licked her lower lip, then nibbled there until she opened for him. His tongue thrust between her willing lips to explore and tease her. When her breathless whimpers increased and she started pushing frantically against his hand, he carried her to the bed and laid her upon it.

Mereck's tarse pulsed in painful demand that he satisfy its need.

Easing himself between her legs, he gave his tarse a gift.

He let it beg entrance to paradise.

If he did not leash his desire, she would soon have the rest of him begging. Wanting Netta's pleasure in this mating, he nudged his shaft aside, ignoring it. He focused on her responses as his fingers circled and caressed her. When she gasped, thrusting her hips upward, he entered slowly, then withdrew even slower. He played with her tiny pleasure nub until her gasps turned to moans of delight.

Her hands grabbed his shoulders and she tugged at him, striving to pull him closer. He held back, not giving her what she wanted. She bit his neck, wrapped her legs around him and lunged upward. He chuckled and seated himself firmly. She cried out in satisfaction and jerked up against him. Her unschooled rhythm was spasmodic. Holding her hips, he showed her the way.

Netta tensed, her eager cries increased. He happily obliged her when her movements became more urgent. His thrusts quickened and became demanding, his gasps louder than hers, his own cries building. Only when her muscles convulsed and squeezed around him did he allow his release. She arched, rigid with her climax. He lunged faster, deeper; his seed exploded from him and flooded against the entry to her womb.

"Ohh, saaaints!"

He would have laughed, but he was too occupied trying to catch his heart afore it burst from his body.

Mereck made love to her again that night, and he did so with amazing frequency. On feeling the first tremors of release, Netta grabbed his hair and pulled his mouth to hers.

Netta's loud responses each night to Mereck's lovemaking embarrassed her, for surely the whole castle heard her. It did not help her dignity having Connor and Eric grin each time they saw her. She was too mortified to worry about Roger and didn't think it strange that Brianna or Meghan was always at her side.

After breaking her fast one morn, she and Meghan practiced archery in the rear bailey where Mereck had provided a target for their use. The castle overflowed with guests for Elise and Connor's wedding. So many strange men were about that Mereck did not want her in the outer bailey.

She decided a young warrior, Thomas by name, had very light duties, for he was always nearby. After Meghan sent him for goblets of cool water, a strange warrior approached to deliver a message.

"Milady, the falconer Rory asks that you come at once. Something is amiss with your sparrowhawk." Gesturing with his hands, he urged Meghan to hurry.

"Dinna leave the area, Netta," Meghan warned. "Thomas will return soon, and I canna take ye with me. The mews be full to burstin' with falcon handlers the guests have brought." When Netta nodded, Meghan took off at a run, the man behind her.

Netta sat and leaned back against the target, thinking to rest until Thomas and Meghan returned. Archery training was strenuous work. Her every muscle ached from strain. Though not all were from archery. Most were from another type of practice. She blushed thinking on the praise Mereck had given her newly acquired skills.

Last eventide, he claimed she had near killed him.

Netta knew it was praise, because he groaned when he said it.

A sound intruded on her musing. She tilted her head, listening. A most piteous wail. She stood and walked closer to the sound, but it seemed to draw farther away. Hurrying, she followed the little cries, for now she recognized them. Her Sprite meowed as if needing her help.

She neared the postern gate and heard the kitten on the other side. With surprise, she noted the gate was unbarred and the lock missing. She looked around, hoping to see Thomas returning, but did not spy him or anyone else she could turn to for help. She feared leaving the castle walls, but she couldn't leave her helpless kitten to fend for itself.

Netta shoved the old gate until it opened enough for her to peer around. Sprite was close to the edge of the cliff, caught in a bush with nettled leaves. In her struggles to free herself, she became even more entangled. Poor little mite. Netta squeezed through the gate and rushed to her. She crooned, soothing the kit while she worked to free her. Finally, she clasped Sprite to her breast. The kitten quivered from the cold wind, and the sounds of the pounding surf below. Knowing it would feel more secure, she put her in her tunic pocket.

The postern door slammed shut. Startled, Netta spun to see the hunched shape of a man coming toward her. Her feet slipped on the loose stones. She lost her balance. Frantic now, she scrambled for firmer footing. The ground crumbled. She started to slip off the edge of the cliff. The man's fingers clawed at her shoulder, the nails digging furrows in her flesh. Still, her leg scraped over the side. She screamed and grabbed for the prickly bush. The limb she clung to snapped.

She hurtled downward and soon came to a bone-crunching stop on a narrow ledge, a ledge blessed with a small bent tree that stayed her from falling onto the breakers below. Though it seemed a far drop, it was not.

Her pulse raced, and terror had such a firm grip on her that she fought nausea. When she stopped screaming long enough to gather her wits, she swallowed, afraid to turn. If she pressed her back to the cliff wall, she would face the vast emptiness and the pounding surf below. To turn her back to the edge was as frightening. She had best stay on her back.

Netta gasped, then bit her lip while she checked Sprite. She tried to shield the kitten from seeing their dire predicament. Wrapping her arms around it, she ventured to look up to find how far she had fallen.

She cried out in surprise.

Mereck had not killed him!

The man who had abducted her was very much alive.

As if he had not already been repulsive enough, his huge nose was even more offensive than before.

"Stupid bitch," he snarled at her. "Stand and give me yer 'ands so I can pull ye up. I warn ye, if ye don't get yer skinny arse up here, I'll kill ye flatter'n a cesspit rat."

Seeing she did not intend to obey him, he rained curses down on her. He darted fearful glances over his shoulder at the gate. Assured they were yet alone, he hurled rocks at her head. She raised her hands to block them. They struck her forearms, her elbows. She cried out with pain. He scuttled away. Afeared he was going to find a way to get to her, she screamed until her voice almost left her. Unknowing, she cried out one word again and again.

Mereck.

She looked to her left. Fear sent vomit spewing from her lips. A very long way down was the teeming ocean. Huge waves burst over the rocks, sending foam and spray flying. She swallowed, determined to look only at the sky. Gulls circled above, their cries raising such a clamor she feared no one would hear her own.

She squeezed her eyes tight and redoubled her efforts. If she was loud enough, her Mereck would hear her. Finally, the sound of her name came to her. Clutching Sprite to her neck, she blinked between the kit's ears. Mereck smiled down at her. How could he be so calm? Did he not realize she could plunge to her death?

Damron, Connor, and almost every man in the castle was there above her. Mereck had a thick rope looped between his legs and knotted around his waist. Damron, Connor and Baron Hugh of Carswell held the other end. They lowered Mereck to the foot of the ledge so falling stones would not strike her. How had he reached her so swiftly? Soon he cradled her against his chest, her head tucked beneath his chin.

"You may stop screechin', wife, or I willna hear for the next sennight." He patted her head when she shut her mouth. "Do you know you howled near as loudly as when we are lovin'? 'Tis how I knew it was you and not some lovelorn lass pining for a tall Highlander to come to her."

His outlandish remarks had the desired effect. She didn't notice she was dangling in her husband's arms—over a cliff.

When they stood on firm ground, he waited to have the rope removed.

"Sweet Christ, woman. Why in all your blessed saints' names did you decide to sit on a ledge?" His shouting near blew her hair back from her face.

Netta was not frightened anymore. She was angry.

She snuggled Sprite between her breasts and glared. She told Mereck exactly why she was laying, not sitting, on the cursed ledge. When she finished her story, she was no longer angry at him.

Mereck was angry, though. Beyond angry. He was livid. Nay, furious was more like it. The other men were livid.

After her husband carried her to the keep, he left her in the women's care. Soon after, they heard the thunder of galloping horses pounding over the drawbridge. Tripping over their feet in haste, the women raced to the window.

"They go to find the bluidy bastard. Ye need not fear the man again, for I ken *he* willna return without him." Meghan spoke with calm conviction.

Netta's gaze followed to where the women stared.

M'Famhair streaked ahead of Damron and the warriors.

His lips drawn in a snarl, Baresark straddled the steed's bare back.

Chapter 25

Fools! They believe I search for Lynette's attacker to avenge her. Roger knew where the lout hid, but he would not lead Blackthorn's warriors to him. Thinking of his plans, his heartbeat quickened. He slowed his mount until he dropped behind, then eased the horse around and made his way to the meeting place.

Late evening found Damron's searchers a short distance from their northeastern border. Damron's squire, Spencer, found the body. When the young man retched all he had eaten that day, no one blamed him. To distract him, Damron sent him to gather the rest of the warriors to this spot.

The body lay in a small clearing, with arms and legs tied to four different trees. The killer had crushed the victim's hands. A bloody rock rested beside the left wrist.

He must have stuffed the man's mouth with cloth, for the material now rested beneath the bloody head. His tongue lay stretched across his forehead. The eyes were missing. The bulbous nose no longer adorned his face, nor were his ears where they should be. The three lay between his legs where his sex had been. The killer had stuffed the man's prick into his mouth. His ballocks lay one on each side of his head.

"Lucifer's pox'd tarse. What manner of man could have done this?" Connor's horrified voice interrupted Damron's study of the body.

"No sane man, but one embracing madness." Damron glanced up as Mereck squatted beside him.

Mereck studied the body in the same detached way. He, Connor and Marcus agreed it was Netta's abductor. Mereck raised his eyebrows questioningly at Damron.

"Do you see the pattern, or do I imagine it?" When his brother nodded, Mereck continued. "His was no random killing. For certs, it relates to my wife. The madman tortured the varlet for failing his duty.

"He plucked out his eyes for he saw Netta unclothed; his nose because he smelled her scent; his ears for hearing her voice; his tongue because he dared try to kiss her; his hands for touching. Not the least was his sex."

"Aye, but how did his master learn of it?" Damron asked. "He couldna been stupid eneuch to tell the man his deeds?"

Connor raked his fingers through his hair and shook his head.

"He had no need. We passed many men on the paths when we brought Netta back to Blackthorn. Any one of them could have seen her battered condition. Word could have reached him on how the lout treated her." He rose and frowned a warning that someone approached.

"Merciful God! If this is the Highlander's way of taking revenge, I must tell you it is monstrous." Mortain held a lacy, perfumed cloth to his mouth and gagged daintily.

"Don't be an ass," Baron Carswell voice lashed out. When Roger drew up his shoulders in shock and stepped back, his expression fearful, the baron glared at him in contempt.

As was his habit, Mereck kept his face impassive. Roger disgusted him. Did the man pay the king a scutage tax to avoid the sight of blood? Mereck strove to hear his thoughts, but it was as if the man kept his mind on naught but trivial happenings apurpose.

They cut the ropes binding the body to the trees. They did not bury the remains deep. The wolves and animals of the forest would clean the forest of carrion.

Since it was too late to return to Blackthorn this night, they rode west for several leagues before making camp. In unspoken agreement, Damron, Mereck and Connor kept their eyes on the Englishmen.

Netta feared Mereck delayed his return because he did not trust himself to deal with her. She should have found someone to go with her to search for Sprite. At the time, its cries had frightened her, and she had not thought it through.

Feeling far too alone to be comfortable, she couldn't fall asleep. And she was cold. She missed his massive, hot body alongside hers.

She padded to the door and looked out onto the hallway to find Sir Thomas, a Saxon knight who came in Brianna's original escorts from England, posted there. When she told him what she wished to do, he nodded and escorted her to Meghan's room. She would sleep with her and Elise. They would never know she was there.

They knew.

Burrowing under the covers like a squirrel hiding from a hawk, she crawled between the two sleeping women. Her sigh failed to awake them, but when she could not get warm, she scooted tight against Elise's back. Unfortunately, she nudged her off the bed. Elise's shriek of alarm brought Thomas, sword in hand, charging into the room.

The poor man's eyes stretched wide at the sight of three beautiful and scantily clad women, their hair tumbling about their faces. He swallowed and backed out of the room.

Shortly after the sun rose on a misty morn, the warriors returned. Netta was glad she was in the hall with the other women. She didn't want to be alone with Mereck when he remembered she had broken her word and went outside the postern gate. By chance he had not yelled at her before because he had seen how affrighted she had been.

She hated that everyone knew her weakness about heights. Meghan did not have this fear, for she had watched the Scotswoman climb to the highest point of a tree. Megan's reason was very strange. She did it for the fun of it.

Netta studied the warriors entering the hall. Not a speck of blood stained any of them. Seeing Mereck bore no new cuts or bruises on his face, she sighed with relief. Before the men retired to Damron's solar, Mereck told her they found her abductor. He had been killed in an accident. He didn't explain what the accident had been.

Netta started to leave the room with Meghan and Elise when Roger's loud voice speaking to the blacksmith stopped her.

"Sharpen my sword to a fine edge. It appears Blackthorn harbors a berserk murderer close. Why, did you know he trussed and butchered a man much like one would a boar? Even plucked the eyes from his head. When we came upon the scene, Baresark still knelt beside the body."

Baron Carswell came through the doorway startling

Elise into a shriek. With lips compressed in disapproval, Carswell glared at Roger.

Heartsick at what Roger inferred, Netta ran from the room and kept on running until she burst through the doorway atop a winding flight of stairs. Surprised to find herself at the highest point of the castle, she blinked away the light drizzle of rain and stared around. Knowing how far above the ground she was turned her knees to porridge. She leaned back against the wall and slid down to sit on the damp stone.

Oh, saints! She was going to be sick.

Mereck had promised never again to lose control. But that was when she could see him. She hadn't been with him the day before. How could he have done such a thing? He could not, of course. He was far too gentle with her to be able to commit such a horrible act as that foul murder.

The door beside her scraped opened. She glanced up, but instead of the bare calves of a Highlander, Roger's skinny shanks stood there. He bent close to her ear.

"I thought to bring you the man's prick as a token. But unfortunately your insane husband lodged it too deeply in the dead man's mouth. I did not want to bloody my hands removing it."

She covered her mouth and gagged. His small, pale eyes gleamed at her. His long nose twitched. He reached out sickly white fingers and grasped her chin, forcing her to look at him.

"What do you here?" Sir Thomas' hand grasped Roger's shoulder and thrust him aside like he weighed no more than a small child clinging to his mother's plaid.

"I thought to comfort the lady." Roger sneered at her. "She is distressed over her beast of a husband."

She did not have to think about it anymore. This foul man had cleared her doubts.

Mereck could never be so vicious. Roger could.

"Nay. You lie. Mereck would not do such as you described." Netta shoved him with both hands as she shouted the words.

If Sir Thomas had not stepped between them, she knew Roger would have struck her. Before she turned her back on him, she grabbed Thomas by his sword belt and tugged. She knew he would follow her anyway, but she wanted to be sure.

Since leaving Wycliffe she had turned into a coward. Hopefully no one would notice that she didn't intend to ever be alone with the baron again.

They noticed.

For the rest of the day, she made sure Sir Thomas knew her every move. If she went from one end of the great hall to the other, she was not content that he kept his eyes on her. She marched over to him, cleared her throat and pretended she wanted to talk to him as she went about her business. She wore him out. As distraught as she was, she started to do one thing, forgot it and started another. When he reminded her, she apologized and declared she didn't usually act this empty-headed.

Netta wore herself out, too. Walking to their room that night, Mereck told her he wanted to talk to her. Fearful he intended to lecture her about the postern gate, she asked him to make love first. Actually, she didn't ask him for the loving.

She demanded it.

He showed her what an accommodating husband he could be.

She showed him her gratitude.

After her usual vocal release, she sighed and went to sleep.

* * *

"Netta, you will not believe all that is happening. Look at the burning crosses in the front bailey. Do you hear Meghan? She plays that lovely wailing thing, and Brianna says Mother and Father are coming, and are you not excited?"

"Elise." Connor, standing beside Mereck, scowled at her from the doorway.

"Uh-oh, I forgot. I'm not supposed to bother you." She streaked across the room and disappeared behind the screen.

Connor followed. Elise scrunched down, and when his big hands clamped on her shoulders, she howled.

"When will you learn to obey me, Mousie?"

"Netta heard the screeching and saw the crosses too. She was staring out the window. How could she not look with those great beasts with their shaggy horses and bare legs right there in the bailey?" Elise blushed. The wind had lifted more than one plaid and bared its occupant's posterior.

"What did you see that brought the pink to your cheeks?"

Connor hauled Elise close to kiss and nibble her lips, cup her backside and lift her to grind her against his hardened sex. "You willna look at the men when the wind is high. Dinna think I willna punish you if I see you staring at their bare skin."

They went below to the great hall to greet guests. Before the sun was at its full height, all the rooms in the keep, the towers and the outer buildings filled to bursting with men and women representing their clans. Lesser clan members set up their tents in the open baileys between the curtain walls and the inner walls. The tubs in the bathing room would not be adequate for the huge crush of people. Mereck recommended the close-by lake, the water troughs for the horses, and the buckets at the wells.

"I will be most angry if I find you lurking beside a doorway peering at naked men about their bathing." Connor eyed Elise. "If you must needs spy on a man's body, you are welcome to bathe mine."

Elise elbowed him in his ribs. "I will not sneak looks at naked bodies, you horrid man." Her voice rose in indignation. "Why, if Father heard you suggest such, he would smash your nose and maybe even break that proud head of yours. That is what he would do, and he would not let me marry you on the morrow."

Soft snickers and loud guffaws of laughter burst out in the room. Elise tried to flee. Connor held her still.

"I hear the piper calling a Sassenach tune. Your father is about to enter the gates. Do you not want to greet them as they come, so he can start beating me to a pulp?" She ran for the door. Chuckling, Connor followed his bride.

Netta cried through Elise's wedding. The more she cried, the more nervous the bride became. Mereck scowled.

"Wife, you insult me with your weeping. You should smile and show her that marriage is a happy affair." He hesitated and looked uncertain. "You act like she is being sacrificed on the altar."

The minute the couple repeated their vows and the family went inside the chapel for the nuptial mass, Netta's tears dried. He decided it must be a woman thing. He changed his mind when tears rolled from Elise's father's eyes. Sassenachs. He snorted in disgust. No man worth his salt would shed tears o'er a woman.

Though Netta pleased him, he refused to acknowledge how important she had become to him. He dared not love her. That he felt rage was a natural thing when that offal had again tried to harm her. When someone threatened his possessions, any man would be angry.

For truth, it was the only reason he kept her clamped to his side. He wouldn't allow Mortain anywhere near her. The man told anyone and everyone how he could not wait to secure his alliance with Netta's sister. If he was so impatient, why in Hades didna he leave?

Mereck doubted how interested Roger was in taking a wife. His short strides were unmanly. Most of all, Mereck disliked how Roger watched Mereck's squire Dafydd.

The visitors would spend another day at the castle for the men to enjoy a hunt. When they returned and before Roger dismounted, Mereck would suggest he hie himself back to England. He scowled and realized he could not insist the man leave. He needed to consider Baron Carswell. Had he not promised Netta to control his rage, he would toss the skinny bastard off the cliff.

Mereck hauled Netta close against his side.

"Husband, you are hurting my arms." Netta pinched his waist, demanding his attention. When he glanced down, he appeared surprised to see her there.

"You willna leave my side, wife. Should you need to seek privacy, I will go with you." His face was set in hard lines as he righted her and patted her shoulder.

Netta gasped at such an indelicate remark. And how was she going to get Elise alone and explain mating to her? She didn't want to tell Elise with Brianna or Meghan nearby. If they learned of her foolish beliefs about mating, they would laugh.

The only time Mereck left her side was during the afternoon games to decide the strongest warrior. The men refused to participate unless Mereck also entered. He would be the last to compete, for none had ever bested him at the caber toss.

He hauled her by her hand over to Damron's side. "I would deem it a favor, Damron, if you would hold to Netta." Hearing Netta snort, he narrowed his eyes at her. "She has a habit of wandering off alone." He pushed her closer to Damron and left.

"Netta?"

Damron's tone was harsh and demanding. When she looked up at him, his jaw looked carved in stone as he crossed his arms over his chest. His sea-green eyes stared into hers. How did Brianna ever have the courage to crawl between the sheets with this man? She wasted no time nodding to him.

"I dinna believe in hangin' on to a lass like me foolish brither. Ne'ertheless, ye willna move from this spot now, will ye?"

Damron waited for her to nod. Smiling, she did. In a short while she could talk to Elise without a man listening. When she saw he was occupied watching the events, she inched away.

"I wudna hesitate to thrash ye if ye disobey me, do ye ken?"

Damron's voice was mild. His eyes were not.

"I will not move a hand-width away. You have my word."

That settled it. Elise was on her own. Netta didn't doubt the laird would do as he said.

She sighed and resigned herself to watching the men's games. Holy saints! Why, they were truly brainsick, that's what they were. This caber toss thing was not a weapon like she thought.

They threw trees. Oaks stripped to their trunks.

She watched as a man would squat down, get a firm

grip on the thin end of the trunk and lift it. When he balanced it to his satisfaction, he surged forward and heaved it upward. If tossed strongly enough, it would somersault through the air to land on its heavy end and fall forward. They judged who had thrown their tree in the straightest line.

Of course, Mereck won. He was not arrogant about it. He didn't act like it was an unusual accomplishment.

It was a very long day. She never had the opportunity to talk to Elise alone. After the banquet, when the women took the bride to help her prepare for bed, Netta gave up. She hoped her friend wouldn't be too horrified when Connor did more than bump against her arse.

When Mereck immediately turned her toward their room, he surprised her. Before they got to their door, which was across the hall from the bridal couple's, he looked blatantly sensual. He sent Bran away and stripped both their clothes off before Netta could whisper a brief prayer.

She was on the bed in a flash, and his mouth and hands touched her everywhere at once. Mereck was ravishing her, she decided, and doing a thorough job of it. When his lips slid from her stomach down to nuzzle the tight curls between her thighs, she almost sprang from the bed. He lifted her legs to place them over his shoulders, and he clasped her waist to hold her still as he burrowed lower.

His deep growl when his lips and tongue began to torment her already swollen flesh proved his sensual arousal. His rumblings sounded much more satisfying than the puny whimpers she couldn't control. She had no time to ponder the reason women didn't make the same sound. She tried to bite her lips to keep silent, but he teased her nipples between his fingers and thumbs until she was beside herself. To Hades with being ladylike.

Netta came undone in his hands.

As he glided up between her legs, his long shaggy hair flowed about his face, and his hot, passionate eyes gleamed at her. He looked like a giant tawny cat covering his mate as he edged closer to her lips. Just as he reached them, a shout stopped him.

"You are going to do what?"

Elise's voice. They didn't hear Connor's reply.

"They are going to do this," Mereck whispered and thrust into her eager center.

"Oh, yes. Please keep doing just that."

He was more than willing to oblige her.

When Netta awoke at dawn, she was glad Mereck had already left with the men on a hunt. She had need of a bucket for she had eaten too much the night before. After she finished gagging and retching, she wiped her face with a cold wet cloth and took deep breaths. She waited until her stomach calmed before she dressed and went to Elise.

"Why did you lie to me, Netta?" Elise demanded after a swaggering Connor handed Brianna the wedding sheet and left the room.

"When we talked about it, I didn't lie. I truly believed it at the time."

"You did too lie," Elise huffed. "How could you not have known? You were married when you told me such a giant untruth. When I prepared myself and proudly told him I was ready for him, I thought Connor was going to die of shock. He turned purple and kept gasping for breath."

"What in the world did you do?"

"You are not listening." Elise huffed indignantly and frowned at Netta. "I told him I was ready. What else do you think I did? I got up on my hands and knees, said some quick prayers and waited." Elise groaned and turned red. "When nothing happened, I crawled around to discover he was having a fit. I sat beside him and slapped his back. He put his head on my shoulder and gasped a couple of times until he could breathe better."

"So? Why is that bad? He could not help it if he was sick."

"Easy for you to say." Elise glared at her a second and then shouted, "He was not sick, like in *really* sick, Netta. He was strangling from trying not to upset me by laughing."

"I am so sorry, Elise. Truly I am." She wrung her hands. For their friendship's sake, she told how her own wedding night ended. In the telling, she realized how thoughtful Mereck had been not to make an issue of her ignorance.

They remained silent for a while. Elise giggled first, then before they knew it, they howled with laughter.

Meghan burst into the room, demanding to know what was so funny. Elise peeked out to make sure no one stood in the hallway and shut the door. Netta didn't think they should discuss their marital experiences.

"Tsk." Meghan's disbelieving sound started them giggling over again. "I learned about matin' when I was a young girl in the French court. You wud need to be blind not to see the couplin' going on all but out in the open."

When they told Meghan of their first nights, she laughed until tears streaked down her face. They stopped guiltily when a worried Brianna came to tell them sentries had spotted the men returning from their stag hunt.

A warrior rode at their lead. Supported in his arms was a limp, injured man.

Chapter 26

Netta didn't draw a sane breath until Mereck vaulted off *M'Famhair.* The great brown warhorse stamped and threw his head about, unwilling to end his outing. Dafydd waited while Mereck soothed the mount, then handed him the reins. An assured smile flashed on Mereck's wolfishly handsome face as his confident, long-legged stride ate the distance between them. Netta had had a terrible fright thinking a wild boar had savaged him. Now, recognizing the injured man, she didn't feel guilty about being glad.

"Oh, thank you, thank you, God."

Her pleased litany stopped when she realized Roger would be unable to leave this day. She saw no blood. He could not have a serious injury. She shoved her hands on her hips and scowled.

"Well, I hope he gets nibbled by every one of Lucifer's fleas and rats," she muttered. Hearing his high-pitched whining, she tugged on Meghan's sleeve.

"Saints' alive, he is a coward. I will gladly give his leg a well-aimed kick to give him something to whimper about."

* * *

Netta spent the next fortnight keeping close to Brianna's solar. Even Meghan avoided Roger's constant presence in the hall, where he lounged with his foot atop a padded stool, demanding attention. Brianna kept Guardian nearby, for the wolf snarled and slavered every time his golden eyes spied Roger.

Time passed so quickly that Netta paid little heed to a strange sickness that plagued her. Each dawn and when time for the evening meal, she hugged a wooden bucket. She reasoned that if she did not eat, she would have naught to return to the outside world. Sadly, it didn't work.

Everyone noticed she had lost her robust appetite. Mereck and Damron shared knowing grins. How could they find her wasting sickness amusing? Early one bright golden morn, Mereck left his brother's side to come to her.

"Meghan is going hawking, and she thought mayhap my lovely bride would enjoy an outing. What say you, wife?"

Delighted that she could take Tuan for his first real hunt, she ignored her queasy stomach. Throughout the morn, they took turns freeing their raptors to catch unwary prey. Meghan's Simple seemed in awe of Glider, Mereck's graceful falcon.

When time for Simple to hunt, the sparrowhawk plunged for a grouse flushed from a bush. So engrossed in her zeal for the catch, the raptor failed to see the tree around which the wily grouse flew. She flapped to the ground, a surprised look on her face. Hearing Mereck's laughter made Netta smile with pleasure.

When she freed Tuan for his flight, Netta watched with motherly pride while the little kestrel took to the air in sweeping curves. The raptor soon spotted his prey. Netta held her breath as Tuan swooped down, caught a mouse in his claws and returned to drop it at her feet.

Netta intended to praise Tuan for being such a smart hunter. One look at the dying mouse sent her racing for cover behind a large rowen tree weighted with orange-red berries. Mereck followed to hold her head and whisper soothing words while she retched. His kindness made her realize that this eve she should warn him the Baresark curse intended to claim another bride.

Rain drummed against the outer walls and lightning flashed close in the woods while Mereck made passionate love to his wife. She waited till her heartbeat slowed to prepare him for her death.

"Husband, I have a dreadful sickness." Noting his surprised look, she patted his cheek to comfort him. "You see, I cannot eat. I can only bear to look at food at the noon meal. I will soon waste away. God wishes to punish me for my sins," she whispered.

"Are there other symptoms of this alarming malady, wife?"

What ails the man? She was trying to prepare him that he will soon need another wife, yet he dared look amused? No Saxon would greet his wife's tragic problem with such ease.

"Aye. Everything exhausts me. Likely it is because of my weakened condition. I have hid it from you."

When he did not soon reply, she started to sniff. He seemed to mull the problem over in his mind. While she waited for him to think of a suitable reply, she rested her head on his chest to listen to his lulling heartbeat. Before he could tell her his thoughts, she fell asleep.

Mereck gave her the comfort she required.

She snored too loudly to hear it.

He hugged her tight and rubbed his chin on her head. Whispering into her sleeping ear, he told her how happy and proud he was.

If it was a son, he will have a father who will acknowledge him. He will not be a bastard, unable to inherit. Mereck grinned, thinking of a daughter he could coddle and give a father's love. Love Netta had ne'er known. The babe's sex mattered not. A son or daughter would have an abundance of love.

He had noted the changes in Netta's breasts and knew her courses had not come since they first mated. She knew nothing of the signs of expectant motherhood, for Wycliffe had kept the women thickening with babes away from the castle, knowing his wife would rant about his many bastards.

Mereck would take his Netta out alone the next day. They would go at midday when her stomach was the most settled. After they supped on cheese, bread and wine, he would explain to his darling that she was with a child.

With any luck at all, Roger, that sorry excuse for a man, would leave before they returned.

"What?" If not for the masking sounds of the waterfall, everyone back at the castle would have heard Netta's shout. "I'm not dying? Why did you not tell me sooner? I have worried this last sennight for naught?"

"Love, if you had confided your fears to me, I would have set them to rest." Mereck grinned at her. "Have I told you how very happy I am?" It was more than pleasure over knowing they were to have a child. He loved her. His wife had become important to him. What proved to him it was love was the first thing he had thought when he suspected she was increasing.

The Baresark legend. How could he live if he lost her?

The thought sent waves of fear through him. He hugged her tight and vowed to warn Bleddyn he was not to let anything happen to her. He had faith in the Welsh mystic, for he was the only person alive who could have saved Brianna when she lay so near death. He knew, for he had been with them through it all. He grimaced, remembering the terrible fear.

Mereck clasped Netta to his chest and started to tell her how much he loved her. He had little warning over the roar of the waterfall, only a startled awareness of evil thoughts. No sooner had they registered in his mind, than his head exploded with light. Netta screamed. With a tremendous strength of will, he fought the blackness creeping over his consciousness.

Forcing his eyes to focus, he saw the bastard strike Mereck's love across her face. He roared in fury, drowning out her cry of pain. He lurched to his feet. Drew his sword.

Roger whirled and lunged at him.

"You rock-headed Welsh bastard. Why are you not dead?" Roger's high-pitched ranting shrilled above the noise of the falls. "Caer Cadwell and its gold will be mine. I will tear your heart from your body. Lynette will carry it to her father. I will force him to give her to me." His eyes flamed with triumph.

Mereck parried Mortain's thrusts and forced the baron back from where Netta lay. It was not easy. To his surprise, the baron was a skilled swordsman. With lightning speed, Roger's blade whipped across Mereck's forehead. Hot blood flowed from the gash, threatening to blind him, while dizziness from the blow to his head unsettled him.

"Shall I tell you how she will pleasure me?" Drool seeped from Roger's lips. Evil gleamed in his eyes. "I will take a finger from your hand each time she does not draw my tongue into her mouth." His lips twitched. "What think you of this fine idea, Sir Bastard?" The madness he had kept hidden was surfacing out of control.

"Think? I will rip your tongue from your mouth for such thoughts, Baron Simpleton." If he could inflame Mortain's fury, it would make him careless. His blade flashed out, leaving a trail of blood across the baron's chest.

"Simpleton? Simpleton?" Startled by his shrieks, birds squawked and scattered leaves as they flew from the trees. "Who else but I would have punished the lout the way he deserved? I am exceedingly cunning."

"Cunning? 'Tis laughable. E'en a child could have outwitted that pitiful wretch." Mereck opened a slash on Roger's leg.

"Laughable? You will hear laughter. I will laugh while you watch her luscious mouth service me. She will. And happily, else I will give her your severed balls to fondle."

How dared the devil's spawn speak such filth about his Netta? Mereck unleashed his hard-held temper. Fury erupted. His eyes narrowed, his nostrils flared. His lips flattened to a hard, thin line.

He whipped his blade out to slash Roger's left cheek. He would rip open Mortain's chest and feed his heart to Guardian. He felt like he grew with his rage. His savage snarls rent the air. He lunged and parried. Both dripped blood from wounds to their chest and arms.

From the corner of his eye, he saw Netta shake her head and push herself up. Shuddering, he struggled for control remembering his vow never again to become a berserker in front of her.

"Little man," he taunted Roger. "Dinna think you have the strength to satisfy a woman. Your worm of a prick couldna pleasure a widow long deprived of a mate. I hear it is no larger than a child's member that hasna learned to swell."

Roger's face purpled. Mereck grimaced and near dropped his sword, for Roger's deranged mind shrieked at him. Locking his fingers around the sword hilt, Mereck goaded him again.

"Such a pitiful body. Your bony chest and skinny shanks puts to mind a chicken. My squire is more manly than you."

Mortain's demented thoughts crashed through Mereck's mind, blinding him with searing pain. He could see naught but dull lights weaving afore him.

"A squire? A squire?" Mortain screamed and lunged.

Mereck lurched aside, dizzy. His knee bent. The blade missed his heart, but cut deep into his shoulder. He grunted. His hand jerked open. He bellowed in fury and pain. His sword fell. Blood spread over his tunic; it flowed off his fingers. He swayed. And fumbled for the short sword that always rode at his side. It was not there. He shook his head trying to clear blood seeping over his eyelids into his eyes.

Netta clutched a rock and watched for an opportunity to help Mereck. She gasped, horrified, when his sword clattered to the ground. Not daring to think, she hurled the stone. It crashed into Roger's temple, startling him. In those brief moments, she dove for the sword at Mereck's feet and grabbed the hilt tight with both hands.

Mortain, sneering with triumph, lunged at Mereck.

"Nay! You shan't kill him," Netta screamed.

Halfway to her feet, she braced herself against Mereck's legs, held tight to the sword and raised the point. Roger had drawn his blade back, ready to thrust it into Mereck's chest. She lunged forward. Her blade sank through Roger's gut. His forward momentum pushed the blade deep to grate against his spine.

Shock and utter surprise blanketed Roger's countenance. His lips moved, without sound. He fell to his knees. To his face. The protruding hilt struck the ground, rocked Roger to his side. Air gurgled from his lungs.

Mereck fell beside him. Netta screamed and tried to roll him over. She couldn't move him. Taking a deep breath, she gripped his good shoulder and arm and tugged with all her strength. At last, she got him on his back. He lay on the edge of her tunic. Rather than yank it free, she grabbed the neck opening and stripped it over her head.

Netta sobbed so loudly she couldn't hear herself think. She couldn't see either. She swiped her arm across her blurred eyes. Spying Mereck's short sword Roger had seized and thrown aside after striking Mereck's head, she grabbed it and cut her tunic into long strips. She made a thick pad and held it tight against the wound. So much blood! It soaked through, hot beneath her fingers. Desperate to stop it, she folded more strips of linen and added it to the pad. Leaning hard on it, she prayed it would slow his bleeding.

"Please dear God, please do not let him die." She repeated her prayer between whimpers of fear. She was not afeared for herself. Aye, she was. Now was not the time to lie.

She desperately feared losing him. She had come to crave his presence. How could she bear not having his compassion, his magical kisses? To never again feel her heart quicken watching his arrogant stride as he crossed the bailey? Not having him beside her in their bed would be more than she could endure.

"Please God, do not take him." Tears dripped off her chin. "Not until we are old and gray and our children and grandchildren are old too. When you do, take us together." She felt him spasm beneath her hand. Thinking his spirit was fighting to be free, she shouted her prayers even louder.

"You cannot have him, God. He is mine. I'm not asking anymore. I'm telling You. You had better listen to me," she threatened.

"Do you seek to drown me, wife?" Mereck's voice was weak.

"Thank you, God, thank you." She leaned forward and rained kisses over his face, soaked with her tears. He tried to kiss her back. His effort reassured her.

"Are you hurt?" Fear gilded his eyes.

"Nay, but I know not what to do for you." Her voice quavered.

"My wound," he whispered. "Tell me of it."

"'Tis through your shoulder. The blade entered above your ribs." She stroked and patted his cheek with a shaking hand. "Never have I seen so much blood."

"Love, remove the pouches tied to *M'Famhair.* Send him to Blackthorn." He repeated the command in Gaelic for her to say to the great war horse. She hurried to do as he bid her. Before the destrier disappeared through the trees, she returned to Mereck.

"The flask." He gasped out the words. "I would drink."

She grabbed the pouch from the bottom and dumped everything out in her haste. After removing the plug on the flask, she held it to his lips. He took a healthy swallow of potent whiskey. If it would dull his pain, she would give him all he wished. When he could not swallow fast enough, and it spilled from the sides of his lips, she realized she was being too generous.

"Press your knee to my wound, my love. Cut my plaid to bind the pads tight."

While she cut long strips of the plaid, he clamped his teeth together. He tried to help her as she wound them around him. Each time he flinched she cried out as if it was she who suffered. When he fainted, she worked as fast as she could.

After she finished, she found corn meal, a plate and flint in the second pouch. She ran to get a blanket tied behind her own saddle. Skittering around Roger's body, she used the blanket to cover Mereck. The sun would soon set, and 'twas cold next to the falls.

Without letting him out of her sight, she gathered every branch and twig she could find. Every few moments she raced back to feel his face and listen to his heartbeat. When she had collected enough wood, she fought with the flint until a spark ignited twigs and a small branch.

Saints be praised. She soon had a decent fire.

What were those horrible sounds? Gasping, she looked up. Wolves! They howled in the distance. They scented blood. She didn't know how to keep them at bay. By chance, if she pulled Roger's body deep into the woods, they would be occupied with it and not come for Mereck? She shuddered and rubbed her arms.

She stared at Roger's body. His sword remained clenched in his death grip. Mereck's sword stayed embedded where she had thrust it. Gagging, she turned Roger and grasped the hilt. She pulled. It wouldn't come loose. After several attempts, she placed her foot against the dead man's ribs and tugged it free. She carried it over to

Mereck, placed it on the ground near to his hand and returned to stand over Roger.

Netta grabbed Roger's limp legs, closed her eyes and pulled. Before she moved him more than five paces away, she slipped and fell. Scrambling to her feet, she turned around, grasped his ankles beneath her armpits and pulled with all her might. When she could drag him no farther, she dropped his feet and ran back to Mereck.

Along with his sword, she placed a large branch beside her. If wolves came close, she would frighten them away with fire. If the fire did not work, she would kill them all. Just see if she did not!

Each time Mereck opened his eyes, she dribbled whisky into his mouth. It helped his pain, for he slept soon afterward. She waited. Hearing the wolves draw closer, she decided to make such a ruckus it would frighten them away.

She sang. Loud. It was quite impressive. The sounds of the wolves diminished. Proud that she had thought of the trick, she sang and shouted until she realized horsemen were surrounding her. Her voice cut off in mid-word.

"Ye can stop caterwauling now, Netta. Did ye and Mereck have a wee disagreement?" Damron leapt off Angel and stooped beside his brother before it registered on her that he thought she had done this dreadful deed to her husband.

"Do not dare say I would harm even the smallest hair on his head." She bellowed so loud it startled her husband awake.

"Please, for the love of God. An armorer is pounding a white-hot blade betwixt my ears." He eyed her warily while whispering to his brother, "She sings God-awful loud, does she not?" Seeing Damron's grin, his eyes narrowed in warning. "Be careful, brother. She killed a man with mine own sword."

"Well now, Netta. Ye didna do the damage. But where is the body of the one who did? I dinna ken ye lettin' the man go who would cause such a paltry wound. 'Tis an insult, it is."

"Paltry? You call his horrid wounds paltry?" She fisted her hand, lunged across her husband and struck Damron's chin as hard as she could. Lord! Her hand hurt. Damron's brows lifted. He smiled. Her tears stopped. She was too angry to cry.

He had achieved his purpose.

"There is a body. If the wolves have not carried it away. I dragged it as far as I could."

At the thought of what the wolves might have done, she scooted around so her back faced them and hung her head between her arms braced against a tree trunk. She was sick again. When she turned back, Connor wrapped a warm plaid around her. Soon after, Marcus and several warriors returned. They had bundled Roger's body in a blanket and tied it to his horse they found tethered downstream.

Had they needed to fight the wolves to collect the corpse?

Damron and Connor kept up a steady stream of insults to Mereck while they helped lift him up on Angel. He whispered back in kind. His brother mounted behind him. Damron wrapped his plaid around them both and put his arms around Mereck to hold him secure against himself.

Fortunately it was a short ride to the keep. For every twitch Netta spied on her husband's face, she cried out.

"For truth, Netta, yer shouts and makin' Mereck laugh with yer curses hurts his battered head more than Angel's gait. I dinna ken jumpin' Jehoshaphats or flippin' gators. What manner o' beasts are they?"

"Beasts? I'm not sure. I must ask Brianna."

"Lucifer's toenails," Damron shouted. "She is teachin' ye to curse? One of these days that lass will drive me to beat her, just see if I dinna."

Fortunately for Mereck's pounding head, they arrived at the drawbridge to Blackthorn. Everyone awaited their return, but the crowd cleared a path for them. Mereck insisted Damron let him walk. When his feet touched the ground, his brother stood on one side, Connor on the other. Holding him around his waist, they kept him upright. They waited to see if he blacked out. He did. With Marcus' help, they carried him to his room.

Damron and Connor cut away Mereck's clothing. Netta was grateful to have Brianna's skill in caring for him. Bleddyn had not yet returned, for he had gone with Elise's parents to Ridley Castle. He delivered a copy of the signed marriage contract to Netta's father.

Baron Wycliffe could not invalidate the union.

As Brianna mixed a potion to dull Mereck's pain and help him to sleep, she soothed Netta.

"Before I came here to live, I often worked to heal wounds. Bleddyn and I have found that frequent washing of hands around an illness helps to prevent further distress. We boil all dressings for wounds and keep them in the herbarium. Bleddyn has taught me all he knows of herbs and potions. Rarely do our patients have infections or fevers." Her words reassured Netta.

Damron lifted Mereck's head so he could drink the potion Brianna held to his lips. While they waited for it to take effect, Brianna explored the swelling on Mereck's head and tended his other injuries. When he was in a deep sleep, Damron and Connor held him still as she probed and cleansed the gaping wound on his shoulder. Satisfied, she began sewing his flesh together.

With each stitch used to close it, Netta cried out. Brianna continued talking in her calm voice as she worked.

"Only when a wound becomes contaminated after an injury do we have a problem. You did a splendid job of caring for him before Damron found you. Mereck will have no trouble."

Netta would not leave Mereck's side. At nightfall, Brianna insisted she sleep. Netta curled up alongside him, keeping one hand touching him. She woke at his slightest movement. Brianna dosed him with her potions and soothed Netta with assurances that Mereck would soon be good as new. At the end of the fifth day, Brianna declared he was healing without problems.

"E'en if I live to be that hundred-year-old man you begged God for, I will ne'er tire of hearing you love me, wife," Mereck said one eve a fortnight later. "But I will soon become hard of hearing if you hum from morning till night, my heart. Could you not do so quietly?"

Netta's outraged gasp was so strong it was a wonder the bed curtains didna flap.

"Rats! You are stealing my thoughts again."

"I would have no need to steal your thoughts if you would but give them to me. Canna you tell me you love me?"

"You would have to be witless not to know I love you," Netta whispered. "Did I not kill a man? When I must leave the room, I run every step of the way until I'm back again. If that is not love, I know not what to call it."

He smiled and grasped her hand to pull her down beside him.

"Have I told you this day how much you mean to me?"

"This day? You have never told me any such thing."

"Nay? Hmm." He rubbed his chin. "Then have I told you lately how much I love you?" Seeing her blush, he grinned.

"Lately? You have never told me that either."

"Nay? Hmm. When I call you *mo gradh,* my love, dinna you know its meaning?" He rubbed his face against her hair and inhaled her sweet rose scent. "You have been my love from the day you put the worms in my stew. You will be my love when our grandchildren are old and gray."

"Worms made you love me? You are most strange, husband."

"Nay. Not the wiggly things, but the deviltry in your eyes when you did it."

"Yet you let me eat from your trencher, with worms, when you knew all along the disgusting things were there?"

Horrified at the thought that mayhap a worm had been on her first bites of stew, Netta slapped her hand over her mouth. Jumping off the bed, she grabbed the nearby bucket. Mereck held her head and assured her that, before she could eat it, Elise had knocked the lone portion graced with a worm out of her hand. When she had control of her stomach, she grabbed the water pitcher from the bedside table.

"If Elise had not stopped me, would you have kept silent?" She peered at him through narrowed eyes.

"Of course."

Poised to pour the cold water over him, Mereck grabbed her. They laughed and tussled over the pitcher. The water spilled, drenching them both.

"You didna let me finish, love. I wouldna have spoken, for I would have taken your hand and lifted the onion to show you what you drooled over. Hmm. Knowing your hearty appetite, I wondered if you would have popped it into your mouth anyway? Extra meat, mayhap?"

Netta howled with laughter. Mereck pulled her beneath him and began to kiss her witless.

It was a beautiful night for loving.

Mereck proved how much he loved his Netta.

Again and again and again.

Epilogue

Bleddyn reassured Mereck, for nigh on the hundredth time, that Netta's labor progressed smoothly. They did not need Bleddyn's presence in the birthing chamber, for Brianna saw no signs of trouble.

He also assured Mereck, time and time again, that helping Netta through her travail would not harm Brianna's babe. She would labor with her own bairn in another month, and she glowed with health.

Mereck wondered if Brianna and Bran's hearing would e'er be the same? Netta made up curses of her own instead of borrowing from someone else. He sighed when she shouted she would kill that "flipping, mind-eating, savage barbarian."

Conner grinned and rolled his eyes at the other men. Netta's last shriek proved too much for Mereck. He shoved past Eric and Marcus, whom Brianna had stationed outside the room to keep him from entering, and crashed through the doorway. He stopped dead in his tracks.

His wife's bloodcurdling scream did not divert his attention from the sight of his bairn entering the world. Seeing the blood, his mind screamed with memories of witnessing Brianna's terrible ordeal, and of the Baresark legend.

Hearing a loud crash, the men ran into Netta's room.

The bed had not fallen. Mereck had. He lay passed out cold on the floor, his face as white as Brianna's roses.

Damron shook his head in disgust as they left the room. Some time later, a very sheepish Mereck awoke and squeezed his eyes shut. Damn. His head hurt. He pushed himself to his feet, gripped his head with his big hands and wove his way to his wife's side.

"You have stopped screaming curses about me, love. Does it mean you forgive me?"

He sounded so hopeful that Netta laughed. And she cursed him again with the pain the laughter caused.

"Did you enjoy your rest, my fearless Baresark? Had you slept any longer, you would have missed our son's christening."

The two brothers stood beside the bed where Netta slept. Mereck held his swaddled son in his arms. Even a blind man would have sensed the pride radiating from every pore in Mereck's body. Grinning, he peeled back the plaid to show Damron what a beautiful son Netta had given him.

When the bairn lay naked to their gaze, Mereck pointed out that he had beautiful black hair like his mother. His eyes would surely be her lovely violet color, for now they seemed deep indigo.

He had all his fingers. Mereck counted to make sure.

And all his toes . . .

"God's holy teeth!" The words were a whispered shout, if such a thing exists. "Look at me puir wee Donald, brither."

Mereck stared down at what marked the babe his heir and not his heiress. His eyes misted and he gulped. The fact he reverted to a Scottish brogue proved his distress.

"Dinna tell me darlin' Netta, but our bairn has a dreadful deformity."

Damron looked at his brother's son and frowned.

"What deformity, brither? I see no extra limbs or strange marks."

"Blessed sweet Jesus. Look at his ballocks." Mereck whispered so low Damron leaned closer to hear. "Do ye no' see how huge they be? Oh, me puir son," he groaned. "The lad will ne'er be able to walk with sech a burden betwixt his legs."

Brianna chuckled behind him. He turned and glared at her.

"It's no deformity, Mereck. All wee boys are born with swollen, er, ballocks. In a sennight they'll be normal."

Mereck's relieved sigh whooshed so strong it fluttered the hair over Brianna's forehead.

Everyone tiptoed in to see his treasure, then left him alone with his loves. He went to lay beside Netta, the babe snuggled tight to his chest. She woke after a time and smiled at him.

"What think you of our son, husband?" Netta's voice was hoarse from all the shouting she had done.

"He is the most beautiful bairn I have e'er seen." Mereck didna consider he had seen few unclothed nurslings. "Look, Netta. See how perfect our wee bairn is."

He stripped the babe of his swaddling to show her their bare-arsed marvel.

"Oh my word, love," Netta exclaimed, staring down at her naked son. "He is your very image."

Seeing her wide eyes, Mereck's heart was near to breaking.

"Do ye think we have made another Baresark?"

"Nay, love. Not a Baresark." She reached up and kissed him between his eyes. "One day, our Donald will be exactly like his father—a kind and gentle man."

Author's Note

Before the usual blather about using words appropriate for the time period, I thought you might be interested in the old crone from the prologue. This character comes from my childhood in Key West, Florida. My sister, Dolores, and I used to run when we'd see her shuffling down the sidewalk toward our house. If she followed us as we raced down our driveway to the backyard, we'd run like our lives depended on it, yelling for our grandma.

We weren't being mean. Old Beyahita—that was her true name—was really scary. And from the time we could talk, we'd heard the old conchs whispering that she was a witch. We weren't taking any chances that she would cast a horrendous curse on us and . . . oh my. Mayhap she did! That would explain all these characters prancing around in my mind, demanding I bring them to life in my tales of love through the ages . . .

As usual, dear reader, please keep in mind that it is not always possible to use only eleventh-century words found in *English Through the Ages,* by William Brohaugh.

For instance, *trencher* wasn't in common usage in 1073. The *Encyclopedia Britannica* described it as ". . . originally a thick slice of bread, used as a primitive form of plate for eating and for slicing meat (hence its derivation from "trancher"—to cut, or carve) . . ."

In narrative, I do not believe it necessary to be so stringent with word choices.

Baresark was the early spelling for a berserker. In excerpts from "The Saga of King Hrolf Kraki," translated by Jesse Byock, ". . . berserkers seem to have been members of cults connected with Odin in his capacity as god of warriors."

They further detail: "His men went to battle without armor and acted like mad dogs or wolves. They bit into their shields and were as strong as bears or bulls. They killed men, but neither fire nor iron harmed them. This madness is called berserker-fury."

Relax and let my stories transport you to another time.

Sincerely,
Sophia
Visit me at www.sophiajohnson.net